FINDING AMERICA

Out of the Ashes, A Nation is Reborn

Sequel to *Searching for America*

R. THOMAS ROE

Finding America
by R. Thomas Roe

Signalman Publishing 2011
www.signalmanpublishing.com
email: info@signalmanpublishing.com
Kissimmee, Florida

Publisher's Note:
This is a work of fiction. Names, characters, places, and incidents are
either the product of the author's imagination or are used fictitiously,
and any resemblance to actual persons, living or dead, business
establishments, events, or locales is entirely coincidental.

Interior layout and design by John McClure

ISBN:
978-1-935991-24-3 (paperback)
978-1-935991-25-0 (ebook)

Cover design by Duncan Long
www.duncanlong.com

Signalman
Publishing

R. Thomas Roe is also author of

The Gaelic Letters

Palm Beach Gold

Searching for America

Available for the Kindle, Nook, and Apple iBookstore as well as in paperback on Amazon.com and BarnesandNoble.com

CHAPTER ONE

Robert Thomas poured himself a glass of Brandy as he relaxed in his apartment in Portland. He took over the simple quarters that were previously occupied by Stuart Martin who was the beloved leader of the WestPac organization until his fatal accident two years before. Stuart had been a leader, a catalyst, a thinker, and above all the person responsible for guiding the men and women on their torturous journey from Florida to Montana to successfully found the new political entity known as WestPac. The United States of America passed into oblivion over seven years ago and since then anarchy reigned supreme throughout the country except for isolated areas of the continent of which WestPac comprised one. Stuart had been the primary organizer for the new political entity.

WestPac encompassed parts or all of the Dakotas, Saskatchewan, Wyoming, Montana, Idaho, Utah, Nevada, Oregon, Washington, and Northern California. It had grown from a small group of Florida emigrants into a political entity encompassing a fairly large land mass.

The leadership skills of Stuart Martin had been primarily responsible for this expansion but Robert Thomas had been a major factor as well. His insight and political savvy contributed greatly to the success of the development of WestPac. The two were a very effective team with Stuart being the front man and Robert being the ideas man, the propaganda minister, the bottom line economics wizard. It was Robert's ability to target profitable ventures and to bring into WestPac people that either could produce or could provide assets or territories beneficial to WestPac. There was absolutely no jealousy between the two men. Stuart knew who he was and who he was not. Robert believed in Stuart without reserve yet was also confident about his own abilities and of his contributions to WestPac. Both men were quick, intelligent and both were outstanding speakers with the ability to convince and sway a crowd. The only difference between the two men was that Stuart was, for the most part, guided by principle and Robert used principles when they favored what he wished to accomplish. In the course of the years they had worked together, Robert had learned that many of

Stuart's guiding principles were effective in producing good results far quicker than the sleight of hand or trickery that Robert had primarily used in attaining his success before becoming part of the original Florida team that eventually became WestPac. As a result, Robert had been very slowly assuming many of these principles of life such as fair dealing, patience with subordinates, tactfulness, and many others including honesty. Robert was having the most difficulty with trying to absorb honesty into his own core values as it was one virtue that he had spent many years of his life ignoring and he was having difficulty taking it on. As Robert thought to himself many times, he respected the idea of one being honest with other people, it was just that it was very impractical to practice honesty with any degree of continuity. He decided early on in the process to try to be honest when it would not destroy whatever goal he was trying to achieve. Stuart on the other hand was almost boringly honest and was aware of Robert's shortcomings in this area but he was very fond of his friend and was aware of the battle he was fighting to upgrade his character. Stuart had the ability to accept the good and ignore the bad in anyone. That was just one more characteristic of Stuart that Robert envied.

At the time of Stuart's unfortunate passing, most of the listed States above were in a state of transition. They were not yet fully stabilized but they were all in the process of becoming organized, secure, and contributing political members of the WestPac organization. When Stuart died, Robert, who had been second in command and jointly responsible for bringing most of the politicians, leaders and bureaucrats in the Northwest into WestPac, saw opportunity knocking. He voluntarily and eagerly assumed the mantle of leadership. He immediately became the man in charge for many and a pariah for others. Most of the bureaucrats in the Northwest fully expected Robert to take over the helm of the new nation when Stuart died. He had been the most visible man in the organization second only to Stuart Martin.

Unfortunately, others in the WestPac leadership group always considered Robert Thomas as one that could not be totally trusted to act on behalf of the men and women that comprised the organization. Robert was never what one would call a 'team player'. He was more of a 'one man act'. There was no hard evidence supporting this lack of trust by his critics in WestPac and it was not a matter of animosity, it was rather a questioning of his motivation. While he was respected as a person who could deliver under very trying circumstances, he was also considered one who would likely see to his own well being if that became an issue. These were clearly intangible complaints that his critics had difficulty explaining but they carried weight and when he thrust himself forward as the new leader of West-Pac, key players in the organization had other plans and blocked his path to the seat of power.

Robert's most visible antagonist was Irene Covington, the very liberal minded member of WestPac who had always been ready and prepared to block moves by Stuart or Thomas designed to give them more power and control over the group. Irene was always arguing the personal freedoms espoused by the former national Constitution to limit the expansion of power being assumed by Stuart and Robert. She used as support for her arguments the freedoms guaranteed by the Bill of Rights including in particular, freedom of speech, right to counsel, voting rights and other rights espoused and used before the collapse as tools by the liberal left to advance their liberal agenda. Amazingly, it was the liberal left that was taking away those freedoms from the mass of the citizenry at the same time as they were espousing them and Irene had always been a master at using the basic principles of liberty upheld by the right to frustrate their ambitions and further her own. Irene was more a strong believer in Democratic Socialism and less a believer in Constitutional Federalist Capitalism. In her hierarchy of heroes, Che Guevara placed much higher than Thomas Jefferson although she did not make it a point to publicize this fact.

Irene was successful in gaining the support of Sarah Taves the number three person in WestPac as well as Anders Jensen, one of the original founders and a number of other influential actors in the WestPac organization. She worked on their subliminal distrust of Robert Thomas and picked away at it until they caved. With that support, Irene succeeded in placing a roadblock preventing Robert Thomas' takeover of the leadership and inserted first Anders Jensen and eventually Sarah Taves as the President of WestPac. She herself was eventually appointed to the number two spot in the organization and Robert was permitted, as a bargaining chip, to retain his position as the Economic Administrator which primarily involved promotion, recruitment and economic development for WestPac in the western states areas. It was a very important position, one that had led to the success of WestPac's growth in the Northwest.

Robert Thomas had been very successful as the Economic Administrator in bringing areas of the west into the organization and following his attempted takeover, he continued to succeed in this endeavor. While Robert had been frustrated in his takeover attempt, that in no way changed his intentions for eventually winning command of WestPac. He concluded that he had not prepared properly and would make sure that when another opportunity arose, he would be fully prepared. The fact of the matter was that he had been taken totally by surprise with the unexpected passing of his mentor and friend, Stuart Martin.

Others in the organization were also disappointed by Robert's failure to take over the helm, in particular, Ross Perry the former Green Beret member. Perry had been in control of the rapidly growing military arm of WestPac and he fully supported Robert's ambitions and agreed with his aggressive approach to the politics of leadership. Perry, for similar reasons, likewise managed to maintain his position as commander of the military forces following Robert's attempted takeover. He had done an excellent job in the past and was recognized by all as the most competent military leader in WestPac. His continuance in his military post was a sop to gain his allegiance to the new leadership of WestPac with Thomas presumably out of the picture.

Following the leadership transition to Sarah Taves, Robert had meetings with Ross Perry wherein the two continued their discussions regarding the need for more effective leadership and planned how they would proceed in the future. They both decided that they had to obtain the backing of certain key officials in WestPac in order to eventually take over the leadership with their support and backing. One person, who both men admired, that was key to the success of this endeavor, was the President, herself, Sarah Taves. Sarah had cooperated fully with Stuart Martin's rather aggressive politics and Robert figured that with some effort on his part, she would work with him as well. Sarah was, by no means, a follower of Irene Covington. Rather, Sarah had a profound respect for the freedoms encompassed by the Constitution and the Bill of Rights. She was aware that Robert Thomas had limited affection for, particularly, certain aspects of the Bill of Rights and this was the main reason she agreed to block the assumption of Thomas to control of WestPac. Robert figured that given time, he could convince Sarah that his proposed changes for some of the Bill of Rights provisions were not only substantial improvements but would in time protect the very life of the Constitution. Sarah supported Ross Perry regardless of any misgivings she may have with respect to Robert. Andy Moss, a top leader in the military units, always supported Ross Perry as did John Barnes who was the 'go to guy' when it came to obtaining scarce materials, an important position when everything was scarce. Monty Wyatt, an upper level military figure, highly respected by the military, also supported Ross Perry and Robert Thomas. Hans Frick, the head of the rapidly growing air arm of WestPac was considered an important figure whose allegiance was not known but who, nevertheless, could be won over.

All in all, Robert Thomas and Ross Perry looked upon their goals as attainable, being fairly evenly balanced against the opposition. The individual that could tip the balance in their favor was WestPac's main enemy, Frank Turner, the former President of the United States of America and presently the leader of the massive Federal Security Police. The FSP were aggressively moving in force across the continent to again take over the lives of the former citizens, including those in the West. Rational citizens of the former nation looked with favor upon strong leaders such as Robert Thomas as the head of an organization that could defend them from the life of slavery and servitude that Turner offered. That support for Thomas could tip the balance in his favor with respect to taking over the leadership of WestPac. The other regions of the country formerly functioning under the auspices of the United States of America continued to be in a state of chaos other than the few regions where functioning political entities, such as WestPac, were gaining control. WestPac's presence was certainly felt throughout the region they occupied. Nevertheless, instability, crime and anarchy still reigned and would continue to reign until new leadership under Robert Thomas and those working for him were successful at reestablishing a functioning, respected government throughout the region. Much needed to be done before that goal was to be achieved.

"All tyranny needs to gain a foothold is for people of good conscience to remain silent."
—**Thomas Jefferson**

CHAPTER TWO

As Robert sipped his Brandy, he was reading the latest intelligence bulletin sent out by the Riverton, Montana, Office of the President, Sarah Taves. Her communications setup with extensive radio and other communication links across the continent provided in depth information on what was happening politically and militarily. There was information in the bulletin concerning FSP battles against the Muslims in the Great Lakes region, ethnic riots in the depressed former manufacturing cities of the former nation and the conditions existing in South Florida where the Cuban forces led by Paco Morales were in combat against the counter Cuban force of Ricardo Ortega. Frank Turner's Federal Security Police, popularly known as the FSP, as well as sub clients thereof, generally maintained a semblance of order by extreme force in Northern Florida, Georgia, Mississippi, Alabama and Louisiana. They had also spread their forces in more limited numbers on a wide swath from Colorado throughout the Mid-West and the eastern States. Their organizational headquarters were said to be in Macon, Georgia, at the former Robbins Air Force Base.

The bulletin noted that while the FSP controlled large sections of the former United States, their iron thumb rule led to frequent but isolated revolts by their subjects and continual pockets of guerilla activity particularly in the South. That was a matter of great interest to Robert as he foresaw the day when WestPac and the FSP would be involved in mortal combat and the discontented populace living under the thumb of the FSP could become valuable allies. There was an extensive article on the FSP's continuing struggle to take over the Southwest. The forces of Louis Donley, the Hispanic leader, had been suffering losses in combat with the FSP ever since Stuart Martin had passed and the new leadership of WestPac had taken over. Stuart had been a staunch supporter of Donley and provided him men and materials to support his army right up to the day of Stuart's death. After that, the WestPac leadership that took over power did not see the connection between a successful Hispanic defense of Colorado and the future well being of WestPac. This was a thorn in Robert's side and it irritated him to read that FSP forces were now involved with fighting in parts of Wyoming, Utah and Nevada. The FSP had driven the Hispanic forces close to the assumed borders of Westpac. It was only a matter of time and they would be moving into Northern Wyoming and on into Montana. Robert knew they would have to act fast to turn the tide against the forces of Frank Turner and the FSP.

Robert took a drink from his glass of Brandy and decided what he was going to do. He would contact Ross Perry and set up a 'come to Jesus' meeting with Sarah Taves. He would enlist Ross, Barnes, Moss, and Nix to meet in Riverton within the next week or two for a sit down with Sarah Taves. They had to convince her that Robert needed a free hand in dictating WestPac moves to counter the intentions of the FSP. WestPac had to join with Louis Donley and stop the FSP in its tracks. Materials and state of the art weapons had to be delivered to Donley ASAP. WestPac had new rockets that Barnes believed would be effective against the tanks that the FSP was using. The older rockets would not penetrate the thick hard shell of the modern tanks. Frick could be providing effective ground support for the Hispanic and WestPac forces. He had the aircraft now that could do the job together with the trained crews and effective weapons. So far, Robert had not heard that the FSP had any effective air support for their Western operation. He had heard they were using a limited number of drones but was not aware as to how effective they were. That could soon change.

Robert reloaded his drink as his mind sped with moves that he could make if given the freedom to do so. He also needed the necessary authority to clamp down on the bureaucratic bumblers that had long been stealing from the producers in the Western States. They no longer heeded his requests or advice. They had realized that he was no longer second in command behind Stuart who supported his every move. That had come to an end with the death of Stuart and Robert's failure to acquire command. Their increasing insolence and failure to return his calls was a growing painful irritant to Robert that was getting worse by the day. He sent a message off to Perry to fly down from Seattle where he had been meeting with WestPac troops operating in that area. The message said, "As soon as possible."

Four days after sending the message to Perry, he was notified that Ross would be landing in Portland that afternoon at three o'clock. When the WestPac courier flight landed and taxied up to the terminal, Robert was standing there waiting for Perry. As Perry walked down the stairway from the aircraft he waved at Robert and soon the two were in Robert's car driving to his office. After covering the normal introductory remarks, Perry looked over at Robert and said, "You don't even have to tell me what is on your mind. I was just going to send you a note suggesting we get together and the sooner the better."

Robert smiled. "Great minds think alike, Ross. Yes, I am damned concerned as to what is going on. We should be kicking ass getting these new areas of WestPac under control and most of all, we should be helping Donley in the battle against the FSP. Donley has been backed up to the Western part of Nevada and that is not good. When the FSP takes care of him, they will be laying their sights on us."

Robert raised his voice even further, "We aren't helping Donley with anything. We aren't doing a damn thing. I am fed up with it. Stuart would have had this operation completed long ago. Sarah is sitting there with Irene Covington and her pals doing nothing. I am for getting some of the principals together and meeting with Sarah either in Riverton or here and letting her know that we need a change of command and we need it now. I would like to have the meeting here but that may not be possible. Also, no Irene Covington. She will not be present." Robert ran through the list of names of the men he wanted at the meeting. They were all members of WestPac that were clearly in Robert's court.

"Robert, I totally agree. Furthermore I am of the opinion that we should phrase this with Sarah as a non-negotiable proposal. I say we go in there with the intention of walking out of there with control of WestPac. We should have all of our horses lined up so that if they balk, we actually forcefully take over. I can have my troops stationed in Riverton to provide total support as soon as we need it. I would rather have Sarah see the light before we push her into a corner. I have a lot of respect for her and I know you do as well. I don't want to insult her."

"I agree, Ross. Let's go over who we want to have at the meeting. I would like to have Anders if we could swing him over. He is a big fan of Sarah's and he may not want to work with us but he must see what is happening."

"Yes, Robert, and Matt Parker is another one that could be of great assistance but he does not like to get involved in disputes such as this. I doubt he would participate. Now, I have already spoken with Moss, Barnes and Nix about the problems we are facing and the problems that are developing as a result of our inactivity. They are hotter about what is happening than even I am and I'm hot."

"OK Ross, we need some cover for all showing up in Riverton at the
same time. I suggest you call for a military conference to resolve the issue
of attacks on supply convoys in the new Northwest Territories. I am invited as it is affecting my dealings with the County and State Bureaucrats.
Maybe in the day or two before the grand event, we feel out Anders and
maybe even Parker and decide then if we are going to let them know what
we have planned. We should by then have most of the power players on
our team and they may just decide to hop on board. That's the way I see
it."

"I agree, Robert. We should demand that you take over as the Chief
Operating Officer of WestPac and I will be reporting to you and to no
one else. Sarah may remain as President with downgraded duties relating
solely to the administrative offices in Riverton. That way Sarah won't look
as though she was fired. You handle all external matters as you did after
Stuart died. Irene Covington may continue to report to Sarah for whatever
the hell she is involved with but we must see that it is nothing important.
Above all, these issues are not negotiable."

The two men scheduled their next meeting for the following week in
Riverton. Perry indicated he would pass the word to his associates to be
in Riverton the same day as he and Robert were arriving and prepared to
back up the demands placed on Sarah. He would arrange the meeting with
Sarah and would let her know that Irene Covington was not to be present and there was no need for Anders or Parker to be present although he
would speak to them beforehand to see if they wished to be involved in
support of the change of command.

"An association of men who will not quarrel with one another is a thing which has never yet existed, from the greatest confederacy of nations down to a town meeting or a vestry."

—Thomas Jefferson

CHAPTER THREE

After Perry returned to Seattle, Robert cancelled appointments and stayed in his office in Portland preparing for the showdown meeting in Montana. He knew this was a one shot attempt at taking over WestPac and if he failed with this move, he was permanently done as far as holding a position of authority in the organization. He had made one mistake before and another mistake would not be tolerated. He had to make this count. He drew up a list of names of people in WestPac with influence and power. He reviewed the entire list and noted those that he knew he could count on to support him and those that he could not count on. For those that would not support him directly, he gave considerable thought as to how he could influence or force them to support him. Of the five persons on that list, he figured at least three could be maneuvered into his court. Anders and Parker could be convinced of the necessity of his proposed changes. They were both logical men with knowledge of what it took to get a job done. Something that appeared to be in short supply in WestPac leadership at the moment.

Beth Sloan was a close friend of Sarah's but she was smart and had been a strong supporter of Stuart and could be a strong supporter of Robert for the same reason. Stuart gave her the clear authority to do the job she had and Robert would meet with her beforehand and offer her the same support. She had run the education system very successfully until Stuart died. Then Irene Covington had come into the picture and had effected some changes that were counter-productive to what Beth Sloan was trying to accomplish. Robert knew that would sway her over to his team when he would tell her that Irene Covington was no longer a player.

After Robert assessed the lineup of people that would be involved in any changeover decision, he concluded that he was in at least a decent position to make his move. What he had to give most thought to was how he was going to deal with Sarah Taves. Sarah was highly thought of both within WestPac and externally across what had been the United States of America. She was one of the original pioneers on the trek west from Florida Her intelligence operation was very highly regarded and was sourced to powers outside of WestPac. Her influence was extensive to say the least. He decided that he would meet with Sarah alone and tell her what she already knew. The FSP was making great gains in the west particularly since Stuart had died in the accident. They had been basically stopped in position before that happened and there was a reason for that. Likewise, the new territories in the west that had come under the umbrella of WestPac were now beginning to lose their interest in continued association with West-Pac due to the fact the relationship seemed to be stagnating. Robert had three large areas in Washington and Oregon that were threatening to leave. They were not being supported militarily nor with promised food supplies. Perry was not getting the new recruits he had been promised and weapons development had about come to a halt. There was clearly a lack of support for the expansionist policies of the new Confederation among the present leaders of WestPac and it was leading to disastrous results if not checked now. WestPac needed to grow in strength and numbers and it had better start soon or the FSP would be in charge. Robert decided he would first try his best to reason with Sarah and if that didn't work, he would have to force his hand. He did not want to do that as he genuinely cared for Sarah. He admired her as a classy woman with brains who was adept at handling difficult people. She was a great asset for WestPac and he wanted to keep her as a helpmate and not have her as an enemy. He continued to give thought to exactly how he would approach her in their meeting.

In the few days remaining before his trip to Montana and his meeting with Sarah, Robert was busy communicating with various leaders in the west that needed propping up for their continued association with West-Pac. He assured them that he was sympathetic to their complaints and was in the process of meeting those complaints head on. He expected to have some news for them within the next five days that they would like to hear. In closing, Robert assured them that he had the same complaints versus WestPac as they had and he was moving to resolve them as soon as possible. They assured Robert that they trusted him to get the job done and they would hold off the critics until they heard from him again. Their last conversation with Robert was mostly in double speak. Both parties had the impression that something of importance was about to take place and they knew what it might be but neither would bring it out in the open.

The evening before he was to leave for Montana, Robert relaxed in his living room with his favorite bottle of Brandy. He was more determined than ever to bring an end to the downslide that had taken over WestPac since Stuart's death. He was sick and tired of the growing bureaucracy, the liberal thinking that had begun to sneak back in and permeate all aspects of WestPac, bringing growth, economic development and political expansion to a virtual halt. He hated Irene Covington for being the prime mover to bring back the laws and administrative proceedings that had paralyzed the former nation prior to the collapse. He would see that she was relegated to a job that gave her no authority to any longer interfere in the rightful progress of WestPac.

Robert wondered where he was going in his own thinking. He had strongly admired Stuart for his strong allegiance to principals of right and wrong. Robert had even tried to adopt many of those principals in his own life when he saw how effective they were for Stuart but was unable at this point in time to assume all of them. He was firmly attached to a belief that what really counted was the bottom line. How you got there was of lesser importance than getting there. He had assumed Stuart's dedication to fairness but even that had some limitations for him and maybe for Stuart as well. He would have to give that some thought. Maybe Stuart was not as perfect as Robert thought he was.

Politically, Robert was very closely allied with Stuart's thinking. To be an effective leader, you had to take control and rule with an iron hand. Be fair but be firm. Give orders but only once. Arguments were not allowed. He would be the leader of the pack and would not turn that responsibility over to anyone. He would listen to advice but only to advice. Some he might even accept. He and Perry thought very much alike as well and he knew that Perry respected him for his ideas on leadership and the future development of WestPac. Robert had commented more than once regarding the philosophy of many in WestPac regarding how decisions were to be made, "They can have their democracy. Just don't bother me with it."

Presently since the death of Stuart, nothing was happening in WestPac that did not pass through the long drawn out democratic process. Consequently nothing was happening in WestPac or if it did, it was so watered down as to be ineffective. Robert had taught Stuart how to play the role of the man in charge and he saw how effective that had been. He would follow his own intuitions on leadership and they would work for him as they had worked for Stuart. As he always told Stuart, the time between idea and action is wasted time. Committees are the ultimate waste of time. If you need to discuss a decision, you are not a leader. Once you make a decision, take action and accept the results, whatever they are.

One thing Robert had was confidence. He never saw a challenge as insurmountable. His entire life had been dedicated to overcoming challenges and this upcoming battle was just one more he had to conquer. He would take over WestPac and would put it on the right track. As a result everyone involved would benefit. There would be pain and no gain for slackers but for those dedicated to the cause, he would reward them fully.

One other aspect of Stuart's philosophy that Robert had initially questioned was his devotion to morality. Robert had viewed Stuart's stance on moral training and its introduction into the culture of WestPac with some question as to what Stuart was up to. Robert at first questioned that emphasis on morality had any potential positive goals. As time passed, he began to see that it definitely did have very positive effects. It had a stabilizing effect on the families and the youth of WestPac. Beth Sloan had been instrumental in producing those results with her incorporation of moral principles in the school system. Irene Covington had, since Stuart's death, watered down some of the school programs and graffiti was again appearing on walls and buildings in Goodland. Robert would point that out to Beth as further proof of the need to return to the principles he and Stuart had implemented for WestPac. He knew Beth Sloan was of similar mind on that point.

Robert thought about his own opinions regarding morality. He had certainly violated most rules related in any manner to the principles of morality. Yet, after observing the progress Stuart had been making in governing WestPac, he had been convinced that adopting moral principles could be put to very good use. However, in order to accomplish what Stuart had accomplished with morality, he would have to make some changes in his own thinking. He concluded it was difficult to fake morality. You either had it or you did not. Yet, many aspects of morality he figured he could adopt and incorporate in his own persona with little effort. His main problem with morality was that by nature he was a liar, a cheat and a thief. He knew it and so did everyone else. He resolved that henceforth he would lie only when absolutely necessary to accomplish a very worthy goal. He would cheat only under severe circumstances or maybe even not at all. If you were known to be a cheat, you would never be trusted under any circumstances and that could interfere with one's ability to lead. He would not give up theft as in this day and age, you had to take property that was not yours on a daily basis in order to survive. He would possibly consider paying for the stolen goods if that was feasible. Generally, Robert was of the view that he was basically honest. He had no difficulty honestly admitting that he had lied about something. That made him laugh as he thought about it, but yet, it was true. In time he would strive to reduce the frequency of his lying. Add to that his admiration for hard work and a great respect for fairness that Stuart had engendered elevated him considerably from his former well known persona. He would never be just like Stuart but he could come damn close. He would continue to work on becoming as he called it, "A better person". He reloaded his Brandy glass and chuckled at his new persona. The new honest, trustworthy Robert Thomas. Well, he would work at it and maybe it would happen.

The following morning as Robert awaited the arrival of the WestPac courier flight in the terminal at the Portland Airport, he looked over at the other passengers awaiting the flight. Some he recognized and some he did not. The courier flight had been set up by Sarah to accommodate travelers working on WestPac business who needed transportation between their main Bases of operation. Robert knew that the operation had expanded beyond those limitations to now providing transportation for others not working on WestPac business but who had access to the powers that be in Riverton and were provided transportation for their personal convenience. He smiled to himself as he made a mental note to end this gravy train tomorrow if not sooner. WestPac was still a hand to mouth operation and had access to very limited amounts of jet fuel that were purchased in exchange for valuable commodities produced by hard working farmers and ranchers primarily in the Riverton, Montana area. There had been a deterioration in dedication after Stuart had died and it was about to be rediscovered if Robert had anything to say about it. It angered him to see people awaiting the flight that had little if any involvement with WestPac business. If they were effective, producing men and women, he would know them and he did not.

Finally the twin jet transport taxied up to the terminal and a number of passengers deplaned, most of whom Robert did not recognize. After the passengers had departed and the baggage was removed, the pilot entered the terminal and checked the passenger's passes and told them to board the aircraft. Robert did not have a pass but it was generally understood that he did not need one. The pilot knew who he was and welcomed him aboard.

As Robert entered the cabin of the transport, he saw Ross Perry motioning to him to come join him. Robert walked back to Perry's aisle and said, "I thought you just might be on this flight seeing as how it came from Seattle."

"I should have told you when I was going to make the trip so we could have some time to chat. Are you all ready for the party we are about to have?"

"Ross, let's hope it is a party. Actually I have been giving this a lot of thought and I am very optimistic we will be able to put this one together. This entire operation is coming to a halt. I was looking at the people getting on this flight and I only recognized a few of them. This is ending. If you are not a producer for WestPac, you walk or ride a horse. Jet fuel is hard to come by. Playtime is over. Our great organization is in tatters and we are not going to let that go to hell right before our eyes. I am pissed."

"Righto, Boss. So what is your schedule for getting this job done? Most of the guys will be in today or tomorrow morning."

"I'm planning on meeting with Sarah tomorrow after lunch. Just the two of us for a heart to heart talk aimed at her retirement. It won't look like that as she can stay on as president but she will have few if any responsibilities. I'm going to make this as soft a landing as possible but that is very difficult to do when you want to take over the entire operation."

The two talked over the changes that had to be made in the coming days and weeks in order to get back on the track that Stuart had in operation at the time of his death. Perry had quite a bit on his plate as did Robert. Both men would need the assistance of competent, efficient staff to effectively regenerate WestPac. Neither man had any doubt that he could do the job or that he could not do it quickly, effectively and efficiently. Perry already had his staff lined up but Robert was continuing to consider just who would take the number two spot behind him. Sarah could handle that position very well but Robert was questioning that she would want to take that on after being rather summarily fired. He would pose it to her just the same.

Robert had lined up the administrative personnel that would be needed to immediately fill the midlevel offices of WestPac to continue their operation according to his policies. He also had one specially chosen person to track down Irene Covington, review her areas of interest and responsibility and ensure that she was no longer involved in any of those activities. They were all to be in position and to move into their respective offices exactly one hour after the time of Robert's meeting with Sarah. That was planned for three p.m. Perry's troops would be in position around all administrative offices and inside all office buildings no later than three p.m. If anyone hesitated in turning over materials or facilities to the new administration, they would be immediately detained and removed. Sarah's office would likewise be secured by Perry's troops and no one would enter or leave after three p.m. without Robert's permission. Everything was set up for the takeover and this time it would be done right.

At three p.m. Robert arrived at Sarah's office and announced himself to her secretary. Her secretary had never been one of his fans and took her time in letting Sarah know that Robert was there. She had been filing her nails and did not make the interphone call to Sarah until she finished the task. After she had done that, Robert leaned over her desk and suggested she pack up her personal items from her desk as she was being replaced. The secretary only smiled and said, "In your dreams."

Robert smiled at her as he walked to Sarah's office door and said to her, "You're done."

"Every citizen should be a soldier. This was the case with the Greeks and Romans, and must be that of every free state."

—**Thomas Jefferson**

CHAPTER FOUR

As Robert entered Sarah's office, she was standing at her desk and welcomed him back to Riverton. "It has been a long time, Robert. We should meet more often. How is everything in the West?"

"Sarah, that is just what I want to talk with you about. Thank you for meeting with me on short notice." Robert paused a moment to get his thoughts in order. "Sarah, I have some very serious matters to discuss with you and I want you to know first that I have the greatest respect and admiration for you. I consider you an indispensable figure in the WestPac organization."

"Well, Robert, you make it sound as though I am being fired."

Her comment stopped Robert for a moment. He had not anticipated getting into the guts of the meeting quite so quickly. "As a matter of fact, Sarah, that is exactly what is going on. I am not going to go into the details of what has been happening to WestPac, vis-á-vis the lack of growth or absence of industry, transportation, economic well being, public safety or whatever. I receive complaints from the powers that be in the west about these issues all the time. Or, for that matter the issues relating to the advances the FSP is making in all regions to the east, the south and in some cases to the west of us. All of us in WestPac are fully aware of the precarious position we have put ourselves into. When Stuart was alive, we were moving rapidly to success in all of these areas. I hate to say it but, and I know it is not all your fault, but WestPac has not been successful since Riverton took over the management of the operation."

Sarah appeared a bit stunned by the severity of Robert's complaint directed at her. She was silent for a moment during which moment it dawned on her that she was, in fact, about to be terminated as the leader of West-Pac.

Sarah immediately questioned in her own mind that Robert had the power to do that. "Ok, Robert, just what do you have in mind as a solution? I am aware we have problems and I have been working on those problems. I was anticipating success in dealing with them but I am curious as to what your proposed solutions are. You undoubtedly came in here with some form of proposal. What is it?"

"Sarah, my proposal is this. You are done as the leader of WestPac. I will be taking over the leadership from my offices in Portland. At this very moment, Perry's forces are present here in Riverton to ensure the takeover of power. Various administrators are at this moment visiting all offices of WestPac wherever they may be, here in Riverton, Portland or in Seattle or elsewhere and taking over administration of all functions of Westpac. We have the entire support of all senior officers in the military organization and most administrators, all of whom admired Stuart and want a return to his policies. As for you, I would hope and pray that you would stay on board as my number two person doing what you so ably did for Stuart. I strongly admire your talents. You are a brilliant organizer, you have imagination and you know intelligence operations inside and out. We need that. We are facing difficult problems in trying times. Sarah, I am a good leader. You know it and the citizens of WestPac know that. So do the clients we are trying to gather up in the West. Let us use our separate talents and get back on track to where we were when Stuart passed. By the way, virtually everything Stuart was doing or saying that was so productive came from my suggestions. Right down to the clothing he wore at the rallies. Think about it. I will meet with you in one hour for your decision. You may even maintain your title as President but I will be calling all the shots. By the way, I just fired your secretary. She is a real jackass. I have to leave now as I have other meetings. I will be back later this afternoon. Think over what I have said and I hope to God you will decide to work with me and bring WestPac up to the level it should be operating at. See you later. Don't bother looking for support from Anders or Parker. They agree with us. Later."

After Robert left Sarah's office, he met with Perry to ensure that all takeover moves were in motion. They were. All offices of WestPac were now managed by Robert Thomas' chosen staff. He inquired as to Irene Covington's location but no one seemed to know where she was. That was fine with Robert. As long as she was out of sight, she could not cause too much damage. Most likely she was still unaware of what was taking place. Robert told Perry that in one hour he would return to Sarah's office for her decision on what she was going to do. He did not believe she had too many options and most likely would accept the position she was offered. He hoped that was her decision. Robert visited the various offices of WestPac that were now operating under his leadership. He also visited Anders and Parker to ensure that they were accepting the changes that were taking place.

When Robert walked into Anders' office, Anders stood up and the two men shook hands. Robert took a seat on the couch and said, "Anders I am going to need your support to make WestPac work as well as we both know it can. Right now it is not producing as it did when Stuart was running the show. Hopefully we can get it back on speed in the very near future. If we can't, we have a major problem."

"You have my support, Robert. I hope you can get Sarah to work for you in the future. She is a great contributor to WestPac and we both know that. I will talk to her myself if she is hesitating on joining up with you. You know how some people are when these issues develop."

"I know it firsthand, Anders, and I would appreciate any assistance you could give us. Anything you need, let me know. Good luck, I have to check on my assistants and see how everything is coming along."

When Robert met with Matt Parker, the reception was a little chilly but then Parker had never been one of his major fans. Nevertheless, Parker told Robert that he knew they had to do something in the leadership of WestPac as it had been losing its touch ever since Stuart died. He had been against Robert's removal from the presidency following Stuart's death but he was in a minority on that issue and could not prevent it. Parker, likewise, assured Robert of his cooperation and backing. The two men shook hands and Robert left for a meeting with Barnes, Perry, Nix and Hans Frick. He was curious as to how Frick was dealing with this takeover in view of the fact Sarah was his wife.

As Robert walked down the hall to the conference room, he became aware of the fact that staffers in the Admin Offices were looking at him with greater interest than they had been doing before. Word apparently was getting out that he was back in the saddle and taking over the leadership position. Many would undoubtedly be in favor of that move and there were always a number that would not. He still had not seen Irene Covington and could hardly wait for her icy comments regarding his latest assumption of power.

When Robert entered the conference room, all of the men invited to attend were in place and stood as he entered and took his place at the conference table. All were smiling as was he. They all were enjoying this moment of apparent success in the transition of power back to the leaders that were known to get the job done. Robert had spoken at length to Perry through the course of the events that had taken place and he knew that Barnes was in support of the change but he was curious as to how Nix and Frick were reacting. They appeared to favor the move and Robert had assumed that both would support it, but he wanted to hear it directly from the two men themselves. He asked them directly for their opinion. "Well Jack, what are your thoughts on what we have been doing here."

Nix smiled and said, "I'm totally in support of what you are doing and I was about to contact you with that in mind when Perry told me what was coming down the pike. I am eager to get rolling on the job ahead. Count on me one hundred percent."

Robert looked over at Frick who had been silent up to this point. "Hans I hope that you understand, I am a major fan of Sarah's and she being your wife presents some problems for you that others in our group do not have to deal with. I understand that but I hope that you can support us in what we are trying to do. I want to get back to what Stuart was building in West-Pac before he had his accident. I have great respect for you and admire the advances that you have made in the war fighting capability of our aviation component. I hope to hell that you can work as enthusiastically for us in the future as you did before. Are you going to be able to do that?"

"Robert, Sarah is a bit disappointed as anyone would be. She was working very hard to correct some of the failings in WestPac leadership and I have not had much of a chance to talk with her since your meeting, but she does understand that changes had to be made. As for myself, I totally supported Stuart and you when the two of you were working together so successfully and I fully intend to continue that in the future. I have great confidence that you possess the leadership we need at the present time and we have great problems that call for strong leadership. You can count on me completely."

"Hans, thanks for your comments. That means a great deal to me. I offered Sarah the number two spot in WestPac and I hope she takes it. She has talents we all need and I hope I can be working with her in the future."

"I just spoke with her for a few minutes, Robert, but I had the impression she would be supporting you in any capacity you chose for her."

"I sure hope so. How about you Ross or John, is everything under control now or are we having major problems anywhere. Any word from Seattle or Portland on the takeover of the offices out there? I have heard nothing but maybe that is good news."

Perry smiled and responded for the two of them. "Robert, I spoke with Andy Moss who is in charge of the Seattle operation and he said that all he had heard was that it was about time somebody did something. Total support. Likewise Mark Campbell and Roy Yates were handling Portland and that had gone smoothly. After all that was your main support in the initial move to take over the leadership. They always wanted you to be running the show."

"OK, that is good news. Now this is what I want. Jack I want you to work with Sarah, and I am assuming she will be on the team, and get West-Pac back into the support role for the new Western territories. They need food and material goods and they have been receiving nothing. I don't care how you do it but I want trucks rolling immediately to Washington and Oregon in particular. Get medical teams out there as well and whatever happened to 'WestPac Corp' with their teams of younger people coordinating between our offices and the new locals in getting them equipped, fed and up to speed on carrying out our mission. Jack follow up on that. We should be drafting those kids for that very important mission as we speak. I don't know if that effort was terminated or what. Maybe Irene Covington killed it. Who knows? Also Jack, find out who in the hell has been painting graffiti on the walls and buildings here in Goodland. When I see that, it just pisses me off. Find the little bastard and put him to work removing the graffiti with a tooth brush. Then when he is done, throw the little bastard in the klink for a few months to think it all over. Ross we need military recruits, recruits, recruits. We will be in the fight of our lives in the near future and we will need an army of at least five hundred thousand or more combat ready soldiers and airmen to defeat the FSP. That is coming right down the pike. I hate to ask what our military numbers are right now. I have been taken out of the loop on that other than what info Perry has. He hasn't been in the loop either which is amazing in view of the fact he was in charge of the entire military operation until we were canned. Now I know this takes food, material goods, weapons, ammo and WestPac dollars. Find what you need and take it, buy it, steal it, whatever, I don't care but we will have progress on this or we will die. Do you all understand that?"

The group responded enthusiastically, "We're with you Boss. We will be on this big time."

"Hans, one more thing. The WestPac courier flights are now only for official business. We are going to have plenty of that so let's get the free loaders off of the courier flights. No more of that. Also I want a plane and a crew for my use and for Ross Perry's use alone. Both of us are going to need rapid, accessible transport. Just a good, safe, fast, six to eight place aircraft will work just fine. They should be based at Portland with repair facilities there and in Seattle as Perry will be using the bird quite a bit as well. We may eventually need two aircraft. I want that made available tomorrow morning when I leave here to make a show the flag appearance around WestPac."

"Also, Barnes I will need offices equipped to handle my staff in Portland. I would anticipate no more than five staffers with five secretaries. By the way, we will be working in all offices or people will be canned. If people do not produce, they go. We are also back to Stuart's morals training programs. I will be discussing that with Beth Sloan later today or tomorrow morning. I want the school curriculum to replace that as it was when Stuart died. From now on this is a clean living, hard working, conservative group of people intent upon getting the job done. Don't worry, you don't have to start going to church but it might help if you do. You will all make damn sure you are devoted one hundred percent of the time to getting the job done. OK? Does everyone understand that? By the way, speaking of show the flag, I have not seen one of our flags anywhere since shortly after Stuart's death. Obviously someone did not like the flag idea. I like it. Nix get those flags out to all WestPac offices and facilities. If we are short of flags, get the ladies together to sew up hundreds of them. All gatherings will now be showing the WestPac flag. Now, Nix, we are going to need Matt Parker's full support with what we are doing. We will need food, clothing and materials for export to the West. Most of that will come from here. We will need those shipped by truck or rail if it is available. We were making rapid progress on rail transport again that was when Stuart died. Ross, I want you to assign people to seeing that all areas of our new territories are supported by rail lines. I know that is a big job so work with Barnes and assign someone that specific task. Let me know who that is so I may contact him directly. My office staff will also be working on this. Advise whoever you assign that I, or my staff, will be looking for immediate progress on that task. Now the work of extending rail lines and getting rail equipment back in operation is the responsibility of the local communities serviced by them. Ross, whoever is in charge on this operation, make sure they know that their involvement should only be supervisory. If your supervisors don't see progress, make sure they let the locals know that they can be replaced quite easily by people who give a damn. No excuses."

Robert paused and thought for a moment to remember if he had left anything out. "OK, enough is enough. We will get together at least once a month to check on progress. If any of you have any problems, contact me immediately. Don't wait until things get worse. Let's all get to work."

When Robert departed the conference room, he went directly to Sarah's office and was admitted immediately by the new secretary who gave him a great smile and said, "Welcome back." He thought to himself, "That's a major improvement." When he went in, Sarah stood and said that she had decided that in the interests of WestPac, she would be totally supportive of Robert and his program."

Robert smiled and said, "Thank God, Sarah. I need your brains and enthusiasm. We have so much that needs to be done. I gave Jack Nix a number of tasks to take on so if you would, let me know how that is going. Also, we are going to need a lot of help from Matt Parker. I am going to see him before I leave but I will be contacting you regarding how that is going. Another item we will be needing is fuel. I'm going to get together with Louis Donley in Colorado or wherever he is fighting the FSP these days and work out an agreement for increased fuel shipments. We may also have to set up a rail line between here and the South that would be dedicated to shipments of fuel to the North and food and clothing to the South. Start giving that some thought. Also I'm going to need an efficient, smart secretary down in Portland if you happen to know of any that could fill that bill. Have them call my office down there if you would."

When Robert left Sarah's office he went to see Beth Sloan in the Education Office and have her reinstitute her morals training program that she had functioning so well when Stuart died. She informed Robert that she had already heard the news of the change in management of WestPac and had already taken steps to accomplish exactly what he was after. Beth was a close friend of Sarah but she knew that Sarah had been having difficulty preventing Irene Covington from forcing her political beliefs upon the system. She was extremely pleased to see Robert back at the helm. Robert also impressed upon Beth the need to increase the number of schools in the west teaching the curriculum that had been working so well in the Montana area. Perry was aware of this need as well and he would provide troops to secure areas she wanted to target for new schools. Robert told her to work with Perry and to let Robert know if she needed equipment, workers, or materials to accomplish her task. His words before leaving were, "I consider your work essential to the success of our efforts in the West. The morals training program you had going in the west was working wonders with the children and teenagers until Irene began undercutting it. That will not happen again. You have our complete support for your curriculum. Keep up the good work."

Beth smiled at Robert and said, "Consider it done."

That evening, Robert sat in his quarters in the company of Anders and Matt Parker discussing his plans for WestPac and some of the very difficult challenges they needed to overcome. He had been eager to meet with Parker as he had to get him on the team as he was key to producing and providing the material goods and food that WestPac would be in need of in the coming months and years. Parker assured him that he would be doing his best to fill the storerooms for the deliveries to the west that would be taking place very soon. His problem was in dealing with the farmers and ranchers for the crops that would go into the storerooms. Robert told him to give WestPac dollars, IOU's or whatever it took to get the warehouses filled. "We will be paying these people back in time. We might be able to work a deal on the fuel the farmers and ranchers will be needing. Louis Donley down in Nevada and Colorado will be needing weapons that we will be delivering to him shortly and that will be in trade for fuel. We will be able to deliver that fuel to our ranchers and farmers and pay them back that way. That will take a little time but the fuel will be arriving in the next few months I would estimate and I know they will be happy to get it."

The meeting with Anders and Parker went fairly well and when it ended, Robert told the two men that he would be giving them a call in the next week or two with a status report on conditions in the West. Robert had been receiving a great deal of criticism from the Western bureaucrats for failure to provide security, food and medical care to their citizens as originally promised. Robert was fully aware of the needs that existed in the West. He had driven in armed convoys through various areas in the west and witnessed first-hand the lack of activity, the boarded up homes, businesses, schools; scarecrow people staring vacantly at the convoy as it passed, holding children obviously in need of nourishment. Sarah had been sending out convoys of food throughout the west but it was never enough. Robert was fully aware that the real answer to the problems of the west was stability and economic growth. The West had to develop their own food production, security organizations, their own products that would produce the income necessary to buy everything they needed to live their lives comfortably. Without stability, there would be no production, no marketing of products and no economic growth. He would see that come to pass and soon.

"That government is the strongest of which every man feels himself a part."

—Thomas Jefferson

CHAPTER FIVE

The following morning, Robert was up bright and early for one final meeting with Sarah. Everything had been happening so rapidly that he wanted to be sure that Sarah was on speed with everything that he hoped was happening. She would provide another pair of eyes to ensure that progress was being made. In their meeting, Sarah called in her new secretary, Sandy, and had her take notes so that both she and Robert had a copy of what needed to be done. Robert rehashed all conversations and instructions that he had participated in the previous day. Sarah assured him that she would see that work was progressing as he intended it to progress. She also advised him that she had contacted a very efficient secretary in the Portland area that would work well with Robert and would contact him in the next day or so in Portland. As Robert was leaving Sarah's office, Sandy assured him that she would be sending him a copy of her notes no later than tomorrow morning.

When he went out to the terminal, the clerk told him that the aircraft was ready to go whenever he was. Robert told him that he was ready and the clerk buzzed the pilot who soon came into the terminal, greeted Robert, took his bag and the two headed for the aircraft. The pilot confirmed that they were going to Portland and told Robert that weather was not an issue today. Within minutes the twin engine jet aircraft with two pilots was airborne and heading west for Portland. Robert noticed that the only people boarding the aircraft were those he recognized as WestPac officials authorized to access the flights. That was the first visible sign of his new administration taking effect and it pleased him to see it. Ross Perry and two other military staffers were already on the aircraft when Robert boarded. Robert greeted the three men and asked Perry if he was staying over in Portland.

"No, Robert, your pilot is flying me on up to Seattle when we drop you off assuming the plane is available for that. If not, I can wait until it returns."

"No problem Ross. My plans are to operate out of Portland for a few days at least but I can see that we are going to need another plane in the West. We both are going to have to be covering a lot of bases out here in order to be effective. I will contact Hans as soon as I land and have him send another plane out and that can be based up at Seattle or wherever your main Base is. The two aircraft should well handle our needs in the West and also for the trips back to Riverton."

As the aircraft flew to the west towards Portland, they passed over Butte, Montana and Walla Walla, Washington, before commencing their descent into Portland. There were extensive fires burning in both cities which was a surprise to Robert who was yet not fully apprised as to the conditions existing in the new Western territories. He had been informed by the politicians and representatives from these areas that they continued to exist in unstable conditions but actually seeing the devastation they continued to experience and the widespread fires was a bit of a shock for Robert. "Ross, that has to stop immediately. Why is that still going on? Are we short of troops or do we lack cooperation from the locals? This is terrible."

"It's a combination of both, Robert. We do not have control of the local leaders as you well know we were getting when Stuart was around. They don't want to totally side with us and then find themselves standing alone facing their constituents as they have been finding lately. We need strong, continuous and reliable leadership. They are begging for it. We also need the troops. I could use one hundred thousand troops out here right now. If I had them, those fires would not be burning."

"OK Ross, then get them and get them working. We can pull experienced men out from Riverton and put them to work out here right now. We can use our lesser experienced troops to guard the fort in Riverton until we get them on speed and totally combat ready. What do you think?"

"That sounds good to me, Robert. I tried that in the past but was refused. I will get them out here and put them to work. We can take care of these larger city issues rather quickly."

Robert went back to scanning the smaller communities from the cabin window and they did not seem to have the same problems. He could tell there were some unstable areas even in the smaller towns but not like the terrible scenes in the larger cities. He was also studying the rail lines between cities and noted that there were periodic interruptions in the lines from time to time. He mentioned that locals were dropping the ball on protecting rail lines and that had to stop now. Ross agreed and said that was a related problem and quipped, "Hard to crack the whip when you don't have the whip."

Robert sat back in his seat. "It seems as though we lost about half the progress we had made in the West with Stuart at the helm. What the hell happened, Ross?"

"Too many people took advantage of the gains we had made and decided it was time to collect. It doesn't do wonders for your confidence in your fellow man does it."

"Sure as hell doesn't, Ross. It's time to kick ass big time. You crack the whip on the troops and I will land hard on the Admin types. As for the bureaucrats out in the countryside, I will take care of them, some with gloves on and some with brass knuckles. I'm going to make a tour of the West in the coming weeks and I'm going to want some troop support as I anticipate that some people will not like what I am going to say and I may want them sent directly to camp for further training, if you know what I mean."

"Gotcha Boss. Let me know when and where and you will have all the help you need."

When Robert arrived in Portland he said goodbye to Perry who was traveling on to Seattle and told him he would be in touch in a few days. He first wanted to get his team set up and would then be moving about the State, Oregon first and then up to Washington or down to California. He reminded Perry to have a well trained military unit available on call in Portland should he be in need of them. Perry assured him he would take care of that.

When Robert returned to his home which had also served as his office, he placed a call on the WestPac com line to Hans Frick in Riverton. Hans was soon on the line and Robert told him he wanted one aircraft in Portland, about a six passenger job for me and my staff, and a second aircraft placed in Seattle. "Talk to Perry as to where the plane should be based and also the size of aircraft that Perry would normally need. Hopefully it would be relatively small. You can quote me on that."

Robert then began giving some thought to who he was going to bring into his operating team as he knew he was going to need some help and soon. There was one young fellow that had assisted him on projects in the West that had been impressive. He was a quick thinker and agreed very much with Robert's philosophy on leadership which meant that he was basically bottom line oriented. How you got there was secondary. He picked up the com line and told the operator to get a hold of Clay Daley. Within minutes, Robert was talking with Clay and they were bringing each other up to date on their whereabouts. Robert finally got down to business.

"Clay, I need an assistant as I have a ton of work to do. I take it you are up to date on the changes in management in WestPac, right?"

"So I Hear and I am mighty pleased to hear you are back in the saddle. I would love to be working with you Robert. I like your style and I like where you want to take WestPac. When can I start?"

"I can use you just as soon as you can get set up here, Clay. You know where I am. I am going to have to move my office as it will be too large for this small pad. That will be your first job. I anticipate having a relatively small staff of around ten people total. Find a building, preferably out at the airport. That will work fine. Make my office large enough and private enough so that I can live right there. Then get four other go getter guys, get a secretary for each one that can keep tabs on them and keep them organized, arrange offices and equipment for them. By the way, I mentioned that to Barnes as well that I would need those people. Check with him first to see if he lined anyone up. If not, tell him you will take care of that for me. He may have lined up office equipment as well, if not, tell him you will handle that one too. As for the three other guys you will be hiring, let them know that they will be spending most of their time on the road. Oh, one more thing. No screwing around by anyone. This is a working operation. Just like it was when Stuart was around. Make that clear to anyone you bring on board. They start screwing around with their secretaries or anyone else and they go."

"I'll pass the word, Robert. Consider it done. I will be on this tomorrow morning. Com will be able to locate me if you need me. Otherwise you can assume I am working on getting us all set up."

As Robert settled back in his chair getting his thoughts in order as to where we go from here, the com phone rang and it was a woman who identified herself as Toni Norton. Sarah had contacted her and suggested she call Robert regarding a secretarial or office management position. She was not totally clear on what it entailed. "But, here I am."

"It is good to hear from you, Miss Norton. I assume you know of me and I take it you know I am not an easy person to work for. Right?"

"I have heard that but I have heard nothing bad. Just that you are very demanding. But then, I am as well and I understand demanding people."

"OK. Well if Sarah sent you, she must have OK'd you for the job so I will assume you are qualified. I am very busy right now and will be for the next whatever. Contact Clay Daley on the Com line. They will know how to get in touch with him. He is what I guess you would call my Administrative Assistant. Good guy, you will enjoy working with him. Help him in setting up our offices somewhere out by the airport in Portland. Tell him I told you to call. You can start in the morning. If you need some funds right off, talk to Clay about that. By the way, I assume you are aware that I am again running WestPac so we have a lot of work to do."

"I am aware of that and I like to work."

"Good. I will talk with you again down the line."

Robert sat back in his chair again. "Well, things are rolling right along." He began making out a list of 'to do's to be accomplished the following morning. The first item on the list was to notify all of the bureaucrats in the Western offices that he was again in charge and to let his office know what problems they were having in their separate district. He generally knew what they were but he wanted to get all the bitches out in the open so that they could work together on getting them solved. He knew that in many cases 'working together' would not always work. He would have to resolve the problems on his own. Fine. Then he would know which bureaucrats needed reprogramming and he could get that started as well.

"And for well over a hundred years our politicians, statesmen, and people remembered that this was a republic, not a democracy, and knew what they meant when they made that distinction."

—Robert Welch

CHAPTER SIX

In the morning after his return from Riverton, Robert pulled out his files on the Western State officials and bureaucrats. He had the information broken down into files by State and by locality. Robert selected the Oregon files and began looking over the maps and materials to determine how he was going to tackle the problem of rebuilding the enthusiasm of the Westerners for WestPac. Most of the population of Oregon resided along the I-5 corridor, or whatever remained of it, and the I-84 corridor to the east and then down to the Southeast part of the State. He decided to work on the larger cities first which ran to the south from Portland down I-5. He had maintained contacts throughout the State in connection with his work as the Economic Administrator after his termination from the leadership role of WestPac so he was not starting from a blank slate. He had the com operator make contact with Bert Connors who was the County Commissioner in the Salem area. Bert was a classic bureaucrat who had been quite successful at filling his own coffers prior to the economic collapse and who had continued his accumulations afterwards but on a much smaller scale. Connors was not a complete waste of time for Robert as he was susceptible to persuasion provided there was some quid pro quo involved. The operator called him back and said Bert Connors was on the line.

"Bert, Robert Thomas here, how are you doing?"

"Same-o same-o, Robert. I hear you are back running the show."

"That's right. How are things down that a way? How are you coming along with the rail line extension? We have goods to ship your way and no way to get them shipped."

"If I'd known that, Robert, I would have had the lines laid. We have had very little coming from WestPac other than promises."

"Bert, you get those lines in and I will see that you get what you need. Remember though, it is not a one way street. I don't know how you all are living down there but I do know it could be a hell of a lot better than it is.

Now, I'll just be real candid with you, Bert, because we have a big job to do. The FSP is knocking at our doors and we have to react fast. That is why I'm back in the saddle. I intend to see that we do what's gotta be done. You with me on that?"

"Yeh, Robert. But what the hell's in it for us? Hell we're short of food, clothing and we have these wild ass young gangs that are raising holy hell with everything. You promised us peace and plenty and we haven't seen any of it. I know when we lost Stuart and you were bounced that created some problems for everyone but hell's bells, everyone here is yelling at me and wondering where the WestPac operation is."

"OK Bert. I tell you what. I'm gonna have Perry send troops down to the Salem area and I guarandamntee you that we will lay the law down immediately. Now in the meantime, I want you to get the track laid down proper between you and Portland and then on down south of Salem so we can deliver to you what you need and so that we can haul the crop and materials out of Salem and get it marketed throughout the West. That way we can all turn a profit. Are you with me on that?"

"OK Robert. I'll tell the boys to get rolling on that but when may I expect Perry to come in and I hope he will leave some troops here to quiet things down and not just march through town like Sherman and be gone."

"Bert, they will station troops in Salem. Now I'm counting on you to get that track laid. We need rail lines to ship goods. Now get those lines laid or I'm going to turn Salem over to the glue sniffing kids. You got that?"

"OK, I'm counting on you, Robert. No bullshit on this side. Send me word in two days as to when Perry's coming."

"I'll do that and I'm going to have my flyboys checking over that rail line to see that it's going in. Good times are ahead for us, Bert, but let's get this operation up and rolling."

"I see the light, Robert. Send the troops. I will kick ass down here."

"OK Bert and also, get those trains up and operating. Get your railroad people back to work. Get that Roundhouse in Salem back in operation. We are going to need engines to pull those rail cars. We will float you a West-Pac loan if necessary but get them out working right now. I want progress and I want it right now. If I don't see progress, Bert, I may have to hire some hotshot down there. Now I'd rather deal with you, right?"

"You damn well better not hire someone else. I'll get it done, Robert. You can count on it."

"Good. I'll call you back on Perry's troop arrival."

Robert called the com operator and told her to get Perry on the line for him. Within minutes Ross Perry was on the phone. Robert gave him the information on Bert Connors in Salem, Oregon and his need for troops now. Perry asked how many would be needed and Robert estimated fifty based on the size of the town. Robert told Perry to contact Hans and have him fly the DC-3 with the troops over to Salem for an extended stay in that area. They could also operate down into Corvallis and Eugene to extend the rule of law into those areas.

"Ross, assign Monty Wyatt or someone with a brain as the honcho of the group so that we can have confidence that our interests in that area are being met. If so, have them contact me through com so I can tell them what I want them to watch for. OK?"

"Wyatt is in Riverton right now getting the new recruitment program going. I don't want to lose him on that but Barnes is there as well and he had it rolling full steam before we all lost our jobs. I'll talk with Wyatt as soon as we hang up."

"OK, Ross. I was thinking about using Campbell and Yates for the recruitment and training program as Barnes is overloaded right now. I'll talk to you about this later."

Robert made notes of his contact with Connors and Perry and made a note to talk with Wyatt as well as Campbell and Yates hopefully in the next day or two. That was a productive few minutes spent and if he could duplicate that about a hundred more times, he would be making some good progress. One problem he would have was that of troop availability. WestPac had approximately one hundred thousand combat ready troops and a huge area of landmass for them to stabilize. They had to go on a crash mobilization program to meet their needs. He would talk with Perry about that later in the day. While he was pondering these issues, his West-Pac staffer that monitored incoming calls and communications knocked on his door and advised him she had the latest Intel Bulletin from Sarah. Sarah would send these out every day or more often if something hot was in the mix.

Robert took the four page bulletin and began reviewing it. He focused immediately on FSP activities in the Colorado, Utah and Nevada area. It was clear that the FSP was on the move to the West and would soon be entering California if they were not stopped. He placed a call to Barnes for an update on the status of weapons development and inventories of the more sophisticated weapons that Louis Donley would most likely want to receive. He also instructed the com operator to attempt to contact Louis Donley for a telephone conference.

The Intel Bulletin indicated the Muslim forces were making inroads into the Wisconsin and Minnesota areas. There was very little resistance to their aggressive moves in those two bastions of pacifism in the North. There was some question in Robert's mind if the Muslims were interested in the Dakotas. If they were he was going to have to take action to protect his eastern flank. With everything going on and the poor state of readiness of WestPac, it was becoming increasingly apparent to Robert that they may have to declare martial law and go on a war footing to prepare for combat.

There was also an article on attacks by local gangs in various parts of the Westpac zone of control on government officials and on military personnel operating in areas that were not totally pacified. That immediately angered Robert and he had the com operator connect him to Sarah. When she was on the line, Robert told her to immediately send out notices on the Voice of WestPac and also in the Word of WestPac that any incidents of violence exhibited towards lawful representatives of WestPac would be met immediately with overwhelming force and long time confinement. He assured her that he would talk to Perry about that as well as he was now awaiting a call from him on other matters.

Shortly after hanging up with Sarah, Robert was on the line with Perry. "A couple of important items, Ross. I know you are working overtime on boosting troop strength. We must get that built up as soon as possible. Whatever you need to expedite that, let me know and I will see that you get it. There will be many other communities just like Bert Connors in Salem that are going to be yelling for troops to protect their citizens from the animals. Also, you are going to have to have a roving squad of troops to go after these jackasses that are attacking local officials and even attacking troops in various areas of WestPac. Sarah is sending out a public notice to whoever is doing that to be aware that they will immediately be hunted down if they pull that kind of crap. When that happens, I will be calling you. When you catch those losers, come down hard on them and then lock them up in one of the retraining centers. No privileges. You can load up your airplane or have Nix send a plane out from Riverton with the troops to do the job. If we have to we will start an immediate draft. Let me know if we need to do that right away and if we have the training facilities and materials available for a rapid influx of new recruits."

"Robert, I talked with Sarah about that and she believes we have the materials, weapons and training facilities available for a substantial increase in recruits. The Northern area of Riverton was pretty well completed for the influx of troops when Stuart died and much of it is still empty. I suggested that Sarah advertise on radio and on WestPac Word that there are openings in our military for young men and women. She tells me they have been receiving many calls, particularly from refugees fleeing the combat areas south of us. Nix and Moss have both been working on that project so we should start seeing progress in troop numbers soon."

"Sounds good, Ross. I have been reading over Sarah's latest Bulletin and it sounds as though Louis Donley has his back against the wall with the FSP. We are going to have to start playing a role there or pretty soon it will be us alone against the FSP. Ross, next time you talk with Nix, tell him to lay the law down on those graffiti boys in Riverton. No trials, just a short hearing before a panel of military officers. Just pick them up, throw them in the klink and tan their hides a bit and send them out to clean up their work. If that doesn't wake them up, send them out to Boot Camp and let them learn to be soldiers, the hard way. OK?"

"Will do, Boss. We have a lot to do."

"Yes. I know I'm laying it on you pretty heavy. When you need more help, let me know. Talk to you later."

That afternoon, Com called Robert and informed him that Louis Donley would be calling him within the hour and to be available. "He has to talk with you." Robert assured the operator that he would be in his office until the call came in. Within the hour, Robert was on the phone with Donley.

"Louis, I'm reading Sarah's Bulletin that I assume you receive as well and it sounds as though you have your hands full with the FSP. What is going on there. Maybe we can offer assistance. You may have heard, I am again in charge of WestPac and I am back in position where I may be of assistance to you."

"Robert, I need your help now. We are short of good state of the art materials and troops who know how to use them. The FSP is now also using drones and ground support helicopters. We were able to defend against the helicopters with the rockets you gave us but the drones operate at much higher altitudes and the rockets are not as effective with them. They arm the drones with bombs and missiles. Both weapons are very accurate and I assume are guided. Let me know if you have anything we could use against them. They are our biggest problem right now. We don't know they are around until the bomb or missile hits. The only thing in our favor right now is that they are operating with a very extended supply line and we are able to interdict that quite a bit. If we could defense the drones, we could turn them back."

"Louis, I will talk to my supply and weapons expert, Barnes, and get back to you. We are in a rebuilding program with our military but we could probably spare fifty thousand combat ready troops if that would get the job done. I will talk with Perry about that. I'd rather fight them now when you are out there than when we are fighting them alone. How many troops do you have in combat against them now and what is their troop strength?"

"Robert, we have around one hundred thousand troops in combat at this time and I estimate the FSP force to number about double that. The main difference is that they have better equipment. Let me know what you could do for us. We sure as hell need the help."

What Robert wanted to do was to send a sizeable force straight south out of Montana and split the FSP force operating to the west from their supply line coming from the east. He also wanted to keep that North South line open so that WestPac would continue to receive the fuel shipments the Hispanics were providing to him. WestPac needed that fuel badly and they were beginning to run short ever since the FSP had made their Western advance into Utah. If WestPac could come in behind the FSP forces and the Hispanics could counterattack from the West, they could annihilate the FSP. This appeared to Robert to be an opportunity to send the FSP back to the East for good. He would talk with Perry about this in their next tele-com. He would also get a hold of the Utah military commanders to learn what they were doing or not doing. They should be joining forces with WestPac and the Hispanics against the FSP.

Robert made notes of the instructions he had given to the various members of his staff so that he would not forget what orders he had passed out to whom. He had been running ever since he took over the leadership and it still looked like a brick wall looming in front of him. He did have some good people working for him though and hopefully that would bail West-Pac out of what appeared to be a gloomy situation.

It was already eleven p.m. and he had been working at top speed since six in the morning. He poured himself a glass of Brandy and water and tried to relax as he thought about where they go from here. The major problem that he needed to solve was the shortage of trained, combat ready troops. He would lay down hard on Moss, Nix and Perry to get that resolved soon.

If he had the troops, he could pacify WestPac and he could march down on the FSP's supply line and destroy those bastards. Well, he would work on that and hopefully that was just what he would do.

As he sipped his Brandy he thought about the nationwide conference that he needed to have so that the citizens could see who was running the show and what kind of a show he could put on. He would again have the local bureaucrats in but this time to Portland as that was more convenient for the Westerners and he would bring back their enthusiasm for WestPac. He would have that telecast for the ordinary citizens so that they could see their local leaders happily supporting the team that was guiding their new nation. That would alleviate many of the problems he was currently facing.

In order to do that, he would first have to repair the transportation grid at least between the major cities so that attendees could safely attend the conference and to see to the safety and security of the citizens throughout WestPac so that they had greater confidence in what WestPac could do for them.

As he drank his Brandy, he thought that he was never again going to turn loose of the leadership of WestPac. He was fortunate to get back in control in time before it completely reverted to the sad state it was in when he and Stuart first got to work. It was amazing the damage that had been inflicted on WestPac after he was dethroned by the institution of bureaucracy that had immediately taken over after he was gone. Many of them were still functioning from their offices and that would be taken care of just as soon as he got the ball rolling on the repairs to the military and the infrastructure of WestPac. He would run the entire show from Portland and all personnel responsible for the various departments would be right where he could watch them. Any empire builders would be terminated immediately. Anyone cheating the system or found stealing any goods or the property of others would be summarily canned and convicted by military courts. No appeals. No defense attorneys. There would be no fancy trials, only hearings involving the parties themselves and the military Judge. There would be some mistakes made, but that beat the hell out of the endless appeals that tied up the court systems. This entire matter had reaffirmed Robert's belief that the mass of humanity needed to be controlled by a strong leader. Stuart had showed him that worked very well and Robert had learned his lesson well.

Robert was becoming more and more convinced by the moment that there was far more work that needed to be done than he could handle by himself. He was wasting his time trying to work on the mountain of problems that he faced. He needed to use his time organizing a team of people with the same drive that he had for getting the job done. He had known that for some time but he realized he was not making progress on correcting the situation. He needed movers and shakers at his beckon call that would serve him as he had served Stuart. He had brought Clay on board with that thought in mind and he would have to discuss that with Clay as soon as the two of them were together. Clay had a reputation for getting the job done and knew how to do it when normal channels were closed. That was key to the position that Robert had in mind for him. He would find others as well. It just took time but he would find them. Right now Robert had about four major jobs lined up for Clay to take care of but soon they would get together and have some time to talk.

"Freedom is never more than one generation away
from extinction. We didn't pass it to our children in the
bloodstream. It must be fought for, protected, and handed
on for them to do the same."

—**Ronald Reagan**

CHAPTER SEVEN

The next day, Robert placed a call to John Barnes to find out what he could do to help Louis Donley with weapons and materials. Barnes informed him that they had been working on some ground to air missiles that would reach up to Drone operating altitudes but targeting the missile was then another problem. They were presently using radar to locate the Drone and target the missile to the Drone. One of the problems was that the drones did not present a very good radar target due to their size. Nevertheless, they were fairly successful operating at about a fifty percent success rate and that would help Donley quite a bit.

He could send some of the units to Donley with instructors to train his people in operating the equipment if that was what Robert wanted.

"You sound as though you are not in favor of sending the goods. Why not?"

"Robert, it's the old story. You don't want to arm your enemy. Right now Donley is very helpful and cooperative but what happens on down the road. It might pay to be a little careful as to what we provide Donley so that we are not looking down the barrel of the gun we gave to him. We could give them the weapons but they are ineffective without the radar control mechanism which is quite high tech. I suggest we would be better off sending our techs to work with Donley's military. They could maintain and operate the equipment and that way we have not given away the whole works. What do you think?"

"You have a point there. I trust Donley but then you can't be too careful. Your friend today may be your enemy tomorrow. OK. Send the radar techs with the missiles and radar systems and tell them to secure the operating manuals. Only our people will operate the equipment. OK John. Keep me informed and you deal directly with Donley. By the way, we need more fuel and we need it soon. Our inventories are being depleted as you well know. I'm going to talk with Perry about securing the rail line so we can transport the fuel up here. Clear all of that with Donley while he is screaming for help. Talk to you later."

His next call was to Perry. He discussed his plan to send a strong force south with a two-fold purpose. One to help Donley by attacking the FSP rear that was battling Donley's forces in Nevada and also to open up and defend our rail lines to the south that we need to ship our petroleum product up to Montana and out to the West. "This may be a good opportunity to seriously damage the FSP with our forces and Donley's hitting them from the front and the rear."

"I've been thinking of that myself Robert. Our problem is that we are short of combat ready troops. We have enough to do the job but it would seriously deplete our operating troop levels. We could gamble on it but it would be a bit of a gamble. The FSP could really hurt us right now but I don't think they would stop going after Donley's troops and just turn on us when they have Donley sort of on the run."

"I agree. Check it out and let me know what you think. Also, give the Utah military commander a call and see if he can contribute troops to that mission as well. His ass is on the line just as ours is. Keep me posted. One more item Ross. I am planning another WestPac conference. I think we need one with the change in command so everyone will know where we are going and how we are getting there. We must open major roads throughout WestPac. You could use half trained troops to do that if necessary. Get one of your dependables to honcho that operation and let's get going on that now. OK?"

"OK, Robert, will do."

Robert thought of calling Sarah but with access to an aircraft now, he considered flying to Riverton and meeting with her instead. He had Com deliver a message to her that he would be there in two hours to meet with her. Also com was to instruct Wyatt to meet with Robert in Riverton at the airport for a brief meeting if he was still in Riverton. If not, Robert would meet him in Salem later. Com confirmed the meeting with Sarah was on and Wyatt would be at the airport in Riverton when he arrived. Robert told the operator to have the pilot ready to take off as soon as he could get to the Portland airport.

Two other WestPac staffers needed to get to Riverton so Robert allowed them to join him on the flight. He was glad to accommodate them. The trip to Riverton was relatively short. Within an hour and a half, they were on final for the Riverton Airport and when he emerged from the plane he saw Monty Wyatt waiting for him on the ramp. Wyatt greeted him and said, "I understand you want me to do some business in Salem, Oregon. Ross gave me the details and I am ready to go. I have the troops lined up and Hans is going to fly me over there with the troops as soon as you and I have finished our business."

"Monty, this Bert Conners that runs the show over there is the typical bureaucratic windbag but he is doable. He will get the job done if you see that he is taken care of. There are many ways to do that. Find out what he wants and if it is within our budget or if it is something we can put together without ending up with one hundred more enemies, then do it. He is big on 'quid pro quo'. The main thing that I want him to do is to get those rail lines put back to the north and to the south. He has the troops to get the job done and I want him out there doing it now. If he just gives you crap and is not working with us, let him know that he may soon be out of a job. If he then refuses to do anything, throw him in the klink. I am not taking any crap from those local jerks. He will see the light quickly. He isn't going to stay long in any jail. He wants to be out and on the take. Another matter, I'm putting a conference together in Portland along the lines of the one I did for Stuart in Riverton and we need good safe ways for people to travel. We also need those rail lines to haul goods, both north and south. Whatever you need, let me know. Take some medical types with you and load up with food and material goods as well. Tell Connors he would be getting more if he would get those rail lines in. Another job you have to handle in Salem is to knock heads with the scum that are preying on the residents there. Connors says they are ruining everything. Kick some ass there and if you have to, put a few away. If you can't convert the troublemakers, set up a place to hold them. Not too comfortable but I don't want to be hearing it was an inhuman way to treat another human being. Just use your head. I don't know how long you will be down there. That depends on what kind of success you are having. When you feel the work load lightening up a bit, expand your area of interest to the south, Corvallis, and find the local honcho down there and deal with him the same way. Do all of this quickly as I need you on the military operation in the South. We are going to need a lot more troops very soon and I was thinking of using you there but I think you would be more valuable working with Nix down South. I may even have you run the operation down into Colorado to protect the rail line. I'll talk with Perry about that."

"Interesting. I'm ready for whatever you want me to do, Chief. Just give me a call. I will be here for another hour or so if you have anything else you want to tell me. Then I will be down in Salem. Most likely find something close to that small airport they have there. I will let Com know how to contact me. Have a good visit here."

Robert said hello to Anders and then went down to Sarah's office. She was in and expecting him. The secretary got Robert a cup of coffee and he sat down in front of Sarah's desk with his notepad out. There were a number of matters he wanted to talk with her about and didn't want to leave anything out. The primary purpose of his visit was to impress upon her the need for an immediate buildup of the military and the need for energizing the WestPac coalition. He explained to her his great concern that if all the leaders in WestPac did not get behind these two major problems, they very well might not be a functioning entity within a year.

"Sarah, I spoke with Louis Donley and he needs troops, weapons and materials. The Montana area has been the big provider so far and it looks as though it will continue to be that for the near future. Keep massaging Parker's back and keep him happy as we are going to be asking a lot of him. I am going to be working on the Western States for materials as well but right now that is a hard sell as they are still not pacified and have many transportation problems. Few rail lines are in place and motorized shipping is about non-existent. Perry is working on improving that and I have others out especially in the major cities trying to get their support. They all want troops stationed in their city for security, which they need, and they want food and other materials. They are not just crybabies, they really do need what they are asking for and we have to get it to them in order to get them back in business. When we do that, the West will be producing what we need elsewhere. Crime is still quite rampant in the West and I have told Perry to crack down big time on that. Which brings up another point, Sarah, I have no intention of providing civil rights to the scumballs that are dragging us down. It is arrest, investigate and punish. I know that in time the criticism of how we operate will commence. That is just too bad. We are on the ragged edge of losing this battle. Are you with me on this?"

"I know what you are talking about, Robert. I have had many conversations with Ross and also Jack Nix on this. They have the same opinion as you do as to how we deal with the problem. I would only suggest that when the time comes that you can edge off the hard line a bit, that you do so. You don't want the populace turning on you and that can happen. Right now, I would say the populace sees the problem much the same as you do and, I might add, as I do."

"Good, Sarah. Now I mentioned to you in our telephone call that I want to set up a large conference of the type we had here in Riverton. But, this one I want in Portland as it is more convenient for the Western States and they are the ones I want to impress. I want you to organize and manage the conference generally along the same lines as before. Jack Nix can also help you. Again it is a sales operation to get the attendance of all the local Western bureaucrats. I want all of them here so do what you have to do to get them here. Nix can help you on the persuasion business. I have also spoken with him. I would like that soon but we have work to do first in pacifying areas and improving transportation. Again we are going to need to haul people to the event so we will have to have buses or trucks placed around the West for the convenience of the residents well outside of Portland. I know we are low on fuel but Perry and I are going to run a military operation south to open up the shipping lanes so we can get our fuel needs met. We will also be fighting the FSP with Louis Donley in the process so we will be very busy in all quarters. The battle in the South against the FSP must take precedence over the conference so allocate your time accordingly. I consider the conference as very important to add stability to our fledgling nation. But we have to be realistic, first things first. Again, impress upon Matt Parker that we need all the help we can get. Impress upon him that these are very trying times for all of us. You know the name of the game. By the way, Toni Norton contacted me. I didn't interview her but I figured if you sent her, she had to be qualified. She is working for me right now and we still have not met. She sounded sharp for whatever that is worth."

"She is sharp. She is also a hard worker and has common sense to go with her brains."

"What more could I ask for. By the way, she is presently working with Clay Daley getting our offices set up in Portland. At the airport or close to it I hope. I have to go see Barnes before I leave here. I did not tell him I was coming. I hope he is here."

"He is. I just saw him a few minutes ago. I told him you were going to be here so he is most likely expecting you."

"Good, Sarah if you think of anything else you and I should be talking about, get the word to me and I will be right back. Otherwise I expect to head back to Portland in the next few hours. Stay in touch."

Robert went over to Barnes office and found him with piles of papers and inventory books on his desk. He looked frazzled undoubtedly from all the requests for men, materials, weapons and food placed on him by everyone.

"John, I'm not going to ask how you are. I can see you are busier than hell. A few things I would like to talk to you about and then I'll get the hell out of here. Regarding the missiles and equipment that Donley would like to get. Have you made any progress on that?"

"I talked directly to Donley to get whatever information he had on the drones, altitude, airspeed, etc., and some data on their weapons. He told me what was known and I think we can help him out. I am sending a team with the necessary equipment to maintain and operate the radars and fire the weapons. I will let you know how that works out."

"Great, John. Now I don't know if Perry told you, but we are considering running a sizeable force down into Colorado to secure our shipping lines and also to attack the FSP from the rear while Donley counter-attacks from the front. I think this would be an opportunity to wound or finish off the Western force of the FSP. Your thoughts?"

"Robert, I'm sure you know what the problems are. We discussed them briefly. We are strapped for men and materials right now. Yes, we could field a force of twenty-five to fifty thousand men but God save us if the FSP gathered their army together and came after us. I'm not convinced Donley would come to our rescue. But, and it is a big challenge but, it could work. I will support it as I know we are going to face them someday and it may as well be right now while Donley is out there."

"John, how soon could you have that force ready? You and Perry that is. Also, you might bring in Hans. He may have some ground support aircraft that could come in very handy."

"I've already spoken with him. I would say we need at least a month to get everything together. That includes, men, materials, food supplies, weapons, trucks and fuel. They have some armored vehicles but we can handle that. Someday I am going to build us a tank. Wish I had that right now. I can armor up some of the trucks but only for small arms fire."

"Good, John. Keep me advised. I will assume we will be rolling sometime in a month or so. I told Perry to talk to the Utah military commander and anyone else that could be of assistance. I suggested Monty Wyatt as the commander of the group heading south to protect the rail lines. You and Perry might give that some thought. Wyatt is a very sharp guy and the troops respect him. With all of this going on, you are going to have to find someone else to manage the buildup of the force. Have you thought of that?"

"Of course. I have been talking to Yates and Campbell about that and they are ready to move on recruiting and buildup of the force. They have assigned trainers for the camps in the north and supplies have already gone up there to handle the influx. I have an arrangement with Perry to send me the junior criminals that he is arresting out in the field. We have just the right people to give those guys a new outlook on life as they enter basic training. We have actually been having good luck with them. Also, Robert, Perry and I believe we have the answer to the military buildup. Refugees are flowing into Montana and the other Westerns States as a result of the FSP invasions of Wyoming, Utah, Nevada and now knocking on the door of California. They know and hate the FSP and are signing up by the hundreds. We do not think we have a recruiting problem any longer and, in fact, have been raising the standards for what we accept. No more trainable scumballs for the military. I was never in favor of that from the get go."

"John you have no idea what a relief that is for me to hear that. Bring them in and get them trained. We need security in the West now and we need troops to fight the FSP very soon. Get whatever help you need to get those men and women trained to fight. I could use fifty thousand at least spread across the West to stabilize that area and to get the productive capacity of that part of the country moving again. Let me know when I can have those troops or even some of those troops. I can set up Bases around the West just as soon as they are available. I'll get the hell out of here, John. Thanks for your help. We are really up to our noses in problems right now but we will work our way out of it. What is it they used to say, some day we will look back at this and laugh. Well; I'm not laughing yet but I am starting to occasionally smile."

"Discipline is the soul of an army. It makes small numbers formidable; procures success to the weak, and esteem to all."
—**George Washington**

Chapter Eight

When Robert stepped off the plane at Portland, Clay Daley was there to meet him. Clay had called Sarah to find out when he was leaving Riverton so was able to be in position at the airport for his arrival time. Clay was not alone. He was with a young woman, attractive, about Clay's age, 30 plus or minus, who he introduced as Toni Norton.

"I understand you have never met your secretary Robert. She has been working with me for the past two days putting our offices together and she is doing a great job."

Robert introduced himself to Toni and welcomed her on board. "I hope you find what we are doing as interesting and as necessary as we do. We have a tough fight ahead of us and I hope you are ready for that. Sarah gives you very high marks so I am assuming you will do just fine."

"Mister Thomas, I am looking forward to working with you. I am very familiar with your general philosophy on government as I followed very closely what you and Stuart Martin were about. I totally support that. Thanks for bringing me on board."

"Great, Toni. Please call me Robert when we are with staff. I will do the same for you. Great. Work with Clay for the time being and I know he will keep you busy as he knows where we have to go and how to get there."

Clay continued bringing Robert up to date on what he had been about since they last spoke. "Empty buildings are a dime a dozen so we had no trouble finding one that I know would fit your preference. Like all buildings these days, we first had to send some of our boys in there to throw the tenants out. Calling them tenants does a disservice to that term. Anyway, it is that large building next to the hangar which is where the plane is kept so it is also very convenient for us. I have had some of our WestPac troops secure the area, including the building and hangar, with guards and fencing so that we don't have trouble with visitors. There are carpenters in there right now setting up the offices and Toni has managed to locate the necessary business equipment for the offices to function. John Barnes also sent over some equipment from Riverton that he thought we could use. He was right, we were looking for many of the items he had sent. Toni says the offices will be habitable within the coming week and that is good timing as I also have three apparently qualified men to work as your assistants and they are likewise in the office space setting up their work stations and waiting at your beckon call. Hopefully we can have a meeting this afternoon and you can get them off and running. We have a conference room ready for use now as I knew you would want that first. They are working on your personal quarters now and I told them you wanted that Spartan but sound proofed so office noises did not bother you. I told the new troops we would meet with them in about an hour and a half from right now. That will give us some time for something to eat and discuss business with you."

"That's great, Clay. I take it you know the territory here. Take us to a restaurant if such exists anymore and maybe we can get something to eat."

Soon the three were seated in a small café close to the hangar. It was a café that existed solely by reason of the airport and its very limited operations. Portland was still barely functioning and that was due to the special emphasis placed upon it by WestPac. Very few businesses were operating even at a minimal level in Portland and most areas of the city were still without electricity but that was slowly improving through the assistance of WestPac troops. The main problem with electricity was getting the transformers, wiring and other apparatus that had been stripped by the scavengers when anarchy reigned in the city. Finding replacement parts had been a major problem.

Most areas of the city had water and sewage as Stuart and Robert had concentrated on getting those basic services up and operating quickly particularly for the larger cities. Most of the smaller towns had their own wells and people who knew how to maintain them. There were only a few other people in the restaurant as the economy continued to be in the doldrums and no one had any funds. Robert asked the proprietor how business was going seeing only a dozen or so people in the restaurant.

"What you see is one of the largest crowds I have had this week. Barely surviving is what I would say. We have high hopes for you Mister Thomas."

"I do as well. It is going to take some time and a hell of a lot of work, but we will get it back. Of that, I am quite sure."

The three ordered a light lunch and while they were waiting for their food, Robert brought Clay and Toni up to date on what had transpired in

Riverton with the transition of leadership in WestPac. He did not spend much time on that as he wanted both of them to understand what was really important was what was occurring with respect to the military buildup, activities of the FSP in Utah and Nevada, fuel needs and the solutions they were working on there. He also added the need to upgrade living conditions particularly in the new territories of the West was a very important goal. The bureaucrats in the West were not a happy lot, having been promised benefits at the conference held in Riverton when Stuart was alive and then being ignored when he died in the accident.

"Clay I want you and Toni to organize a visit by me as soon as possible with the leaders in all of the larger communities here in Oregon, Washington , Northern California, Utah and the parts of Nevada that we can still get to. I want to visit the leaders in every such State that will have the influence to draw in those people of the State that I just don't have the time to meet with. I have Perry setting up Bases all through the West as we speak to stabilize those areas and to start bringing in very needed supplies of food as well as medical services. Let whoever you talk with know that help is on its way. This is an absolute necessity or we will be losing the support of these people. We can weed out the dead wood later but right now anyone that has a position of influence in any community, I want to be speaking to them. Another important message we need to get across to them is that we need the agricultural products and material goods that they can produce. They must get their production up and operating and that must get shipped to areas of the country that cannot produce those items. That calls for rail beds, lines, diesel engines, cars and repair facilities, tractors, lumber, everything that makes a community function. Also we need roads repaired so that trucks can haul to cities that do not have rail connections. Tell them we are counting on them for their help and it will benefit them big time."

Robert paused to gather his thoughts. "I can cover three or more areas a day with the airplane. I want to get that all covered before the conference that I have been talking with Sarah about setting up here in Portland in approximately two months. Now the scheduling of that is dependent on our military operation in the South but we will get to it eventually and the sooner the better. Clay, I have files on many or most of these people from when we set up the Riverton conference. Those files would be a good place to start. Some of those people may no longer be around. Well then, find who has taken over. I will give you those files when we get over to the new office. We can stop by my apartment and pick them up so that you can get these new staffers working on this business right now. Understand?"

"I do, Robert. We will be on this big time. When can you start out on this visit?"

"I need this week to get organized on a number of other items. Start in one week and give me a break of a few days every now and then to return here and put out whatever fires are going here, Riverton or Seattle. I am counting on both of you to honcho what is going on and to keep me informed. We will be in contact almost daily. Perry can handle many of the problems if I am out of touch. Also, Sarah, and Nix, and Wyatt, Barnes, Moss, they are all capable of dealing with these problems, so use them."

An hour later, Robert was seated in the conference room of the new offices. He had already delivered the files of local administrators to Clay and had met the new associates that Clay had hired. They were an impressive appearing group of three young men with excellent credentials. Robert was generally impressed but as he always said, you don't know the cook until you've eaten the food. Robert gave the three young men the same talk he had been delivering to all staffers regarding the seriousness of their present situation and that WestPac was on a war footing to get back on speed immediately. "You are the key people involved in this battle at this time. We need the West and you are the ones that have to deliver it to us. You need your sales skills and you need your common sense. Some or maybe even many of these local bureaucrats are basically system suckers and scammers. If they have influence, use them. Sell them. Later on we can replace them but we don't have time to fire all of them right now. Let them know, however, that their performance is crucial to what responsibilities they will be handed in the future. OK, get your offices set up and Clay will assign your contact areas. Work with Clay on the schedule that I will be working with. If we are running behind, then you men are going to have to cover many of the communities that I wanted to take care of personally but won't have time to get to. I want the entire area surveyed, visited and sold on WestPac within the next six weeks. That is a high hill to climb. After that we hopefully will be working on the conference which will be here in Portland and Clay, we will need a suitable site for that. I would estimate two to four hundred people. We will need housing for our guests as well, something decent and it should be in the same building as the conference site. Maybe a good conference center hotel that is shut down for lack of business. Clay, I also want full time security for our headquarters building and hangar. I'm talking internal security from our own WestPac military. No civilian guards. I want guards here and in the hangar. I want people who are working here at midnight to be completely safe, 24/7. Any questions from anyone?"

Later as Robert sat in his apartment office, packing up his papers for the move to the new office facilities, the phone rang and it was Com announcing that Monty Wyatt was on the line. Robert took the call.

"Monty, what's the word from Salem, Oregon?"

"Robert you sure do know how to call 'em'. This guy Connors is a piece of work. I dealt with him as you suggested. He gave me crap from the time I walked into his office until the time that I told him he was going to a Retraining Center in Montana if he didn't wise up quickly. When he realized I was not kidding, he changed his tune a bit. I don't know how far you could trust this guy though. He is just so full of it and if you leave him alone, he will be back to the old game. I have spoken to some businessmen here in Salem and they tell me that he is in shake down mode constantly. They all want his sorry ass out of there."

"Monty, is there anyone else around there that can run the show the way we want it run?"

"I think there is. The Mayor of Salem seems like a sharp guy that understands what needs to be done. I'm for shipping Connors to camp and we then work with Lyle Richards, the Mayor. He is a long time fan of Stuart and of you as well. Do you know the guy?"

"I recall the name but that is about it. Fine, meet with Richards and make sure he is ready and able to carry the ball for us in Salem. Then if Connors is not singing in tune with us, send him east, as a prisoner of WestPac. Assure him that if he passes retraining with glowing marks, he may possibly return to Salem but that is not for certain."

"Now Monty, you brought forty troopers with you I believe. That is what Sarah said anyway. Have them silence that gang of kids that Connors was griping about and then have them move out through the city, the County and out into the State and do the same there. Gotta go. call me after you iron everything out with Richards and the street toughs."

Robert then placed a call to Perry up in Seattle. The two discussed the situation in the South involving the FSP and Louis Donley's forces. Perry had sent Guns and Ammo down to scout out the situation along WestPac's train line and supply route for petroleum deliveries from Donley. The line was still there but the area was under the control of a light force of FSP rear-guards that were primarily guarding their own supply line to the West. Those guards could easily be removed when the rail line to Montana was needed. Guns and Ammo were now setting up for the rear guard action in support of our campaign against the FSP

"Ross, how are the supplies to the FSP being transported. Any rail lines down there running to the west."

"Robert, there are some but most of the hauling is being done by truck."

"OK, Ross, then we could mine the roads well to the west of our supply lines. I say we hold off on that until we decide what we are going to do regarding getting fuel up here?"

"Robert, that would be possible. If we ran a trainload of tankers up to Riverton before we started blowing up their roadways, they might not be aware of the fact we were shipping fuel through their lines until the job was done. That might be the best way to do it. If we could get about ten of those tank cars up to Riverton, that could support our needs for sending a sizeable force south to help Donley. Once we had the force in place down there, then Wyatt with his force of Rangers could provide security for future shipments."

"OK, Ross. Let's do that. You contact Donley and make all the arrangements with or through him. Tell him we will be moving south after we get the fuel and will be attacking the FSP from their rear. That should be coordinated with Donley so that he can also then put pressure on them from the front. First things first, we need the fuel. Have him set up that shipment ASAP and when it comes up through Donley's territory, Wyatt and his troops are going to have to protect it as it passes through the FSP rear guard area. Guns and Ammo can interdict the supply lines coming from the east for the FSP troops. If they need some extra help on that, Wyatt can give them a hand. Have Guns and Ammo making up their plans for how they are going to accomplish that. Have you decided on who is going to run the offensive against the FSP down in Nevada?"

"We are all busy with everything but Jack Nix would be a good man for the job. He has good experience and is respected by the troops. Guns and Ammo as well as Wyatt have all worked with him before and they worked well together so that should work out."

"Ross, sounds good to me. You deal the cards on that and talk to those people. Get Nix on that right now as he is going to have to do some heavy planning. I would like that operation rolling about the time of the conference in Portland and that would be in about two months. We should have around another two hundred thousand fresh troops by then according to Yates and Campbell. I spoke to them yesterday. Is that the same information you are getting?"

"That is what I am told Robert. We picked up a ton of new recruits from the men and women fleeing the FSP advance into the West. They see us as the answer and they are more than willing to do their part. Many of them have military or combat experience as well so we are very fortunate to be getting them at this time. Robert that is about it for now. I will talk with you later unless you have something else."

"No, that's it, Ross. Have a good one."

Robert contacted Com and told them to get Mark Campbell or Roy Yates on the line. He would be in his office for the next hour or so. Within minutes his phone rang and it was Mark Campbell. "You rang, Chief?"

Robert briefed Campbell on what was taking place regarding the FSP operation and the planned Portland Conference. "Mark, Sarah told me about the increase in troop strength coming out of the Training Bases up at Riverton. In the very near future, we will be needing about another three hundred thousand or more well trained troops for combat operations that will be taking place. As you are well aware, we have been flooding our training camps with new recruits from the South. Apparently the ones fleeing the FSP operations in the Southwest, primarily against Donley. I am told there are more coming on their way and willing to join our forces. We need them trained, equipped and run into combat units. You and Roy Yates have done a great job on getting our numbers increased but our needs will only increase as well. Keep up the good work and if I can help in any way, let me know, OK?"

"Robert, we would be glad to do whatever you want done."

"Good, Mark. Go to Riverton and meet with Sarah and Barnes. They are the ones primarily involved with the recruitment programs right now. The problem is they are overloaded with ten other jobs to take care of as well. Tell them I want you two operating the Recruitment and Training Program to bring in qualified recruits and to deliver well trained troops to units as soon as possible. Tell them you are ready to take over the reins of the military buildup program or if either one of them wants to participate as well, which I doubt, then inform them that they are free to help. Barnes is up to his eyeballs in gearing up for delivery of uniforms and equipment. I suspect he is already doing that. Sarah is working on Matt Parker for his support and help. You two are going to have to oversee the operation and crack the whip on everyone to see that the production line of new troops is running smoothly. I am told that we have more recruits than we have openings in the system right now due to the refugees streaming in from the South. Clear up the bottle necks and get the new recruits into training camps. We can build more training camps if the ones we have can't handle the crowd. Check out the training facilities and solve any problems they may be having. I also want at least one hundred thousand trained troops available to act as security in the West within the next six weeks. That does not give you much time, so get rolling. OK?"

"Chief consider it done. Roy and I enjoy a challenge and this sounds like a good one. I'll get ahold of Roy and we will be opening any bottlenecks in Riverton tomorrow."

"Good Mark. I will let the Aviation office know that you need transport to Riverton so give Hans a call when you are ready to go. Good luck."

Robert had Com contact Jack Nix to call Robert as soon as possible. Nix always stayed in close contact with Com as it seemed everyone was after him at all hours of the day and night.

"Chief, you called?"

"Jack, yes I did. I know you are on a number of projects and we have a major one coming up soon that we want you to honcho. First of all, regarding all the tasks I assigned to you when I was in Riverton, get a hold of Roy Yates and Mark Campbell as they are coming over there tomorrow. Pass all of those jobs onto them. They are taking over control of the recruitment and training program as we are getting a large number of recruits mostly from the flood of refugees coming in from the South. They are fleeing the FSP and have no great love for them. As you may know, we presently have Guns and Ammo down South checking out the security of our supply rail line that we use to haul primarily petrol from Donley's refineries up to Riverton. Now the FSP supply lines for the forces to the west of those lines run right through our rail lines going north. Guns and Ammo are right now just reconnoitering the situation down there and report that the FSP has only light security over the area of their supply lines coming from the east. We are going to try to run a fairly sizeable load of fuel by rail up across their supply lines and Wyatt will be down there with a force of Rangers to provide protection for it. Guns and Ammo are confident that should do it provided it can be handled quickly and doesn't cause problems before then. If it is done right, the fuel should be run north before there is any combat with the FSP rail line guards. Now after we have the fuel, we want you to run a sizeable force of troops south from Riverton and follow up on that FSP supply line to the west and nail the FSP forces in their rear. Coordinate what you are doing with Donley's commanders. They should likewise put on their pressure at the same time. Hopefully you will have around two hundred thousand troops or more to help you get the job done. This is our chance to nail the FSP big time. We are going to face them sooner or later and this looks like a good time. Work out the plans, anticipate your supply needs and coordinate those needs with Barnes. Coordinate also with Hans Frick so that he can provide some ground support with his Air Force. Also, the FSP is now using drones with guided munitions. Coordinate your timing with Donley so that the two of you are working the same plan. He is aware that you will be moving on the rear of the FSP force. You want to be hitting them at the same time as Donley is counter attacking their frontline forces. Talk to Barnes about the drones and get what you need to defense against that threat. This is a very important mission and that is why we picked you to run it. If you need anything you don't have, let Barnes or me know. OK?"

"Chief I will do that. This is the mission I have always wanted to have. I assume Guns and Ammo will be under my command as well, correct?"

"They are all yours, Jack, including Wyatt. Good luck and keep us all informed. We want that mission in progress in about six to eight weeks from right now, so get to work. You have a lot to do."

"Effective leadership is not about making speeches or being liked; leadership is defined by results not attributes."

—**Peter Drucker**

CHAPTER NINE

Robert had been living in his new quarters in the office building and was enjoying his surroundings. His staff was working in adjoining offices and his airplane was in position in the hangar adjoining the office building. The plane had been kept quite busy since the staff had begun functioning according to Robert's directives. Of the four young men working in the office, at least two or even three were out, at all times, meeting with and persuading local bureaucrats to increase their effectiveness as contributors to WestPac. That was not an easy task and it was usually met, at least initially, with total refusal. After further threats by Robert's staffers, they usually saw the light. There were around ten percent that never did see the light and in those cases, Staffers located other personnel in the County or State office that had more common sense and were willing to take over the job of being the WestPac Officer in Charge for that area. The former bureaucrat in charge was then sent off for retraining at one of the four camps situated around WestPac. These camps were set up especially for uncooperative bureaucrats, gang leaders, trouble makers, law violators, or other such problem cases. The camps all had a high success rate for converting problems into solutions. The newly converted were then assigned to other jobs in WestPac commensurate with their abilities. The others, usually a small number, were terminated as employees of WestPac and released into the general population.

Robert's living quarters, if you could call them that, in the office complex were very similar to what Stuart had before his accident. Robert's quarters were very simple. He had one large room. The only furniture in the room was a small bed, a television so that Robert could stay abreast of the news that was delivered over Word of WestPac, and there was a large desk with a comfortable desk chair and computer for his use. Off of that room, there was a small bathroom and shower for his private use. The walls in his quarters had been sound proofed so that he was able to sleep at least four hours a night in total quiet. Robert had realized years before that he could function quite well with four hours of sleep a night. Occasionally he did not get his four hours of sleep and that was not a great problem as long as it didn't happen two nights in a row. The office building also had quarters for the office staff on other floors so that they could stay close to their work when the pressure was on, which was often.

The entire complex was closely guarded by WestPac Rangers so that the staffers did not have to worry about being robbed or attacked at all hours of the night. As a result the staff tended to use these quarters more often than their own homes which did not provide commensurate security. Crime continued to reign supreme in Portland with gangs of young thugs roaming all neighborhoods at all hours of the day and night. As soon as Robert could get the one hundred thousand troops he had requested, he would establish a curfew and tight security throughout WestPac, certainly starting with Portland, Oregon.

Robert was beginning to see progress as a result of his efforts to reorganize WestPac. Primary offices handling important aspects of government of WestPac were now firmly in his control. That had not happened without difficulty or complaints from some men or women that Robert referred to as 'empire builders'.

When he had been terminated as the leader of WestPac following Stuart's death, the bureaucrats took advantage in the absence of critical management to invade many political positions across WestPac that offered opportunities for the unscrupulous. He had managed to remove many but there were many more to go.

A few of them were also enjoying retraining in one or more of the camps. It was an ongoing struggle and his phone rang often in his office from many local leaders wondering when the food supplies or clothing shipments would arrive. His problems were compounded by not only the unscrupulous bureaucrat but also by the ever present shortage of materials as well as medical and food supplies.

Transportation continued to be a major problem and lack thereof interfered with virtually everything. He thought about the conference which was now about six weeks away. Would people travel if it was very unsafe to do so? No, they would not. He had to cure that problem for openers. Campbell and Yates assured Robert that he would have his troops needed to stabilize the west by the end of the coming month. All troops prior to those now graduating from Boot Camp were going to Nix who had priority on whatever was available. Sarah was sending out convoys of foodstuffs, clothing and medical supplies in response to Robert's requests for shipments to the cities and towns in the West and they needed protection as well.

Robert looked at the stack of papers on his desk that he had been ignoring for the past few days. He went through the messages sorting out those that appeared to have some matters of importance that he should pay attention to. One of the letters bore the official address of WestPac, Riverton, and the caption, National Ecological Administration Office. As Robert broke the seal on the letter, he commented to himself, "Just what in the hell could this be?" He unfolded the letter and noted that it was addressed to him as the Economic Administrator of WestPac, apparently referring to his government position before the change of command. The letter was apparently an introductory letter from the woman who had been assigned the post with the title of the National Ecological Administrator and was informing Robert, as the Economic Administrator, to be aware of the implications of the recently authorized NEA Office. The letter read as follows:

We must all work together to ensure that the new companies that are being developed in WestPac fully comply with all of the Administrative Procedures designed to protect the environment and that they are fully complied with. It has come to our attention that companies in your West Region are continuing to use coal and other non-renewable natural resources for the production of energy, fuels and heating purposes. Such uses of our natural resources are not permitted without waivers and we note that none have been granted to companies in your area of operation. You are hereby instructed to inform all companies that your office is in contact with to immediately cease and desist in the use of said resources.

```
Failure to abide by the terms of this
letter may result in fines, criminal
penalties or termination.
Signed,
Jocelyn Sanborn,
Administrator, National Ecological
Administration Office.
```

Robert called Com on his office phone and instructed them to contact Miss Sanborn and have her call him immediately.

Within fifteen minutes, Com was on the line and said that Miss Sanborn was calling, "Should we put her through?"

"Send her through."

Soon she was on the line. "Mister Thomas, you requested that I contact you. What is this in reference to?"

"You sent a letter to the Economic Administrator regarding their failure to inform companies in their region of their obligation to abide by your regulations. I take it that is your area of responsibility?"

"Yes and did you comply with the referenced requirements contained in the letter?"

"No, I did not."

There was a pause for a few moments and then Miss Sanborn replied, "Do you realize there are severe penalties for failure to abide by our required regulations? Do you need the citations for those regulations so that you could be more familiar with them before you proceed in violation?"

"No. Apparently you have the wrong person. I was the Economics Administrator and your letter was addressed to the Economic Administrator. Sounds the same but the person you were looking for had no "S" at the end of Economic. Must be someone else."

"Mister Thomas, this is no joke and you are in no position to be joking about this."

"Miss Sanborn, or is it Mrs. Sanborn?"

"It is Miss Sanborn, Mr. Thomas."

"Miss Sanborn, it is very important that we address our letters properly. Don't you think that is important? You could be arrested for improper addressing of letters."

"Mister Thomas, I am pursuing a violation of the National Ecological

Administration Regulations against you for willful violation of our regs. It is obvious you have no respect for the laws."

"No. I believe in laws, I don't believe in regulations so I am just going to ignore them."

"Mister Thomas, you are acting in blatant disregard of the law and if you persist, I will have you arrested. I have that power."

"No, Miss Sanborn, you don't have that power. Furthermore, you no longer have a job and furthermore, your NEAZ office or whatever the hell it is called is now defunct. No longer exists. Now let me ask you, do you know who I am?"

"I am assuming you are Robert Thomas the Economics Administrator and you appear to be continuing your practice of operating as the Lone Ranger. I thought you had learned your lesson when you tried to take over the government and were thrown out of that office."

"Well, I hate to tell you this, Miss Prissy, but I am now the government and you are out of a job. I suggest you read the papers and I believe you will discover that I am number one again and I do not have any Administrative Agencies in my government so you are unemployed. I am busy. Go find a real job." Robert hung up the phone. Robert chuckled to himself. "There are some things about this job that I really enjoy." Robert made a note to Clay to make sure the NEA or whatever the hell it was called was immediately shut down.

As Robert sat mulling over the problems he needed to solve, the phone rang and Com said Monty Wyatt was on the line for him. Robert told the operator to put the call through. He was soon in contact with Wyatt who was now in Corvallis, Oregon. "Robert, I'm down in Corvallis and have been working with the County Commissioner here on his problems. He is a good man and has the rail lines complete to Salem and South for about a hundred miles. Others down there need to get to work. Anyway, I have had the same problem both in Salem and Corvallis and that is youth gangs. They roam the streets, terrorizing everyone and they are dangerous. They have no respect for human life and I am talking about kids that are somewhere around fifteen years of age. Both boys and girls. Their attitude is that we can't touch them because they are minors. What is our policy regarding these kids. If they were older, I know what I would do. What are your thoughts?"

"OK, Monty, here is what we do. First of all, they are hard to catch but get one or two out of the pack and throw them into your jail. Most likely they will tell you to go screw yourself. No problem. Anytime they mouth off, just deny them food. After a while they'll realize that mouthing off is not a good thing. Then tell them you want the names of all members of the gang and no B.S. or they will feel it big time. Oh, I almost forgot. No food until they start singing like canaries. That includes providing you with names, addresses if they exist and that sort of thing. Kids love to eat so while they are starving, eat in front of them. They also like water. Just give them enough of that to stay alive. Let them know that when they start helping you out with information, they can have some water. You will end up with the entire gang. Then send them all to charm school at the retraining center. Problem solved. Oh, almost forgot. There are no trials. Used to have those, not anymore. At the most, give them a hearing before three military officers. Tell them this is the new form of Juvenile Justice. If some attorney comes in there demanding you release the kid, throw his ass in with the kid. If he and the kid don't eventually shape up, send both of them to retraining. Tell them they will stay there until they become model prisoners. That system works quite well. If their parents bitch, send them as well. By the way, I take it that Lyle Richards worked out fairly well in Salem, right?"

"Righto. Model citizen. Good man. He has completed the rail line between Salem and Portland and is running three engines and a number of freight cars through his rail yard in Salem. They will have their roundhouse up and operating soon. They do need diesel fuel but then so does everyone else. I told him we were working on the fuel issue but we could deliver goods by truck so if you can detail a truckload of food, clothing and some medical supplies to Salem, you would have a very effective convert there. Where do you want me to go after I clean the kid gangs out of these two towns? I have about forty combat ready troops that love dusting off these gang bangers so just tell us where and we will be there."

"Monty, just pick your targets. Head for the larger cities as we are out to pacify the population and the smaller towns have less problems with gangs. They take care of them in their own way. Do talk to the small town mayors or what have you and tell them to get those rail lines in so that they can have train service and supplies coming in there. You might take a look at the towns on I-84 that run to the east out of Portland as there are some good sized cities on that route to the east and eventually down to the southeast. That is what we need to hit in Oregon. Then move on down into California and do the same. I will have Perry work on Washington and then Idaho. One slight problem. I need you in the operation down in Colorado. Perry can fill you in on that and you are going to have to head down there soon. Coordinate with Nix on the move south as he will be leading a substantial force down as well and you should be in position about the same time. But, while I am talking to you about what needs to be done in the West, find someone capable for the job to take your place and give them the instructions I have given you. Include the following as well."

"There are two problem areas that I want you to be aware of. We are presently short of security forces for the West but we should have plenty of troops soon to cover all areas of WestPac. Matt Parker tells me they are loading trucks for shipment west right now so that means food primarily. Some of our Western States should be able to provide good supplies of clothing and other materials when they get up and running. Right now they need food and protection from the gangs. Hopefully a year from now we can have WestPac stabilized. Let's hope so anyway. When you clean up a city or an area, Monty, be sure and leave a security force in place. Either the local Sheriff's Office, Police Department, or leave a temporary unit of troops there until those other offices are up and operating. In the meantime, Monty you or your replacement should send in reports on what you are finding regarding effective leaders in the communities you are working. These are the people we will invite to the conference. Give us all the necessary contact information and a brief summary on what the person does and his level of enthusiasm for WestPac. Send that report to Toni Norton who is my Admin Assistant in Portland at our WestPac airport office. Good luck to you and keep up the good work. Also, Wyatt, make sure you find someone with a brain in your cadre there that can take your place on very short notice when we ship you south to support Nix. Stay in good contact with Com as we may need you on short notice."

"Will do, Chief."

That evening as Robert was watching the news in his quarters, Com called and said Sarah was on the line. He picked up his desk phone and said, "My my but you are working late."

"You have to be kidding, Robert. This is just another normal workday."

"I know, Sarah. You are a hustler and we all know it. What can I do for you this evening?"

"Guess who was asking about you today?"

"You don't have to tell me. Must be the wicked witch from Riverton."

"So right you are. Needless to say, she is ballistic at the dictator from the

West being back in power. She will not be doing you any favors, Robert. I told her to cool it as we needed to make some severe changes and she of course doesn't see it that way. I will keep my eye on her but I wish there was some out of the way job we could send her to that would keep her out of trouble."

"Sarah we have four out of the way spots for her. If she keeps causing trouble, we may have to send her there."

"She means well, Robert. Many of her ideas are commendable. Her problem is that her liberal philosophy is not what we need right now. Maybe sometime in the future."

"Yeh, way the hell in the future. Her thinking is just what destroyed our country before and damn near destroyed WestPac after Stuart's death. She is the sales person for disaster. Just keep your eye on her and if she starts gaining converts, we may have to send her out for counseling, or whatever. Keep me posted. Anything else?"

"No, that is about it. There are a million other problems but we are working on them. Two weeks ago we had five million other problems so we are making progress. Talk to you later."

The following morning, Robert was moving his files and personal items to his new quarters in the office building. He decided to take a tour through the city to get a glimpse of life in Portland. There were very few vehicles on the streets and they appeared to be WestPac trucks or privately owned trucks hauling materials of one type of another.

Very little traffic other than many bicycles ridden by adults apparently going to work or on a mission of some sort. They were not out for a pleasure ride that was obvious. They were on bikes because fuel for their automobiles, if they still ran, was very expensive and rare. There was an occasional gasoline service station open but they did not come out and wash your windows or check your oil. They were bunkered down in their building, shielded by sandbags and coverings over the windows, if they had windows left. There were guards in secured positions around the station wearing protective vests and carrying assault rifles. Their bicycles safely parked inside the station. No more credit cards. Everything was cash and carry. Gasoline was obtained by the station owners from various sources both instate and out of state. It was sold for WestPac dollars, former American dollars, gold, silver, bullets, and virtually anything recognized as having transportable value.

Very little sign of life in the city either other than the fairly frequent sight of residents tending their gardens. It seemed as though every home or apartment complex had its own garden. Robert concluded that the citizens of Portland were now growing their own food. Deer and other animals had been a problem munching on the very edible green stems and shoots of the growing plants in the backyard garden. That didn't last very long as the homeowner soon discovered that venison was a very tasty dish and as a result, a deer was seldom seen within the environs of a small town or city. As Robert drove through the city, he occasionally saw a small cluster of five or more young men or boys standing around the street corners with their hands in their pockets. Doing nothing. That was not good. Robert made a note to have these gangs of adults and kids picked up and put to work doing something productive. He would have one of his staffers handle that. This scene was repeated as he drove through the city towards his new office. Definitely a depressing view of Portland.

Robert thought about the problems the youth of the country was facing. Under the previous regime of President Turner and his predecessors, there was virtually no religious training of any kind. It showed in the behavior of the kids. The violent crimes committed by teenagers soared over the years when there was no ethical training of any kind going on; none in the schools and very little if any in the homes. Religious teachers had been suppressed by the government and made to look like clowns by the media. Some of the church schools, such as the Catholics or the Mormons and others, did provide morals training but the government had been restricting their influence more and more every year. Robert made a note to talk to Sarah about again supporting the Christian and Jewish schools specifically with respect to their educational systems. The youth of today had no guidance from a previously instilled morals training program. The Christian Faith in particular had been the target of a long term cultural attack by the powers in government and in the media in the years before and after the collapse.

Robert would do what he could to counteract the effects of the attack on Religion. He was not what one would call a religious person but he was a firm believer in the good that morals training did for the youth of the country. He had witnessed over the years an increasing problem with youth crime. Violent crimes perpetrated by teenagers, both boys and girls, on the elderly or others not capable of defending themselves. He recalled the case of the young girl that had been arrested for the murder of a small town grocer. She and her boyfriend had decided to rob the store and in the process, she had shot and killed the grocer. He was a family man with three small children and the gravity of the crime shocked everyone. When she was arrested, she immediately confessed that she had killed the grocer and furthermore that she had "gotten a kick out of it." She was laughing about it which amazed all the arresting officers. "You should have seen how scared he was." She was about eighteen years of age, attractive, a high school graduate, decently dressed and lived in a moderate income housing area. Both parents at home and they were as surprised as everyone else at what their daughter had done. Robert attributed her actions to the fact that there was a complete absence of any morals training in her life. No church affiliation, none in her public school and no other alternative source. At first he had been shocked by the news items, but after a while when he had been subjected to hundreds of articles reading the same as the one about the young girl that murdered the grocer, he became almost immune to the repetition. It was Stuart that got him thinking about the connection between youth crime and violence with the lack of morals training in the home, the school or the nation. Stuart's programs of instilling ethical principles in the young appeared to be having a beneficial effect but that all came to an end with his death. Now that Robert was back running the ship of State, he would carry on Stuart's ethical programs.

After Robert moved his files and other items into his new office he went to the main part of the office to see how his staffers were coming along. Three of the four were there and they were all on the phones, apparently in contact with local political leaders getting status reports or trying to solve problems. Toni Norton was in her office typing up reports prepared by the staffers following their contacts with local leaders.

Robert asked how that was going and Toni replied, "Some good reports and some rather negative but for those, the staffers had provided suggested solutions, so generally good. These young men are pretty good at dealing with people who talk a good game but produce nothing. I am rather impressed."

"Well, Toni, Clay hired them and I've known Clay for some time. He can see right through a phony and about half of these city or state bureaucrats are genuine phonies. Some are damn good people and those are the ones we want to end up with."

"Individual commitment to a group effort - that is
what makes a team work, a company work,
a society work, a civilization work."
—**Vince Lombardi**

CHAPTER TEN

In the past month since his offices in Portland had been set up, Robert had traveled extensively through Oregon visiting the leaders in the larger cities of the State. As he had experienced previously with Stuart, some of these visits were successful and enjoyable and some were not. On this day, Robert was traveling to Yakima, Washington for a scheduled visit with the County Commissioner and Mayor who he had been informed were the persons with power and influence in the area. Robert was accompanied on this trip by Ross Perry and a substantial number of military personnel. Robert had decided to boost the number of troops that were traveling with him on these visits for two reasons. First, some areas he had been visiting were not particularly friendly. The second reason was that many, if not most, areas of the West were not stable and needed to be stabilized. At virtually every large city they had visited, they had left a security force of WestPac troops to ensure that stability was regained and maintained. This had a profound effect on how the local leaders viewed WestPac in general and Robert in particular. He was clearly a person who did what he said he would do.

As they were traveling into Yakima, Robert observed numbers of young, teenage, boys and girls standing around the corners apparently doing nothing. He told his driver to pull over in front of one group of about seven boys and a few girls. He stepped out of the car and approached one youth who appeared to be a bit older than the rest. "What are you kids up to?"

The youth obviously did not consider Robert to be a person deserving of his attention. "What's it to you?"

"Just curious. Maybe you need something to do."

"We're doing it. We like doing just what we are doing."

"Do any of you have jobs?"

"What the hell is that?"

"OK, that's fair. Do any of you live at home with your parents?"

"Why don't you go give some other kids this test, we aren't interested."

Robert decided not to waste time anymore and went right to the point. "Do you know who we are?"

"The new army people I suppose."

"Close enough. Now give me your name and address and cut the B.S. If you give me a phony name, it will only make it worse. What is it?"

The boy said nothing so Robert asked the others for the same information. The kids now looked at one another wondering where this was going as Robert was realizing it was going nowhere. Robert told Perry to load the group into one of his transport vehicles and to instruct the troopers to keep them there until Robert told them otherwise. As they drove on into the city, Robert told Perry to have his troops take the kids over to the county jail and lock them up there. "Then tell the ones that actually have parents to call them and have them come and pick them up. Tell the wiseacres that they had better be real parents or they would be in the next cell. When the parents arrive, have someone notify me and I will come down to the jail for a discussion with them on child raising. No child is to be released until I say so."

After dropping the youth off at the county jail and advising the custodian there as to how to contact him when any parents arrived, Robert went on with Perry to the county offices to meet the Commissioner and the Mayor. Robert's concerns for Yakima were primarily providing security for the city, transportation issues, food issues and material shortages. The four men discussed these topics for about three hours and Robert was impressed with the serious nature of the shortages Yakima was experiencing in all categories and the high level of competence of the two men he was meeting with. Crime was again a major issue in Yakima. Stuart had Perry meet with the people responsible for ensuring the peace and tranquility of the city and told Perry to take care of that problem. He stayed with the Mayor and Commissioner to press his on-going problem with road and rail transportation. He assured them that supply shortages were coming to an end soon but it did take time. He placed a call to Sarah to do what she could to increase food supplies going to Yakima. Sarah told Robert the Riverton Office was working on that for Yakima and the other cities of the West but they had to start producing crops of their own to feed themselves. That would be the best solution to their problem. Robert agreed but pointed out they needed a boost in supplies to tide them over. Robert was aware that Yakima had been a major food producer in the State of Washington and he strongly pushed the issue with the two locals that they regain the high levels of production of fruits and other agricultural crops they had produced in the past.

The County Commissioner reminded Robert that they needed diesel fuel to run their tractors and other farm equipment and that was very hard to come by these days. Robert assured him that they were working on that problem. It was well after nine in the evening when Robert left the County Commissioner and Mayor for his temporary quarters. On the way there, he received a call that he was wanted at the jail. One of the parents was there and he appeared to be in a high state of irritation.

As Robert entered the offices of the county jail, a red faced, overweight fellow began yelling at him, "Just what the hell is this all about?"

Robert walked up to the fellow and said, "Normally when I meet someone to discuss matters with them, they introduce themselves before they start yelling at people."

"I'll ask you one more time, what is this about. You have my son locked up in jail and as far as I can tell, he has done nothing."

Robert smiled and said, "You are right, he has done nothing. He and his pals were loitering on the corner of a street in Yakima in the middle of the day, doing nothing. Do you as a parent take an interest in your son's activities during the day?"

"Course I do, now who the hell do you think you are throwing my son in jail?"

"Well, do you know who I am? I don't think you do or you would not have been quite so impolite. I am Robert Thomas and I am the CEO, the man in charge of WestPac and we have a major problem in WestPac right now with youth gangs. Kids in their mid teens and older raising holy hell in all of our territories. They have been assaulting the elderly, stealing almost anything they can get their hands on, doing and selling drugs, and committing virtually every crime known to man. When I see kids today, standing on street corners, I figure they have just committed a crime or are about to. Unfortunately the statistics on that say that my opinion is most likely correct. Now, let me ask you what you do to keep your son out of trouble because I really haven't seen that you do very much along that line."

"I try to keep an eye on him and he has had some problems but hopefully he is coming along."

"Well, at least you are here. I don't see any other parents around. Are any of the others here?"

"Not that I know of."

"OK, tell the jailer I said it was OK for your son to leave. Tell the jailer I am here if he wants to talk with me first. In fact, tell him to come out here. I would like to talk with him before he releases your son."

When the jail custodian came out, Robert asked him how the boy, whose father had come to the jail, was acting. The jailer indicated he was not a particular problem. A few of the others were but not him. Robert then told the jailer to release the boy to his father, which he did. When he came out with the boy, Robert asked about the behavior of the others. They all, more or less, were basically obnoxious brats. That was about the extent of their misbehavior. About that time, Perry walked in and Ross told him to send the remaining youths to retraining centers for a course on how to act properly. Perry confirmed that was the wording that Robert wanted on the order for punishment and when informed it was, he said, "Consider it done."

Robert again addressed the jailer and asked if they had spoken with the parents of the other boys and girls. They were only able to get in touch with four of the parents and they had no interest in going to the jail to pick up their offspring. One of them said, "Been there, done that, too many times." They said they would check on the kid the following day. Their interest level was minimal according to the jailer.

Robert replied, "Just what I thought".

As Robert and Perry drove to their temporary quarters for the night, Perry explained the results of his meetings with the Chief of Police and the County Sheriff. Both men were dedicated professionals but were dealing with a society that had basically run off the track. People had none of the basics of life and were surviving on next to nothing. Consequently anything not nailed down was community property and that created problems for the community. Gangs were running rampant and were well armed. Road travel was dangerous. Travel by foot was more dangerous and there was very little gasoline available for vehicular travel. Unemployment was to the moon and not seeming to improve. There was little, if any, respect for law enforcement and communities lacked funds to pay for more and better police officers. The local government had WestPac dollars but they were not always negotiable for goods and services. That was another problem Robert had to tackle soon. He had already spoken to Sarah about tying the value of the WestPac dollar to the price of a bushel of wheat. A bushel of wheat in these times of food scarcity was one commodity virtually everyone could assign a dollar value to. Sarah and her staff had not yet decided what valuation they were going to assign to the WestPac dollar but the mere indecision gave some respect to the WestPac dollar that allowed it to serve as a mostly negotiable currency.

In the meantime, while he was attempting to solve the problems of the new nation, Robert told Perry to support the local law enforcers by leaving a number of WestPac troopers under the further direction of the Sheriff and Police Chief but with the additional powers to enforce WestPac rules and regulations without local direction. His trust level of the local authorities was not very high.

"Assign an officer in charge that is dedicated to our goals and tell him that he has our authority to act as he deems necessary to enforce stability in the region. He does not need an order of the local authorities to do that. We want this area stabilized and soon. He should also ensure that efforts are being made by the local communities served thereby to improve transportation with increased rail beds and maintenance on the streets and highways. Tell him to send us reports of his progress."

"The two worst strategic mistakes to make are acting prematurely and letting an opportunity slip; to avoid this, the warrior treats each situation as if it were unique and never resorts to formulae, recipes or other people's opinions."

—Paulo Coelho

CHAPTER ELEVEN

Robert had been working out of his new offices in Portland for six weeks and was just beginning to receive the newly trained personnel from the military training camps in Montana. Perry had supported his request for pacification troops that had been assigned to various posts throughout the Western areas of WestPac and were extending their influence throughout surrounding cities and towns. Local officials were providing quarters and food for the troops stationed in their areas. Sometimes the local officials didn't realize they had this obligation until reminded by Robert and they rapidly saw the light. The troops immediately took steps to bring peace and security for the citizens living in the surrounding cities and towns. With the return of stability, much work was being done to improve the infrastructure of the local area including the transportation system. Trains with food and materials were running at least frequently if not yet on schedule between the major cities of the West. There were occasional problems of organized bands of thieves attacking loaded rail cars but Perry's reaction to that was swift and punitive. That was on the decline as more troops became available.

Certain areas of the West were still plagued by gangs of youths and adults and that was slowly decreasing as well. Youth gangs were being rounded up as the troops became available and they were being carted off to retraining centers that were work oriented rather than punishment focused. The youths were assigned to work projects that had been neglected and that provided a beneficial effect on the community. In time, the youths involved began to take pride in what they were doing. They were also paid a small remuneration for their work and by the time their retraining period had ended, they had accumulated a small savings and a new outlook on life. They were then sent to Beth Sloan's educational system for more learning, depending upon their previous educational experience. Many of the youths had very limited experience in any school which was just further evidence of their need for retraining. When they had completed the retraining program, they were definitely wiser for the experience and most hungered for the education that they had previously avoided and that WestPac now offered to them.

Robert had concluded that his plans for the WestPac conference would have to be delayed by a few months. The issues with transportation and stability, while markedly improved, continued to stand in the way. With the rate of progress being what it was, a conference of the magnitude Robert desired would be possible within a few months. Another impediment was that Jack Nix was in the process of organizing a large force of troops for the Nevada Offensive against the FSP planned for the current time frame. The Nevada Offensive was going to tax available resources to the max and to try to schedule a well publicized and presented conference at the same time was not going to work. Robert wanted the entire country focused on the conference and following its activities on their local television stations and that was not going to happen in the middle of a major offensive by WestPac forces.

This offensive move against the FSP was the brainchild of Robert Thomas who viewed this action as a great opportunity to injure or destroy the FSP. He was also aware that it was a risky move. His troops were for the most part young, inexperienced and not battle hardened. Everyone was aware of these limitations including Robert. And as a result, those in support of the plan were in the minority. Were it not for Robert's absolute control of major issues such as this, the plan would never have seen the light of day. Irene Covington had been working overtime to make everyone question the wisdom of what Robert was doing. She raised all of the issues well known to all. The lack of experience of the troops, the lack of fuel for the mission, the load the mission placed on WestPac for the supplies needed for the troops, the tons of food and expendables that needed to be stockpiled and replaced as used. Many of the farmers that had been producing for the benefit of all and reaping very little, if anything, for their labors were beginning to question where this was taking them. Irene constantly raised the question of, what would happen if the FSP defeats our young boys. She constantly raised the rationale that the FSP has better equipment and certainly more experience at warfare than do these young recruits. Robert countered that argument with, our young men in the military believe in our leaders, our mission and they will do what is right for our civilians and our country. It was true, everyone did have that attitude in WestPac and it was well known that the FSP controlled their troops primarily with threats and fear.

Out of these conflicting views of going to war against the FSP came more active forms of dissent. Rallies against the war had sprung up in isolated areas of WestPac. This was particularly painful for Robert to observe. Political rallies for or against virtually anything had long been a part of the culture of the former nation. At first Robert was going to let it pass as he assumed active support against the war was the viewpoint of an insignificant part of the populace. Unfortunately, as time passed the rallies seemed to increase in frequency and in the number of participants. The anti-war leaders were becoming more vocal, more aggressive and their efforts appeared to be paying off. Robert realized he had to act to shut them down or they would shut down the military mission to fight the FSP.

Robert told Perry to begin arresting the leaders of all rallies against the war and to also arrest protestors who were making an issue of the arrests of the leaders. When this was initiated, there was a loud outcry from the citizens of WestPac questioning Robert's authority to arrest law abiding citizens engaged in peaceful rallies. Robert spoke on television to the nation and said basically that the rallies were damaging to the morale of the nation's fighting men and it had to stop. The arrests were made and the leaders were sent off to retraining centers for rehabilitation. They would only be released when they had shown a significant improvement in their attitude towards the goals of WestPac. In the meantime, they were utilized to work on the many areas of the infrastructure that needed repair. As they improved in attitude and spirit, they would be released back into society but would be monitored to ensure they did not relapse into their old destructive activities.

The troops being assigned to the Nevada operation were being gathered together in the Northern Mountains adjoining Riverton. These were all relatively new troops led by experienced men and they were being subjected to vigorous military exercises carrying full combat gear in the rugged mountains north of the training Bases. They were living and training in full combat mode; foxholes, MREs, full packs, deep snow and pup tents. Both Robert and Jack Nix wanted their troops to be battle hardened veterans by the time they entered combat with the FSP. Guns and Ammo were two of the top military leaders on Nix's staff at the Training Center and were respected by all of the senior NCOs in the unit. They were adept at instilling a fighting spirit in the new recruits, a task they pursued with vigor. Fol-

lowing Thomas' theory regarding how to build camaraderie, every trooper
who survived the forty-five days of pain and deprivation in the below zero
mountain snow with limited food and shelter was given a symbol of their
accomplishment, the unit beret, a dark green beret with the WestPac sword
and shield centered in front bearing their own unit designation, The 104th
Ranger Brigade. The 104 designation referenced the grueling 104 day trip
across the United States to establish their new nation in Montana. The
men in the unit were very proud to wear the beret and other troops that had
been smiling at them previously as they marched off to "Hell in the North"
were very envious of their new status. At the time the troops were preparing to deploy, Robert's popularity in WestPac was at an all time low due
to the popular opinion that the proposed Colorado combat was extremely
risky and possibly unnecessary. The country, in general did not support
the forthcoming combat. There was no doubt it was in the offing and the
Administration was certainly not denying it. On the contrary, they were
calling on the citizens to tighten their belts and help in the Grand Struggle
as Robert referred to it in his television chats with the public. As for the
criticism that he was taking for sending the nation's youth into combat, his
attitude was, "Who the Hell cares what they think? I know what I am doing is right. If we win this battle, we will be well on our way to defeating
the FSP." Robert knew that with success in major combat operations, his
poll ratings would be elevated. That was not an important consideration
with him but he was aware that his staff followed polls quite closely. As
Clay had mentioned a number of times, he didn't care for them either but
when the ratings were high, his job became much easier.

The troops were being transported by truck down to a staging area in
Northern Colorado where supplies of food and armaments had previously
been positioned and placed under guard by the original reconnaissance
troops of Guns and Ammo. The plan was for approximately fifty thousand troops to be deployed protecting the North South Rail Line and the
rail shipments of fuel moving to the north destined for Riverton. Fifty
thousand troops to be held in reserve in Northern Colorado with the balance of one hundred fifty thousand newly formed, freshly trained troops
to advance to the west and make contact with the rear of the main force
of the FSP that were presently engaged in combat with Donley's forces
in Nevada. The FSP was at a definite numerical disadvantage once all of
the troops were engaged in combat. There was also a unit of Utah ground
forces that merged into Nix's WestPac troopers. When the forces were

engaged in their planned positions with Nix attacking the rear guard of the FSP in Nevada and Utah and Donley counter attacking the front lines of the advancing FSP force, the FSP was caught in the classic squeeze play with attackers on all sides. The battle raged on all fronts and continued for seven days and nights with heavy losses among the FSP. They were being attacked day and night, front and rear, and had lost their artillery support early on in the battle when their artillery units operating in the rear were overwhelmed by Nix's troops attacking them from the east.

The FSP was running short of ammunition due to the fact their supply line from the east had been severed by Nix's troops guarding the rear. No FSP rail or truck transports were reaching Western Nevada. Furthermore, the WestPac rail tankers were now carrying fuel without interference from New Mexico and Texas all the way to Montana where it was being trans-shipped to Western areas of WestPac. FSP helicopters were being knocked out of the sky with ground to air missiles and the drones were present at the start of combat but were withdrawn after seven were taken down by the newer high altitude radar guided missiles provided by Barnes. It was also at about this time that Nix's forces securing Northern Colorado and Nevada discovered a drone base in Western Utah with four drones in hangars on the airfield together with their control equipment, manuals and captured technician operators. That was considered a major find and Barnes ordered the drones with all support equipment and personnel immediately sent up to Seattle for study.

When the outcome of the struggle became obvious, The FSP Commander suggested a cease fire and offered to withdraw his forces to the eastern border of Colorado. Nix agreed to a temporary cease fire, in position, while he messaged the offer to Robert Thomas for his decision.

Robert immediately called a meeting in Riverton for the principals to discuss the situation. Robert was against allowing a withdrawal of the FSP troops as he reasoned that he had them right where he wanted them. Irene Covington who had been informed as to what was going on, was lobbying hard for a permanent ceasefire and withdrawal of WestPac troops from the zone of conflict. At the same time, Sarah was receiving information that supported Robert's opinion. Her staff had intercepted messages to the FSP forces in Western Nevada from Turner's FSP offices in Georgia in response to their requests for support due to lack of ammunition, food and water. The Western forces were instructed to adopt delaying tactics as a sizeable FSP force was moving to the west and about to enter Colorado.

This was a substantial force that presumably would overcome the WestPac and Hispanic forces then controlling the battle in the West.

With this information, Robert's mind was firmly made up. He sent a message to Nix demanding an immediate surrender of the FSP forces involved in the battle or they would be annihilated. "Give them no more than three hours to decide and then attack from all sides. We don't have much time before a large force of FSP arrives from the east to rescue them. Then gather all forces, including Donley's, and lay a trap for the FSP coming towards you. If you have any prisoners, which I assume you will, send them under guard up to Oregon. Advise us how many and when you expect them to arrive in the Portland area. Good luck and keep us advised."

Nix ordered his troops guarding the rail lines in Utah and Colorado, numbering approximately sixty thousand, to cut the rail lines heading to the west to deny the eastern FSP force transport of men and materials. They were undoubtedly relying on rail support for this operation. They then laid out their troops in the high country along the assumed FSP route to the west so that the WestPac forces had the advantage of the high ground. Hans Frick also sent high altitude reconnaissance aircraft to monitor the progress of the FSP force moving to rescue their Western units.

"There is no instance of a nation benefiting from prolonged warfare."
—**Sun Tzu**

CHAPTER TWELVE

Five hours after the cease fire was terminated and battle had recommenced, The FSP battlefield commander surrendered. He was sustaining extremely heavy losses and further combat was senseless. Furthermore they were out of food and water and in the desert heat, his troops were becoming overcome physically, principally from lack of hydration. Approximately, eighty thousand FSP troops were captured. Nix was concerned at the terrible shape those men were in as they needed food and water immediately or they would be dying before they were moved anywhere. He advised Robert that they needed at least two days to get many of them back on their feet. Robert told Nix that was about all the time he had to get them moved as the FSP coming in from the east would soon be a threat. Robert was torn between advising the eastern FSP commander that he no longer had troop support in the West in order to dissuade him from his rescue mission or from letting him proceed. He finally decided not to send the message as that would interfere with the possibility of achieving a significant victory over what appeared to be the main force of the FSP.

With the large number of troops surrendered to WestPac, Nix's mobility was definitely hampered but he was taking steps to provide a secure area for the prisoners while at the same time moving the bulk of his force into position to do battle with the rescue force. He now also had leadership of the Donley force as well as the original troops securing the rail lines. With the additional men coming from Riverton, Nix had a combined force of over four hundred thousand troops. He moved most of these troops into positions to the east of the North-South Rail Lines so that they would continue to have fuel supplies flowing to WestPac and available for military operations. His intention was to meet his enemy well to the east of his rail supply lines.

In the meantime, Perry had sent every school bus, city bus and truck he could locate in Oregon down I-5 and over into Nevada to pick up the surrendered FSP soldiers under guard. It was his intention to bring them to Portland and interview the prisoners to see if there was interest in fighting for WestPac. Nix had advised him that he was getting comments from many of the prisoners that they had more or less been 'Shanghaied' into the FSP force. Many of them were not big fans of Turner. They would present less of a problem if they joined the WestPac military than if they remained in Westpac as prisoners. Another advantage was that if they could convert them, with the current turnout of the training Bases they could soon field a force of seven hundred thousand men. That was good news to Robert as it was his intention to proceed with his military operation and recapture eastern Colorado and then move east against the FSP through the center of the country. He was beginning to think long term about destroying the FSP permanently and reuniting the country. He had spoken to Anders about his plans for defeating the FSP and Anders supported him but cautioned him not to get over confident based on the one major victory in Nevada. Robert's opinion was that the FSP had suffered a major loss and this was the time to strike them with a fatal blow now that WestPac was operating from a position of strength.

As Robert had predicted, his poll numbers took a major leap with the victory in Nevada but as word began to leak out that he intended to press the attack on the FSP and hopefully regain control of the entire country, the polls began to fall. The citizens of WestPac had lived through very difficult times following the collapse and they did not want to gamble the gains they had achieved in the past year since Robert had taken over operational control of WestPac. Regardless of growing criticism, Robert gave the green light to Nix to engage the FSP rescue force.

As Nix's troops moved to the east through Nevada and into Utah, they began encountering FSP advance reconnaissance units for the main FSP rescue force. There were a number of these limited actions all the way through Utah and into Colorado. Nix was receiving word from Hans Frick and Sarah regarding the progress of the FSP force to the west. It was a large force estimated at three hundred thousand men or more together with armored vehicles including tanks. The FSP force was still located on the east side of the Rocky Mountains but making rapid progress. Nix wanted the major battles with the FSP to take place in the high country where he still had time to position his troops in favorable defensive positions. This was about to become a major battle and Nix made up his battle plans to take advantage of the terrain. Nix sent smaller guerilla units comprised of twenty or more Rangers each to harass the FSP force as it made its way

through the higher country on its route. The FSP was following two separate routes, one along Interstate 70 and the other following the course of
State Highway 50. Basically these were the only two routes through the
mountains that were available for the FSP force to take in its journey to
the West. Apparently their intention was to join forces at Grand Junction,
Colorado where the two routes came together. Nix had his guerilla forces
strengthened by the 104th Brigade Rangers in the mountains to the west of
Vail, Colorado along I-70 and also in the mountains along the increasingly
difficult terrain of State Highway 50 west of Gunnison, Colorado. His plan
was to ambush and decimate the FSP force at every choke point to the
west of those locations so that by the time the two forces met in mortal
combat, presumably at or near Grand Junction, Colorado, the FSP would
be substantially weakened.

Nix's plan which he had worked out with the assistance of Robert was
to strengthen the passes along both routes where the roads narrowed due
to the cuts made in years past along the canyon walls for the roadways.
Nix would place mortars in the upper levels of the cliffs on either side of
the roadway targeted for the narrow pathway the FSP troops would have to
take in their journey to the West. They would also locate sections of both
highways that were very susceptible to avalanches and would target those
areas for their artillery to bring down tons of rock on the roads rendering them impassable and then destroyed by mortars secreted in the higher
elevations of the mountains. Included in the mix in these locations, Nix
had highly trained sniper teams secreted in the rocks and ledges above the
roadways to target the FSP troops most of whom were moving west on foot
as the roads both on I-70 and Highway 50 were virtually impassable by
normal vehicular traffic. In many areas they were overgrown with brush,
the roadways were littered with boulders and small, to in some cases, large
rocks as well as avalanches of dirt and rock with absolutely no road repair
by anyone for years. IED's were also dug into narrow sections of the roadway that were now mostly dirt and that were exploded by compression
switches or radio signals from above. Traveling through these sections
of Colorado on these roads defended as they were was a very hazardous
undertaking by the FSP but these were the two available routes west for
Turner's forces to take.

Nix's intention was to incur as much damage to the westbound FSP
force as he could and then to retire his rangers working the heights when
their risks of loss were unsustainable. These Rangers would safely move

further to the west to previously selected and fortified positions to perform their deadly mission yet again. The FSP had helicopters and drones which could counter the threat of the WestPac sniper and mortar teams working up in the heights above the roadway provided they were not being interdicted by the defenses available to the Rangers. Barnes had equipped these Rangers with hand held missiles capable of downing the helicopters and low flying drones. The drones were a greater threat than the helicopters in view of the fact that they could operate at higher altitudes with guided smart bombs and rockets. For them, Nix had set up anti-Drone teams at distances of a few miles north and south of the affected roadway. These would be smaller, well camouflaged units that were difficult to detect and were capable of radar targeting the drones and destroying them with high altitude missiles.

Again, as before, he sent smaller combat units around the presumed areas of combat to position themselves to the rear of the FSP forces and harass or completely stop any resupply. It was Nix's intention to use the mountains of the west to his advantage and destroy the Army of the FSP in country they were not familiar with.

Jack Nix stayed in constant communication with Robert Thomas throughout the campaign and Thomas completely supported the plan of battle that Nix had prepared. The complete plan was kept under wraps and did not go further in Riverton than to Robert Thomas. He was still being severely criticized for this risky maneuver and Robert did not want to take any chances that some of his enemies in Riverton would pass on vital information to the FSP.

There were approximately fifty armored vehicles in the FSP caravan. By the time they had arrived at the major choke points being west of both Vail and Gunnison, they had already lost twenty or more tanks and other armored vehicles primarily to road side bombs and heavy mortar fire from well hidden sites up the sides of mountains. The FSP had countered with helicopter attacks on any signs of WestPac troop activity in the upper slopes above the routes of travel. In the process they had lost a number of helicopters as a result of ground to air missile strikes.

The FSP were suffering major losses to the WestPac guerilla sniper teams occupying the high ground along their routes and finally they took action to bring that to a close. The FSP began airlifting thirty to fifty man teams to the west of presumed locations of guerilla forces who then fought their own guerilla battle against the WestPac teams. This back and forth between the smaller units of each side continued as the main FSP forces proceeded along their westward journey. They continued to suffer losses from the attacks of Nix's troops but not as severe as it had been. When the FSP convoy reached the major choke points of Vail and Gunnison, the battle greatly increased in intensity. It was no longer a guerilla battle between smaller units. This was all out combat. Nix's artillery, camouflaged and set in place long before the arrival of the FSP, bombarded the troops and armored vehicles now trying to hunker down in the passes alongside the cliffs and mountainsides. The FSP was again successful in outflanking some of the artillery units and the WestPac troops were, in some cases, forced to abandon their positions and move to the west. The battle between the two forces continued unabated and seesawed with one side winning some firefights and the other side winning others. There were casualties on both sides but Hans Frick had rescue helicopters moving back and forth into the battle zones removing wounded WestPac troops and taking them to emergency medical care centers set up in safe areas to the rear. There did not appear to be any such care for the wounded FSP soldiers.

It was Nix's intention to follow Thomas' suggestion of maintaining contact with the advancing FSP force while slowly pulling back in the direction of Grand Junction which was being strongly fortified in anticipation of the major battle between the opposing sides. Hopefully, the FSP would take this as a sign of weakness. During this slow pullback of the WestPac forces, they continued to exact a heavy toll of dead and injured on the FSP troops. The WestPac losses were minimal compared to what the FSP was experiencing but from the reports taken from captured FSP troops, their commanders were becoming very confident of victory as they continued to advance to the west. That was exactly what Nix wanted them to do.

The reports of the battle coming back to Riverton did not appear favorable to WestPac. Wounded troops were coming into Riverton for medical treatment daily and together with the reports of the FSP advancing to the west and WestPac Rangers continuing to retreat, soon the criticism of the entire venture began to grow. Irene Covington was calling for the removal of Robert Thomas from the executive position he occupied and the removal of Nix as the commander of the WestPac force fighting the FSP. There were no moves being made to meet her demands but there was no move to oppose it either. It seemed as though both sides on that issue were awaiting the outcome of the battle.

Thomas remained quiet and let Irene criticize to her heart's content.

Even Anders and Sarah were beginning to question Robert as to what they had gotten themselves into. Robert only responded with, "Let's see what happens when the main forces meet. That will be soon."

Robert was confident that the plan he and Nix had laid out would be successful. But, then one never knows for sure what will happen. He knew that his future was at stake if the FSP was the major winner in the forthcoming battle but, in his mind, it was a battle that had to be faced. "Let the nay-sayers bitch all they want. That is the one thing they are good at."

Later in the day Sarah called him and said that Irene Covington was getting up a petition to have Robert removed from office. "I am expecting that on my desk any day now."

Robert chuckled and said, "Great. That is perfect. Only Irene could be that stupid. I want that petition when you receive it or a copy would do. I want to know the name of every jackass in Riverton or elsewhere that I cannot count on. What a wonderful way to know who is against you."

"I will send it to you Robert but I will warn you, there are quite a number of names on that list."

"That is no problem, Sarah. I have never let polls influence me in any way. I might add, Stuart viewed them the same way. By the way, Perry and I spoke yesterday about the troops that will be sent south soon to support Nix in his battle with the FSP. We are sending Wyatt from Portland to Riverton to take command of that unit. There should be about one hundred thousand or more of those new trainees. They will be learning fast when they get into combat. Make sure they have all the gear they need. We still have plenty of rifles and combat equipment from our original supply but uniforms, packs, and all the assorted gear to be fully equipped I am not sure about. Make sure that they have whatever they need. Also I assume food and fuel supplies are getting down to Colorado OK, Right?"

"Robert that is all taken care of. Matt Parker has been working overtime to make sure supplies are going to the troops. He has been great on this. By the way, he didn't sign the petition."

"I didn't expect that he would. I will be over there tomorrow. Tell that jackass Irene Covington to not show her face. She is on the ragged edge of going to Retraining Classes. If I catch sight of her, she is going. See you tomorrow."

When Robert arrived in Riverton in the company of Wyatt, Ross Perry had already arrived. Robert wanted Perry with him when the battle was joined down in Colorado in the event that any major decisions had to be made regarding military strategy. Robert was well aware that Nix was a topic of many conversations throughout WestPac as the battle in Utah and now in Colorado was the number one conversation piece throughout the new nation. He was a bit concerned that Perry may have considered himself to be a bit out in the cold when it came to military matters. He had spoken to Sarah to publicize Perry's heavy involvement in what was going on in the South and that many of the tactical decisions that were being played out in Colorado were coming from him and from Robert Thomas. This was publicized heavily on WestPac Radio and Word of WestPac published throughout the new nation.

The publicity for Robert and Ross Perry did have some beneficial effects. The criticism of Robert continued but it did not seem to be growing in intensity.

When Robert ran into Perry shortly after landing in Riverton, Perry jokingly commented that, "I see you are trying to share the blame for any loss down in Colorado by having Sarah put you and me in there with Nix."

"Right, Ross. Actually, I didn't want Jack Nix to get all the credit if it ends up as a victory for us. I figured if that happened, you would be pissed, right?"

"Not really, Robert. I am quite impressed with how Jack is handling matters down there. I knew he was a sharp guy and furthermore he is not a glory seeker. He doesn't need to wade ashore in full view of any cameras. That is just not important to him."

"Yes, Ross. Both of you are confident as to who you are and that is the major reason you work so well together. You are as important in this battle as Nix is and I am fully aware of that. Monty Wyatt is another good troop and I told him we would be meeting with him in the Admin Building so let's get over there."

As they walked over to the Admin Building, Robert asked Perry how the interviews with the new FSP prisoners went. Perry said that almost all of them wanted to join with our military and fight the FSP. Apparently, very few of those men were fighting for the FSP voluntarily. It was decided that all of those that appeared willing to fight for WestPac would be sent for a familiarization course on WestPac, its rules and regulations. If they were still willing to join the WestPac military, they would be sent through boot camp in Riverton as any other new recruit so that they would thoroughly learn our systems, procedures and chains of command. Their progress would be closely monitored and if there was any question as to their loyalty, they would be removed from the program. If removed from the program, they would be allowed to return to their home area wherever that may have been. They would first be photographed and finger printed. Should they ever again be captured by WestPac in battle, they would be imprisoned on labor details for a number of years.

"Obviously, the greater the length of a **war** the higher is likely to be the number of **casualties** in it on either side."

—**Douglas Haig**

CHAPTER THIRTEEN

Perry, Robert and Monty Wyatt sat in Robert's Riverton office discussing the battle in Colorado. The FSP had continued their slow advance to the west and were expected to be in the Grand Junction area within the following week. According to reports coming in from Nix, FSP battle losses continued to climb. WestPac sniper teams were exacting a terrific toll of FSP dead and wounded. Barnes had designed and issued a new fifty caliber light weight bolt action sniper rifle armed with an infrared/ lazer computerized scope that was deadly at over two thousand yards. Every combat squad had one Ranger sniper qualified and equipped with the WP50 rifle who was also assisted by a spotter with day and night range finder equipment which was wi-fi connected to the rifle computer system. The spotter was able to feed range and wind information into the gun scope that would adjust the gunsight reticle accordingly as well as to compensate for altitude and heading variation. They were proving themselves to be a deadly duo in the Colorado Mountains above the westward moving FSP troops.

It was estimated that the FSP had already lost about twenty percent of their troop strength and about one third of their armored vehicles. They were now suffering from limited resupply from the east as that was blocked by Nix's forces harassing the rear of the WestPac advance. Robert was wondering why they continued to advance. Ross said it was due to the hubris of the leaders of the FSP force. He knew some of them from his years in the Federal Army before the collapse. "They are an arrogant, obnoxious group of men and that is a very serious weakness in a military commander."

Monty Wyatt was eager to join the battle taking shape down in Grand Junction and Ross and Robert walked him down to the embarkation point which was at the town center. Wyatt's wife, Tracy, was waiting for him at the convoy operations center along with the senior officers leading the convoy. Thousands of troops were saying goodbye to friends and family for those who had them. Many thousands had no family living in the WestPac region as they were refugees who had led lives in other parts of the former nation and had fled the FSP to Montana or Oregon to save their lives and lives of their families. Robert had taken steps to make these men feel part of WestPac by having civilians in Riverton and Goodland handing them gift packs and talking to them as they prepared to depart. As those troops departed Riverton, they waved to the citizens and gave thumbs up signs showing their intention to right the wrong done to them and their former nation.

When the three men approached the staff vehicles, Monty Wyatt introduced Robert and Perry to his wife, Tracy. Perry had met her years before when she was a young girl that Wyatt had rescued during one of his patrols out of the Control Zone. When Perry and Robert were walking back to the administration building, Perry told Robert the story of her rescue. Her entire family had been killed by the gangs roving the streets of Melbourne and it was a miracle that Wyatt had been able to rescue her and bring her back to civilization.

As they returned to the Admin Building, Robert was soon seated in Beth Sloan's Education Office. "Beth how are you doing here? I want you to know that I consider your work in education to be one of the major responsibilities we have."

"I know you do, Robert, and I appreciate it."

"Beth, I was reading in the local newspaper that there have been some local rallies in other areas of WestPac criticizing the war and raising the question asking if we have what it takes to battle the FSP. That in my view borders on treason. I don't want to pull those critics in and send them to re-training camps but I may have to do that if it does not stop. I would rather see them get educated to know better. What is your view?"

"Mine as well, Robert. I would say most if not all of those young critics of our military and our government would not be out at those rallies if they had attended our school system."

"Beth, I certainly hope you are right. We need to instill a knowledge of what happened to our former nation and the difficulty we have overcome to get this far in building up this one. Also, and equally important, young people today need to have a set of moral principles that they can use as guides for their future lives. That seems to be missing in many of them. Look at the violence that young people, boys and girls, are continuing to commit throughout WestPac. It is senseless violence with no redeeming value whatsoever, totally meaningless. They need to learn right and wrong and what to do if faced with having to choose between right and wrong. That has to be instilled in them so that their reaction to evil is automatic. They must have the background to be able to distinguish good from bad. It is amazing, that so many people lack that. I am starting to think that a good basis in morality is not naturally instilled in people. They must learn it and if they don't learn it, they don't have it. People criticize me for being a religious nut. If morality is religion then I am guilty but they are completely separate bodies of knowledge. Morality is a body of ethical principles. Religion involves a belief in a God. I am all for believing in God. I do myself, but right now I am pushing morality. The people can decide what God they want to believe in or not to believe in. That is their business."

The two talked for another hour and when Robert left, Beth understood that teaching moral principles in the school system would be brought back to the curriculum and emphasized immediately. Robert thanked her for her efforts and the progress she was making in the school system and he departed her office. On the way out of the Admin building, he stopped in to see Anders. Anders welcomed him in and shut the door so that they could have a few moments alone.

"Robert, are we doing the right thing down in Colorado? I sure as hell hope so."

"Anders, I do as well. Personally, I have great faith in Jack Nix and in our troops and their leaders. The FSP leaders lack the great respect leaders need from their troops to win battles. You don't win wars with troops that do not trust you and that is what the FSP has. Our discussions with the Nevada prisoners makes that very clear. Many of them are coming over to our side and are now in boot camp learning our war making ways. Furthermore Anders, they know they can trust us because they have communicated with some of their soldiers we have captured and released and are back home and they know the FSP would never have done that. They have seen our citizens and how hard they work and how well they are treated and they want some of that for themselves. When some of them on the trucks going to fight down in Colorado received gift packs from our citizens, some of them began to cry. What the hell does that tell you? We will win. Count on it."

"Robert, why don't you tell that to the people who criticize you for fighting a losing battle?"

"I want them to prattle on so that when I boot them in the ass after we win, people will understand what I am doing. That is not what I wanted to talk to you about, though. When Stuart was alive, we used to spend much time talking. Actually we were very much alike in our political philosophy. I was shattered when he died as I saw him as our future. He was truly a good man. Since his death and my reinstatement as the leader of WestPac, I have given the position I occupy, and the responsibility that comes with it, a great deal of thought. I have not always been a quote unquote good man but I always respected fairness, equality, charity, honesty…now don't start laughing. I always have respected honesty but, in my view, there are times when it may be excused due to circumstances. All along, Anders, I have tried to be a better leader. That does not mean to be a better person. Sometimes a leader must do difficult things that may not appear right or ethical. But a good leader must always try to achieve ethical acts. You two used to talk quite a bit and Stuart would relate your talks to me. I would like it if you would continue participating in these discussions. Not right now as my plane is waiting for me but save up some of your comments, theories, issues and let us talk them over. I could use that as Stuart used it. Not that he agreed with you at all times, but rather that you made him focus on some issues that would have slid past him, to his loss. Also Anders, if you disagree with me on issues as to how I govern, let me know. I may not agree with you but I would like to hear your take on it. Your voice is one of the very few I would like to listen to. I have to go now. Stay in touch."

As Robert left his office and went out the building, Anders leaned back in his chair and thought about what Robert had said. After a while, he mused, "Yes, Stuart was a good man but maybe we have another good man taking his place."

Robert flew back to Portland to deal with the local bureaucrats and problems with transportation and food shortages. He also had to begin focusing in on the conference that he wanted to hold following the battle in Colorado. He intended to be in Portland for only a few days and then return to Riverton to be available during the battle that was forthcoming in Colorado.

Robert was soon back in his office and meeting with his staff, Clay Daley and the other three young men that had spent the past month traveling the far flung communities of WestPac handling transportation, security and food problems. Getting the local bureaucrats moving to solve the new nation's problems was a difficult task. Clay had prepared a report summarizing his findings and those of the other three men. Approximately half of the local community leaders were survivors from the pre-collapse days of the former nation. They were educated by years of experience holding themselves out as hard working, responsible citizens striving to improve the lives of the people they represented while at the same time striving to improve their own lives even more. Unfortunately for them, they were now being appraised by critics that were fully aware of exactly what was going on.

Of the total number of community leaders reviewed, approximately one-third had been summarily fired and were sent to retraining camps or, as Clay referred to it, sent out for makeovers. Another third were considered as capable of being rehabilitated and were placed on probation. They were advised to make severe changes in their operations immediately or they too would be going to retraining centers. The remaining third were considered to be responsible leaders attempting to do a good job in their communities. The most enjoyable task Clays assistants had dealt with was telling some overweight, well fed, arrogant bureaucrat to clean out his desk, leave the check book, and get the hell out of his office and to be on the bus leaving in the morning for the Retraining Center. At first there was disbelief, next came anger and threats followed shortly thereafter by pleading and begging.

Clay and his staff had covered Washington, Oregon, Idaho and Nevada and the net result of their work had been the installation of a number of hopefully competent men and women into leadership positions where they were needed. There were some hard feelings on the part of some of the citizens who did support some of the men and women that were summarily dismissed. That was to be expected because everyone needs a support base, even the crooked politicians and the support base needed to be taken care of or it would no longer function. Likewise some of those on probation were not considered strong supporters of Robert Thomas and his staff of reviewers after they were told to shape up. No one had ever told them that before. The vast majority of citizens of all involved communities were, on the other hand, very impressed by what Robert was doing and strongly supported the actions he and his staff had taken. That was what Robert was after so he was quite pleased. Clay's report on transportation issues was not pleasing. The inspected areas in the mentioned States still needed rail line and rail bed replacements for lines between most major cities. Some progress had been made but much more needed to be accomplished by the very bureaucrats begging to be reinstated. Supplies of food and clothing were not getting out into the areas where they were most needed. Robert told his assistants that had to be solved immediately. If they had to, they would mobilize the work force from the communities involved and get the job done that way. He sent his staff out again to visit the communities most directly impacted by the lack of rail transportation. They were also to ensure that roadways were in good enough shape to handle truck transports. If any of these important needs were not being met, Clay and his three young men were told to draft the needed labor from the involved communities. The preferred alternative was to let the new local leader handle the selection process. Clay was to oversee that project and to communicate with Sarah regarding shipment of needed food supplies and materials. Clay was also detailed to visit areas that had high levels of food production in years past and determine why they were not producing at those levels currently. Clay knew that one of the prime reasons was that their supply of diesel fuel for tractors and agricultural implements was very limited. Needed truck transportation was scarce. That was improving with the rail line shipments from the south but it was going to take a long time to get all the fuel reservoir tanks in WestPac filled. In the meantime, there would continue to be shortages.

Robert told his staff that he would confer with Sarah about getting fuel shipped into WestPac by pipelines from the Alaskan oil wells. To his knowledge those wells were not pumping any fuel to anyone and he wanted to know why. If need be, they could provide protection and security for those lines if they were being interdicted. There was no doubt that whoever owned or controlled those wells would want to make them profitable. Sarah said that she would check that out and would get back to Robert when he returned to Riverton. Robert was anxious to return to Riverton soon as he wanted to be where the action was when the battles began down in Colorado. He would leave for Montana first thing in the morning.

That evening, Robert tried to relax in his office-quarters. He had told his staff not to bother him unless it was a true emergency. That was one problem with living in your office. You just couldn't get away from it. He could not ignore the desk with the piles of papers lying on it awaiting his attention. Well, he would have to ignore it. The day would come, sometime, when his life would again be his own. He now understood what Stuart had gone through. He was going to have to be careful not to let that happen to him. Clearly WestPac needed him. He smiled as he thought about that but it was true. There was no one else in the administration of WestPac that he was aware of that had the drive, the brains, the leadership qualities, the understanding of the problems and the balls to do what had to be done to make WestPac succeed. There were some young guns coming up the pike but they still needed some weathering. Clay was competent and so was Nix and Wyatt, but they all needed overall experience. They were getting it now and hopefully in a few years they would be ready to take on larger tasks. In the meantime he thought, "You are it big boy so enjoy."

"All successful revolutions are the
kicking in of a rotten door."
—**Kenneth Galbraith**

CHAPTER FOURTEEN

Robert drank from his Brandy glass while he stared out the only window in his office. The sun was just going down so he could still clearly see the streets, the houses and the smoke rising from some that were using wood to heat their homes or their rooms. There was very little traffic. Actually there was virtually no traffic other than a very occasional pickup truck or a person on a bicycle. WestPac was now a nation of bicycles. Everyone used them as their main mode of transportation. Gasoline was hard to get and very expensive. Money was another problem. Money consisted of primarily the WestPac dollar, some U.S. dollars, gold, silver, bullets, food and anything one could use for barter. That was virtually anything of value that was transportable from one hand to another. Sarah was working hard on getting the WestPac dollar recognized as the national medium of exchange. She was having some success but there was obviously work to be done. The main issue with the WestPac dollar was that it needed to be backed by something of recognizable value. A bushel of wheat had value, so did an ounce of gold or of silver. This problem was still being worked on by Sarah and her financial advisors and in the meantime the WestPac dollar was worth various product volumes depending upon any particular area of the country. The product volumes were likewise interdependent in that a bushel of wheat was worth two bushels of apples and one rubber bicycle tire was worth two bushels of wheat and that could change tomorrow. It was a very complicated process and that had to be stabilized.

As Robert stared out the window at the streets below he noticed all of the children playing in the streets. They now considered the streets as their playground. Before security was increased in the cities, the children did not venture forth out of their homes as it was too dangerous to do that. Stray bullets were prevalent and occasionally a child or a pedestrian was struck and killed. Seeing the children on the streets showed to Robert that life was returning to the nation at least to this extent. As it improved and motorized traffic again predominated on the streets, he would have to make the children realize that they no longer owned the streets. Robert thought, it is always something. He knew then that the day would never come when he could sit back and say to himself, "I have done it, I am now done."

The following morning, he was sitting on the airplane as it flew east to Riverton. Monty Wyatt was seated next to him and they talked about the reports coming in from the battlefield. They were not good but then they were not bad either. Robert understood what Nix was doing down in Colorado even if the reports did not spell out that what was taking place down there was exactly what Robert and Nix wanted. A gradual retreat from one secured bastion to the next while taking a heavy toll on the enemy. Not much of a retreat but enough so that people, particularly the FSP and Robert's critics in WestPac would know it was a retreat. In the meantime, the overanxious generals of the FSP would see the retreat as a sign of weakness and thrust their forces forward faster than would have been prudent. The FSP generals knew they were taking high losses but they considered the ground gained to be worth the sacrifice. Many of the troops, on the other hand, were beginning to see the light. Some platoons of the FSP force had been completely decimated and were now filled with the fourth layer of troops. All previous replacements had been killed or wounded and were no longer around. Company losses every week were generally mounting to one-third of the unit strength. Semi-trained replacements were coming up from the rear but these were likewise being taken out by the guerilla tactics of WestPac troops under the direction of Guns and Ammo who operated to the east of FSP forces who were moving to the west on I-70 and State Highway 50.

It was a weakened FSP force that was moving into contact with the well dug in main force of Nix's WestPac line. The area immediately to the east of Grand Junction, Colorado had been fortified by Nix's forces in preparation for the major battle that would be taking place there. Artillery emplacements had been dug into the hills surrounding Grand Junction targeting the roadway of I-70 where the FSP force would come in contact with Nix's Rangers. Mines had been laid in the roadway as well as IED's. Well camouflaged and protected sniper team bunkers were cut into the mountain sides above the roadway awaiting the arrival of the FSP soldiers. Longer range artillery was also set up west of the city to fire on the FSP force coming up to Grand Junction on the relatively flat ground of Highway 50. The terrain in that part of Colorado was a major change from the narrow canyons they had traversed almost all the way west to Montrose on Highway fifty. The turn north on highway 50 at Montrose in the direction of Grand Junction gave the FSP generally flat terrain, less difficult for them to traverse but it also provided little if any shelter from air strikes or artillery rounds for a force that had been seriously damaged by the losses taken in the narrow canyons west of Gunnison. WestPac Rangers were also dug in on either side of Highway 50 just south of Grand Junction to bring the FSP forces to a halt in the hot deserts of that area. The FSP would by then be running short of food, water and ammunition due to the interdiction of their supply lines by Guns and Ammo's forces attacking the rear of the FSP force as they had been doing all the way from Gunnison and south on 50.

Finally, both armies were about to face one another in the mountains and foothills of Grand Junction, Colorado and the flat plains to the south. The primary battle was already beginning on the very east and south sides of the city of Grand Junction where the FSP force that had been moving west on State Highway 50 and the FSP force following I-70 combined with the intention of crushing the WestPac troops. In actuality the WestPac force again occupied the higher ground, was well dug in and was stronger numerically now than the FSP. While this battle waged, Nix radioed to Guns and Ammo to advance north on 50 from Montrose and west on I-70 with their troops in full strength to strike the rear of the FSP. Wyatt's troops coming from the north were protecting the flanks of Nix's main line of defense and were pouring mortar and artillery fire on the FSP troops below the ridge lines. Nix had been expecting air support for the FSP ground troops but Sarah had advised him that radio messages had been intercepted indicating that the FSP was running very low on fuel. They did not have access to the Hispanic wells of the Southwest or the Texas wells and their resupply from the east was nil. WestPac was, in fact, much better off than the FSP with respect to fuel supplies and for the final battle, Hans Frick was launching dozens of ground support aircraft loaded with missiles, bombs and bullets as well as a number of drones. Nix's heavy artillery dug in the mountains above Grand Junction were taking a deadly toll of FSP troops as were the isolated snipers of the Ranger teams and the aircraft and drones flying overhead. This slaughter continued for seven straight days with no let up in losses for the FSP. The FSP made a number of thrusts along I-70 with massed troops in desperate attempts to break through the lines of WestPac Rangers defending Grand Junction. These assaults were repulsed by the advantage of massive fire power on the part of the Rangers and in some cases with hand to hand fighting and always with overwhelming losses for the attacking force.

Again, the main problem for the FSP force was that it was running short of water, food, fuel and ammunition. Their supply lines no longer existed. The FSP commander was experiencing the same problems the previous FSP force had experienced. They were literally being wiped out. Eventually they were forced to discuss terms of a surrender. After a pause in the fighting, an offer was delivered via an FSP Officer under a white flag. Nix advised the FSP that the only surrender that would be considered would be an unconditional surrender of all of their forces in the West. President Turner, safe in the East, was messaging them to fight to the death and that he was sending additional reinforcements as well as air support. The commander of the FSP forces knew this was not happening. There were no forces in reserve. Most of them had been used to build up this rescue force that was to save the FSP in Nevada and Utah, now that was gone as well. Finally he agreed to surrender and shortly thereafter the firing stopped.

Nix sent word to Riverton of the surrender of the FSP force. It was decided by Robert that the FSP soldiers would be secured in the Grand Junction area and interviewed individually to determine if any were willing to join up with the WestPac army. It would be a matter of join up or possibly go into an internment camp. For those of lower rank that did not appear to hold any desires to fight again another day for the FSP, they would be allowed to return to their families in the east. Nix requested that additional food and water supplies be sent down to Grand Junction as the FSP soldiers were in very poor condition again due to lack of sustenance. The demands on the Grand Junction community for food particularly was well exceeded by the WestPac military needs now combined with the FSP prisoners. The intention was to take as many of the FSP soldiers having an interest into the WestPac military and then to intern the remainder for a period of time and then release them provided they swore an oath of allegiance to not rejoin the FSP. As for the harder cases, they were to be sent to the retraining centers. That included all of the FSP officers.

While the battle ground was being stabilized and the soldiers were given a well needed rest, Robert had Nix return to Riverton alone for a conference. When he arrived in the city, he received an enthusiastic hero's welcome. They had a parade down the main street of Riverton with people coming from all over WestPac that had any means of transportation for getting there. The entire city was in a celebratory mood. Totally different from what Nix had seen before he left to take command of the force in Nevada. There were no signs protesting the war and condemning Robert Thomas for attacking the FSP. The new flags of WestPac were out in great abundance. Robert had seen to it that they were readily available for everyone. All along Main Street in Riverton and in Goodland, the flags were being flown.

Robert had Sarah set up an interview of Nix on WestPac Radio which was broadcast across the nation. While receiving accolades himself, Nix praised the leadership of Robert Thomas who he said was the figure responsible for the victory over the FSP. Nix said that all praise for the defeat of the FSP in the West went to Robert. Much of the strategy for the winning tactics he claimed were authored by Robert Thomas. The effect of this interview and other interviews of Nix for the newspaper, Word of WestPac, and other media for the following weeks was a giant uptick in the popularity of Robert Thomas. Part of this was initiated by Ross Perry who saw in Nix's popularity an opportunity for Robert. On the other hand, for Nix, these were his genuine opinions and beliefs. He had great respect for Robert Thomas and was driven to make sure that everyone in WestPac was aware of the qualities of the man.

Irene Covington and a few others, on the other hand, concluded that this was just another trick by Robert Thomas to gain power and influence in the nation. Irene was still alive and well and continued in her quest to chip away at the weaknesses of Robert Thomas.

Following the interviews of the FSP soldiers, over half chose to join the WestPac military and were sent to training camps north of Riverton to learn the goals of WestPac, its rules and regulations as well as to learn WestPac military procedures and tactics. This was a major project for Ross Perry to support. There were approximately two hundred thousand new trainees for him to work with which also laid a heavy load on John Barnes for the massive amount of supplies of military hardware that would be needed to equip these new men. Both men attacked this giant challenge with their usual vigor and in no time at all, progress was being made. Matt Parker was sending uniforms and other material goods to the training camps by the truck load. Supplies of food, clothing and military hardware were coming from some of the newly developed areas of the West. Rail transport had been improving there daily and factory production had commenced in many cities and towns turning out clothing, tools, weapons, and other items needed by the new military personnel and also needed to replace lost or damaged materials for the WestPac Army in Colorado.

There were approximately fifty thousand new detainees in the Retraining Center representing the Officers and some recalcitrant FSP soldiers who held some allegiance to their former employers. Robert assumed that given a little time, most of these detainees would see the light and would either take the oath of allegiance to WestPac to be released or would join up as recruits to fight for WestPac. None of them were difficult prisoners to detain and Yates and Campbell were soon able to assign them to work details improving the infrastructure of WestPac roads, bridges, rail lines and community buildings. All personnel working with the detainees were soon of the opinion that they would be released from the Centers within less than one year.

Robert held an important conference with Nix, Perry, Barnes, Parker, and Sarah to map out where they would go next. The FSP force in the West no longer existed. The road was clear except for the usual small gang activity all the way to the Nebraska border. Louis Donley was stabilizing his part of the West and resting his battle weary troops. It was Robert's intention to honor the geographic limits of WestPac as laid out in Stuart's meeting with Donley as Donley had always dealt fairly with Westpac and never questioned the agreement he and Stuart had made years ago. Nevertheless, that agreement had nothing to do with the rest of the former nation to the east of Colorado. Robert was well aware that now the WestPac Army with the addition of the mass of new recruits from the south and the former FSP troops in training in Riverton now numbered close to one million men. They were fairly well equipped. They were very limited in armored vehicles and in late generation combat aircraft but then so did what was left of the FSP. On the other hand, he viewed the WestPac force as a dedicated, patriotic, high morale group of young men that believed in what they were doing. This was an invaluable quality in a fighting force and Robert firmly believed they were capable of extending WestPac to the limits of the former nation with the exception of the Hispanic Southwest that was currently under the control of Donley. For the time being, he would not interfere with that.

Robert made his views clear to those in the meeting. Generally they were supportive as they all realized that if they did not strike now, in time Turner would rebuild his military and they would be back. Turner was not going to let WestPac off the hook. Robert totally agreed with that opinion. Sarah suggested that the military needed some time off. They had been involved in heavy fighting for months now and their equipment must be showing the effects of that if their bodies were not. She inquired of Robert as to what sort of time table he was considering.

"The sooner we move, the better off we will be. There is no doubt that Turner is anticipating such a move on our part. He knows he is weak at this time and he knows we are aware of his weakness. I say in one month, no later, we move to the east, in force. At the same time, or sooner, we adopt the guerilla tactics that worked so well for us in Colorado. We send our Rangers out in smaller units of one thousand to five thousand man packages into the South, into the North, and across the nation to harass, interdict and destroy the FSP supply lines and to seek recruits for the fight from the millions of subjugated people who we know hate the FSP with a passion."

"As our Army moves to the east, we must be prepared to bring these people on board. Again, that takes food, weapons, clothing, all of the military hardware we have been producing. We must continue to produce that. There should be no letup in our production of military goods. We are going to need them. Furthermore, we should begin to plan the delivery of resupply items so that our Army is constantly being supplied. This is going to be the hard part. We are going to move into an area of the country that has been ravaged, stolen from, cruelly crushed by the FSP and by the many gangs roaming uncontrolled through the cities and towns of the former nation. We all saw it when we moved to the west from Florida. Consider that it is only worse now, far worse. We are not going to be able to live off of the land that we will be traversing. There are no bountiful crops out there according to Sarah's intel reports. Furthermore, the FSP knows we are coming. No sense in trying to keep that a secret. They know we are coming because we have always done what was right and taking back the nation from those animals is the right thing to do. They know we will do the right thing again. So, along that line, I want WestPac Radio and WestPac Word to drum up support for the major action. Get broadcasts and leaflets out to the major cities and towns to the east of Colorado and tell them we will put them into our armies and they can fight with us to regain the country that was stolen from all of us. We want recruits and we will provide the arms and materials just as we have provided those weapons and support to our young men and women in the Ranger companies. Come, join with us and take part in the great victory. Help us bring back the country that we all remember. We need your participation in this great effort. This will take a long time, maybe up to a year, maybe more. I hope not but we also need the total support of our WestPac nation to work overtime to produce what we need to do the job. Any comments from anyone?"

Sarah indicated she had something to say. "Robert, we all have been hoping for such a move at some time and apparently the time is now. My staff has been studying the mood of what is left of the United States of America and the hope is out there. Hope for a rescue from the anarchy, the gangs, the demands of the FSP and their bureaucratic stooges. It won't be easy but we will definitely find support out there for what we do."

Ross Perry commented, "The morale of the troops in Colorado could not be higher. They definitely want to continue moving east and get back to the homes and the life they remember existed there. They hate the FSP as they always had. They are ready to move. We are daily sending reinforcements from our training camps down to Colorado by the truck load. In another month, we will have huge numbers of new troops from the FSP that are in the retraining centers. They are dedicated, battle hardened and the word I am getting from the centers is that they are eager to join the battle and take the country back. We are getting the materials we need to resupply the troops and that goes for the troops in Colorado as well." Robert addressed Nix, "Jack, you have a good handle on the condition of the troops in Colorado supply wise, what is it?"

"As far as our losses in combat of the dead and injured, we suffered a number of casualties. Our KIA's numbered around three thousand. Many good men, enlisted and officers. We have an additional ten thousand injured. Some severe, some not. We have filled all units back to full strength with the new troops coming from the Riverton camps. Since the surrender of the FSP, we immediately began inventorying our military hardware and weapons in the hands of the troops. We had definite needs following that review and that is being met as we speak. Equipment is lost and destroyed in battle and we are now replacing that. It is in the pipeline. I would say that in less than a month, we will be back at full strength with respect to our war making materials. We captured quite a few weapons and ammunition as well and much of it is similar or identical to our own equipment, particularly the rifles, machine guns, rocket propelled grenades, mortars and such. We will be ready to go and believe me, we are eager to get moving."

"He who is prudent and lies in wait for an enemy who is not, will be victorious."

—Sun Tzu

CHAPTER FIFTEEN

Robert had pretty much dropped the idea of having a nationwide conference. There was just too much going on. He would have to deliver his patriotic messages by radio and by television. TV reception was expanding across the country rapidly with the construction of towers and relay sites. Licenses continued to be very scarce but Robert wanted to keep control of that or he would be seeing Irene Covington on various channels blabbing her liberal message. Lately her message delivered in person to whoever would listen to her had been leaning even closer to support for the FSP than it ever had before. Her hatred of Robert Thomas had driven her in that direction. Robert had Sarah meet with her and advise her that she was cruising dangerously close to being sent to a retraining center for a long term confinement.

When Robert returned to Portland, he told Perry to prepare the force and to launch it just as soon as it was ready but to keep Robert informed as to the status of the force as he would be giving some television addresses and wanted to keep the nation informed as well. Perry agreed with the television addresses and told Robert he would have current information as the situation changed. Robert gathered his Portland staff for an important meeting. Some of the assistants were out in the field augmenting the improvements in production and transportation that Robert had dictated some months ago. Robert was very interested in hearing from them as to the progress that had been made.

Finally the day arrived when the key players in the Portland office were present for the meeting. The assistants as well as Clay all gave reports on the improvements in transportation, food and material production from their respective areas of the West. The reports were all very favorable with rail lines having been substantially extended in all areas. Likewise rail assets of engines, cars, tankers, repair facilities and needed supplies had improved markedly. There was now functioning rail service between major cities of the West. Food production had increased markedly and production of material goods, hardware, clothing and tools was substantially higher than the last report.

Robert again made it very clear that they were preparing for a massive assault on what remained of the FSP in the east. This would be a long term commitment and was going to take all the energy, resources and talent of WestPac to be successful. Furthermore there was no alternative to being successful in this mission and Robert expected every one of the leaders of WestPac to be devoting one hundred percent effort to the task and that included every one of his staff members as well as himself.

Robert told them about the television addresses he intended to make informing the nation of the sacrifices necessary to carry out this noble mission of retaking the country from the very scoundrels that had run it into the dirt. The public was to be informed that they would be expected to perform to the maximum in producing the food, the materials, and the war making tools required for this noble venture. "I want you four to fan out among the leaders in the west and impress upon them their great duty of instilling enthusiastic support for this mission in their citizens. Should any one of these leaders balk, remove them from that position of influence and replace them with someone that will get the job done. This is not a game. This is serious business. If they don't understand that, they go. If they don't go quietly, they go to a retraining center immediately. Take a squad of Rangers with you so that everyone understands the seriousness of your mission. Does everyone understand what I have said?"

All of the staff were of the same mind as Stuart on the mission at hand. By the following morning, all had left Portland and were spreading out in the west to send the message. The office was quiet except for his secretary Toni who was busy completing reports that would be sent to Riverton and for disseminating Riverton bulletins and messages for various departments in Portland and Seattle. There was the usual security document from Sarah which focused primarily on what was going on in the former United States of America. The FSP was not going to be the only enemy that Nix would face in the east. There were hundreds of gangs, primarily opportunists, intent upon retaining and expanding their geographic areas of control as that was where they were acquiring their wealth. As well, there were the Muslims in the Northeast and the area of the Great Lakes, from Minnesota to New York. The Muslims would fight to the death to retain their control of that space. They would not be giving up without a fight.

Robert thought about the Cubans under Paco Morales that controlled lower Florida. According to Sarah, the population from Orlando south to Miami was predominately Cuban. Their control of South Florida had been characterized by stability, economic growth, prosperity to a degree and fair treatment of the non-Cubans living in their area of control. Robert considered the situation in South Florida to be much the same as the Hispanic control of the South West. As long as conditions remained as they now existed, he would treat them as potential allies in his fight to control the rest of the United States. They could then decide what they wanted to do, retain their separation or join the new federal Union.

Robert began working on his television introduction to the nation that would be taking place in Riverton. He first called Nix who was still in Riverton and told him that he wanted Nix to deliver the introduction along the lines of what Robert had delivered for Stuart at the first major conference in Riverton. Nix had been present for that and saw the impact delivered to Stuart from Robert's powerful introduction. He said he would be proud to deliver that and would review some of the basics of his introduction with Robert. Robert then called Sarah and told her to set up the broadcast days and times. She already had done that and had a number of dates available depending upon Robert's wishes. He picked one that was four weeks away. Robert told her to advise Nix of that date so that he could plan on being in Riverton at that time. The campaign to retake the east would proceed shortly after Robert's address to the nation.

Robert worked on the layout of the speech. Where he would give it; the length of the speech, the lighting of the venue; the music that would be performed and how it would be crafted for the different phases of the event; the audience in attendance, he would leave that to Perry. He wanted this speech to be a major production that would unite the country to deal with the task at hand, the retaking of the United States of America and the defeat of the FSP. Robert knew exactly what he wanted the speech to say. He had been saying the words of the speech to his staff and to the key figures of WestPac for weeks and months. It was to be an energizing speech, the goal of which was to lift up the spirits of the nation following the victory over the FSP in the west and now challenging them to rise up and fight the battle to win back the United States of America. He considered what to wear and concluded he would wear the uniform of the Commander-in-Chief. He wanted that message sent loud and clear to anyone watching the television. He wanted them to say, there is our Commander and Chief and he does look the part. He would have Nix wear a similar uniform but one with a bit less gold ribbon. He would also complement Nix for his bravery, his patriotism and his love of country. Both Countries, the new and the old.

Robert took a break from making notes on his speech and placed a call to Perry. He was soon on the line and Robert gave him a report on his staff operations in Portland. "Ross, I'm working on the speech I will be giving in four weeks. I want you to staff the new conference hall in Riverton with our trustworthy enthusiastic friends. I will be in uniform as the Commander-in-Chief and I will send you a description of that uniform so that you can dress accordingly. Nix will also be in uniform and the rank structure should be apparent from me to you to Nix. I also want you running the lights as you did before and stage the music appropriately as well. Drum rolls on introductions, that sort of thing. I will get you a copy of my speech when I have it finalized so that you can adjust your team, the orchestra, what have you. You did great work at Riverton before and let's even do better work here. This is very important. I want the nation to see a very impressive leadership group that is enthusiastically supported by everyone there. If you have any questions along the line, give me a shout. I'm sure you are quite busy with the expansion of our military and dealing with how and where we proceed to the east. Sorry to burden you with this but this is also very important and you do great work."

"You are too kind, Robert. I am eager to assist in this as well. I know how important it is to get the support of the country in what will be a difficult task. Anything you want, I will deliver."

Robert worked on his speech the rest of the week. He filmed himself delivering parts of the speech, practicing various postures, voice inflections, pauses and finding which seemed to be the most effective for the part of the speech involved. He adopted many of the poses that he had Stuart use in his speeches to great effect. During this week, he also had a tailor measure him for the uniform he intended to wear as the commander in chief of WestPac. The uniform would bear a resemblance to the WestPac formal uniform worn by WestPac troops at the previous Riverton Conference. His would be solid black as well with gold leaf shoulder boards with three stars signifying his rank as Commander-in-Chief. A WestPac gold emblem on each lapel and his last name, in gold, above the right breast pocket. Over the left breast pocket, the WestPac shield in green and gold below which was "WestPac" spelled out in gold letters. Robert also notified Nix and Perry to adopt the shoulder board insignias of one and two stars respectively. When Robert's uniform arrived, he did a practice session in front of the video camera to see how it looked. It was very good and he made no changes in his speech, its delivery or the uniform.

Sarah had been covering all areas of WestPac with the news of Robert's major address to the nation. The Conference Hall in Riverton was being cleaned and polished and covered with WestPac flags. The Honored guests in formal attire were again sitting against a backdrop of WestPac flags and behind them, the speaker's podium which was on a walk out platform that extended from the stage in the rear of the Conference Center. The podium was again a very impressive affair facing a sea of dining tables for the attendees. The WestPac Symbol of the vertical sword in a field of green was on a plaque situated on the front of the heavy wooden podium with fluted columns carved around the symbol and along the sides of the podium. A great deal of work had gone into the carving of the podium and that was readily apparent. The podium was elevated some four feet above the level of the floor in the Conference Center making it the obvious focus of the event.

On the evening of the event, everyone was in attendance which included the leadership of WestPac, Riverton and Goodland, many in military formal dress uniform, civilian leaders from around and outside of West-Pac, specially selected, including Louis Donley and Paco Morales, that had been invited with formal invitations to ensure their loyalty to Robert Thomas. The Riverton Symphony Orchestra was playing soft music while the guests finished their dinners and awaited the beginning of formalities. Again, wine was in abundance having arrived by special delivery from the best wineries Northern California had to offer. Seated among the WestPac dignitaries directly in front of the podium were, Sarah with her husband, Hans Frick; Ross Perry, Nix, Anders, Matt Parker, and John Barnes. Behind them sat the two hundred or so civilian guests, military guests, honored dignitaries and other WestPac officials.

After a while, Nix had left the group of WestPac notables and apparently was conferring with Robert Thomas behind the curtained stage. After a period of time, the lights were lowered, then darkened and the spot lights began circling the attendees and the stage as the symphony drums began their slowly increasing beat and the lights began to hover over the split in the drape upon the stage. After the drums had achieved a crescendo of maximum volume and pace a cymbal produced a resounding ringing sound followed by silence. The crowd's eyes were focused on the stage and after a moment or two, Jack Nix, resplendent in his impressive formal dress uniform wearing the gold shoulder board rank of General of the Army, stepped forth to tremendous applause from the audience who were now all standing and cheering him as he walked forward to the Podium. After a lengthy period of time and on the third or fourth attempt by Nix to quiet the crowd, he finally succeeded.

"Welcome friends. It is so good to be back home." The crowd again broke out in a loud wave of cheering and applause that took Nix more time to silence the crowd so he could proceed. He then went into the introduction of the real Commander-in-Chief of WestPac, the general that laid out the tactics that led to victory in Nevada and Colorado. The man that had advised and assisted Stuart in his successful leadership of Westpac prior to his fateful accident. The crowd interrupted Nix's introduction at least ten times with lengthy and loud applause. Jack Nix went through a litany of Robert's achievements over the years that Robert had never spoken of before. The audience was definitely impressed with Robert Thomas from the many accomplishments he had made over the course of the previous years that had gone unpublished but were generally known by all. All of his accomplishments were significant to all in the conference hall. They had all led to better lives for the citizens of WestPac who were well aware that Robert was not one to tout his own accomplishments. At the conclusion of his introduction Nix left the stage, returned to his seat and then many in the hall began the chant, Robert Thomas, Robert Thomas. This grew in volume spreading throughout the large gathering and continued for minutes. Finally the curtains parted a second time and Robert appeared resplendent in his new black and gold uniform. It made a very impressive appearance. Robert was not smiling. He stood straight looking over the mass of people who were now standing and cheering. He raised both arms to signal for them to take their seats. Most complied and finally the room was totally silent. Robert approached the podium and placed both hands on the rostrum and said, "Let me first give praise and appreciation to the wonderful troops of WestPac, many of whom gave their very lives in achieving the great victory in Colorado over the Federal Security Police and let me also congratulate General Nix and General Perry for their outstanding leadership in achieving this victory." The crowd was again on its feet for a very long time. Robert stood silent only to nod his appreciation to Nix and Perry who were seated directly in front of the Podium. Both men stood and clapped for Robert.

When the audience was again silent, Robert went on with his speech which was primarily directed at the far flung television audience of West-Pac telling each and every one of them that they were needed in the forthcoming great battle to retake the nation from the clutches of the FSP. He impressed upon them their need to sacrifice for the good of the troops fighting on the front lines and for the rescue of the millions of people in the former United States of America that had been held in captivity for so many years by the arrogant thieves of the FSP under the leadership of former President Frank Turner. Robert consistently throughout his speech asked the attendees if they were ready to give the one hundred percent of their time and effort to the great battle ahead. The audience yelled in unison back to the speaker that they were ready.

The term The Great Battle was used time and again by Robert as he wanted that to be the title for the difficult years ahead for all in WestPac. "These are not going to be easy times. Do not be mistaken about that, but they are not easy times for our troops either. Don't ever forget that." Crescendos of applause and cheering followed that line. Robert finished his speech with a promise. I promise to do all I can to deliver to you the United States of America. It will not be the same as it was when we all knew it before in our youth but in many respects, it will be a better United States of America and it will be the same guardian of freedom and liberty it started out to be. I will ensure you that it will not be corrupted by the greedy and the power hungry politicians as it was before. We will again have that great Federal Democratic Republic with power returned to the States and with a functioning national government with limited powers. Power returned to the people who will again be the focus of government, not the elite bureaucrats with their Hollywood friends and media protectors living lives of wealth and splendor while the citizens scraped and fought to survive and provide for their families. We will revive that sacred document, the Constitution of the United States and it will be honored." This statement brought a crescendo of applause and cheers but Robert went on, "The Constitution will not be subverted by executive orders, by Administrative Regulations, by powerful lobbyists intent upon achieving their selfish goals. It will be a Constitution written by and protected by the People of the United States of America." Again, lengthy and enthusiastic support from the audience for what Robert was saying. Robert continued, "We will bring back our neighborhood schools teaching the basics that provided the foundation for what our great country produced in the nineteenth and twentieth centuries before the social engineers took over the message and real education floundered. That will not happen again but we must forever be vigilant."

The crowd was cheering and Robert stood tall and impressive as he finished his speech and shouted into the microphone, "let us all sing that wonderful song that we all sang many times in our past and will sing many times in the future. It has been a long time so song sheets are being distributed now." Waiters and waitresses passed out the song sheets and the audience gasped. It was "God Bless America."

As the orchestra struck up the music, they played through a bar or two and then returned to the beginning so the audience could get over their shock at thinking of singing a song that many had not heard in the last thirty or forty years. There were some in the hall that were not familiar with the song. Most of those old enough to know the song were in tears as they began to sing.

> *God Bless America*
> *Land that I love.*
> *Stand beside her, and Guide her*
> *Through the night with a light from above*
> *From the mountains, to the prairies,*
> *To the oceans white with foam.*
> *God Bless America, My home sweet home.*
> *God Bless America, My Home sweet home.*

When the full verse had been sung, Robert yelled out into the microphone, "One more time. Let us all join in." He was fully aware that many had been overcome by emotion and were unable to sing a single word. The second time , the walls of the conference center shook with the volume of the voices. As the voices filled the hall, the lights dimmed and a spotlight lit up the Flag of the United States of America which was slowly being raised on a flagpole standing to the side of the stage. As they finished singing and the hall lights slowly came back on, they stood and applauded Robert for minutes. He waved to them and walked back to the curtain on the stage, waved once again and disappeared. As he left the stage, Sarah turned to her husband, Hans Frick and said "That was masterful. He owns this country now."

That evening Robert met with Sarah and Hans, Jack Nix, Anders, and Ross Perry. They had a quiet dinner in the staff dining room as they discussed the day's events. All considered the televised speech to have been very successful and that was the word coming from Sarah's office. There had been hundreds of televised presentations of the speech throughout WestPac, held in schools, theaters, churches, and virtually any building large enough to accommodate the many people that wanted to hear the leader of their country speak to them especially after the great victory over the FSP forces in Colorado. The public that heard the speech was impressed and dedicated to the cause of retaking the country that had been stolen from them. Following the speech, discussions were held and virtually everyone vowed to support the "great battle" in every way they could. Support was unanimous. Robert spoke with Clay and his assistants that evening and they could not believe the overwhelming support he had garnered with the televised speech. It was clearly a major success for Robert and for WestPac.

"There are certain things in which mediocrity
is not to be endured, such as poetry, music,
painting, public speaking."
—**Jean de la Bruyere**

CHAPTER SIXTEEN

The WestPac force in Colorado was fully assembled and ready to move to the east as soon as Robert gave the order. He first made contact with Louis Donley and Paco Morales to advise them of his intentions and to inquire if either or both wanted to participate. Donley denied the request on the grounds that he needed all of his troops to again stabilize the Southwest. Too many people in the Southwest were organizing for their own benefit while Donley's military was fully involved in dealing with the FSP. Paco Morales advised Robert that he would support the fight but thought it best if he kept his Cuban forces in their own territory so as not to arouse suspicions on the part of his neighbors in the South. He did not want them thinking that the Cubans in South Florida had any intentions regarding expanding their territory.

Donley also said that they would be providing material support for the eastern campaign and would ensure that fuel needs of the WestPac military would be fully met. They were already taking steps to stockpile large quantities of fuel in eastern Colorado in anticipation of WestPac's forthcoming needs. He informed Robert that to his knowledge there was little sign of FSP forces anywhere in Colorado after their great defeat at Grand Junction. He stated, "I suspect they are reorganizing somewhere in the States. If you need help in the future for anything, let me know. We are deeply indebted to you for coming to our rescue when we needed it badly."

Robert thanked both Donley and Morales for their support and gave Jack Nix the green light to proceed in his campaign to retake the United States of America. Sarah had been hard at work digesting as much information as she could acquire from her hundreds of radio contacts in the east concerning FSP actions, supply issues, and their mobilization following the disastrous defeats in the West. The one very favorable report Sarah was receiving was that the FSP apparently was very short on fuel. They had been building up troop strength in the Louisiana and Texas border regions possibly to solve the fuel problem but Robert believed these troops would be needed to counteract Nix and would also be meeting stiff opposition from the Texas Militia that had no desire to let the FSP enter their State.

Nix had a force of approximately one million men under arms and was expecting to receive many more as time went on and their needs increased. There was also the issue of replacements for battle losses. He had spoken to Robert about this and Robert had passed on the order to Campbell and Yates who were running the Military Recruitment and Training Operation. Recruiting in WestPac had increased again significantly following Robert's televised address. After the major bump in recruiting from the FSP prisoner group had gone through the system, the facilities were now available to handle massive numbers of trainees. Robert figured that once Nix began entering the newly stabilized sections of the east, they would be receiving many applicants that wanted to join the fight. At the present time, the battle with respect to the million man army was focused on the difficulties and strategy of effective resupply. Not only did WestPac have to produce tremendous volumes of food and water for the troops plus material goods, they had to be able to deliver the resupply to the troops safely and securely. The country was still infested with opportunists who thirsted for the goods they saw on rail cars or assumed were contained in truck convoys moving through Colorado to the troops in the East.

Frick was providing aerial reconnaissance for the advancing force and Sarah was likewise providing intelligence information so that Nix had a fairly good idea of what he could expect for the following days or weeks. He was also using his advance patrols but these were not to make contact with any hostile forces, only to determine if they were out there. For the smaller groups that had fired at his patrols, Drone aircraft operated by mobile technicians traveling west in the troop convoys would deal with them using bombs, rockets and some cannon fire. The main advantage of the drones was their lengthy loiter time and their low maintenance requirements. The drones were reloaded with armament and refueled whenever the convoy came within visual range of an airfield where they could be landed safely and protected during their uploading. Rapid Reflex teams were prepositioned to recycle the drones and other support aircraft in fifteen minutes from landing times which reduced their exposure time from mortar or artillery fire. Nix had a complement of twenty drones, over half airborne at all times, and a number of assault helicopters armed with missiles, rockets and thirty millimeter Gatling type cannons for taking out armored vehicles. The helicopters did require more maintenance but most

of that could be taken care of with engine change outs which could be accomplished in minutes. This was part of the resupply issue. Sending spares
for virtually everything in the combat force so that there were no shortages
slowing down Nix's advance to the east.

As Nix crossed into Kansas and Nebraska from Colorado, he conferred
with Robert as to their further intentions. Nix was running into minimal
defenses from the FSP and Sarah was not reporting any massive troop
movements in front of his force. Most of the opposition was coming from
smaller groups intent upon protecting their own turf. These were fairly
easily overcome and thus far Nix had only sustained relatively minor combat injuries. He suggested separating a force of a third of his complement
and sending them north and east to move into Iowa, Minnesota and then
unite with the rest of the force to take on anticipated Muslim forces in
Wisconsin and Chicago. It would also be necessary to maintain smaller
units of five thousand or more troops in some areas to ensure that they
were stabilized. At the same time, these smaller units would determine the
existence of dedicated leaders from the local communities to take over the
direction and political control of the citizens. All prisoners taken in combat
and non-cooperative political leaders would be sent in returning supply
trucks to new retraining centers setup in Nebraska. These had been created
in the newly stabilized territories in order to be readily available for the influx. Trained personnel were being sent from Riverton to set these centers
up and get them operating.

Nix was reporting that as his troops moved to the east into Kansas, they
were being received with enthusiasm and support. The support was only
limited by the scarcity of materials available to the civilian population but
there was no doubt this would increase tremendously as production was
again removed from the control of the FSP. The troops moving to the north
toward Iowa were beginning to make contact with some Muslim forces
that were using guerilla tactics quite effectively. Quick strikes, night attacks, never standing and fighting, hit and run attacks, and improvised
explosive devices, or IED's, were now coming into play. Nix had his guerilla outfits led by Guns and Ammo take charge of fighting the Muslim
force. They sent troops around and behind the areas where they suspected
the Muslims were operating from. The local populations did not support
the Muslims and they were more than happy to provide any intelligence
information regarding their tactics, location or local area operations. The
Muslims lacked that support although in their normal tactics they tried to

accomplish with fear what they lacked in voluntary cooperation.

The locals would ignore Muslim forces moving through their area but would inform the WestPac guerilla teams as to their location so that drones could be directed for attacks and when the Muslims would retreat to the north or the east, Guns and Ammo and their troops could be waiting behind them for their arrival. The tougher battles were taking place when the Muslims were cornered in these guerilla operations or in the larger cities in Iowa and up into Minnesota where the Muslims were characteristically fighting to the death and using suicide bombers whenever possible. The Muslims had very few Western appearing suicide bombers available and any person with Muslim characteristics approaching WestPac troops was ordered to strip and if they refused to do so, they were shot and killed, usually in an explosion. The Muslims attempted to change the appearance of some of the suicide bombers but generally speaking this was not effective. They were also adept at using human shields or secreting themselves in locations that civilized forces were not eager to attack, such as schools, hospitals or churches. WestPac forces were instructed to do what they had to do regardless of where the action was taking place but to be ready to explain themselves if necessary.

As the WestPac force moved up into Minnesota, they began to run into cases where the Muslims had recruited regular Americans to fight alongside of them and many of these were also quite willing to act as suicide bombers. Western appearing young men and women were more difficult to defend against by the WestPac troops and some casualties were being incurred. Any of these converted soldiers acting on behalf of the Islamic force that were captured were being summarily executed on site. That was with the full approval of Nix, Perry and Robert. As the force moved into more densely populated areas, the regular citizens of Iowa and Minnesota would advise them as to who might have been cooperating with the Muslims. These people were rounded up and subjected to interrogation. For some of these people, there were multiple accusations from responsible appearing citizens of the community, teachers, lawyers, church leaders and so forth, in those cases, the accused were given an opportunity to defend themselves before a board of officers and were then generally sentenced to commitment at a specialized Retraining Center that provided the security required for the situation or if they had been actively involved in warfare against WestPac forces, the sentence could be much more severe. The length of their commitment was left open and there was no intermingling of the prisoners so as to deny them the possibility of gaining converts in the prison. The only reading material provided were Christian bibles. If any of the prisoners in these specialized facilities created trouble, corporal punishment was permitted. If intelligence was sought, water boarding was allowed as an investigative technique. Also, the prisoners that were not considered disruptive were eventually assigned to work details that provided some benefit to the local community.

As Nix's north bound force began entering larger cities such as Des Moines, Iowa, the general appearance of the population changed markedly. Virtually everyone was wearing Muslim garb. Burkas for the women and men wearing full face beards. Nix was advised that these changes were dictated by the Muslim leaders in the involved city and their orders were being complied with under pain of severe punishment. Sharia Law applied to all, Arabs and Americans. Consequently, almost everyone the troops were encountering appeared to be the enemy. Nix conferred with Robert regarding what they were finding, particularly in Iowa and into Minnesota. Robert advised Sarah to set up radio stations in stabilized areas and to immediately start broadcasting to the citizens the behavior expected of them by the advancing WestPac forces. All citizens within sight or range of WestPac forces were to discard Arab attire right down to underclothing or possibly be misconstrued as members of the enemy force which increased the possibility of being fired upon. Any American that was caught actually supporting Muslim military forces in combat with WestPac troops would be dealt with summarily and there would be no appeal before the penalty determined by the WestPac Military would be carried out. It was clear that the intent was they would be shot on sight.

Hans Frick had his planes dropping leaflets in advance of the WestPac troops advising the citizens of the forthcoming combat actions and how they should handle themselves if and when approached by WestPac soldiers. They were also advised that 'Human Shields' would not be respected and the citizens being utilized in that manner were advised to refuse to participate in that activity even if it meant severe bodily harm or death at the hands of the Muslims. Unfortunately there was no other way to deal with that problem. Nix bypassed the fairly large city of Omaha under FSP control in his move north and stationed troops around it to block any resupply by the FSP. They would take the city at a later date when food and munitions had run dry. There was no need to suffer combat losses when they knew the FSP Defenders would be surrendering when their food, water and supplies ran out. They did not follow the suicidal defensive tactics of the Muslims. In the meantime, the city was subjected to constant mortar and artillery fire. drones were also used to locate centers of FSP activity in the city and then to attack them with bombs and missiles. Within days, many FSP soldiers were already coming out of their hiding places carrying white flags of surrender. Again WestPac was witnessing FSP soldiers that lacked any interest in fighting on behalf of the FSP or losing their lives for a cause they did not believe in.

As the WestPac soldiers began entering the Western suburbs of Des Moines, they began entering a different and more dangerous phase of their struggle to retake America. The Muslims were well dug in using homes, office buildings, hospitals, churches or any structure from which to fight to their death. One of their favorite tactics was to let the WestPac attacking force pass by their location and then to come out and attack WestPac troops from the rear while they were also being attacked from the front. Suicide bombers were again an issue and a number of Caucasian American males and females were involved. Nix was very curious as to what made these people apparently change sides in the struggle to retake the country. He had two of them brought to his command center. The first to come in was a twenty-eight year old American white female. She apparently had attempted to discharge her explosives but they failed to ignite for one reason or another. The soldiers quickly disarmed her and brought her in for questioning.

Nix studied her appearance. She appeared to be fit, well nourished, no sign of having been deprived of anything. He asked her where she was from and she said Minneapolis. She did not appear to be frightened of her situation or what might happen to her. She was quite confident. He asked her why she had chosen to fight on behalf of the Muslims. She explained that she was now a Muslim and was willing to give her life for Allah. Nix saw that she was not about to fall to the floor begging forgiveness so he just said, "You realize that you are most likely going to be shot for your actions?"

"We all die sometime. You too will be dying soon. You cannot defeat Islam."

Nix smiled and said "I don't know that we want to defeat Islam but we will defeat the likes of you, Arab or turncoat American. Take her to her hearing. Let her meet Allah soon."

The young man that was then brought in was more understanding of his situation. He was obviously nervous and was not as dedicated to the cause as the young woman was. He was a little older than she was which may have accounted for his understanding of his plight.

Nix asked him, "Where are you from?"

"I'm from Minneapolis."

"Interesting. The young lady before you was also from Minneapolis. Is that some sort of hotbed for turncoat Americans?"

"There are quite a few Islamic Americans up there."

Nix was curious. "Why is that?"

"Well it's a very liberal area and many people in this part of the country look with disdain on the militaristic attitude exemplified by WestPac."

"So you all have studied WestPac. Is that what you are saying?"

"Yes, to a certain extent. Even before the Muslims took over. After they took over they increased the information available concerning WestPac and that had an effect as well."

"Did you consider that they may have been bullshitting you?"

"Not really. There were many aspects of Sharia Law that we admired and many aspects of America that we did not admire. So it was not a difficult transition to make."

"Do you realize the position that you are in now?"

"Yes. I think I do. I know you people are quick to kill anyone that disagrees with you."

"Not necessarily but as for those who try to kill us and are American by birth, we tend to deal with them harshly. Are you sorry now that you bought into the Muslim sales pitch."

"Not really. I am ready for whatever you wish to do with me."

"Interesting. Generally I would say you are in serious trouble but that is not for me to say. You will be judged by military officers and their judgment will be carried out soon thereafter. Anything you want to say?"

"No. I will get mine and you will get yours."

"Maybe. Take him away."

Nix told Robert later about his conversation with the two Americans that were fighting for the other side. He figured from what he had been told that he would be running into many more just like these two. "Very sad indeed." Nix thought over what the young man had said as to why Minneapolis seemed to side with the Arabs. His reason being that Minneapolis was liberal. "What the hell does that have to do with it? Well, maybe he knows something I don't know."

Robert had no answer for that.

The Muslims defending Des Moines were putting up a terrific fight. WestPac losses were climbing and Nix figured they would have to change their tactics or they would be in big trouble. He called Robert for a strategy session and they discussed how to deal with the Muslims. Most of the WestPac Ranger casualties were being killed by IED's, suicide bombers, or aggressive use of hostages. While the FSP would occasionally use IED's the other less humane methods of defense were not their style. Nix mentioned that according to Sarah's intelligence bulletins, WestPac would be facing Muslims all along the northern tier of States and all regions of the Great Lakes. At the rate they were going, WestPac would be bled dry of good combat troops. The main problem, aside from their methods of defense, was that the Muslim troops were holed up in well protected nooks and crannies of buildings and they would fight to the death and before dying or surrendering, they would set off large explosive charges and take as many attacking soldiers with them as they could. On occasion, the Muslim defenders would adopt mass night time suicide counter attacks which increased Ranger losses when it was apparent that their positions were going to be overrun. The FSP soldiers had never fought with this dedication so this was a demoralizing experience for WestPac troops. The two men talked over how to deal with the Muslims and Robert suggested that rather than try to ferret out the Muslim defenders from well concealed and defended positions, it would be better to blow away his position with bombs, artillery or rockets and finish it off with napalm. So we ruin some buildings. Better to do that than lose some good men. Nix agreed and said he would put that into action. He told Robert to make sure that Hans Frick had plenty of munitions as well as napalm to do that job as most of that tactic would fall on Hans' shoulders.

Word was immediately passed to the combat units to provide GPS coordinates of well defended Muslim controlled sites and shortly thereafter they were reduced to rubble. This created what the troops referred to as the Stalingrad effect. Rubble provided great Muslim sniper locations which were then just targeted for napalm drops delivered by Frick's aircraft. Likewise, armored vehicles could clean out some of those sniper nests and when that did not produce the desired results, Hans Frick's support aircraft could take care of the problem with a napalm drop. The beauty of napalm was that it crawled into all hiding places and destroyed everyone in it or at the very least sucked all of the oxygen out of the areas where it was used.

As WestPac troops began to use the new tactics and move across the city of Des Moines, it became very obvious that they were creating a large area of total destruction behind them. A collateral problem was that the Muslims took over homes and apartments as defensive positions that were still occupied by civilian families and individual citizens. The Muslims refused to allow these people to leave the homes and buildings in these battle zones. On the contrary, they would occasionally secure American civilians, men, women and children of all ages to the exterior of the structure and wait for the Rangers to arrive. This would bring the Ranger advance to a halt while the leadership studied the situation to come up with a solution. Again Nix went into conference with Perry and Robert for a decision on how to proceed. After some discussion it was very apparent that there was no reasonable humane decision on how to deal with this Muslim tactic. A number of methods were tried including dropping disabling gas canisters into the home or other structure and then bringing in armored vehicles to literally drive into the structures and kill the defenders. The Muslim response to this was to set off massive explosives killing the defenders, the Rangers in the vehicles and the hostages. In time, the solution boiled down to absolute destruction of the structure and hope for the best. Consequently civilian deaths were very high. There was no solution available to diminish civilian fatalities. Robert had Sarah publish the methods being used by the Muslims and distributed the information in all unsecured large cities of the east by leaflet drops so that civilians could begin to consider how they would avoid the situation if possible.

"The essential act of war is destruction, not necessarily of human lives, but of the products of human labor."

—George Orwell

CHAPTER SEVENTEEN

When WestPac finally declared victory over the city of Des Moines, Nix had his staff locate the civilian authorities of the city that had not previously been acting under the direction of the Muslims. At times this was a prolonged search as many of the civilian authorities were the same bureaucratic bumblers Nix and Robert and the others had been familiar with for years. At times, it took some digging to find the individual that had the interest, experience, principles and intelligence to become the local representative for the new American government. These men had a huge task in front of them. Their city had been virtually destroyed, flattened. What was not flattened was still in flames. Families had been wiped out. Food was scarce, warm clothing was scarce, there was no fuel to either operate vehicles or to heat homes. Public utilities no longer existed and needed to be replaced. Nix assigned his public affairs staff to first of all get the water and sewer systems up and operating. Fortunately WestPac was working with an educated, intelligent group of very interested and motivated citizens so this was accomplished rather rapidly. Again the old problem of laying railroad lines and repairing roads for truck service was key to getting the needed materials and services repaired, replaced and back in operation. Emergency distribution of food and water was being passed out to the survivors. Amazingly there were still many survivors who had been able to secrete themselves from the Muslim defenders or had used other methods to stay alive.

The Battle for Des Moines had cost WestPac the lives of five thousand KIA's and nine thousand injured young men. Most of the dead were killed prior to the change in tactics and that proved the value and worth of that particular military strategy. The loss of so many killed and injured created a ripple in the confidence of the WestPac citizens. Robert realized that they would not be able to maintain the confidence of the citizens if they continued to sustain losses at this level. He cautioned Jack Nix to avoid loss of troops at almost all cost. Obviously there were times when that could not be your primary consideration in a combat action. Another matter that came up during the Des Moines battle was the fact that many residents of the Des Moines area were coming forward begging to be given rifles and ammunition to go after the Muslims. There was no love on the part of the local American community for the Muslims in their midst. Use of these men and women against their former oppressors could alleviate the load on the WestPac troops. It was decided to organize these men and women into combat units and utilize them to clean out pockets of Muslim resistance remaining in Des Moines as well as in the drive north into Minnesota. They could be used as forward operating units to determine where the enemy was situated and their unit strength. Furthermore, many of them were very familiar with the terrain and knew the most favorable routes to take around difficult obstacles and the most favorable locations from which to launch an attack. Nix had special units prepared to organize, supply and lead the many recruits that were volunteering to serve. There was a special training unit ready to instruct the volunteers on the WestPac procedures and structure. This was done in a matter of hours or at most a day or two. Then weapons and ammunition were delivered and instructions given to familiarize them with their use. The volunteers were then organized into squads with a WestPac Ranger in charge to lead them and coordinate them into the main battle plan. After the city had been secured, many of them were needed in Des Moines on a permanent basis to maintain stability in the now ravaged city so a number were detailed to what was left of the former city Police and Sheriff's Departments. This use of civilians worked fairly well although there were the isolated cases of some exercising power without any semblance of restraint. When these cases were reported and reached the offices of Nix's staff, personnel changes and retraining of those involved of the new civilian security force was initiated.

Nix was relatively pleased with how he was leaving Des Moines. It was in tough shape but it was under good control and the Muslim elements that had previously been present were mostly gone. From the information Nix was receiving, it appeared that the Muslim stronghold in the area was in Minneapolis. That would be the difficult fight and Nix would need every piece of intelligence that he could obtain before tackling that hornet's nest. There were also other smaller cities north of Des Moines that were obviously under the control of Muslim forces. As his troops moved north roughly along the I-35 corridor they had some brief skirmishes with the Muslims but after very limited fire fights, they disappeared. Nix had the impression that they had no intention of losing fighters to a vastly superior force when their main force was up in the Twin Cities. On some of these fire fights, a few Muslims were captured. It was a relatively rare occurrence to capture a Muslim in combat but it did happen. If captured, they very seldom provided any information without water boarding although there were some that appeared to be a bit more cooperative. The question always remained, are they telling the truth or not. From the interrogations of these few prisoners, the consensus was that there would be no major confrontations until WestPac began entering the suburbs of Minneapolis. As Nix moved his troops north, he sent out smaller units of five or ten thousand troops to stabilize some of the larger cities along the route. Ames, Marshalltown, Fort Dodge, Mason city and other towns to the east and west of the route were stabilized, cleared of Muslim influence and returned to at least a limited status of civility. Fortunately these cities were not as substantially damaged in the process of driving the Muslims out. They were generally leaving of their own accord to fight elsewhere under better conditions. Another positive factor was that there were many civic minded citizens left in the city or town willing to take on the task of returning the community to a responsible status as a contributor to a legitimate national government. Nix or his staff also met with these leaders and directed them, as before to upgrade and reactivate rail lines, roadways, agricultural production, granaries, manufacturing and to reopen stores, schools and churches and make necessary repairs to the utilities. Small troop units were detailed to stay in position in some of the cities as stabilizing forces to be used as necessary and to ensure that these areas continued to progress and that they helped out with food, water and materials for the more severely battle damaged areas of Des Moines and other cities of Nebraska and Iowa. They were also put on notice that Minnesota would soon be in need of foodstuffs and other material goods following the forthcoming battle to retake that metropolis. Nix had been told that there were approximately five hundred thousand Muslims in Minneapolis and he knew that everyone of them would be fighting to the death to deny him victory. He would have to plan this battle carefully to avoid massive combat casualties. Nix also had Frick dropping leaflets over the residential areas of the Twin Cities advising the citizens to leave and to not wear the Muslim garb so there was no mistaking them when they came in contact with the WestPac soldiers. He again instructed them in using whatever it took to avoid participation in "Human Shield" operations even at risk of injury or death. "Any citizens wishing to participate in the defeat of the Muslims in the Minneapolis area should make their way south and become a member of a rapidly expanding armed group, the Minnesota Militia. They were needed there now. Weapons and ammunition would be provided."

One thing that Robert, Nix and Perry were learning was that the FSP was not particularly involved along the northern tier at least from what they were experiencing in Iowa and Minnesota and which they assumed would be the same along the region of the Great Lakes and to the Northeast. They were learning that the battle to retake the country was going to be even tougher than they had originally anticipated. They had not anticipated the very sizeable, well supplied and dedicated Muslim force that they were encountering.

As Nix's forces moved north into the Western and Southern Suburbs of Minneapolis their unit strength had increased by a large number of attached platoons of volunteers acquired from small towns in Iowa, Nebraska and Southern Minnesota. All young men and some women intent upon driving the Muslims out of their country were volunteering their services. His north moving force had begun with approximately three hundred thousand men but was now numbering around five hundred thousand under arms including reinforcements from WestPac and the new volunteer regiments. The new additions were eager to fight, they were intelligent and many had acquired combat experience in guerilla operations prior to the invasion by WestPac. They mixed well with the WestPac troopers, many of whom were from the same area of the country as the new additions.

Nix was continuing his strategy of using munitions to uproot snipers and Muslims fighting from well defended bunkers or facilities that would normally not be involved in military operations, churches, schools and the like. There was no doubt there were large numbers of civilian casualties as the Muslims were continuing to use them as Human Shields and hostages held in Muslim bunkers. Bypassing these facilities in the hopes of starving out the Muslim defenders was not working. When they became hard pressed for supplies of food or munitions, they would start releasing civilians and then shooting them as they began to run from the facility. This information was passed back to Sarah so that she could inform all civilians in the involved areas just how the Muslims were defending their positions. The advice given to the civilians in areas about to be in conflict was to leave your homes and try to make your way to the south or the west where the WestPac forces were located.

IED's, or improvised explosive devices, were in wide use by the Muslims. Again Robert Thomas and Jack Nix conferred on how to defend against these weapons. This had been a favorite weapon of the Muslims for years and they had become experts at utilizing the terrible destructive force of these weapons. They could be ignited by radio, telephone, electronic signal, by being struck by a bullet, or activation by a suicide bomber, be it a man, woman or child. In trying to come up with defensive tactics to neutralize the use of the IED as an effective weapon, Nix and Thomas came to realize that it was being used both in areas primarily inhabited by resident Americans and also in areas of cities that were primarily Muslim in nature. The two men concluded they had to defense the weapon differently depending upon where it was being used. In Muslim neighborhoods, the tactic was to blow up anything that could be used to hide an IED. That included a parked vehicle, garbage cans, piles of dirt, a dead body, or debris alongside the roadway. A burst of fifty caliber shells into the suspect target would usually produce a significant explosion. The explosion would also destroy collateral structures that the Muslims would most likely only destroy provided they were taking a worthy WestPac target with it. Any structure along a roadway within fifty feet of the travelled portion of the road was totally destroyed before a convoy or military vehicles passed. The Muslims were also adept at burying the IED's in the roadways so as not to present a visible target. The solution to that was to drop containers that would open on descent and spill out hundreds of smaller grenades that would explode on streets or alleyways of the city. The explosion that would result was not large but it was sufficient to set off any buried IED's. This weapon was also valuable as an anti-personnel weapon but had limited use in this conflict where massed troops were seldom used.

For civilian residential areas inhabited primarily by local Americans, Robert had Sarah broadcast a message to the effect that all citizens must be observant for and report the location of suspicious digging, vehicles, construction, or any unusual activity in locations that could be used to hide an IED. They were to make these reports to approaching WestPac forces or risk the same techniques to immobilize those weapons as applied to Muslim areas. Given such reports, the WestPac force could neutralize the weapons using various methods to do so short of exploding them. Hans Frick dropped leaflets in primarily civilian areas advising the residents of the proper procedures to follow. There were some IED's that were buried under remote roadways or in other locations that did not trigger suspicion by their appearance alone. In these cases the Rangers had to rely on the citizens for their warning. In Muslim neighborhoods, such warnings were generally not available although there were reports of some of the Muslims that were reporting IED sites to the advancing WestPac force.

As the WestPac forces moved into the city, they found a population living under terrible conditions. Food was scarce, Clean water was difficult to obtain. There was no heat for the homes and absolutely no fuel for automobiles. Many were ill from dysentery, flu and pneumonia, contaminated food, lack of food, medical care and ill treatment. All fuel for vehicles or any use was controlled by the Muslims for their own military vehicles. All Christian churches had been converted to Mosques for the use of the Muslims. A large number of Caucasians had converted to the Islamic faith either under pressure or voluntarily seeking the easy way out and all Caucasians were wearing Muslim attire whether converted or not. They had been aware of the request by WestPac not to be so attired but they were being instructed under threat of death not to defy the Muslim dress code. The city had been under Sharia Law for the past five years and the brutal punishments under Sharia Law had removed any desire on the part of anyone to challenge the authority of those now in control. Again as the troops moved forward deeper into the city, eager volunteers, willing to risk their lives, came forward to join the invading force against their oppressors.

All of the Mosques were well defended by the Muslims apparently on the supposition that the invading force would not attack a place of prayer. It was the practice of Nix's men to broadcast a message to the defenders in the Mosque, church, hospital or school that they must immediately surrender or they would be killed. Usually the defenders did not respond or replied that they would never surrender. Without delay, the building would immediately be destroyed, absolutely flattened. No single person could ever survive the destruction of the building and if they did miraculously survive its complete demolition, they would not survive the use of napalm flowing over, around and in the debris. Such defensive positions were taken in a minimal amount of time. Homes occupied by defenders holding civilian hostages presented another problem. If it was an isolated structure standing alone amidst other homes that were not an issue, Nix's policy was to turn the attack on the Muslim inhabitants over to the local militia and have them secure the home until the Muslims surrendered or tried to escape. This approach did not bode well for the civilians being held hostage in view of the fact the Muslims normally slaughtered them before making a final charge at their attackers. Unfortunately, there was no other viable alternative.

As the WestPac troops were advancing into the Western Suburbs of Minneapolis, two other bodies of troops were moving around the north and east sides of the city to make contact with a third force moving around the south side of the city as well as Saint Paul to complete the encirclement. In time, the Muslim force was isolated from its supply lines. The Saint Croix River presented a natural barrier against any resupply or rescue of the Muslims coming from the east. There were bridges across the Saint Croix but as the WestPac troops moved in that direction, the Muslims blew those bridges in order to slow the advance further to the east. With the blowing of the bridges, it was clear that the Muslims defending the Cities of Minneapolis and Saint Paul had no intention of withdrawing. Furthermore, according to Sarah's reports, there was no shortage of Muslims to the east from Wisconsin through the Great Lakes Region and into the Northeast. They had made great efforts to increase their population in that region following the collapse primarily through uncontrolled immigration. Shiploads of Muslims over the years had flowed into the eastern ports disgorging hundreds of thousands of Muslims to take over what remained of 'The Great Satan'. All immigration since the collapse was unregulated, uncontrolled and totally lacking any regulatory procedure. Sharia Law governed the population in that area and had been the controlling mechanism for the past seven years. Nix was well aware that they had a very difficult fight ahead to rid the nation of the Muslims. There were millions of them, they were very well armed and they fought to the death. That included their women and children.

There was talk of using nuclear weapons in ridding the East of the Muslims. That would obviously also cost many non-Muslim lives in the process. There was the issue of what nuclear weapons were even available. The FSP had some, that was known and that was an issue of some concern for Thomas and others in the leadership of WestPac. Robert assumed that the FSP would have no major issue with the use of nuclear weapons against the Muslims as long as the FSP was not also the target. The word that was being passed around the country by way of rumor was that nuclear weapons would not be used against Americans, even by the FSP. No one was willing to deliver them to a target and many, even in the FSP, considered their use out of the question. Robert Thomas was aware that there were some nuclear weapons secreted in territory that WestPac controlled. While he could not say that he would never use them anywhere in the former nation, he could not imagine the situation that would compel him to use them. In the meantime, he had small inventories of nuclear weapons stockpiled for emergency use. These were smaller kiloton weapons capable of being fired as artillery rounds or dropped from fighter aircraft using lazer guidance to the target. While they were available to be used as tactical weapons the decision for the present at least was not to use them. Their use in the future was another issue to be decided at another time.

The populations even in Muslim controlled territory were very mixed, blacks, white Americans, Muslims, Hispanic, Asian, plus others, a total mixture. Other solutions would have to be found to rid the nation of the Muslims who were willing to fight to the death to defend their turf. It was a thought that kept Robert awake at night trying to come up with a solution. He and Perry had spent hours discussing the problem. They always came back to suggesting Nix do just what he was doing.

The fighting in Minneapolis and Saint Paul had disintegrated into a house to house battle to clean the Muslims out of their defensive positions. Destruction in the battle zones was total. Homes, buildings, any form of structure was either flattened, burned out, or terribly damaged. Obviously there were thousands of civilian deaths and there were a number of West-Pac casualties in the process. In order to limit WestPac losses, a single shot coming from a home or building was grounds to totally destroy the entire structure and all people that were inside. There was no talking to the Muslims about releasing their hostages. They were not about to do that. Following this procedure, WestPac units were able to finally reach the eastern limits of the Twin Cities. The area behind them was a wasteland. It was estimated that three hundred thousand or more Muslims or more had perished and an equal number of civilians had died as well. Four thousand WestPac soldiers had died in battle and thousands more were injured. One benefit of the battle was that the cities and towns north of the Twin Cities in Minnesota were freed from control of the Muslims as the ones that had been there had joined the battle to the south and apparently perished along with their Muslim brothers. WestPac Civil Affairs Officers began the difficult task of bringing food and water to the limited number of survivors that existed in the city. Again good leadership was sought from volunteers that had experience in city government and administration of city services. Water and sewer services , as usual, was the immediate concern. Also, getting food to the city from undamaged areas of Minnesota and Iowa was of great concern. Transportation, communication and stability were all major challenges. By this time in the battle to retake the country, WestPac had expected all of the problems they were facing in the Twin Cities and had prepared to provide immediate solutions even before the battle was over. Truckloads of needed food, clothing, medical supplies, water and experts familiar with the problems the devastated area presented were stockpiled and ready to go to work as soon as the shelling had stopped.

Nix scheduled a meeting with the newly appointed authorities to manage Minneapolis and Saint Paul. He had hoped to have one entity in charge of both cities but soon found that the competition between the two cities had not been reduced by the war. Another surprise for Nix was that the new civilian authorities did not look upon him as the great savior. They held him at least partially to blame for the tremendous destruction laid upon the cities. That was a matter of considerable irritation to Nix. He also found that in the Twin Cities, there was a substantial residual affection for the FSP. He attributed that to the long standing connection between that area of the country and the Liberal leadership in Washington. At the conclusion of his meeting with these civic leaders, he advised them that while the war continued in the former nation, he expected total commitment on their part in support of the war with men, materials, production of war materials and their complete support of the war effort. If he did not see that, they would be out of a job. That threat did not seem to be a matter of concern for the local politicians. They believed they had the full support of the survivors that remained in the city and would be calling the shots regardless of what WestPac had to say. There were a few of these politicians in Minneapolis particularly that were not shy about voicing these opinions. When they did so, Nix summarily ordered their incarceration and had them sent down to the Nebraska detention centers and that shut up the few with similar opinions that remained.

In a follow-on meeting with civic leaders where he was laying out what needed to be done to rehabilitate the city, Nix studied the disbelief showing on some of the faces of the civilians in the room. He again restated what he expected of them. "I want these rail lines reestablished within six months. I want trains running at the same time and I want to see food production, and increased supplies of everything a society needs for survival flowing out of Minnesota to areas of the country that we will be stabilizing. Those people need what you can produce here. Furthermore, there will be no Unions, there will be no critical media, no critical television or radio. There is a war going on and my troops are giving their lives to win it. I expect the same dedication from the people in this area. If I see or hear some loud mouth in opposition to the war, or trying to instill dissent, he or she will be sent away. As you well know, a number have already taken up residence at centers in Nebraska. When the war is over, we will discuss what kind of a country we want to have. Until then, you take direction from WestPac." Nix asked if everyone agreed to comply with what he was saying. Of the ten men and women in the room, three said they could not agree with that. Nix said, "Fine. Pick up your things. You are out of here." Three more volunteers with the correct attitude were brought in and filled their shoes. As the three left the room, one sneered at Nix and yelled out, "Good luck". Nix motioned to one of the troopers to arrest that person and send him to the Detention Center in Iowa. The now concerned prisoner yelled out, "You can't do this to me." Nix only replied that "We are doing it to you. Goodbye." The other local citizens were now fully aware that while their lives were to be markedly improved, their total allegiance was to WestPac and they had best not forget that. Before ending the meeting, Nix introduced the new civic leaders to the representatives of WestPac that would be in charge of seeing that Minnesota was developing as rapidly as it was known they were capable of and also to oversee compliance with WestPac directives.

The WestPac teams that remained in the Twin Cities immediately took control of the local television stations and the local newspaper, all of which had been operated by the Muslims for their own purposes. Many former staffers from these media outlets stepped forward to move back into the positions they previously held. The WestPac teams allowed some to return but by no means all. Many of the former staffers were known to have been highly critical of WestPac before they fell under the control of the Muslims. They were advised to seek another profession.

Nix reported his experience in Minnesota to Robert who was back in Riverton dealing with the issue of providing the tons of materials needed by the troops in battle as well as the emergency aid for civilians in newly controlled territories. Nix was quite surprised by what he termed the lack of enthusiasm for what WestPac was doing for the civilians living in the previously Muslim controlled areas. "I really thought they would greet us as their saviors, their rescuers, but hell no, we were part of the problem. We may have trouble with them in the future and my suggestion, Robert, is that we don't screw around with them. I have already sent a number off to the Retraining Center we just created down in Iowa. Fortunately there are also some good people there and another plus is that the civilian community in Minnesota is generally comprised of a skilled, hard working, goal oriented population that is capable of delivering much of what we are going to need in the future. So we also have to be a bit careful in how we deal with them."

Robert had great confidence in Nix and told him to do what he saw fit for the situation and anytime he wanted to chat about it to just give him a call. The two men discussed other matters regarding the campaign in the former nation and Robert wished him well.

At about this time, Robert had an interesting conversation with Sarah regarding moves the Muslims were making to strengthen their forces. They were still in control of a number of harbors in the Northeast including Boston Harbor and New York Harbor along the Hudson. According to Sarah's intel operation, the Muslims had been becoming increasingly concerned about the growing strength of the WestPac military operation vis-á-vis the Muslim force. While their numbers of Muslim fighters had increased significantly in recent years in the Northeast and Great Lakes Regions of the United States, there remained a question as to whether or not they had grown to sufficient numbers to be able to destroy the new WestPac force.

Consequently the Muslims were making moves to significantly increase their troop strength in the Northeast. They had been bringing in larger freighter loads of Muslim fighters from the Mid-East to eastern Ports primarily in Massachusetts and New York. They had already off-loaded another hundred or more thousand of their fighters in both Boston and New York. Word had it that a dozen more ships were currently en-route to America to strengthen the Muslim Force. This presented a very serious problem for Robert. He had no idea as to what options were available to him to defense against this threat. The WestPac forces were still thousands of miles to the west of the shipping lanes being utilized by the Muslims with their reinforcements and their aircraft lacked the operating range to effectively counter the threat.

Needless to say, there were no naval forces operating in the Atlantic under the control of WestPac or any friendly nation. He asked Sarah for her thoughts and for once, she had nothing specific to offer. She suggested that they needed to find out what ships or aircraft were available that could operate at great distances and interdict the ships bringing the troops. Robert said he would get back to her after he talked with Perry.

"The essence of war is violence.
Moderation in war is imbecility."
—John Arbuthnot Fisher

CHAPTER EIGHTEEN

As the WestPac force was reorganizing after the combat in Minnesota and re-staffing positions they began moving to the east and preparing for operation in the former State of Wisconsin and the large city of Chicago over in Illinois. In the meantime, the main force of the WestPac Army led by Ross Perry had battled the FSP through two major large cities successfully. Both Oklahoma city and then Kansas city had been taken with substantially fewer casualties than Nix was experiencing in the north. The FSP was not known to fight to the death and when facing overwhelming odds, surrender was definitely an option. Again the troops fighting for the FSP were known to take opportunities to change sides if they could do so without loss of life. The inner strength of the FSP was falling apart. When their only motivation for fighting was to gain some material benefit over their neighbor, loss of life was just too high a price to pay for that. The previous advantage the FSP had on the battlefield was the availability of armored vehicles. Unfortunately, these vehicles used a great deal of fuel and the FSP no longer had huge resources of fuel. Furthermore, WestPac had developed weapons that were designed to penetrate the thick armor of these vehicles. The FSP also had limited use of air power for the same reason, no fuel. Consequently their strength, or weakness, lay in their foot soldiers who were primarily concerned with surviving the battle. As the FSP was under attack on a wide flank in the center of the nation, they were drawing upon troop resources from elsewhere in the country. Up to this time, those resources had been enjoying the luxuries of being in total control of the wealth and pleasures that yet remained in what had been the United States of America. They had very little interest in trading that for the gun and helmet that were thrust at them and told to get out there and fight to the death.

Sarah had been researching the morale issues of the FSP force for some time. According to her information, desertions were at an all time high and morale among the soldiers was very low. Even high ranking officers were deserting their posts and were listed as missing. Infrastructure problems in the East had never been fully addressed and consequently transportation, communication and production continued to exist but at a low ebb. According to Sarah's bulletins, it was almost impossible to get a message delivered from New York to Chicago in under ten days. Radio continued to be the most reliable means of communicating across the country and this was just not available in sufficient quantities to replace telephone or internet services which were in a condition of disrepair. Sarah issued opinions to the effect that the FSP control of the East was capable of crumbling even before the attacking WestPac forces defeated them in battle. She also added that President Turner was nowhere in sight and there was some question as to whether or not he was still within the borders of the United States of America.

Robert finally had a chance to meet with Perry and the first item on the agenda was the issue of the Muslim controlled ships bringing Islamic troops to the ports of New York and Massachusetts. Perry said that he had heard rumors to that effect but had discounted them. Based on Sarah's reports, he conceded that apparently they were true. He estimated that it would be another six months before WestPac had control of the East Coast and even that was questionable. Furthermore, he understood there were some combat ships and submarines that were dry-docked in the Carolinas that would be able to do the job but they needed a great deal of work before they would be ready to perform in that operation. Ross suggested that manned airplanes or drones would have to be used. He suggested that Sarah should check out what the situation was with respect to Goose Bay Air Force Base that operated up in Labrador for years. If that was still operating at least as an airport, possibly long distance bombers, recon aircraft and drones could be sent up there to carry out the mission. drones had very long operating ranges and could stay airborne in loiter mode for up to twenty-four hours before needing refueling. Westpac had already recaptured Offut Air Force Base at Lincoln, Nebraska and there were a number of mothballed B-52 and B-2 aircraft that could be rehabbed for the mission. Some work had already been done on those aircraft as Perry wanted to put them in use on the Northeast Muslim targets and possibly against the FSP if they ever showed up again in strength in the center or the south of the country.

Robert agreed with Perry that operating out of Goose sounded like a very feasible plan. He would discuss it with Sarah and let him know. He immediately called Sarah and she said she would talk to her Canadian contacts regarding operating conditions in Labrador and the condition of the Airport at Goose Bay. She also suggested Gander as a possible base in Newfoundland, either that or Saint Johns. There was also Halifax in Nova Scotia any of which bases would be better operating distance wise for the bombers operating in the North Atlantic than Goose. Robert told her to line it up with her Canadian contacts and to also keep in mind the weight limitations for the involved airports. The B-52's would most likely be a problem but possibly not. The drones would present no problem and it was possible they could handle the job. Sarah said she would get back to him within the week with answers.

Perry's forces were making rapid progress to the east and were approaching the environs of Saint Louis. While they were in the process of softening up the defenses of that city, Perry sent a third of his force south to move through Louisiana and along the southern row of States. Perry anticipated support from guerilla organizations in the key Southern States of Mississippi and Alabama. He was a bit concerned about Alabama as that had been the fiefdom of Richard Johnston and the Pioneers making their way across the nation to Montana had a close one with Johnston in Western Alabama. At that time, Johnston, who was Black and presumed to be a Muslim, controlled a very substantial and well armed military force, both Black and White, operating primarily out of Montgomery, Alabama. He apparently controlled a large area of Alabama from the Western Border across the State to the Eastern Border and down to the old Fort Rucker Army Base which was located in the Enterprise-Dothan area in the southeast part of the State. The old Army Base was the recruiting and training center for his operation however, he preferred to spend most of his time in Montgomery and Birmingham as this was where the money was that financed his operation. His force numbered between twenty and fifty thousand troops that were well equipped with state of the art weapons as well as some armored vehicles that he had acquired when he took control of Fort Rucker. According to information that Sarah had been able to obtain, the FSP had given him free reign to roam provided he contributed periodically to their coffers and performed on their behalf militarily when they requested him to do so.

In any event, Perry was aware that while Alabama was generally considered a conservative State and assumed to be friendly to the goals of the WestPac forces, the Johnston controlled areas of the State were going to be another matter. Perry attempted to send messages to Johnston advising him that the WestPac force was willing to discuss an arrangement whereby he could maintain his position as the local administrator for WestPac in the areas of the State that he controlled. After a prolonged period without any reply from Johnston, Perry advised him that if he did not wish to peaceably discuss a resolution of the issue, WestPac was prepared to defeat him should he refuse to surrender his arms and equipment and cooperate with Westpac. After another prolonged period without any response, Perry sent a final message to Johnston to respond or WestPac would be moving forcibly to remove him from power within twenty-four hours.

At the expiration of the grace period, hundreds of Drone recon and attack aircraft swarmed over Montgomery, Rucker and Birmingham leaving all three heavily populated areas in ruins. Anticipating the usual Muslim tactics, Perry had leaflets dropped on those population centers advising the citizens to flee to the west and the safety of the WestPac force. By this time, Hans Frick had three B-52 aircraft in operation at the former Offutt Air Force Base in Nebraska and upon Perry's request, he had all three performing round the clock bomb and napalm runs on Rucker, Montgomery and Birmingham. The bombing missions were limited to military targets or to facilities in the target areas that would be of military value to Johnston. Robert instructed Perry to limit damage as much as possible to avoid basic infrastructure or civilian assets that WestPac would have to rebuild at a later date.

After five days of intensive destruction of anything that appeared to have military value, Perry initiated the ground attack on Birmingham and Montgomery. Again, they were facing the IED's, suicide bombers and a willingness on the part of the defenders to fight to the death. Perry initiated the tactics that had worked best for them in Chicago and WestPac losses were minimized. Within two weeks both Birmingham and Montgomery were taken. The Fort Rucker area was more difficult for Johnston to defend as it was mostly wide open training areas that were easily targeted by Frick's drones. Within one week the Rucker area was under WestPac control. The KIA's in the entire campaign had not exceeded five hundred WestPac Rangers lost. Unfortunately, the Civil Affairs people were not happy with what they had to work with. Again due to the house to house fighting involved in the two cities, the destruction was extensive. Food and water were again in scarce supply and Perry had Sarah send out an emergency allocation to feed the few survivors that remained. Many civilians and defenders had been killed as again, the Muslims had refused permission to the civilians to evacuate. Instead they were used as hostages. There were very few prisoners taken in the battles which was fine with Robert and Perry as they had no place to hold them before continuing their trek to the east. Of the few that they did capture, they were mostly American born blacks and whites that had adopted the Muslim faith. These few were returned to Riverton for detention and retraining. They were very uncooperative prisoners and there was little doubt they would ever be rehabilitated. Johnston was never captured and was never found. Word was that he had been killed in battle while in Montgomery and his troops had buried him somewhere in the city. No one was willing to talk as to where he was buried.

Meanwhile the resistance to Perry's main force outside of Saint Louis had been stiffening. The force was temporarily under the command of Wyatt while Perry was busy in Alabama. Wyatt was finding that IED's were again becoming a problem and Nix's methods of dealing with them were rapidly put into operation. Fortunately the population of Saint Louis provided information regarding the location of most of the deadly IED's and they were becoming an ineffective weapon for the FSP. Also, many FSP prisoners or those that surrendered to the attackers knew where the IED's were located and gave the advancing troops that information as well.

As the WestPac troops began entering East Saint Louis, it was learned that there were some units of Muslim troops defending certain areas of that city. The problems associated with the Muslim troops in East Saint Louis resembled on a lesser degree what Nix had experienced in the Twin Cities. In the north, Nix had made rather rapid strides through Wisconsin with the exception of the Madison area and was moving to the south and entering the Northern Suburbs of Chicago. At the same time, Wyatt's force was cleaning up the Saint Louis operation and then moved in a northerly direction headed for the Southern Suburbs of Chicago. Perry returned to take command of the force and Wyatt took over the Southern Command. As Perry's force moved north, they began running into stiffer opposition at Gary, Indiana and it continued as they moved around the south end of the Lake and headed for the city proper. The total force aiming at Chicago now numbered some seven hundred and fifty thousand men. Estimates of Muslim strength in the Chicago area was between five hundred thousand and seven hundred thousand men.

Nix and Robert had decided that in order to hold down casualties fighting the Muslims in the Great Lakes Region and the Northeast, they would have to come at them with an overwhelming force. Their tactic was to hit them from the front, the sides, the rear and above. Hans Frick had moved a number of Air units to stabilized areas to the South of Chicago and had seen to it that sizeable supplies of jet fuel were available for his ground support aircraft and for his drones. Frick's Recon drones had provided great intelligence on the locations of Muslim forces defending the city and his combat drones had also dropped tons of ordnance on their positions throughout the city. It was expected that civilian casualties would be high but there was just no way to avoid that and take control of the city. The fighting was very intense all the way from central Indiana north. Whenever the Muslims held fast in one position, Frick's planes unloaded tons of bombs and napalm on their positions. Slowly but surely the two forces, Nix's and Perry's continued their advance to eventually meet very near to what had formerly been the Chicago loop but was now a wasteland of flattened collapsed buildings, rubble and carnage. The Wrigley Building that was located on North Michigan Avenue near the Chicago River was nowhere in sight. Destroyed in toto, gone. Michigan Avenue was indistinguishable from the former locations of Loop office buildings. Just one flat, endless land mass of bricks, rubble, concrete, broken furniture, cars, and debris from virtually any source. Nix had acquired some new armored vehicles produced by factories established by Barnes in Montana to deal specifically with the Muslim forces in Chicago and the Lakes Region. They were tractored vehicles equipped with canons as well as flame throwers that could hurl their deadly flammable jellylike substance over three hundred yards at rubble protected pockets of resistance sucking away the oxygen and incinerating anyone within their range. These well protected armored vehicles rapidly increased the forward motion of the advancing Ranger force, no longer held back by well defended hidden Muslim troops. They were capable of traversing virtually any terrain and were capable of climbing over obstacles and impediments to progress that would have stopped the battle tanks of World War II. From the time the armored vehicles were introduced in the Chicago Operation, the operation consisted primarily of a mop up of residual pockets of Muslims dug into the wreckage of war or individual Muslim snipers operating on their own. After the major fighting had concluded, the Civil Affairs staff again took over. The problems were the same, only the names had changed. The surviving civilians in the Chicago area were a pathetic appearing lot, undernourished, lacking nutrition, without food and taking water from Lake Michigan which was obviously a very unhealthy practice causing widespread cases of Typhoid Fever, Dysentery and Respiratory Problems. Nix called in the Civil Affairs teams to immediately address the health of the citizens of Chicago and had potable water trucks hauling to areas of Chicago that were still considered dangerous due to the presence of snipers but people were dying of thirst and hunger on the streets and they had to be dealt with immediately.

Other than the sad plight of affairs of the citizens, Nix was very satisfied with how the battle for Chicago had gone. His troops were becoming battle hardened and savvy on how to defeat the Muslims at their game. Their losses in taking the city were approximately one thousand dead and three thousand wounded. The difference in Ranger strategy in Chicago versus their strategy in Minneapolis was that they no longer stormed strong points of Muslim resistance, they instead held back, then bombed and obliterated their bunkers or ruins. They then brought out the napalm either dropped by planes or launched by the armored vehicles and watched all forms of life drift skyward from the Muslim hiding places in black clouds of smoke.

It was decided by Robert, Nix and Perry that the country to the south of the Great Lakes Region and the Northeast would first be retaken before engaging in what was anticipated to be the bloody battle of the war. They wanted to move on the center and the south of the former nation first as they believed, based on information available, that the FSP was not only seriously weakened by their losses in Colorado, but was about to crumble. Nix left a sizeable force in place in Chicago and Indiana while the balance of the force rapidly swept through Indiana and on to the east through to the District of Columbia. The larger cities bordering the Great Lakes were left to be conquered after the central and southern part of the former nation were retaken. In the meantime, they would be subjected to continuous bombing attacks by drones supplemented by Recon drones. The troops that entered the nation's former Capital were amazed at the destruction. The Administrative Buildings, such as the IRS, FBI and so forth, still remained for the most part but they were gutted on the interiors and bore the marks of habitation by animals. Filth and debris were present everywhere. All of the doors and windows were gone. They stood as monuments to the self destruction of the human race. Over one entryway was scrawled, "Only Sub-humans Live Here." The White House and the nation's Capital Building were totally destroyed and burned to the ground They were only recognizable by the location of their rubble. The former national monuments in honor of the founders and principals of the country were basically unrecognizable. Many had been partially or substantially destroyed by vandals and haters of liberty and basic human rights.

Civic Affairs personnel put in an emergency request for additional personnel as they were obviously being overwhelmed with the challenges they faced in the newly retaken areas of the nation. Nix and Perry were traveling east and then south in parallel thrusts to retake the country. As they advanced, they left units from their command to provide stability, security and protection for the citizens in their areas of control. They were also in great need of additional troops as the country needed the stability that only the troops could provide and they were running short of armed soldiers to leave in position. The large cities bordering the Great Lakes, such as Detroit, Cleveland and north of the Pittsburgh to New York city line were left for the final campaign after the rest of the country had been retaken. Those were all Muslim occupied and heavily defended sites that would require a very strong force to clean out. In the meantime it was a known fact that they were being strengthened daily by the influx of new fighters from the Mid-East.

Sarah had gotten back to Robert and Perry with the information on the Canadian and Maritime bases in Nova Scotia, Newfoundland and Labrador. Goose Bay was considered operational and the runways had been specifically strengthened for the B-52 aircraft years ago and were considered useable with some maintenance. Gander was also available as was Saint Johns, both in Newfoundland. Perry instructed Hans Frick to get a B-2 Wing and a Drone Wing operational; and located either at Gander or at Saint Johns immediately. That would take some time and in the meantime, he had Frick send a reflex team to Saint Johns to prepare to operate a squadron of recon drones and tactical drones out of there pending receipt of the operational B-2 Bomber Wing. They had the range and should be able to locate the freighters plying the waters between the Mid-East and the narrow range of ports between New York and Massachusetts. There was some question as to the route the freighters would be taking but there was no doubt as to where they were going and that made their targeting more doable. The Recon drones were equipped with long range radar and would have no trouble picking up the slow moving freighters. Perry's plan was to monitor the freighters and then warn them by radio or leaflet drops to put in at Halifax, Charleston or Miami where they would be searched. WestPac units were located at the referenced harbors as Charleston had been taken earlier and the Cubans under Morales granted Robert access to Miami Harbors and the Canadians granted access to Halifax for this mission. If Muslim troops were found on board, they were ordered to return to the Mid-East or some port other than the North or South American Continents. If the ships failed to abide by these instructions, they were sunk. A number of the freighters had to be sunk and in time, the Muslims discontinued this resupply method as the losses were unsustainable. The problem was actually solved by the drones before the B-2's were returned to combat ready status which was good news to all involved.

Robert advised Nix that his request for additional troops was being answered and they were on the way. Yates and Campbell were turning out new recruits from the Training Center in Riverton as fast as they could. Barnes was supplying the new trainees with current weapons and ammunition from the factories in Washington and Oregon. Matt Parker was now in charge of the production of uniforms and all accessory equipment for the new troops. Parker was managing hundreds of small to large Plants operating across WestPac producing the variety of products needed to sustain the now huge army of WestPac forces. The total military force of WestPac as it now existed was in the neighborhood of two million men and women under arms. They had made a large expansion from volunteers who joined WestPac as members of militia units from territories of the nation that had just been retaken. Some of these had come back to Riverton for training but most had joined militia regiments acting under the command and control of WestPac troop leaders.

Robert had made a number of television and radio broadcasts across the landmass of the former nation directed at FSP soldiers telling them to leave their posts and join in the fight to bring the country back under the control of the people as it was before the FSP took control. These broadcasts were very effective and they produced a steady river of new troops wanting to be on the side of the victors. Everyone now knew that WestPac was winning the battle to retake the nation. Robert was now treated almost as a God not only in WestPac, but throughout the former nation. He also gave broadcasts directed to the civilians in territories of the former nation that had not yet been retaken. He told them to be patient and to assist the WestPac soldiers as they entered their part of the country. He impressed them with the fact that relief and supplies of food, water and clothing would soon be arriving. Medical care was coming as were schools, peace and security. He also stressed upon them their responsibility to rebuild their own communities and cities. They had to organize and provide the leadership, the food, clean water, utilities and all the benefits of good government. WestPac would provide training and emergency supplies to sustain them for the short term and would protect them until stability returned to their communities. The long term was their responsibility.

Robert wanted to address the issue of the Cuban held territories before the troops began to enter the South. He did not want to create any problems that they could easily avoid. He had Sarah contact Paco Morales and discuss with him the status of Florida south of the Orlando-Tampa line. Morales informed Sarah that his forces had been in control of that portion of Florida for the past five or more years which confirmed the information that Sarah had. His main opposition had been Ricardo Ortega and he had been defeated four years prior. They had been successful in keeping the FSP at bay and had no problems with them. Morales indicated that he had no ambitions to extend his area of control but at the present time he also had no desire to withdraw from any portion of it. Sarah indicated to him that she had no knowledge of any desires on the part of WestPac leaders to move into Southern Florida and to her knowledge it was their intention to maintain a peaceful relationship between their two governments. When peace was established, they could then discuss the future of South Florida and if there was any interest in becoming part of the new United States of America. She also said that she would keep Morales informed as to the geographic locations of the WestPac forces as they moved south so that there was no accidental conflict between the two forces. She also told him that a separate Army Group was advancing to the east along the Southern Corridor of States and that also was under the command of Generals Nix and Perry. That force would likewise honor the Orlando-Tampa line pending further discussions.

As the troops under Nix and Perry's commands moved south on a line extending from Chicago to Washington, D.C., they were meeting with minimal resistance from remnants of the FSP and from independent gangs attempting to maintain control of their particular fiefdom. The usual experience the WestPac troops were having with these two groups was that the FSP fighters were surrendering in droves without hesitation. The gangs on the other hand would temporarily put up a fight but would soon realize the futility of battling a far superior force. The manner of dealing with these surrendering gang members Depended upon the particular group involved, the WestPac officers in charge of the involved area would either send the gang members with their leaders to retraining centers for indoctrination or they would be sent to a facility that offered stricter retention and more control to ensure a change of attitude on the part of the prisoners. The idea being in both cases to attempt to develop law abiding citizens following the retraining.

Again, the Civic Affairs Staff was working behind the lines organizing the local community leaders to help get their cities and towns working productively for the benefit of the nation as a whole. All areas of the nation had different assets and opportunities for growth and development. West Virginia had coal mining and other mineral resources of great value to the country. Some areas were primarily agriculturally oriented or were primarily involved in manufacturing, or at least had been. The Civic Affairs people attacked all areas based on their potential contributions to the country. The citizens in the center of the country were generally very supportive of WestPac and their mission to retake the entire country. There was an isolated dissenter and WestPac was also prepared to deal with that element as they had dealt with them in Minneapolis.

When WestPac entered Georgia and moved on Atlanta, they expected to run into more opposition from the FSP than they had thus far due to the fact the area had been the center of FSP activity in the recent past. Surprisingly, there was little opposition and the FSP had apparently vacated the city shortly before the troops entered it. The question on Nix's mind in that phase of the operation was what resistance would they run into in the Macon area which had always been the primary center of FSP operations. He also assumed that most likely former President Turner would be located there. Nix learned from interrogated FSP prisoners that Turner had been seen in the Macon area within the past month. It was assumed by them that he was still there. As Nix's force proceeded south following the old I-75 highway towards Macon, they were running into fairly large groups of FSP soldiers carrying white flags. There was virtually no opposition as they moved south except for the isolated sniper that usually turned out to be nothing more than a mentally disturbed fellow with a grudge against someone but he didn't know who.

Nix moved his main force directly at the former Robbins Air Force Base which was the presumed center of FSP operations. The former Base was totally unguarded and his advance elements moved onto the Base without a shot being fired. Obviously they had been expected as there was much evidence that FSP troops had just vacated the base. The food in the Chow

Hall was still warm and there were a few FSP soldiers who stood around and studied their new hosts with curiosity. No one tried to interfere with the Rangers taking over occupation of the Base. There were a number of aircraft in hangars and maintenance equipment for the aircraft appeared to be intact. Hans Frick landed on the airfield a short time after it was taken and said the facility was a gold mine of needed aircraft maintenance equipment. Everything appeared to be in workable condition and fully capable of handling current needs. There were also extensive supplies of ordnance and weapons including AR-20 rifles by the thousands, missile launchers, rockets, bombs, radars, communication equipment and a wealth of other electronic items that would be of great use in rebuilding and defending the country. As the Base area was secured and stabilized, former technicians apparently employed in the past at the Base began coming in and offering their services to WestPac. This again was a valuable find as they included aircraft mechanics, electricians, and technicians of every possible stripe that were always in short supply in WestPac.

It was clear to Robert, Nix and the leaders of WestPac that Turner or the current leaders of the FSP, if they were not one and the same, were no longer interested in putting up any resistance. They realized the mood of the country, the strength of WestPac and the low morale of their own troops were factors that denied them any chance of victory in combat with WestPac. Robert had Sarah broadcast a request to the leaders of all FSP forces to surrender their men and war fighting equipment and they would be treated fairly. It was very obvious that the people that were responsible for the destruction and collapse of the United States of America would be treated accordingly and would likely be sentenced to long prison terms. The mid-level soldier or administrator would have nothing to worry about under normal circumstances. Likewise all leaders of irregular forces which included criminal gangs and non-criminal self protection troops were advised to contact the WestPac military leaders in their area and submit to their further direction. Some of those would require retraining and many would not.

Within days, WestPac units were on the southern border along the Tampa-Orlando line. Their rapid advance, north to south, across the center of the United States showed them the condition of total disarray that existed everywhere. The FSP had been in control a short time prior to the arrival of the WestPac forces and they made all decisions in all areas on behalf of the local citizens. Everything was done for the good of the FSP and the welfare and livelihood of the citizens was secondary or totally irrelevant. Food supplies and material resources were in very scarce supply. Water and sewage services were in great need of repair or total replacement. There were no public services in effect to provide sustenance for those incapable of providing for themselves. The infrastructure of the former nation had seen no maintenance or repair for well over ten years and required virtually one hundred per-cent replacement. It would be years before the infrastructure was brought back into normal operating condition.

The WestPac troops were being met by hundreds and thousands of starving citizens begging for any scrap of food. They were again seeing mothers holding up starving infants and begging for the troops to take them. There were no operating hospitals, no police or fire protection. The FSP ran everything and they ran it solely for their benefit. The advance of Westpac to the south line across Florida was not hindered by FSP defenses. It was slowed a bit periodically by better organized criminal elements that had to learn they were too ill equipped to tangle with WestPac Rangers. But, the main holdup to the advance of WestPac was the need to provide some stability to the newly acquired landmass and to feed and protect the citizens that lived there. Housing was also an issue but food and water were immediate needs. The sick, the young and the aged were at the mercy of roving gangs of thieves who saw nothing wrong with beating and killing anyone that had anything of apparent value to the thieves, be it food, liquor or material items. Added to the confusion the WestPac Rangers were already facing were the thousands of FSP soldiers trying to surrender to them. The Rangers lacked the personnel and the facilities to care for the surrendering FSP troops and after a while, they refused to take them in.

The problem of dealing with the situation the citizens were facing extended from the Great Lakes Region down to the Southern Border and from east to west across the center of the nation, all citizens in all States that were now occupied by WestPac.

The task ahead was daunting but Robert was confident they could meet the challenge. For openers, he decided that the District of Columbia would no longer be the focal point of government in the United States of America. The new center of government in the United States would be located appropriately in the center of the country at the former Scott Air Force Base in Illinois, outside of Saint Louis. Robert wanted to destroy all vestiges of the former center of mismanagement and corruption in the country. He was certain that this move would be very demoralizing to the many lobbyists and bureaucratic opportunists who had already taken steps to locate homes and offices in somewhat stabilized Washington, D.C. Robert had further decided that the new government would be a government for the people. It would not begin its new life as a government of the people as how that was to be created would require further study and thought, primarily by Robert and the Study Group.

Pending the reorganization of the nation, Robert had the military spread across the country to act as a stabilizing force for all citizens. Crime was not to be tolerated. Dissent was not to be tolerated at least for the immediate future. Constructive criticism was acceptable provided it was truly constructive and was directed at offices capable of making the desired changes. All political gatherings required permits. For the time being, Unions were considered illegal. The military was authorized to enforce the new rules of the Administration. Basic Rules of Conduct were printed up and disseminated throughout the nation. The violations for punishment were appended to the Basic Rules. Some newspapers and radio or television stations ignored the rule against dissent and sharply criticized the new Rules of Conduct. Each person, newspaper or media source that was publicly critical immediately received a visit from the local military authority and they were politely requested to terminate dissent or be put out of business. It was also suggested to them that trying to frame their dissent in the form of constructive criticism would not pass muster if there was any question as to its validity.

Robert had Sarah organize another national radio and television speech for him and to ensure that facilities were available for all citizens in the newly emancipated territories of the former nation to hear or see the speech. The date, time and facility for viewing or hearing the speech were broadcast hourly through the Voice of WestPac. Leaflets were dropped on the larger cities by Hans Frick to ensure that everyone knew of the speech and where they might go to hear it. On the night of the speech, Robert had organized the event to take place in the Conference Center of Riverton. The hall was inundated with WestPac flags and also with flags of the United States of America. The American Flag that was being flown bore the fifty stars of the nation at the time of the collapse. Questions remained concerning the West, South Florida, Alaska and Hawaii but Robert was confident that in time, these areas of the former nation would be back in the fold. Robert was wearing his formal dress uniform as the Commander-in-Chief of WestPac Forces complete with the gold braided epaulets. Again he had

General Jack Nix handle the introduction and the hall was filled with supporters, both military and civilian. The audience gave Robert a rousing reception as he stepped forward to take the microphone. Again he was speaking from the carved rostrum he had previously used to such great effect.

Robert began his speech by welcoming Americans back in their own country. "The FSP has been defeated and most of the soldiers that had been serving in their armed force have joined with us in rebuilding the country. Everyone should realize that the FSP soldiers were with rare exception not serving the defeated government voluntarily. We welcome them back to the country and rejoice with them in their new freedom. We still have military actions that will be taking place soon to retake areas of the Great Lakes Region and the Northeast. We expect that those will be difficult battles and we trust our fellow citizens across this great land will support our forthcoming war effort and will provide the food and supplies we will need to defeat the Muslim force. We are also aware that some of the Muslims in the area we will be moving against are not the enemy. The problem is that it is difficult to identify them. I urgently request all peace loving Muslims to refuse to fight against our soldiers and to surrender to them immediately upon coming in contact with them. You will be treated fairly."

Robert paused and took a moment before proceeding into what he considered the real meat of his speech. "I am aware that our new Rules of Conduct that have been distributed throughout the nation are a matter of some concern. I cannot tell you how long they will be the controlling guidance for all or if and when additional rules will supplement or amend them. We need stability across the country. There are many who do not intend to help us do that. Let me advise them that we will deal with them severely. For the law abiding citizens of our new nation, the Rules of Conduct should not be presenting any problems. As to how the new nation will be governed, that will be explained in the future. In the meantime if you question what the immediate future holds for you with respect to governance, let me suggest you look at WestPac. What we have been doing in WestPac, we will be doing in the rest of the nation at least for the near future."

"Right now we have work to do in rebuilding our cities, our services, our schools, and our communication systems. We will not be having a government that dictates all actions for everyone. We will be writing a national Constitution which will list the powers of the national government.

All other powers not listed will be in the hands of the States. The national government will ensure that the States honor, respect and abide by the rights and privileges written in the new Constitution. If you American citizens need anything, food, housing, medical care, look to your neighbors, your city or your State for your needs. All citizens who are now flocking to our new site of Government at Scott Field in Illinois for some form of largesse, you are wasting your time. Look to your State and convince your fellow citizens there that you need a free ride for one reason or another. As to what you might expect in the future, I generally support the former Constitution of the United States of America. We will make some changes that we believe are needed to preclude the problems that developed as a result of some of the wording of the old Constitution. Let me just say this. We are no longer a nation of victims. Political correctness is no longer in vogue. We are not Native Americans, or Black Americans or Irish Americans, we are Americans. There are no special rights for anyone based on ethnic, religious or sexual preference. Anyone wanting that can leave the new United States of America and live somewhere else. We are basically a Christian nation but we do not prefer one religion over another. All are entitled to respect provided they honor and respect all laws of this nation. All laws presently on the books of the former nation are now null and void. That includes Administrative Regulations, and all Court decisions. That does not mean all behavior is lawful and acceptable. Such is not the case. Our Military is instructed to arrest and imprison anyone acting in an immoral, anti-social or criminal manner. Those are very general terms and the Military has been allowed a liberal interpretation of each of them. All judicial appointments are hereby nullified, all Administrative procedures and offices are no longer in existence. All State Officials are now being appointed by the WestPac Military and will serve until elections are held sometime in the future. Matters previously handled by Administrative entities will now be handled by State governments operating within the restraints of the new Constitution and there will be no Administrative Regulations enforced again for the foreseeable future. Administrative Law as it existed before the collapse was just another means of avoiding the Constitution. All legal matters, criminal or civil will be handled by the Military. Prisoners are not to be released pending further hearings by the Military. All jail sentences will be reviewed by the Military. The Military has been instructed to enforce ethical human behavior. If you do not know what that is, you had better be careful. As problems develop, the national government will decide how to deal with them. What we need now is to re-build, to restore peace and security across the land. We must work together to accomplish that and when we do that, we will succeed. Everyone must help carry the load. I wish you all well and God Bless America."

The reaction to the speech was generally very favorable. Some who were used to operating on the edge were a bit concerned that there were limits being put on their personal behavior. In a follow on interview by the Word of WestPac, Robert admitted that "Yes, human behavior is not without its limits." Later Robert commented to Anders, "Is common sense a casualty of our former national government?"

"Government, even in its best state, is but a necessary evil; in its worst state, an intolerable one."

—**Thomas Paine**

CHAPTER NINETEEN

After the speech, Robert returned to his Riverton office where he met with Ross Perry, Jack Nix and Sarah Taves. The four of them studied maps of the eastern United States and discussed the strategy for the forthcoming military operation. Sarah pointed out that the primary centers of Muslim military strength would be Detroit, Cleveland, Pittsburgh, New York and areas of Southern Connecticut. She did not expect any major opposition from the Muslims elsewhere in the Northeast and no other opposition from other groups other than the usual criminal enterprises that had existed elsewhere in the country. Sarah estimated the combined Muslim strength in that area to be around five hundred thousand men or more under arms. She said that her reports were devoid of any sightings of armored vehicles or aircraft. Strictly men under arms and the usual IED's.

Robert suggested that they gather a force of one million experienced soldiers and hit Detroit, Cleveland and Pittsburgh all at the same time but with primary force first directed at the western most city, then moving east. Using aircraft, artillery, armored vehicles and foot soldiers. "Soften up all targets to the max with bombs, rockets, napalm and constant artillery shelling. They are not going to be surrendering but we want to make them think about it. Again, destroy anything and everything that affords them shelter and use plenty of napalm. That will dig them out faster than anything else."

Nix laughed and said, "You are a real mean son of a bitch, Robert."

Robert replied, "Yes, and remember, when it comes to war, mean usually wins."

Perry assembled a force of five hundred thousand men that he deployed to the south, west and then north of Detroit and then he had Frick drop leaflets over civilian residential areas advising them to leave the city as soon as possible as it would be receiving heavy shelling. There was minimal reaction to the leaflet drop and Perry assumed the Muslims were forbidding the residents to flee following the same procedure they used in

Chicago. After waiting an appropriate amount of time, Perry commenced the shelling and bombing of the known Muslim centers of strength. Frick had his drones providing photo reconnaissance of the Muslim positions and upgraded targeting data based on those studies. In between artillery shellings, the drones were dropping guided bombs, guided napalm and firing missiles. A few had been shot down but they were rapidly replaced. The Muslims assumed they could move their force at night in the dark but they soon realized that infrared targeting was taking a severe toll of their troops.

After three days of heavy bombardment, Perry began moving his troops into the city. The new Barnes tanks were burning out Muslim resistance from bombed out buildings and other sites using their napalm guns. Any potential IED site was destroyed by cannon fire or explosives. The collateral damage to other structures in the vicinity was extensive. After three more days of intense conflict, the WestPac Rangers were moving into the high rent areas of Grosse Point and Saint Clair Shores located on the shores of the lake feeding into Lake Huron. Formerly beautiful lakeside mansions were now being used as fight to the death defensive positions by the Muslims. The Rangers proceeded to level what was left of the structures and using tactical aircraft and Barnes Tanks, they made multiple bomb and napalm runs over the resulting debris. When they finally ended their attack on the structures, there was no way any living human being could have survived the assault.

All of Detroit had been taken by the WestPac force with a troop loss of only five hundred men killed and one thousand wounded. As the troops moved to the south and reformed by unit, the Civil Affairs team was taking over in the city. Civilian losses had been high due to the use of hostages and the total destruction of the city that was required to uproot the Muslim defenders. A stabilizing force of ten thousand men was left at Ann Arbor to maintain security in the Michigan area. In Detroit, a city government was established and they were advised to get to work rebuilding the city and to ensure the safety and security of the citizens. Looting had started in the city as soon as the Rangers had advanced from one area to another. Robert issued the shoot to kill order for all looters. This brought the practice to a halt. Robert told Nix that this was one area of the country that WestPac was not going to waste time with. He did not believe the local citizens would do anything to rebuild Detroit "And you can bet we aren't going to step in and do their work for them."

While Detroit had been under attack, leaflet drops had been made on Cleveland and Pittsburg with the message to the residents to flee for their lives to the south as their cities would be subjected to intensive artillery and bombing. After a week of continuous bombardment, the WestPac Rangers began their advances into the city. Again they followed the strategy that had worked ever since Minneapolis. Everything that could shield an IED was totally destroyed. Buildings from which shots were fired were flattened and napalmed. Within days, half of the cities were in flames but WestPac casualties were minimal. Again both cities were totally encircled almost immediately to preclude enemy combatants from fleeing to fight again elsewhere. As a result only a few prisoners were taken. The word to the troops was not to take prisoners unless there was a particularly good reason for doing so. The few Muslim prisoners that were taken were not carrying arms, were not in the immediate vicinity of where the most intense fighting was taking place, and in the case of some were with Caucasians that verified they were not combatants. Unfortunately these were rare exceptions among Muslims. The battle for both cities was concluded within one week from the day the troops began their move into the suburbs.

Robert, Perry and Nix met briefly to discuss the campaign to retake the New York-Boston-Connecticut metroplex. This had the potential to be the most difficult battle since the fight to retake Minneapolis. Perry gathered a force of one and a half million men to first completely surround the target area and to begin softening up the New Jersey defenses. The plan being to retake the west side of the Hudson up to west Point and then bombard the hell out of New York up to Connecticut before attacking the city. They concluded that with the difficulty of getting troops across the Hudson at New York city, with bridges most likely blown, they would first send a strong force up to West Point while making it appear that the main thrust against New York city would be by way of Staten Island. The Rangers had been battling through New Jersey for days to reach Staten Island and could only assume that getting across to New York city was only going to be much worse. The west Point force would then hopefully be across the Hudson and then move south to either find bridges not yet blown or safe crossing points to bring greater numbers of troops and armored vehicles from one side of the Hudson to the other. This would then become the main force for the attack on the city itself while a companion force would indeed attack from the Staten Island area after the New York city defenders were mostly involved with the force coming at them from the north.

Fighting to retake New York city and environs was indeed ferocious. The Muslim force was fully aware that this was their last stand in America and they fully intended to fight to the death for every man, woman or child capable of firing a rifle or rocket propelled grenade. To add to the problems faced by the Rangers, the use of suicide bombers had increased significantly. Even children were being enlisted into the ranks of those willing to give their lives for Allah. The Rangers had been hesitant to fire at young boys or girls but after seeing fellow soldiers riddled with ball bearings from the bombs worn by the children they now gave only one warning for the approaching child to remove all clothing before coming closer. If they refused, they were fired upon. Needless to say, some totally innocent children who were shy about removing their clothing were killed. It was a brutal war and all the Rangers hoped they would never have to witness this type of warfare again.

The battle for the city of New York including Long Island lasted for two full weeks. When it ended, it, like the cities before it, was virtually totally destroyed with fires burning day and night. There were no longer tall buildings remaining in the skyline. They were all totally obliterated and lying in disarray at their former locations. One could not tell where the streets had run or where buildings had been located, it was one miserable mass of destruction in flames or at least still smoking. A constant pall of smoke and haze lay over the city. The Recon drones searching for pockets of resistance were having problems operating due to lack of visibility precluding their operators from locating targets. Some of the drones were equipped with high tech navigational and targeting aids that permitted them to function in zero to low visibility conditions. For the rest, they were grounded. There was obviously no way to put out the fires and very little interest in doing so. The citizens who had resided in the homes or apartments involved had long ago left or were lying dead in the rubble of their homes. Civilian losses again were very high but it was either that or lose thousands of WestPac soldiers trying to uproot the Muslims from their bunkers or hiding in the rubble. They were very adept at secreting themselves and taking lives of approaching soldiers. When the smoke and haze had lifted a bit, one standing in the midst of New York city formerly surrounded by tall buildings and occasional skyscrapers could see for miles nothing but relatively flat piles of rubble, some fires still burning, total silence, no sign of the former residents, only troops cleaning their rifles and eating their MRE lunches. Even the troops were silent. They had never been involved in such deadly, intense combat before, some with blank stares, sitting wondering if this was the last of it. It had been a brutal battle to take the city and now looking out at it, nothing but total silence. The city was gone.

After the fighting had ended in New Jersey and New York city, the West-Pac force took inventory of their losses and concluded that this had been one of their costliest battles. Ten thousand wounded and seven thousand WestPac soldiers had given their lives. Many were lost to suicide bombers, IED's and snipers. Nix had cautioned his officers to warn the troops that the hidden danger was their primary threat and to watch out for it. Needless to say, one could exercise the maximum caution and still fall prey to the many novel methods being used to take their lives. In one home as the Rangers moved through it, they noticed what appeared to be a Mexican piñate hanging from a lamp in the kitchen of the house. There were other signs that a birthday party was in the making. As one of the Rangers passed through the kitchen, he raised his rifle to strike the piñate to get some of the candy, one of his companions yelled out, "No, don't…" The explosion took the lives of three of the Rangers.

There were very few prisoners taken in the fight to recapture the New York Metroplex. Among them was a Muslim that was taken prisoner with five other Muslim fighters that had run out of ammunition and had nothing left with which to fight. While the five other Muslims had nothing to say and took their fate silently, the one claimed to be an emissary of a Mid-East country assigned to the United Nations and was entitled to immunity pursuant to the UN Charter. He presented a UN Identification Card to prove his authenticity. The matter went to Nix and he contacted Robert for his opinion as to how to handle the matter. In the meantime the Muslim was detained under guard.

"Jack, how do you want to handle it?"

"As far as I am concerned, we don't have a United Nations anymore so this bird has no immunity."

"You read my mind. Tell him he has no immunity anymore and to enjoy his internment until he is packed up and sent back to his Mid-East homeland. Also let him know that they have no rights to counsel, a jury trial or the rules of evidence. Those days are over. If he is lucky, he will be sent back home. That is, if he is lucky. That is most likely what we will have to do with all of the Muslims that were captured on the battlefield. I will talk to Sarah about this but I see no reason to continue any association with the

United Nations and I sure as hell don't want to be feeding these clowns for the next five years or more. I never understood what reasons justified the UN's continued existence at our expense anyway. I always considered it a waste of time and a misuse of good land in New York city."

"I agree, Robert. As for the prisoners, the word coming in from our troops is that the very few prisoners we have been able to take are about to swear allegiance to this country. Send them back."

Perry and Nix spent a week regrouping, reforming and reequipping their force before being ready to move on into Connecticut and Boston. The troops were very tired and were a bit demoralized from the losses sustained in their recent battles. Perry and Nix assured them that all resistance would be destroyed as much as possible before they would be sent forward. The attitude of the troops was "That didn't work before but, what the hell, let's just get it done." As the troops began their move to the north, they were not running into any opposition until they began to come close to Bridgeport. Pockets of primarily Muslim opposition had to be removed but other than that the only opposition had been the occasional gang fiefdom that offered little resistance. Bridgeport offered minimal resistance compared to New York city and within two days, they were on their way to New Haven. The troops were being transported in trucks for most of this Northeastern Campaign. It was obvious the heavy fighting was behind them but they still had to be careful as there were many people yet out there that wanted to kill them. As they moved towards New Haven, they began running into south-bound travelers trying to avoid the conflict. These people told the Rangers that there were still Muslim fighting units in the city but they did not think there were over fifty thousand of them. The Muslims had been busy building their bunkers and sealing their positions with sandbags. As one of the Rangers commented, "More of the same."

The battle for New Haven and Hartford was very much the same. Hartford was not the Muslim haven the other coastal cities had been but they did offer resistance there as well. Ranger patrol units that had gone further north to Providence reported that militia units in that area operating on behalf of WestPac had pretty well neutralized the opposition. After New Haven, Nix assembled a force of ten thousand men to proceed north under the command of Monty Wyatt and ensure that the rest of the country up into Maine was secured and stable. Monty Wyatt reported to Nix within a few days that they had run into minimal resistance and this from relatively small gangs intent on maintaining control of their turf. Wyatt was able to convince them that they would be better off working with WestPac provided they abided by the rules. Again, the military appointed local leaders that appeared to be driven by positive goals of rebuilding their area and providing peace and security to the citizens living there. Nix established a number of Military Bases in the northeast to stabilize the area and again had Frick drop leaflets reciting the Basic Rules of Conduct that everyone would have to follow. These were relatively strict rules but they were required by the situation at least until the nation was stabilized and a Constitution was again in effect. Sarah was also broadcasting procedures for the citizens to abide by in rebuilding their cities and towns and restating for them the Rules of Conduct that were to be observed.

Robert then had Perry establish Bases throughout the country to ensure that all opposition was stifled. He was also authorized to appoint community leadership and to take such action as was necessary to get the States and Cities up and running again. Meanwhile, Robert and Nix traveled down to Scott Field in Illinois to begin reestablishing a national government. There was much work to be done along that line including what Alaska's status was going to be. Robert had communicated with leaders in Alaska but there was still some question as to what their intentions were. At times, they indicated they would be joining WestPac or the future national government and at other times, they sounded as though they wanted to go it alone. Robert assumed that the variation of intentions shown by the leaders in Alaska reflected the amount of attention they were receiving from China. The Alaskans were very leery of the attention they were receiving from the Chinese, yet they continued to listen to their offers. Robert would have to sit down with them and come to some agreement or this could go on forever. There were also very important status issues with Paco Morales in South Florida and the Hispanic territory now governed by Louis Donley in the West.

Robert did not have major ambitions with respect to any of the three outstanding entities. His attitude was that if they were no threat to the rest of the country and the people in those regions were content with their present government, why create a problem that did not exist. He was aware that in time these entities could very well become a problem. That was a possibility and he would have to deal with that when and if it came to pass.

Robert and Nix first took a tour of the former Scott Air Force Base in Illinois just to the east of Saint Louis to see what condition it was in. The Base had been secured by local authorities who had been apparently assuming that in time it would again become operational and it could be a very viable entity with respect to employment which everyone hungered for. The FSP had also used various sections of the Base for their own purposes. These included the runways, control tower and the Aviation Maintenance shops. The temporary living quarters consisting of the Barracks and the Chow Hall were also being utilized on a fairly regular basis. There were some airplanes secured in the hangars that appeared flyable but undoubtedly would require considerable maintenance before getting airborne again, if ever. Again, the local community was aware from news announcements that Scott Field was destined to be the center for the new national government. So regardless of Robert's admonition to people seeking opportunity at Scott Field, they still arrived there by the thousands. This was both good and bad. Robert knew they would be needing skilled administrators to operate the Base and to serve in the new government but he also knew that many of the applicants lining up for jobs had no skills that Robert or his staff would be interested in using. Nevertheless, Robert had grossly underestimated the many slots that WestPac would need to fill at Scott to get the Base up and operating again.

Scott was going to need administrative help as well as aviation services including weather forecasters, mechanics, transient alert personnel, tower operators, air traffic controllers , plus housing staff, utility service operators to restore and service the water and sewage systems and a myriad number of other employees. Consequently one of the first offices opened at Scott was the employment office. Former employees were given preference mainly because they were familiar with the work and experienced at the job. After being hired, the new employees were immediately put to work cleaning, repairing and getting the Base ready for operation. The new mission of Scott Field was quite different from its prior mission as a Military Air Transport Base, yet aspects of the former mission would also be needed.

Robert sent word to the Riverton staff that they should begin the move to Scott Field. They would continue to use Riverton and Goodland for the time being as military training centers but that could easily be managed by Campbell and Yates. There had been some talk of using military training bases used in the past when the former national government was in existence that were more centrally located in the country but that would have to be further explored. Matt Parker was offered a management position at Scott but he declined. He could not leave his home in Montana and Robert completely understood that. Sarah was one of the first to arrive at Scott Field having arranged to fly down there with her husband, Hans. The two of them quickly arranged to take over one of the few stand alone homes on Scott Field. Robert had already picked out his office in the administration building and moved into the former Military Barracks with Perry and Nix. Perry and Nix had no intention of being locked up in some office at Scott and did not want to give the appearance of wanting that to happen. Their interests were with the troops in the field. The Barracks served them as a permanent address that they would be periodically returning to and a place to leave personal items while they were gone. They were most comfortable there and looked at a desk as the end of the road for a true warrior. Robert, on the other hand, intended to be a permanent resident at Scott for the foreseeable future but preferred the simple Barracks life to the comfortable existence a home would provide. He did grant himself the luxury of taking one of the end rooms in the Barracks to afford himself some privacy. He also had a doorway constructed in the hallway separating his quarters from the others so that he could get some rest when that was required.

When the dust had settled on Robert's move onto Scott Field, he sat in his office in the administration building and looked out at the overgrown runways of the Base. It was actually a very pleasing view, very much a pastoral setting as the airfield was now much more grass than concrete and the landscape extended out for two or three miles with no buildings or other man-made structures to interrupt the panoramic setting. There was something very relaxing in looking out at the field of green that stretched for a great distance. There were no buildings to block Robert's view of the sea of green and he thought how fortunate it was that he had selected this particular office. He had a north south view from this office and the sun shining into the office should not become a problem for him other than maybe in the winter time when it would be out of the south and then it would be welcome.

A small airplane could still land on the runways just as they could land on a field of grass but larger aircraft would need the runways cleaned up and repaired first. He would have Hans Frick take care of that project at least pending the assignment of a permanent airdrome manager. Having their own airfield was a major plus for Robert. The Airfield was already secured and aircraft repair facilities were adjacent to the concrete ramp in the huge hangar buildings. As he relaxed in his chair, he thought that this was one of the first times in months or maybe even years that he had been able to kick back and not think about what he had to do right now.

He had many things he had to do but he was not going to let them interfere with his reverie. It was totally quiet in the room and no one else in the building that he was aware of other than the security guard at the entrance. He had been sitting in the chair for some time dozing off when he realized that it was getting dark in the room. He looked at his watch and noted that it was eight o'clock in the evening. He must have been sleeping for at least four hours. That was amazing as Robert had never slept like that before during the daytime. He knew he was burned out from the pace he had been keeping but apparently he was more tired than he thought.

The Staff from Riverton would begin arriving during the coming week and he would have to prepare for their arrival and assign tasks for them to work on so that there was no time lost in getting everyone to work. He had contacted Clay Daley in Portland and told him to make arrangements to come to Scott Field as soon as possible and to bring his secretary, Toni Norton, and his three assistants with their secretaries. WestPac had a number of passenger planes in their inventory and Robert called Hans to have them set up a schedule for bringing staff from Riverton, Portland and Seattle to the new government center at Scott Field. He told Hans that the runways were not perfect but they appeared to Robert to be at least useable. He could have one of his staff head down to Scott in a smaller plane and check them out first if he had any questions.

Nix had the former Base cook get the Officer's Club kitchen up and operating with full staff to serve the members of Westpac presently on the Base and those that would soon be arriving. Robert was still quite drowsy from his long nap and finally thought he should try to get something to eat before the dining room was closed, if it was not already closed. Fortunately it was still open and when he went in, he saw Nix having a sandwich and the staff standing around hoping he would hurry up and leave. Robert apologized for his late arrival and ordered a light lunch to tide him over until breakfast.

Robert sat down with Nix and laughed as he told him he had just crashed in his new office for about four hours. "I must have really been burned out. I have never done that before."

Nix laughed. "You must have needed it. People were beginning to worry about you burning the candle at both ends. Better watch it. That's what got Stuart."

"I know, Jack. There is just so damn much work to be done. The American Public is already beginning to bitch about everything. Sarah's bulletin was loaded with their complaints. Where's the this, where's the that. They drive you nuts. Where the hell is the old pioneer spirit we all read about when we were kids. We sure as hell need that now."

"It is still out there, Robert, we just have to find it. We have to give that some thought. The so called pioneer spirit was destroyed or at least put to sleep by the series of dead beat leaders this nation had before it finally sunk into total collapse. During that fifty or more year period of our government handling all problems and decisions for all Americans, the public forgot that they were supposed to be making their own decisions for themselves and their families. We have to teach them to do that again. That is not going to happen overnight. We have to be patient with them."

"Ok, Jack. Up to a point I will be patient. After that it's kick ass time."

"A little of that is OK too."

"Physical courage, which despises all danger, will make a man brave in one way; and moral courage, which despises all opinion, will make a man brave in another."

—Charles Caleb Colton

CHAPTER TWENTY

Robert returned to his room after his dinner planning on going to bed early. He figured he needed a good night's sleep and then he would be fine tomorrow. There were some old magazines in the room that dated back years to the pre-collapse times. He found them interesting due to their age and after a while they became depressing. The news from those days was so staged and slanted that it was almost humorous to read it now. But it wasn't humorous to Robert and it only angered him more. He put the magazine away and finally went to bed. He laid in his bed and thought about the work they had to do in the coming months and years to rebuild the country. He wondered if he had the energy to do the job or better yet, if he had the patience. He was becoming impatient with the lack of enthusiasm on behalf of the citizens in the newly freed territories to dive into the challenge of rebuilding their homes, cities and country.

Robert was serious about his comment to Jack about missing the pioneer spirit. He had thought a great deal about that in earlier years when he first entered the Western States with Stuart. As a boy, he was fascinated by the western cowboy mythology that permeated the novels , the story books he had read and the Saturday morning movies he always went to see. It was the independent spirit of those men leading lives on the range, taming wild horses, fighting the elements, Indians, and the many risks they were facing on their own with only their courage and their six guns. Robert lived his life as a child believing that those men really were out there in the West. He knew by then there were no cowboys in the center of the country where he lived. Nevertheless, he assumed those real men were still out West. All through his childhood, he had wanted to grow up and be just like them, on his own, taking care of himself and beholden to no one. It came as a bit of a surprise to him when he did grow older and did realize that most Americans at that time did not want to take care of themselves. They lacked the interest for that and the aptitude. They preferred leaving those decisions to others. Robert was still surprised to discover when he moved West that not only was the Western Cowboy a myth but the Western Young Man that he was seeing was dedicated to finding the easy way out. They paid little or no taxes, they used barter to avoid taxable records and they were difficult to hire for any sort of task that required effort especially during elk or deer hunting season. He was sorely disappointed in what he was finding in the West when it came to the so called diehard American Spirit. There were some that possessed the old drive to be their own man or woman but that was not the universal finding. Matt Parker had it but many in Riverton did not.

Robert looked upon people, men in particular, that lacked the drive to provide for themselves as wimps, pussies or worse. He had no time for them and did not hesitate to let them know his view of them. Consequently, he was a loner because by that time most men were following someone's orders, their wife's, their family's, their employer's, or what have you. Robert had none of those people guiding his life. He had always worked for himself, sometimes in legal employment and frequently not. Furthermore he had such strong feelings about such people that he steered well clear of them. He belonged to no clubs, no cliques, did not hang out in bars which he viewed as loser club houses and avoided marriage like the plague as he had by then concluded that was a man's ticket to loss of freedom and independence. He used to voice his opinions on these ingrained attitudes until he had grown older and realized there were many men who had different opinions than his and they were not losers. They were good fathers, good husbands and good providers. They were not wimps. He finally settled back on the opinion that he was just different for whatever reason he did not understand and that was not going to change. He maintained his old beliefs but would try to keep these opinions to himself in the future as he was realizing his frequently uttered generalities were not helping him.

As Robert lay in his bed in the Barracks trying without success to fall asleep, he kept thinking of the task ahead. His staff would come in this coming week and he would have to first organize everything that had to be worked on and then he had to pick the person most capable of solving the problem. His thoughts were just going in circles thinking of the food shortages, then increasing production of goods and services, resolving the money issue which continued to cause problems, then myriad other problems. He had his own ideas on how to tackle the hundreds of problems but that was not the solution. He needed others to do that work and his job was to find them. He finally woke up after a fitful night's sleep when the first rays of light in the new day came into his room. He arose, showered and went over for breakfast so that he could get started on laying out the work assignments.

He had set up a Command Post in the administration building so that someone was always on duty, especially in these early days, to handle the message traffic. After his breakfast he stopped by the CP and there were a number of messages for him. Most of the messages dealt with arrival time for Staff traveling to Scott Field and he had the CP forward those to the Airport Manager that he had assigned to that task yesterday. He told himself he was going to have to start making notes of these assignments or he would be forgetting them. He needed Clay Daley walking behind him taking notes. He did leave a note in the Command Post for Sarah to contact him as soon as she landed. He was hoping Hans had loaded a plane with the basic communication equipment so that she could be back in business overnight on her Intel Operation.

Robert was soon at his desk in his office and tried his phone. He was pleasantly surprised to find that he did have a dial tone. Apparently the night tech staff had arranged that. He was questioning that he would actually be able to make a telephone call either local or long distance but it was sure nice to hear a dial tone. He tried dialing the operator but nothing happened. He would have Sarah get the word to him on what communication services they had available and if they were slim to none, she would have to get her radio equipment up and operating now. It was also possible that some of the Air Force radio gear that served the Base was still available. Possibly her staff could locate that and maybe her staff or Del Sutton could get it up and operating. Robert had absolutely no idea what communication services were available in the Missouri area. This was FSP territory as recently as two months ago and all of WestPac's communications into that territory for years had been by radio.

Robert's first thoughts on what he had to do immediately dealt with the issue of food and medical supplies for the recently acquired territories. The Civil Affairs officers in those areas, whose names Perry had recorded somewhere, would be the ones to talk with to find out the state of affairs in their areas of responsibility. He put a star on that note to see that someone was immediately assigned to give him a status report as to what was going on there.

The next area of interest for Robert was to know if they were running into conflicts anywhere in the country. There no doubt were snipers or Muslim units that they had overrun in the battles to retake ground and they could be causing serious problems. Perry would know about that. Everything he was coming up with involved Perry or people that worked for Perry. He was getting frustrated that he had no way to communicate with him and finally went down to the CP to determine if there was any communication system operating on the Base. He was pleasantly surprised to find out that his phone was in the system and provided Base wide communication if he first dialed 9 and then a three digit number for the particular office. The numbers were in a book that should be somewhere in his office. A little embarrassed, Robert thanked the Ranger on duty in the CP and then returned to his office, located the phone book on a stand and called the quarters to see if Perry was there. He was and in just a few seconds he was on the phone. "Ross I am in my office in the Admin Building, I would like to go over some items so when you are available would you stop by here."

"Be there in about two Minutes, Robert."

Perry finally located Robert's office and commented, "Plenty of room available in this building. If the guard hadn't told me your room number up here, I never would have found it."

"I'd like to keep it that way. Maybe I should fire the guard. Don't worry, this building will be packed all too soon but I will guarantee you, it won't have the scum ball bureaucrats there were in Washington."

"Glad to hear that."

"Ross, a number of things I want to talk to you about." Robert then laid out the problem areas that he wanted Ross and his staff to tackle first. Feeding a half starved population was the immediate need. But Robert told Perry to have strings attached to everything we give out. "I don't want to create another nation of victims. They are going to have to work for whatever they receive. There is plenty of work to be done so put them to work…before lunch. There is always the five or ten percent that is not going to be able to work due to physical limitations. That is understandable. But when the numbers of invalids crawls up to twenty-five percent, forget it. Give those that claim they can't work a thorough examination and if they pass, give them an ID card that cannot be copied so they can show that at the chow line. By the way, I want chow lines. I do not want food stamps. I got very tired of seeing dog food going through the supermarket checkout being bought with food stamps. Make sure the chow lines are accessible to the population. Either put the chow lines where the people are or move the people to the chow lines."

"People will not have money but they can get WestPac dollars for their means of exchange. They can get those dollars for the work they are doing for the community in which they live. Same goes for their housing. If need be, they can receive one free meal so they can then go to work and earn some dollars. Happy times are over. Work time is here. If they don't want to work and are able to work, let them starve."

"Also, watch out for crime. Criminals do not like to work. That is why they are criminals. No first time passes. All crimes of theft, assault, murder, bribery, and so forth are to be punished. You will have to set up prisons. Nothing fancy. Protection from the weather, a basic diet and all prisoners are kept separate. Guard Posts with armed guards instructed to shoot to kill. I don't want any of this wounding business. Wounds mean hospitals and we are going to be short of those. None of this rump riding business; that is no longer allowed in our prisons. Anyone that gets caught doing or receiving that, voluntarily that is, gets fifty lashes right on their bare ass. Both of the loving parties, the giver and the taker, that will remove their interest in that activity. If cliques are discovered in prison let those prisoners be mingled in with the people they hate or fear. That will be the end of the cliques. Any 'in prison' gangs will be separated and members will be left in single secluded holding pens, outside in the yard. When they are about half dead from the weather, they will be cured of their gang issues. Then put them in single cells again on the inside, away from their fellow gang members."

"Also, after 9:00 p.m. it is lights out and total quiet. Anyone making any noise inside the prison after that time goes into solitary. For those outside, they lose one day's food ration. No talking between cells. Period. No exceptions. I was so damn tired of seeing those prison brats on those TV shows blaming their rotten behavior on having been deprived of toys as a child. We'll show them what real deprivation is. Also every now and then review just who the hell is in prison. Historically we sent people to prison by mistake as often as we did for good cause. Make sure all young good looking guys are segregated and safe from the rump riders. No exceptions. Watch your guards as well. They can be as big a problem as the prisoners. That occupation can sometimes have its own rewards. Also, brutal guards should have the opportunity to spend some time in holding pens with prisoners they have brutalized. Also, no visitors and no mail means no drugs.

Sounds pretty tough doesn't it, well, it is. Oh, I almost forgot. No Internet, television or radio. But, here is the real benefit. Plenty of books should be available at all times. Good books, mostly classics including bibles but no Korans. Books should be accessible at all times. With a good book they might even be able to learn to read. I suggest that for starters you write up what I have just told you as a prison rule book for serious crimes. Give that to Sarah and have her publish it as soon as possible so that all those so inclined will know what they might be getting themselves in for."

"Now Ross, I want to talk about the issue of Freedom of Speech which includes all forms of communication. We all know that in former times it was used as a tool to propagandize, incite, spread falsehoods, you name it. Usually it was very beneficial but the misuse of speech in all its forms was very dangerous and I don't want to get back into that situation. Let us talk first about television and radio. I have no problem if one station or one speaker presents facts that I do not like to hear. For example if someone is on TV or radio today and says that I am not seeing to it that food is distributed fairly around the nation. If what he says is factual, that is fine. If it is not substantiated and shown to be factual, he is out of business. So, how do we handle that sort of issue? That is a rhetorical question, Ross."

Robert paused for effect. "I say you in the military are going to have to monitor this and control it. For a single minor violation, a warning is sufficient. The second time, they lose their license to broadcast or publish for one year. A third time, they lose their license permanently. Also, let us be very strict in the enforcement of this especially now in the early times of the rebuilding process. These are critical times for us and unfounded criticism can damage or destroy the good we are trying to create. By the way unsubstantiated factual data that supports rather than criticizes a person or issue, regardless of which side of the issue they are on, is less damaging to any cause and should be treated less stringently."

"Now a good example of one that should be silenced is Chris Masters. We all listened to his blatant B.S. on his monologue show for years. He is the classic offender. I don't know where he is today but if he is alive, he is looking for another TV station. By the way, he does not get a license. If he shows up with a station somehow, arrest that sack of crap and throw him in one of your prisons until he discovers a new occupation."

"Now Ross, I have given you a ton of things to do. I have not been speaking in specifics so use your best judgment on how you apply what I told you to do. We all are overloaded, no doubt about it. Wyatt is here now or coming in shortly. Use him to help you get the things done that I have told you to do. If he is too damn busy as well, find your own people and put them to work. Good smart people that like to work. Your first duty is to see that food is distributed and public housing is made available to many people, particularly in the cities, who lost their homes. The first place I would look to house them would be the former government buildings which we are not going to be using. If any local politician has taken control of those wonderful marble and steel structures, throw his ass out onto the street. If you have no housing available, I suggest you get the public that needs housing to build the old wooden or Quonset type barracks that we all spent time in when we served in the military. Small but private rooms. We all did fairly well surviving that experience, right?"

"We sure as hell did, Chief."

"If you have no questions, keep me posted on how you are doing. Let me know the problems you are facing so that we can take steps to alleviate those. If I am being too rough on the citizens, use your own judgment and relax the rules a bit. But not too much. Good luck, Ross and thanks for your loyalty through the years."

"The reading of all good books is like a conversation with the finest minds of past centuries."
—**Rene Descartes**

CHAPTER TWENTY-ONE

Later in the afternoon, a twin engine plane landed on the field and the CP notified Robert that Sarah and her husband, Hans Frick had landed together with Monty Wyatt and his wife Tracy. Within minutes they were seated in his office very excited over their move to Illinois. Robert's first question to Sarah was how soon could she get her intelligence office operating. She said that she fully expected to have it completely installed and producing information by the following morning. Robert suggested that possibly she was being a bit overconfident but she replied that she had found a fellow that can do almost anything electrical and he was coming in on the next plane with all the gear.

"Just who the hell is that? Electrical issues have always been our nemesis."

Sarah smiled and said, "His name is Del Sutton. I found him years ago."

Robert laughed. He knew that Sutton was one of Stuart's finds during the Exodus trip from Florida and he was a great find. "Del Sutton. Now there is a guy we really need here. This Base has been shut down for years and I can only imagine what shape the electrical system is in here. Thank God we have Del. Well, that is great news. Now before you get too busy and before hundreds of more people start showing up, I suggest you talk to the Base Housing Officer who is in operation in the building down the street and get your housing arranged. The CP can point out the Housing Office to you. Sarah, see me in the morning so we can discuss our plans."

Robert now directed his attention to Hans Frick. "How do you like this Base, Hans? This should fit into your area of responsibility quite well."

"Robert this is perfect. I did peek into the hangar and was amazed at what I saw in there. I have four larger aircraft coming in this afternoon and tomorrow morning with people and equipment and this Base can handle our operation very well. I would like to talk with you in the next day or so and discuss your vision for the Aviation Department so if and when you have time, give me a shout. I will be on the Base helping Sarah or going over the hangar facilities and equipment. I will see you whenever you have a moment. By the way, the runways need a bit of cleaning and patching but they can handle what we have coming in here without suffering anymore damage. I will be working on that in the next few days as well."

"Glad to hear it, Hans. Now Monty, I spoke with Perry this morning and gave him a ton of work to do. He is quartered over in the BOQ but I believe he has an office either in this building or one of the next ones. He is going to need your help and is expecting you. The CP Ranger can tell you how to find him. In closing, let me welcome you all to Scott Field to begin a fresh start with this country."

Later in the day two more flights came in from Riverton and Portland carrying among others, Beth Sloan, Anders and Clay Daley with the Portland staff. The CP had directed Beth to Robert's office and sent Clay and the others to Base Housing to set up their quarters and to meet with Robert at 9:00 in the morning after his meeting with Sarah. Robert had left Anders a note to set up his offices in the administration building and to see him after lunch. Within minutes of Beth checking in with the Command Post, she was up in Robert's office. He pointed to a chair in front of his desk and told her to make herself comfortable.

"Robert, you seem to have picked a great location for the new government. I totally agree with your selection of the center of the country for our nation's capital. The mere thought of the Washington-New York elite mentality guiding the country sends us up the wall. Enough is enough."

"Yes, Beth. It should be interesting to see how Washington handles this with all of their wasted empty buildings. I suggested to Perry that he consider setting them up as homes for the homeless. A decent alternative use for them. I do want to set up part of the former capital as a national park. Mainly to preserve the monuments to our founders that are all over the place and also the memorials to our fighting men from previous wars. Those are worth preserving. About the only thing in D.C. that is worth preserving. The National Archives hopefully are still there as well but very likely they suffered at the hands of the animals that raged in the streets there unrestrained. But that will be it. No bureaucrats. They are a thing of the past. We must exercise great caution that they don't sneak back into business here in Illinois." Robert paused for a moment to get his thoughts together.

"There are a number of items I wanted to speak to you about. First of all, get together with Anders and set up your office in this building somewhere in proximity to where Anders will be. When I am in town, which I plan to be most of the time, I will be right here in this office. By the way, the phone system does work and we will have a current phone directory out soon so that we can locate one another."

"Now let us talk about the schools that we are going to need immediately across the country. Many of the buildings have been destroyed and there was very little education being performed before and after the collapse of the government so it will be like starting over again to even think about educating the young people of this country. For openers, I do not want a national school system of the sort we had before the collapse. They were just bureaucrats who produced a dumbed down nation. I want the cities, counties and States running the show and they'd better run it right. I see the nation's government of the future as not an active participant in the school rebuilding process, rather limited to the duties specified in the Constitution and ensuring compliance of all with the new Constitution. What I want from you is a basic school curriculum established for the teachers to follow in teaching. Again reading, writing, history, mathematics, the sciences and the morals course. History means real history, American history, no make believe history. You know the program. We name the courses, broad outlines of the courses and they do the teaching using textbooks that they publish at their cost. We provide the topical material for the text books but the locals produce them. We do need unity across the country in what material is being published, especially for the basic courses such as history, math, the sciences, literature, and so forth. We only verify the material the books contain to ensure that they meet the criteria of honesty and relevance that we establish. The courses will be the basic courses we stressed up in WestPac. Plus the Morals courses that we added later. Make damn sure they don't try to give short shrift to the Morals courses. Watch for that. There are many people in the country today that will use most any trick to keep Morals training out of the schools. No teachers Unions either. Teachers report to the local school boards. Watch for State Offices that are trying to take over the education function in the States. Schools are locally operated with some direction from your office alone. If people try to interfere with that process including the morals program, find those people and have Perry send them to retraining centers. I am not going to put up with that nonsense and end up with millions of kids running around uncontrolled by any personal measure of what is right and what is wrong."

"Your job as the National Education Administrator is just to see that those courses are, in fact, being taught. This is a little less encompassing than what you were doing in WestPac but what I am trying to avoid is setting up another Department of Education that produced nothing other than thousands of bureaucrats primarily involved with social engineering. Should you find that any city, Town or State is ignoring your demands that the materials we want in the courses be taught, you report that failure to Perry's staff and they will find someone that will see that the courses are being taught. If they don't we will replace them. So, figure out your courses of study for all grades through high school. Hire your staff to write the drafts for the books. Have the local Boards then get them printed up and distributed to the schools. Then send your staff out to meet with the local administrators and verify that they are doing the job."

"As for colleges and higher education, I want you to inform the administrators of those institutions that they will no longer be havens of left or right wing political doctrine. Professors and administrator's wages will be reasonable and college costs will be within the reach of everyone. If they are not, we will adjust them. There are thousands of men and women qualified to teach at the college level that will take the job for a reasonable salary. College profs will teach and the only politics taught will be political science, taught the way it should be taught. Let the administrators know that if the old style leftist college prof shows up again, both that prof and the administrator will be gone. I don't care if they are private or publicly funded colleges or universities."

Robert paused and then continued. "By the way, there will be no nationally funded colleges or universities so I am talking about state funded. If they show a lack of interest in abiding by the new rules, let Perry's troops know so that changes can be made immediately. Also let the administrators know that professors teach. They do not work part time and draw full time pay. They do not have a consulting business on the side with an office in the college or university. They teach or they are gone. I would control that by allowing not more than ten percent of a college professor's income to be from outside sources. One more thing in the secondary schools, physical punishment is permitted provided it is used sparingly and with restraint. If that does not work, send the kid out for retraining and not back to the parent that screwed him up. You cannot have disruption in the classroom and expect to teach anything. Other than that, you are on your own.

Use your own very good judgment in carrying out your duties. If you find this new program, as I have outlined it, as too restraining, let me know and maybe we can make some changes. Any questions?" Beth had none and said she would be in touch and left.

Anders came in after lunch and Robert was eager to talk with him. Robert's secretary Toni was now in the outer office working on her computer and he told her to hold the calls and have anyone that wanted to talk with him come back in a few hours. Robert motioned for Anders to sit down and told him to make himself comfortable.

"Anders, I'm running in circles and all I can do is hope that I am not screwing things up too badly. Running WestPac was one thing but running the entire country is a totally different ball game."

"I doubt you could screw it up worse than it was."

"Anders my biggest problem is that I have no patience with people anymore. I am very disappointed in the reactions of many Americans in how they are dealing with adversity. So damn few are willing to pick up the shovel and clean up the mess. They want you to do it. It's right in their back yard but they want you to do it."

"Sign of the times, Robert. We trained them for years to look elsewhere for solutions rather than from themselves. This is what we get. It will most likely take years to change them back. By the way, I did hear that you are getting a bit more autocratic. One of the Rangers that is working on setting up the prison system was commenting. Not bitching. Just observing. I couldn't really tell if he was in favor of your move to the right or not. Most of the people realize we have to be strict right now and don't have the time to pussyfoot around. Stuart went through the same damn thing. He started out as sort of a Liberal and by the time he arrived in Montana he was the boss and there was no voting on issues. I'm sure you remember that."

"I do, Anders, and I enjoyed it. Stuart just realized that if you wanted to get something done, you did it yourself or you ordered it done. That is what he did. No discussion. No argument. Do it. Yes, I suppose I have moved farther to the right politically. Just let me know if you think I am going too far. May not do any good but I will allow you to do that." Robert laughed as did Anders. "When everything is all screwed up Anders, you have to make decisions and expect them to be carried out now not later. Otherwise, you just continue the problem and the confusion that results. We can't afford that. That is my opinion anyway."

Robert told Anders about his discussions with Perry and Beth on the prison system and education. Anders agreed with the prison program for now but in time the public would be raising hell about it. "Too many people being incarcerated and in time that will be a problem. As for education, that would be the same. Americans in general want to have a say in how their government is run and most particularly with respect to education. I think they will agree with your main points but they are going to want to have a say with respect to how the schools teach and what they teach. As you know, that has always been a hot issue with the public. They are going to want that Constitution and a voice in government. You might as well as plan on it."

"I know. I have been thinking about it. I thought I would meet with the Study Group we set up in Florida and get them working on a Constitution but I have some definite changes I want to put in there. I do not want to get back into the situation where criminals had more rights than law abiding citizens, or more attorneys, or more privileges in jail than people on the outside. As you know, I also have views on freedom of speech, the right to vote and other so called basic rights. Remember when the left was hollering for the basic right to free medical treatment. Look where that took us. It turned out to be a Basic Right into financial ruin."

The two men spent two hours discussing various aspects of the new government and problems they would be facing with the many shortages plaguing the nation. Not enough food, housing, clothing, jobs, lack of health care and many more. After Anders left, Robert had Clay Daley come to his office and he told him to contact Bill Phillips of the original Study Group who were still in Riverton to come to Scott field and to bring the library materials and the other members of the group with him. The sooner the better. Robert also told Clay to remind Phillips that Irene Covington was no longer a member of the group.

For the next month, Robert was busy putting out fires. Conflict had reignited in a number of areas of the former nation that had recently been retaken. That was to be expected as the advancing WestPac forces frequently bypassed areas that were not completely cleaned out.

Shortages continued to plague the new nation and again transportation was a major problem in solving the shortages. Rail lines were damaged, missing, or lacked repair materials and the same problem plagued the road system preventing rapid movement of supplies transported by truck. Economic development lagged behind the need for virtually all materials. Steel production was just beginning to arise from its long sleep. Food production was slowed by the shortage of diesel fuel and tractors. For every want there were ten reasons why it could not be satisfied. Robert searched for and finally found an Economics Minister to deal with those problems. He, of course, needed a staff and Robert told himself, "Here we go again." Robert called the Economics Minister in and told him that he could have a staff of five people. No more, period.

Robert was extremely busy throughout this transition period and the harder that he worked, the more the complaints kept coming in. He had even considered passing on the reins of power to others but there was no one that he could trust to manage the country intelligently and fairly. He was even beginning to consider reestablishing a democratically elected representative form of government but he knew that was creating the same self destructive force that had led to the demise of the former great nation. But the more he thought about it, the more he concluded that with proper safeguards in the new Constitution a quasi democratic federal republic could be made to work.

Possibly it could be drafted up to include provisions that came into place if and when the new government began to outgrow permissible boundaries of some sort. That expansion would trigger automatic events that would revert the government back to where it started from. He didn't know how that would work or how it would be drafted up or how it would be set up. That would almost have to be created by fiat. Were it to be subjected to popular vote or to a commission, the politicians would see it as a juicy plum for them to feather their own nest. It could only be created by a complete dictator. One who had ultimate power and authority in his own hands. It all began to make sense to Robert. He had retained complete power in the decision making aspect of the new government and he must not relinquish that power until the most perfect form of democratic republic possible was created.

A new government, to succeed, needed to negate the natural weakness of a democracy to destroy itself. The new America that was just now emerging from years of obscurity after the collapse of the old America, needed the protections of a Constitution that would last. At the time of the collapse, that existing America had few similarities with the America of the early eighteenth century when the likes of Jefferson, Madison, Franklin, Adams and their associates were still in charge. This new America had to be protected from the likes of Turner, the bureaucrats and the many opportunists that saw in it vast opportunities for exploitation and profit making.

Robert swore on the lives of all the Rangers lost in the battles to recapture the country that he would not let the country be lost from within again.

Robert met with Anders a number of times to discuss the concept of automatic regeneration of freedom and liberty for all. At first Anders considered it an idea that would not see the light of day but after further discussions and giving it a great deal of thought, Anders began to see it as a viable solution to the well known fact that any pure democracy was doomed to fail. In the end, the politicians promise themselves right out of existence. They can never deliver all the things they promise their adoring public in order to stay in office. In their final moments of existence they destroy the very democracy that gave them all of their wealth. They literally eat themselves out of existence. That is the nature of the beast.

Bill Phillips and the other three members of the study group had arrived at Scott Field two weeks prior to Robert calling them in for a meeting. They had set themselves and their library of materials up in the administration building and were busy getting organized in the new facility when Toni told them to report to Robert's conference room at 1:00 p.m. When Robert walked into the room, they all stood and he welcomed them to Scott Field. After being assured that they were all getting situated without major problems in the new facility, he began explaining to them the situation in the country as he saw it. The country remained somewhat unstable but they were making progress. It was going to take a long time before they would be able to say, "Problems solved" but they were getting there.

Robert told them that the time was coming when he would not be around to guide the country in its further development. He had been at it too long and it was beginning to take its toll on him. He had concluded that his final duty to the country was to create a national government that could withstand the assaults of human nature. That being man's insatiable desire for more power and more wealth, That is an uncontrollable constant demand in the soul of man. Not everyman.

"There is the occasional true holy man running around wanting to sacrifice everything he has or will have for his fellow man. There are at least two that I know of. There is one in Ohio and another somewhere out West. I forget their names." Seeing the serious looks on his listeners, Robert admitted he was kidding about the two men. "They do not exist, sad to say."

He paused for a moment to let them digest what he was saying. "Now I have given this problem a great deal of thought and I have concluded that it may be possible to structure a form of government along the lines of our former Constitutional government, on a federal republic format. It would be written basically as it was before but with controls that could not be voided or changed by a majority vote of the citizens or by a unanimous vote of any court including a supreme court nor by any other means. This Constitution would differ in that it would contain limits of government size and power that would trigger automatic fall back positions of reduced size and less power or some other mechanism that would bring government back to the original purpose and size for which it was intended. I know I am speaking in very general terms and I am not yet clear in my own mind how this would be accomplished or how it would be structured. I do know that it would have to be done by executive order, by me, with your assistance and input, as no commission or representative body would be able to produce the pure product required. The inherent weakness of man would interfere."

"I want a Constitution that will provide as many guarantees as possible that the rights and privileges inherent in it will not be abused by the invasive power of politicians. Keep in mind, many politicians much smarter than any one of us will be studying this document to see where they might be able to penetrate its defenses for their own benefit, to increase their power, or to augment their wealth. I will lay out a few of the specifics that I want the document to contain but those are not the only changes. I want you to add changes that you would consider necessary to provide meaning and effectiveness to the document."

"This is what I want you men to work on. First of all, do you generally see where I am going with this?" Obviously the project had only been described in broad terms and the men were confused but they did see generally what Robert was after. He continued, "Do any of you think that you would not be able to produce a Constitution of the nature I have described to you that would be put into existence by my order alone?" No one indicated that they could not work on the project. Robert went on. "I have great respect for the original Constitution of the United States and I would expect that we would start from that point in the rebuilding process. Start at the beginning of that document, then the Amendments thereto, the Bill of Rights. Study each word, each phrase, consider improvements, deletions and constantly revise as you see fit."

"This brings up the matter of the Case Law that has interpreted the Constitution. It is my present intention to void all case law prior to the date of the New Constitution. Some or maybe even all of those cases that interpreted the Constitution may need to be incorporated in whole or in part in the new document. Let me take one example, Issues dealing with Race. I want to see wording in the new document negating any preferential treatment of any race, sexual orientation, or religion. We are henceforth all Americans. Not one better than another. Wording to that effect, better drafted, will incorporate most court rulings dealing with racial issues. As for the religion issue in the wording I just gave you, there is no doubt that this country was founded on the Judeo-Christian ethic. That history should be honored, respected and continued. Our morals course that will be taught in the schools will be based on Christian Ethics. That is not intended to be a religion course. It is intended to be a principles of human behavior course. We will continue to follow the dictates of separation of church and state but with reasonable restraint and that must be drafted into the Constitution. We will not follow that policy to the point that we attack every vestige of Christianity in our nation as was occurring in the years prior to the collapse. Christianity was inherent in the formulation of our initial Constitution and government. We do not have to ignore that fact. Christianity is part of our History and deserves our national respect. The Ten Commandments describe generally accepted ethical conduct and the fact that they are inscribed on tablets of stone is incidental. The first three commandments will stay but will not be drafted to refer to a particular religion. As for the Islamic Faith that we have so recently been at war with, If it is practiced and promulgated in compliance with generally accepted ethical values and does not foment preferential treatment based on gender, or religion, it is permissible. If it does not meet those tests, it will be prohibited. The Koran should be studied by our religious scholars to determine if it is amenable to the objectives of this Christian nation. If it is not, then it will not be placed on a par with the Christian Bible until it is rewritten to comply. There is no doubt it could be modified to comply and you may have to seek out appropriate people to handle that task. Those are just a few issues that you will be encountering in your work. I will now go through some of the matters that call for change in the new constitution."

"First, term limits on Representatives and Senators. We need those. Let us have three terms for Reps and two terms for Senators. Then they may not serve again during their lifetime."

"All citizens will be taxed on their income regardless of source and it will be based on a flat percentage. I say again, all citizens will pay tax on their income regardless of how small or large it is. The percentage will not change based on the type of income. There will be no deductions in the computation of income. All forms of income will receive similar treatment under the Tax Code."

"The government will operate on a balanced budget and may not spend more than it takes in by way of revenue."

"There will be no Administrative Law Courts. Agency rulings are no longer enforceable as there will no longer be any Administrative Agencies. If Congress passes any laws that were formerly regulations, then violations thereof will come under the scrutiny of the Federal Court System. The applicable courts will be the Federal District Courts, The Federal Appellate Courts and The United States Supreme Court. State Court systems will be, as before, established by state legislative bodies."

"There will be no government funding of any media outlet, TV, radio, or newspaper."

"The President will not be permitted to issue executive orders relating to or creating any office, or assignment of any person to any agency outside of the executive branch nor any office that historically required Congressional approval. Executive orders shall only be allowed when applicable solely to executive department matters and must be approved by Congress and the Senate within ninety days of promulgation or they shall thereafter be considered void."

"Lawful immigration to the United States will be strictly controlled and only those persons shall be admitted who meet the qualifications for admission. Preferential treatment for immigrants may be based upon education, work experience, particular expertise, financial standing or family relations presently residing in the United States who will agree to support the immigrant until they are self supporting. All candidates for admission must demonstrate the ability to support themselves for a period of at least three years without the assistance of any other person, entity or the government."

"Any person intending to be a candidate for the office of President of the United States must first prove to the satisfaction of a Federal District Court Judge at a hearing that he/she is, in fact, a natural born citizen of this country. Any natural born citizen of this nation may contest the evidence presented by the applicant and may also present evidence or challenge any document or testimony submitted on behalf of said applicant. The court may limit the number of opposition participants but only to avoid needless duplication of effort."

"The second amendment shall be rewritten into the Constitution to clearly state that all citizens have the right to carry arms at all times and at all places they so desire subject only to specific reasonably restricted areas nor shall they be permitted to carry while under the influence of alcohol or drugs. Reasonable exceptions to the locations where arms are permitted shall be clearly specified by State authorities and shall be supported by clear and convincing evidence justifying the need for the exclusion. A blanket exclusion as to a particular location such as a government office, a restaurant or bar where liquor is served or a location previously noted for such an exclusion will not be accepted without specific clear and convincing evidence supporting the exclusion."

"The tenth amendment shall be rewritten to protect the states from the incessant invasion by the federal government over state authority in matters primarily or solely of state interest. Unless the federal government is acting under the authority of a specific provision of the Constitution that gives to it the exclusive power to act, then the state has exclusive jurisdiction to act under that law. Statutes intended to provide equal or shared jurisdiction to both the states and the federal government shall be clearly written to show that intent and the need for the sharing of jurisdiction. Statutes that do not explain whether the state or the federal government has jurisdiction to administer the Statute shall be construed to be under the exclusive jurisdiction of the State."

"Make the requirements for Constitutional amendments so onerous as to make them extremely difficult to accomplish. As you draft, consider the many arguable exceptions to the right, limitation or protection you are involved with and do your best to forestall the need to change it in the future."

Robert continued his comments regarding the new Constitution. "The other amendments of the Bill of Rights have to be reviewed and amended as necessary to incorporate the above suggestions. Including provisions that establish common sense handling of criminal cases. Now keep in mind that we are going to have a criminal code that you will be drafting and it will be incorporated into the Constitution. That code will contain many of the proscriptions and rights that I have suggested or implied may be contained in the new Constitution here today." Robert put aside his notes and looked at the four men in the room.

"OK, that is it. I know you have questions or will soon have many questions and I will meet with you from time to time to discuss where we are at. I will likewise have additional comments on what I believe should be in the new document or should be deleted. Good luck and if you need anything from me, let me know." Robert then left the room.

The four men began gathering their notepads and materials together when one of them commented, "This is going to keep us busy for a while."

Robert returned to his office and Toni told him that Clay had wanted to see him when he returned if he had some time to spare. Toni told him that Clay wanted to talk to him regarding what Robert wanted him to tackle next. Robert told Toni to have him come up. This was as good a time as any.

Within minutes Clay was coming into Robert's office. Robert motioned for Clay to take a seat and then asked him if he was getting situated in the new offices. Clay said he was and he had taken an office right down the hall from Robert's so that he would be readily accessible should Robert want him for anything.

Robert smiled and said, "In time you may consider that choice to be a mistake. There is so damn much that needs to be done that I don't really know where to start. My real problem, Clay, is that I have delegated out about a hundred rather important tasks to Perry, Sarah, Nix and everyone else and I am losing track of who has what. I do have notes on most of that. I did adopt that tactic in order not to get lost and I am going to find all of those notes and have Toni take them to you for sorting and review so that you know who has what. Then you can contact those people, get status reports from them and summarize periodic reports on their progress. Now how did you and your associates all come out working with the bureaucrats in and around Oregon, Washington, Idaho and California. I heard no squawks coming from the areas you were all involved with so I assume it went without any major hitches, right?"

"Robert, that is because the ones that were really bitching were all sent to retraining centers and not able to whine. Seriously we sent a number of them out for retooling. It amazed me that so many were not working with us to get their territory producing again. We all went out there expecting to find major cooperation from the bureaucrats in the field that had everything to gain and damn little to lose but such was not the case."

Robert shook his head. "Clay, that is exactly what I found in my travels and I discussed that with Anders just yesterday. I frankly was depressed by what I had seen and heard. Where the hell is that grisly American out there on his horse eating raw meat, drinking from streams and sleeping on the hard ground. He is dead. Deader than a door nail. We are left with a bunch of over fed porkers who just want to sit in their big office and wonder where they will be able to scam another fortune from this new administration." Robert paused. "Now, I'm being a little hard on them. There are some damn good men out there too and our job is to find them, put them on our team and get the job done."

"That is what we did find as well. Under every pile of dirt was a gold nugget. In every city where we had problems, we concluded that we had located someone to push the load and get the job done. A lot of women as well, I might add. I think many of them were more pissed about the situation we all found ourselves in than did the men. There are some very sharp people out there and when it comes time to bring people into this government, we can produce some very qualified candidates. All four of us have people like that. We talked about that quite a bit. By the way, Robert, those three guys are mega producers. They got more rail lines laid, boosted more production, saw that more crops were planted, everything than I did. But I'm taking up your time. What sort of activity do you have in mind for me and the others?"

Robert went over the conversations and instruction that he had passed out to Perry and Beth Sloan. "Clay I want you to make the rounds of the new territory in the East that we have retaken in the recent campaign. I want you and your team to do basically what you did in the West. Get those communities and cities up and operating. Rail lines, trains running, roads repaired, housing, jobs, production, all of that. Divide the country up into four packages and you guys go out there and kick some ass. See how the young kids are doing. If they are just doing drugs and getting laid, get them involved in fixing the country. If that doesn't work, tell them to join the military and make something of themselves. If they still don't see the light, send them to Retraining for the Basic Course for people that just need motivation. Let's not let them destroy themselves. You have the authority to hire, fire, call for shipments of food, fuel, clothing, what have you if you see that the local economy is not getting sufficient help. Check on coal production up there in West Virginia. We need that. See if they have decent rail lines to haul the coal out of there and coal cars, diesel, whatever they need. We need that coal to get the electrical grid up and operating around the country and West Virginians need what that coal can buy, food, clothing, housing, automobiles, you name it. That sort of problem applies across the country. But remember the basics, those communities must work to improve their condition. That means they build the housing, they produce the food, they fix the rails, etc. Now stay in touch and send summaries to Toni so she can type them up and I can read them. I never could read your writing. Take some vouchers and get cars for you and your men. Also, carry weapons. That's rough country out there and you don't want to go around unarmed. Make sure that you discuss your proposed routes with Ross Perry. Some areas have not been totally tamed as of yet and you could find yourself as the main course at the barbecue. As to when to get going on this, I would think tomorrow would be early enough."

"Sounds good to me Chief. I will gather the boys, give them the info you gave me and send them out. They prefer the wild life out there to sitting around drinking beer here anyway. As for me, I like activity."

"Be careful out there Clay and if it looks like you are getting into a problem with the locals, have Perry send a team over to help you out. Don't call him when it is too late, OK? He can send a team by plane and they can be there in hours or minutes so use that. I don't want to have to train some other jackass into your job."

"Trust me, Robert. I take good care of myself." Clay picked up his files, shook Robert's hand and said "See you in a month or so. If you need me before then, tell Toni and I will make sure she and Com knows exactly where I am."

When Clay had left, Robert thought for a moment that he had made another mistake. He enjoyed having Clay around as he knew what Robert liked and didn't like and he added a special tone to the mood around the office. There was no doubt that Toni considered Clay a very special member of the management team He was quietly competent which was a rare attribute among most men.

In a year or more, Robert figured that he could pull Clay out of the somewhat risky work of traveling around untamed country without some security. He would talk to him in a week or so and find out what he was running into. If it was rough country as he suspected it might be, he would have Perry assign a couple of men to make sure he was protected. He would do the same for the others. As he thought more about it, he thought what the hell and dialed Perry's phone number. He soon had Ross on the line and conveyed to him the concerns that he had for Clay and his team. Ross totally agreed that wandering around the newly retaken land was no picnic.

Ross and his troopers had been fired on too many times to count and he figured Clay and his men would be even better targets for the Muslims or the local gang leaders that had lost their turf. A number of Rangers had already lost their lives across the country since it was said to have been pacified. It took some time to settle the West in years past and it would take longer to settle the vast plains of the former country. He said he would immediately get a hold of Clay and assign eight of his top guns to Clay's team and further would provide them with good communications gear that could bring help with short notice should it be needed. He would tell Clay to stay put until the men showed up which would be later this very day.

The following morning, Toni rapped on his door and stepped in. She had talked to Clay and he was leaving at that time with his security detail. Clay, of course did not consider the assignment of security to him to be a necessary precaution but Toni clearly did. She had access to Sarah's intel briefs and knew what was going on around the country. She looked at Robert and said, "I think that was a very good decision to assign security to Clay and the other guys. He would be damn hard to replace not only for you but for many people here that know what a class act he is. Thanks, Robert." She gave him a salute and left. Robert thought for a moment. "Well, that was interesting." He wondered if Clay and Toni were becoming an item. He thought about his comment that no one should be screwing around in the office. He concluded that his comment did not extend to normal human interaction. He was really talking about wild parties rather than serious friendships. He would leave it at that.

Within one month the Administration Staff from Riverton and Goodland had been transplanted to Scott Field and were operating as before. Sarah's Intel team were all on duty day and night in the administration building and the Intelligence Reports were being published and sent out as before. The shortage problems continued to exist but gains were definitely being made. Louis Donley had increased production of scarce fuels and was shipping tanker cars across the United States to fuel depots for transshipment to factories and retailers. One problem they were running into was that of sabotage. Intentional derailing of tanker cars and starting fires in storage tanks. Perry had increased the security for fuel deliveries and they had killed or captured a large number of the culprits responsible for the damage. Most of those captured were former Muslim troops continuing the battle or were from smaller anti-government political groups. They were all sent to retraining centers and put to work producing products needed by the new government. If the retraining was not taking hold, the non-cooperatives with Muslim origins were just loaded on boats or planes and returned to the Mid-East. Some of the Mid-East countries were no longer taking them back in which case they were loaded onto Military aircraft, given a parachute and booted out the door over their country of origin. In time the occurrences of sabotage had decreased to rare isolated instances. Furthermore, shipment of petroleum products was now being handled by large ocean going tankers that were hauling from Houston to Charleston, New York and Seattle avoiding the risk attendant with rail transit for thousands of miles through all parts of the country.

Rail transportation had grown exponentially. It was by far the most economical mode of transportation from the point of view of diesel fuel usage and diesel fuel was always a matter of concern. Truck transportation had been growing as well as that was the prime mover of products from storage area to consumers.

Hans Frick had called Toni to set up a time for him to meet with Robert. On the day of the appointment, Hans showed up and was ushered into Robert's Office.

"What's on your mind, Hans? I'm sure you are up to your ears in alligators as everyone else is.

"You might say that, Robert. What I need right now are some air bases where I can base my flying units. We accumulated quite an Air Force in the course of our combat around the country and I need at least two bases where I can keep the aircraft and crews, do the maintenance and do operational flying. I have two former Air Force bases in mind that would work very well and would like to grab them before someone else does. I was thinking of Warner Robbins Air Force Base for my transports and drones and Tinker in Oklahoma city. We may need more in the future depending upon what happens with respect to the West in the future. Also Wright-Patterson at Dayton, Ohio possesses a wealth of technical and aeronautical science talents and materials that we should not let go to waste. I would like to get that reactivated and again forging ahead with innovation and modernization. Your comments?"

"Sounds good to me, Hans and remember to maintain a good transport unit right here at Scott. Obviously we are going to need it. You can pass the word that I approve your taking over the facilities you mentioned. Good luck."

Robert mentioned the take over of the bases to Ross and he agreed with the picks.

Ross also mentioned that he had his eye on three bases for his ground military units. They were Bragg Army Base in North Carolina, Fort Benning in Georgia and Campbell Army Base in Kentucky. These bases were already set up for his units and were ideal locations for training troops. Robert gave him the go ahead as well.

Robert had taken on the additional task of giving a national address via TV, radio and Internet at least once a week. He would provide a synopsis of the intelligence data that was being produced by Sarah and her staff with respect to conditions around the world and within the United States. Conditions in the country were slowly stabilizing. It was obvious that problems would continue for the next several years as shortages slowed down the economic progress of the nation. Internationally, the situation was much worse. Many large formerly advanced Countries of the world were still in a condition of complete disarray with disparate units in charge of smaller areas of the former Countries. The largest controlling faction in most of the Western European Countries were the Muslims. They were clearly very well united in their goals and were autocratically controlled right down to the single combat soldier. It was obvious that maps were being redrawn every day. There was very little international travel and less reason for anyone to attempt it. The European Continent remained in a general state of anarchy except for the Muslim controlled areas. There were pockets of stability particularly in France and Germany. Switzerland was leading the European Countries in reestablishing stability and security and they had prohibited Muslim immigration right from the start. Swiss troops had taken control immediately when the country began falling apart. Both France and Germany had internal problems with diverse ethnic groups, other than the Muslims, that were in constant turmoil and conflict which aggravated the instability in those two countries. In recent years, both Countries were making some headway, particularly Germany which had established a nucleus of autocratic control of the population. In the Far east, Japan was forging ahead of the other Countries of the Region. China had suffered severe instability in the global economic collapse as its society was undergoing massive social changes brought about by a surging democratic movement at the same time as the economic system was in turmoil. Their saving feature was their autocratic government that did not tolerate disruption. Conditions among all world governments appeared to be improving with time. The primary mode of communication between countries of the world was by way of the Internet. Virtually everyone in the

United States communicated primarily by way of the Internet. Hard line telephone service had come back somewhat in larger cities but seemed to have stalled. It was considered something of the past by most Americans. Many people had or were getting the pocket solar phone which seemed to work the best. Postal mail service was also a thing of the past. Private mail and delivery service had replaced government service.

Robert had followed global events for some time with great interest. It was obvious that world peace continued to be threatened by the extent of instability across the globe. As long as the countries of the world were suffering internal conflict, the chances of war breaking out between Nations was a very serious and present danger to all Nations on the globe, particularly when all Nations were suffering from lack of food and material goods.

In Robert's addresses to the nation he was beginning to describe certain tenets of the forthcoming Constitution so that when it did come out, it would not be a major disruptive event. Even his discussions of the document created a buzz in the nation. There was no public dissent being published in newspapers or on the Internet as that was forbidden but for most people it was a popular conversation piece. The major points regarding the Constitution that Robert had spoken about to the Study Group were the items that he was bringing up in his speeches. For the most part, the public agreed with his positions as they too had been irritated by the antics of the former politicians and their abuse of the Constitution.

An item that Robert mentioned in one address that caused a bit of a stir across the country was his intention not to provide voting rights for all. There were criteria to be established laying out the qualifications for a citizen to vote. Robert mentioned that one of these criteria would be that only those that actually paid a reasonable amount of taxes would be able to vote. In view of the fact that he had already informed everyone that all citizens would be paying taxes provided they had some income, that did not cause too great a stir but his further criteria that they had to pay taxes at a certain minimal level to qualify to vote or they had to own property did ruffle some feathers.

Robert utilized his following address to the nation to further examine that issue. "I want you all to understand my reasons for limiting the right to vote to various qualifying requirements. One of which is that in order to vote, one must own property. That would include a house, real estate, a company that produced revenue from the sale or creation of a product, or some other identifiable entity, tangible or intangible, that demonstrated a specified value or worth of sufficient value to qualify. My thinking is that we want people voting who have a stake in the country. They at least have something to protect and in doing so, they would be protecting the nation. We lived in a nation before the collapse where voting was being conducted primarily by people who had no stake in the country or in anything they owned. Just prior to the collapse of that government, around fifty per-cent of the population paid nothing in income taxes and the result was that they were easily used by any demagogue that came along and promised them benefits that would presumably be paid for by those who produced. In time, the demagogue had the support of a majority of the voters with minimal effort and he could do virtually anything he wanted, whether it destroyed the country or not. I do not want to relive that experience."

After the address, he met with Anders. "Well, what do you think?"

"It sounded good to me, Robert. Keep in mind that there will always be someone that will bitch. I agree with your logic on who should vote and who shouldn't. Those that have nothing to lose in society are primarily interested in what there is to gain as they sure as hell aren't concerned about losing anything. You have explained your position quite well and I would just leave it at that. Don't start running around explaining and explaining every time someone starts to bitch."

"Not going to happen, Anders. There are other changes coming in the new Constitution that will produce more complaints than the voting issue. But, I do believe most Americans will approve of them, for example the Balanced Budget concept. If not, I may have to take a look at making some changes."

Anders nodded in agreement and then brought up another issue. "Robert, I just read over the Intel Bulletin. Have you seen it yet?

"No, I haven't had a chance to look at the Bulletin yet. Toni just brought it in. She had highlighted an article but I just hadn't yet read it."

"I'm not talking about the General Intel Bulletin that goes to everyone, I'm talking about the classified document."

"I haven't read that one either, Anders, but I do have it."

"There are reports coming in that they know where Turner may be hiding out."

"My God, Anders, I didn't know that."

"Ross Perry is checking that out right now and I think we should be talking with him and have a plan for how we are going to deal with Turner if and when he is in our custody. Personally, I believe we would be far better off if he put up a fight and was killed in the process. Otherwise, there is going to be a loud clamor for a public trial that could tear this country apart. Remember he had about a fifty plus percent popularity even when the country was falling apart. Furthermore, if you had a trial, what would the penalty be? A death penalty would create a further massive disturbance but to keep him alive would be even more dangerous. Maybe we should have Perry go in there and just finish him off and claim he was reaching for a gun. Even if we had a trial for him, this country might not convict him. He gave a lot of goodies that we paid for to a lot of people. What do you think?"

"I haven't even been thinking about that jackass. I was hoping he had been killed by someone somewhere as we have had no sighting of him for an awful long time. I agree. He is dangerous regardless of whether he is alive or dead. We cannot afford to have a jury trial for him. We can have a military trial if it gets down to that. We can pretty well structure that so that we limit our losses. Let's give Perry a call and find out what he knows about this."

Within minutes, Robert had Ross Perry on the line. "What do you know about Turner, Ross? Anders just brought me up to speed on this."

"Same here, Chief. I was informed just minutes ago that he is believed to be hiding in a monastery in South Carolina. I was about to contact Monty Wyatt and have him get a team together to go there and investigate. I'm glad you called as I was also about to call you. I have put a blanket over this information as I don't want the media to blow it all over before we decide on how to handle it but I don't know how far it may have gone before I learned of it. The media may already have this. Give me a few minutes to make some calls and find out what is known about this. I just hope word of this has not spread out to the wrong people. I also want to detail some troops around the area where he is said to be living to ensure that no one speaks to him and then starts blabbing that he wants to return as President of the United States to again pass out goodies to those that support him."

Robert and Anders continued talking over the problems presented by this reappearance of Turner and within a few minutes, Perry was again on the line with the latest information on Turner's location.

"Robert, I am told that Turner is living as a sequestered monk in a small religious community near Salem, South Carolina. That is a very small town in far western South Carolina, definitely off the beaten track. Word of his presence there comes from a former monk who left the group recently and who rather accidentally discovered who Turner was. This is a cloistered monastery where the monks live alone, raising crops and caring for their own livestock. No communication is allowed and we have no information on Turner's state of mind, whether he genuinely pursues the monastic life or if he is just hiding out."

"OK, Ross. Listen, put a blanket on this information for anyone that is not privy to it. This is very important. Stress that if anyone blows this story around, they will be in worse shape than Turner is. Get a hold of the monk that broke the story and see that he is secured somewhere and is not blabbing this to the media. The media would love to spread this around. They still hate us for taking away their privileged life style. Find out who all knows about it and how far this story has gone. We may be too late to stifle it, but let's find that out first. After we know that, we will decide what we are going to do. Also, get Monty Wyatt heading out to South Carolina with a small cadre of troops and have him pick up Turner if he is there. Best to get him before he knows that we are aware of where he is so he doesn't fly the coop."

About an hour later, Ross Perry was again on the line. "From what I am hearing, Robert, probably around a hundred people have been told that Turner is down in South Carolina. I would off hand say, that is more people than we would be able to silence on this issue. I think we should pick him up, put him in custody as a military prisoner and then Court Martial the guy for treason. That carries the death penalty. In the alternative, I would think that we would have to secure him somewhere that he had no communication with anyone and I don't know where the hell that would be. If he is alive and talking, he will be your biggest headache."

"OK, Ross. Here is what I think we have to do. Send Monty down there to pick him up. Tell Monty that we are definitely better off if this guy tries to defend himself and we have to shoot him. If that does come to pass, tell Monty to make it final, or I should say, terminal. That will be easier to explain than it will be to try him in a Military Court and then to sentence him to death. Tell Monty to get moving down there right now and get him back to Scott Field. No media interviews for the prisoner and keep him tightly under wraps. I don't want the media to know he is here either. Have Monty contact us as soon as he has him. Tell him to arrange a flight down there and I assume he will need choppers to get into the area that Turner is located in. OK?"

"Righto. Consider it done. I will let you know what is going on."

"Amateur bureaucrats are often even worse
than professional bureaucrats."
—**John McCarthy**

CHAPTER TWENTY-TWO

Monty Wyatt was meeting his squad of Rangers at the Scott Operations Office for the flight to Robbins Base in Georgia. From there they were going to board two helicopters for the flight to Salem. They had studied aerial photographs of the area of Salem where the monastery was believed to be located. There were suitable helicopter landing sites within a few hundred yards of the target destination. Monty had spoken with Perry's office regarding the information from the monk and learned that Turner was now using the name Brother Francis. There were only thirteen monks at the monastery and they never left the facility. The monk that came out with the story is now under wraps and being flown to Scott. He has been assured that he will be free to leave there just as soon as Turner is picked up. He seems to be cooperating with his temporary confinement.

Before they boarded the twin engine plane for the flight to Warner-Robbins Base in Georgia, Monty briefed the troops that they were on a very important mission and everything that they learned about the trip, saw or heard on the trip was Top Secret and was not to be disclosed to anyone. He also warned them to avoid any contact with media figures should they be in the vicinity of the destination or be present during any phase of the operation. He assured himself that all fifteen members of the squad were fully equipped for day or night combat operations in mountainous terrain.

When they were airborne, Monty Wyatt explained the details of the mission that they were on including the name of the man they were going to be picking up. They were advised that they would be changing to helicopters in Georgia and would then proceed to Salem's Tammassee High School where they would be landing on the baseball diamond or on another field used for football games if that appeared more suitable for the choppers. They would then use their own vehicles from one of the choppers to drive to the location of the monastery just a mile or two from the High School. Arrangements were already made to pick up the vehicles at Robbins.

Within an hour and a half of departing Scott Field, they were descending down to Robbins Field in Georgia. Weather had not been a problem on the flight and was not expected to be a problem going on to Salem in the helicopters. The choppers were starting their engines as Monty and his squad came down the ramp. The troops were loaded onto one helicopter while two armored personnel carriers were loaded onto the other. After a forty-five minute flight they circled the baseball field in Salem for landing. They immediately off loaded the vehicles from the second helicopter and then drove to the presumed site of the monastery using the GPS map data that Sarah had provided. Within ten minutes they turned off the highway and proceeded down a gravel road for another fifteen minutes before they came to a halt before a gate that was blocking further progress and was under the control of a person assumed to be a monk from the monastery.

Monty approached the attendant at the gate and introduced himself as an officer of the military and a representative of the Office of the President. He said he had to see Brother Francis on a personal matter and to please open the gate. The attendant paused, obviously confused as to what he was expected to do. He reached for the phone and Wyatt reached over and pulled the phone out of its connection in the wall. The monk was temporarily startled and Wyatt then informed him that they did not want to be announced before they arrived at the monastery. Wyatt then ordered one of the troopers to secure the monk and monitor the gate while they proceeded to the facility. From having looked at aerial photos of the facility, Wyatt did not expect to find any buildings other than the main housing structure and smaller buildings for the farm animals. They drove up to the main building and an older monk came out to see what was going on. It was not every day that an armored military vehicle showed up at the monastery.

The monk asked Wyatt his purpose in being there and Wyatt informed him that they were there to see Brother Francis. "Is he here in the monastery?"

"Yes he is but he is not allowed to have visitors. Our monks have taken vows of silence and any dealings they have must be done through me. I am Brother Mathew, the Abbot here in the monastery, and possibly I can help you."

"Sorry Abbot, my orders are to see Brother Francis and that is what I intend to do. Now where is he or do we have to locate him ourselves?"

"I'm sorry but I will have to get him for you. You are not allowed inside the monastery. This is a cloistered monastery and visitors may not enter. I will bring him out."

"Ok, troops surround the building. Make sure no one leaves the building. I don't want someone warning Turner if he is out in the field somewhere. Anyone leaving, detain them. OK, go get him and be back here in no more than ten minutes and if you don't have him here, we will enter the building and search the entire building and grounds."

Within ten minutes, the Abbot came out with another monk. The other monk was introduced as Brother Francis. Wyatt studied his appearance and had no idea if this was Turner or not. This monk had a full face, gray beard and could have been Turner but Wyatt could not be certain. He asked the monk, "Are you Frank Turner, the former President?"

The monk would not answer and the Abbot informed Wyatt that the monk would not speak as that would break the vow of silence that he had taken.

Wyatt thought for a moment and then told the Abbot that Brother Francis was going on a trip and would be gone for some time. He was wanted on serious criminal charges and would be returned if he was not the right person. They would be taking his finger prints and those would be checked out by others to verify his identity. The Abbot protested that Wyatt did not have the authority to remove the monk from the monastery and to immediately leave the property. Wyatt told his troops to cut the phone lines from the monastery and to prepare to leave immediately. He asked Brother Francis if he had any personal items that he would need for a possible extended stay. Wyatt was considering the possibility that Turner, if that was who he was, had medical prescriptions, or other such items, in his room that he would need. The monk made no reply so they cuffed Brother Francis, put him in the armored vehicle and departed the premises. They were in the helicopters and just lifting off when Wyatt saw two police cars entering the school grounds with their red lights flashing. Apparently the Abbot had been able to contact them and report what he considered to be an abduction.

When they arrived at Robbins, Wyatt had called ahead and requested that a barber be available to clean the prisoner up and give him a shave so that he could be identified. They also requested that finger printing equipment be available so that prints could be taken and sent to Scott for verification. Anders had maintained personal data including DNA and finger prints of a number of former government officials that would be facing criminal charges at some time in the future. Turner was definitely one of them. It was Wyatt's intention to clean up the prisoner, photograph him from all views and send the photos and fingerprints to Scott Field. If the identification came back negative, the prisoner would be sent by way of helicopter back to Salem and released. There was no doubt that this was the same Brother Francis as the monk had described. There was only one Brother Francis in the monastery. Whether he was President Turner or not would have to be determined.

They landed at Robbins, put a hood over the prisoners head and face and rushed him into the Operations Office where the barber was waiting. In fifteen minutes, the prisoner had the appearance of a completely different person. The photographs and the fingerprints were immediately sent to Scott Field and a report came back in minutes that this indeed was the former President, Frank Turner. Turner was then again hooded, cuffed and placed on the twin engine aircraft that had flown Wyatt's Squad to Robbins and they were soon airborne en route to Scott Field in Illinois. During his capture, clean-up and on the trip back to Scott Field, Turner maintained his silence. He did write a note for Wyatt to the effect that he was abiding by his Vow of Silence and further that he was entitled to have an attorney representing him. Wyatt only commented that he doubted he would have an attorney representing him as that was no longer considered necessary.

Robert was in his office when Sarah told him that Frank Turner was on his way to Scott Field and would be arriving in about two hours. She had already prepared a special cell and guards for him in the newly constructed prison wing. He was being totally secreted and would have no cell mates or neighbors in his secluded wing of the prison. Robert was surprised at his own reaction which he thought would have been more significant. He only said, "Interesting. Now we have to figure out what the hell we are going to do with him."

Anders came in behind Sarah and said, "We should figure this one out fairly soon as no matter what we do, soon the world will know we have Turner as a prisoner."

"I agree, Anders, and the problem is too damn many people already know that we have him. They can all be our people or people we trust but there are too many of them and word will eventually leak out. Someone will tell his wife or his best friend and it will go like that until everyone knows. At this point I am of the opinion that we have to give him a trial. If so, it must be a military trial and not open to the public. Not even the media. Furthermore, it must be soon. The sooner the better as if there is a delay, then the pressure will mount for a public trial. Have Perry assign a military tribunal, ASAP, complete with Prosecutor and Judge. We should be prepared to start trial in from one to two weeks. We all know what he did so that will not require a lot of preparation. We can issue summaries once a day of what took place in the hearing and then the final decision. I, personally, do not want a death sentence in this case. He deserves it but the fallout could be too great. Anders, do you want to handle this one. If so, get a hold of Perry and have him set up the Military Court Martial and do it soon. Also, let him know I am not wanting a death sentence here. How about you?"

"I agree Robert. But we may just end up with a death sentence anyway. Most thinking people would want that but the others would definitely raise a stink. Let's see what happens. You could always commute the sentence."

Anders and Robert continued discussing the process and decided it would be best to hold the Court Martial proceeding right on Scott Field. The Base was already a secured facility and it would be easier to control the publicity emanating from the trial on the base than from a public court room. There was a court room on the base adjacent to the new prison wing that had served the military in years past and that had been upgraded and rendered more secure for the number of prisoners they had been trying since they took over the Base. Military Rangers were placed on guard duty, both inside and on the exterior of the jail facility. There was no great concern of anyone attempting to rescue Turner but still security was in place should such an attempt be made.

Wyatt informed Robert of Turner's request that an attorney be assigned to him. Robert did agree to have a junior officer from the Ranger Battalion who had received legal training to act as his attorney. The Attorney was restricted to ensuring that the provisions regarding Court Martial procedures were observed. Evidentiary issues were limited to the Judge's determination as to what was fair and what was not fair for the Defendant. The older case law on what was admissible and what was not did not apply any longer. For example, Hearsay was not excluded provided the communication being offered into evidence was "reasonably reliable".

The prosecuting attorney was immediately assigned to the case by Ross Perry and he was a former attorney from the Army Judge Advocate General's staff. He was a very knowledgeable attorney and respected for his thorough approach to trial preparation. He immediately began assembling witnesses for the trial. Anders had accumulated a large number of witnesses that could be used in these trials of former government officials and he had files on their locations for easy reference. Many were former government employees and many were former citizens from pre-collapse times who were prepared to testify to the difficulties of trying to survive during the years of the Turner Administration. Chiefs of Police from a number of major cities were brought onto the Base to provide evidence regarding the out of control crime and the many deaths that resulted from the corruption going on in the Administration.

The defense attorney representing Turner requested the opportunity to question the various witnesses for the prosecution but this request was denied. Instead, he was provided a brief summary of the witnesses experience and the general topic of their testimony. The attorney complained that this was not sufficient and he would appeal. The prosecuting attorney informed him that there was no appeal from the ruling of this Court. The only recourse the defense attorney had would be to seek relief from Robert Thomas but the prosecutor advised against doing that unless it was truly a very important issue, one determinative of the final outcome of the case. "If I were you, I would save that to try to get a reduction from the sentence in the case. He is going to get convicted. Trust me."

The case was ready for trial in record time. Turner had not been on the Base for over two weeks when he was informed the trial would be starting in the following week. A special hearing building had been constructed for the offices for attorneys working on the case, meeting rooms for the attorneys and for their staff. A work room to provide document transmittal and copy services together with word processors, document transmittal machines, telephones and computers for Internet services was included. Rest rooms and quarters for overnight lodging of staff were available in the building. There were no facilities made available for the media as none were expected to be present for any phase of the trial.

The Court Panel consisted of seven military officers, all Rangers, as was the Prosecuting Attorney. The ranks varied from a Full Colonel to a First Lieutenant. There were other support personnel in the court room, all Rangers. There was one member of the general public who was present on behalf of Word of WestPac who would prepare daily summaries for distribution to the media who were hovering around the exits of the Base. The summaries would first be reviewed by Ross Perry's staff. That was the extent of the publication of the progress of the trial. Robert intentionally wanted to suppress the publicity the case could garner in order to diminish the status of the accused in the eyes of the public. In view of the limits on what the media could publish, there was very little furor raised over the manner in which Turner was being tried.

The question in Robert's mind was whether or not Turner would revoke his Vow of Silence and speak in his own defense. Robert hoped he would stick to his word, never to speak again, as that would make Robert's work just that much easier. "What a fool he is," thought Robert. "Sort of like the clowns that decide to go on a hunger strike when they should be reserving every ounce of energy they have to defend themselves from whatever or whoever is prosecuting them."

As the trial began and the evidence poured in concerning the massive corruption, blatant theft and graft that had been taking place in the Turner Administration. Witnesses testified that Turner not only knew of the massive theft of public treasure but that he was also threatening financial institutions and corporations with constant investigations and tax audits if they did not deliver large sums of money to Turner's political party as contributions. Turner used his Vice President, Boo Hicks as his bag man. The former Senator was considered an incompetent dolt by all who knew him but he was apparently adept at delivering messages and gathering up funds for his boss. Hicks was best known for making counter-productive public statements that invariably demonstrated his lack of intelligence. After one episode where he had led a fund raising event at a large Islamic Mosque, Hicks commented that "God does all the work, and we make all the money." It was after that comment that Turner was said to have told Hicks to "Keep your damn mouth shut, just take the money."

The pathetic part of the trial was at the end where the public witnesses testified that they had worked their entire lives building up lawful businesses and the taxes just kept rising to the point where they could no longer come up with the money to pay them. Particularly when they were also trying to cover the massive increases in runaway labor costs demanded by the all powerful unions who were in a "I help you and you help me" relationship with the Turner Administration, losing businesses that they had built up over their lifetimes that were basically stolen from them. Meanwhile the people that had contributed nothing to the economy of the nation were granted free medical care, free housing, and food stamps that could also be used to purchase liquor, jewelry, clothing, and most likely drugs. Hard working people were aware of what it was their taxes were paying for and they were angry, despising both the government and the people who took more and more of their hard earned money every day.

At the end of the evidentiary portion of the trial, it was clear that Turner would be looking at a guilty verdict unless a miracle occurred to prevent it. The officers went into deliberation and after two days of discussion and argument announced that they had reached a verdict. The main issue in the jury deliberations was whether or not to invoke the death sentence or to honor Robert's known request that the prisoner be given only a life sentence without parole. When they did issue their verdict, it was obvious that Turner was having second thoughts about not having spoken in his defense, assuming that he had such a privilege. He appeared to be under great stress and it was clear he had not been able to eat or sleep. He appeared haggard, exhausted and kept rubbing his eyes and scanning the room as though he was looking for a friendly face. When the verdict was about to be read and he was told to stand, he was barely able to do so. He had to balance himself in the process and had a grip on the railing that ran alongside his chair. He was found guilty on all counts and the court set a date for the delivery of the sentence in thirty days. Turner was familiar with the fact that these Court Martial cases delivered the sentence and carried it out on the same day so he figured he had thirty days left to live. He finally blurted out to anyone in the court room that was listening and broke his Vow of Silence. "Why don't they just shoot me right now? Why wait?" The Court admonished Turner to keep quiet. He would have an opportunity to speak at the sentencing. That was news to Turner and it clearly brightened his day. There was no mention of his outburst in the summary delivered to the media, at least in the final form after review by Perry's staff.

Robert heard the news of the verdict from Perry and also that Turner had finally spoken. He was also told that the Judge hearing the case was apparently going to allow the defendant to speak at the sentencing. Perry said that the speech would be suppressed in the published report so not to worry about that. Obviously the speech would be a diatribe against the present government and would serve no useful purpose whatsoever.

In the days following the trial, Robert was finally hearing from Clay Daley regarding his inspection of cities and towns in recently stabilized areas of the country. All of his team of officers were safe although all, had periodically been harassed and in two cases, even shot at. There was no doubt on their part that had they not had the protection of Perry's Rangers, they most likely would not be alive. There were areas of the country that were just not safe. In every one of those situations where the populace was not friendly and was downright dangerous, the Rangers called in a unit known as "Swift Strike". This well armed and experienced unit was choppered into the area and within days of being called, had the situation stabilized and under control. The Swift Strike troops were trained to deal with angry civilians, youth gangs or armed Muslims and were known for being able to deal effectively, fairly, forcibly and swiftly with whoever it was that was causing trouble. Robert had Sarah report the results of Swift Strike missions on Word of WestPac and Voice of WestPac so that their effectiveness would be known across the country.

Before they left an area that they were called in to suppress, they would first ensure that it had been pacified, that law abiding men and women were in charge and were providing security. Clay's team had been required to call in the Swift Strike Team on only five occasions as, generally speaking, their findings from their visits to cities and villages had been favorable or at least acceptable. There were certainly problems but most of the new leadership was goal oriented and progress was being made with respect to economic development. Crime continued to be a factor and particularly violent crimes continued as well. Clay pointed out that many of the murder victims had held positions of power with the FSP or the Muslims and vengeance may have been a factor in what led to the violence. Murders were committed at rates unheard of in prior times and were particularly violent. Murders frequently followed rapes. Even children were being raped and then murdered at alarming rates. When the culprit involved in murders was caught and tried before a Military Court Martial, upon conviction they were immediately taken to the gunnery range and made to pay the penalty. The time interval between arrest and being at the gunnery range was usually approximately ten days. These child rape murder cases were highly publicized together with photos of the defendant being cut down by the bullets and as a result, the frequency of occurrence of this particular crime was dropping rapidly. Perry attributed that to the widespread publication of the penalty phase.

There were a number of cases scheduled for the new court house at Scott Field. The facility had worked out so well, they wanted to put it to use in cutting down the number of cases that were awaiting a hearing. There were ten corruption trials of defendants that were formerly on Turner's staff, including Boo Hicks. These men were all eventually housed in the prison at Scott that had been expanded quite a bit so that each prisoner was housed in a single cell. That was not to provide comfort to the prisoner, it was to prohibit collusion among the prisoners. The cells were sound proofed and were separated sufficiently one from another to render communication between them to be virtually impossible. Every cell was built alongside another cell but the adjoining cells opened to a different corridor so there were solid walls between all cells. Again, the cells did not provide radio, TV, or internet availability. They were furnished with a desk, a chair, a notepad, pen, a Bible, a bed, a toilet, sink and an overhead light. Once a day, they were hooded, handcuffed and taken to an exercise yard where the hood and handcuffs were removed. They could then walk, run and or exercise for one hour and then again, handcuffed, hooded and returned to their cell. They were not provided an attorney but were provided with a printed pamphlet laying out the Court Martial procedure, charges against them and the maximum penalty for the charges alleged. There was a notation that Death Penalties, when adjudged, would be carried out immediately by ten man firing squads. Rules of Behavior in the court room were also appended and they informed the accused that they had no right to speak in the court room without permission of the Trial Judge and then only relating to something said by the Prosecutor or the Judge. Media were never allowed to be present at any of the trials. Only the witness from Word of WestPac was allowed to be present provided that the defendant was a highly visible figure from the Turner Administration and sometimes not even then. Guards were present at all times within view of all prisoners and there was no conversation allowed between prisoners and guards. Any violation of that led to a ten day prison sentence for the guard followed by termination of his job.

The day arrived when the verdict in the Turner Case was to be read. Robert did not attend the court proceeding but Perry did and reported that Turner appeared even more haggard than previously reported. He was gaunt, very nervous and was obviously expecting to receive the death penalty. When the penalty of life in prison without parole was announced, he appeared confused and looked over at his legal counsel for an explanation. He could not believe he had not been sentenced to death. In his confusion, he totally forgot to read his prepared statement or possibly his statement no longer had relevance. He was given multiple life sentences with no chance of parole. There was no mention as to where he would serve his prison sentence but Perry told Robert that it would be in total seclusion at a site not yet selected. The news item released to the media merely stated that Turner had been found guilty on seven separate felony counts and that he was given a life sentence without possibility of parole. There were to be no further public statements regarding Turner. As far as the public was concerned, Turner had just died.

"America's state religion, is patriotism, a phenomenon which has convinced many of the citizenry that 'treason' is morally worse than murder or rape."
—**William Blum**

CHAPTER TWENTY-THREE

In order to stabilize the national economy, it was decided to establish gold as the foundation for the WestPac dollar, now referred to as the National Dollar. How that would be done was a difficult problem for Robert and his staff to solve. It was finally decided that there would no longer be any private holdings of gold allowed. All gold would be the property of the nation's Treasury Office and would be secured at Fort Knox where gold had been held until previous administrations accessed portions of those holdings. Some of the stolen gold had been recovered but it was suspected that thousands of ingots remained in the possession of thieves associated in one way or another with the Turner Administration. Robert issued an order that all gold was to be turned into the government in exchange for National Dollars. One delivered ounce of gold would receive five hundred National Dollars in return. The international market value of gold was obviously much higher but a portion of that was also the result of inflation and not a true reflection of the value of the products it could buy.

The immediate effect of the trading price of five hundred dollars an ounce was to produce increased value for the National Dollar. There obviously were holdings of gold that were not turned into the new Treasury Office and a secondary Black Market immediately developed for trading in gold. Perry's military units cracked down on these trading houses and soon they became very hard to find. Also known holdings of gold were confiscated after the allowed time interval elapsed leaving the owner with nothing for his investment. These activities spurred cooperation on the part of the public to voluntarily turn in their private holdings of gold. As the National Dollar increased in value on the world market, more National Dollars were printed to bring its value back down to the issue valuation. In time the economy began to stabilize and trading became more predictable with the National Dollar that was also being recognized by the world market as the primary means of exchange.

The world economy continued to be in very bad shape with low production, high unemployment and high inflation in most of the larger countries. As they began to shift over to the National Dollar, their economies began to stabilize quite a bit but still were producing at non-acceptable levels. In the United States, the economy was growing at a fast rate. Production of hard goods and commodities was rising rapidly. Coal and oil production was at an all time high since the limits to mining and oil drilling had been removed. Environmental concerns continued to exist and to be respected to a certain extent but the previous cultist approach to nature no longer existed. Unemployment rates were back down to acceptable levels below five percent. The new flat rate tax system seemed to be working quite well. Only one tax was collected and that was paid to the National Government. State governments received a portion of that payment and that was used to cover all State expenses. Some of the States were attempting to add their own tax collections to their revenue but the National Government prohibited any additional taxes from being collected other than the national flat tax. Many of the State bureaucrats complained but the public applauded and the economy soared. States were allowed to charge fees for services such as toll road fees, parking fees and other such programs. A loud outcry was heard to remove all taxes on the low income wage earners. Robert steadfastly refused to do that and reminded everyone in his weekly television address of what the outcome of preferential tax treatment based on income or lack thereof had been in the years before the collapse. He was not about to let the country make that mistake again. He reminded the public that a flat tax on a minimal income produced only a negligible amount of revenue. As Robert noted, even a small amount of tax paid renders the payer a more involved citizen.

In his weekly addresses to the nation, Robert continued to bring forth portions of the Constitution that he was quite certain would raise the hackles on many Liberals who were becoming increasingly disenchanted with his political philosophy. One of these issues had come to the surface in the Turner trial and that was the absence of the legal defenses that had existed in years previous when defendants had numerous and sundry defenses and delaying tactics at their finger tips that caused needless delays and great cost to the government. Robert's position was basically that if the defendant had not violated the law, he would have no need for an attorney. He actually referred to that in one of his speeches and when the uproar came, he casually brushed it off as a poor choice of words.

Robert did go on to explain that providing defendants with legal counsel and hundreds of legal arguments to present to the court in their defense was a tremendous financial burden on the part of the government. Possibly when times were better they could reevaluate the situation but for now, defendants would have to take care of their own defense and besides, they were being provided with a legal summary of the trial procedure, their rights or lack thereof, the charges and the penalties attached in the event of their guilt. This seemed to satisfy the public who were generally not sympathetic to the rights and privileges of the same people who were doing their best to bring misery, pain and loss to them on a daily basis. Another issue that had become a bit of a conversation piece was the very short period of time between the arrest of a man accused of murder and his being shot by a firing squad. Everyone knew that mistakes had been made in the past in courts of law, even when the rights of the accused were amply being utilized. Robert's reply to that was that only in cases where the defendant's guilt was clear and convincing, was not based in whole or in part on circumstantial evidence and was without any reasonable doubt of guilt, was the death penalty applied. In those cases, it would be economically burdensome and unjustified to keep the defendant alive, imprisoned, fed and receiving medical and dental care for the rest of his life that was not available to the average citizen.

Robert had concluded early on that no matter what he said or did, someone would complain and others would listen. After a while, he paid very little attention to the rumblings of a few. As long as he kept a lid on the media it would not get out of control, no matter what he said or did.

One item that did come up in conversations with him by people in authority or educators in particular was the issue of the former States of the Union that were not presently included in the national territory. Those States were Colorado, New Mexico, Southern Utah, Southern Nevada Southern California and South Florida. There was a rising clamor for Robert to use force if necessary to retake those territories. The Western States encompassed areas that Louis Donley had taken control of and that Stuart had, in the past agreed to in exchange for the upper half of California, Nevada, Utah and the San Francisco Bay area which provided an excellent harbor and seaport.

At the time that Stuart negotiated the deal with Donley it was very favorable to WestPac and Robert himself considered it a major coup. As time wore on, however, Robert found himself thinking about how he could renege on the agreement with Donley and still maintain his friendship as the nation needed the petroleum that was flowing in great abundance to the North and to the East from the wells primarily in the Southwest. Robert had brought in the oil experts from Texas and sent them into the Gulf of Mexico to begin drilling in quantity so as to provide the nation with fuel in the event of problems with the Hispanics in the Southwest. He also sent envoys up to Alaska to get them to develop wells and also produce natural gas for the nation. He had already received the fruits of those endeavors but he knew if he had control of the Southwestern wells, his fuel problems would be completely solved.

Robert made the call to Donley during the summer when Americans were again traveling to Colorado on vacations. Good times were not yet back in full swing, but times were definitely better. Donley got on the line and exchanged pleasantries with Robert. They had always had a very good relationship and that relationship had foreshadowed the mutually satisfying business arrangements the two had made for the shipment of products in exchange primarily for fuel. It was a naturally beneficial arrangement for each of the parties.

After the exchange of courtesies, Robert invited Louis to visit him at Scott Field. He would send a plane to pick him and his wife up and would like to discuss a number of topics of mutual benefit to both men. Donley was agreeable to this as he needed greater quantities of some items and a growing number of other items that were not produced in the Southwest. They made arrangements to meet and for the flight to bring Louis to Illinois. Thirty days later, the four engine transport used for the VIP flights landed at Scott Field. The Base had been cleaned up, repainted, and new VIP quarters built with all of the conveniences expected of a wealthy, stable government. The Base Military Personnel, selected for their military bearing, were all outfitted in the attractive new uniforms. Their boots were shined to a gloss and buttons and brass on their uniforms polished. Robert wanted to impress Donley with a well run, efficient government that was doing very well since they had retaken the land.

Robert personally met Louis Donley's plane when it landed. The limousine then carried Louis and his wife to their quarters which were immaculate, very comfortable and were staffed by servants prepared to answer any request they would possibly have. Robert had arranged with Sarah that she would host Donley's wife on behalf of the nation in order to give Robert sole access to Donley to discuss business. After a two hour break to let Donley rest up from the trip, the limousine would again pick up Donley and his wife and take them to the Officer's club for a reception. The key players in the new nation were present and formally attired ready to meet the President of Hispanic America. It was a very friendly gathering and both parties to the event had been through a great deal in furthering the cause of their separate countries. Hispanic America had also made good strides since the FSP was vanquished there. They had especially benefited from their close proximity and friendship with the United States of America. Business dealings between the two had brought economic development to both. Sarah had a very good relationship with Louis' wife who Sarah found to be very intelligent and gracious while Hans found her to be a very attractive lady as well. The cocktail gathering which preceded dinner was a great success and friendships that had existed at long distance were firmly cemented by the opportunity to talk first hand with one another.

Louis Donley was a very personable fellow and Robert was thinking to himself that it was possible that Louis was coming out of this get together as the major winner. He may be walking away with all the prizes tonight. Before the dinner there were toasts to the principals present, including Donley and his wife, and after dinner, Robert invited Donley to visit with him in his conference center for a brief meeting. Meanwhile Sarah took Louis' wife on a tour of the facility and also to a small gathering of the wives at the club.

When Robert and Louis were seated in the conference room, Robert got right to the point. "Louis, we have a great deal in common and we are both doing quite well in organizing our separate communities and developing our businesses. I am amazed at what we are seeing in the growth and wealth of Denver, Colorado Springs and the Front Range and other productive areas of the Southwest. Your production of natural resources is outstanding and God knows we are benefitting from it. Now I have been considering if the benefits to both of us would not be even greater were we to join our land mass and form one united Union."

Seeing Donley draw back a bit, Robert immediately explained. "Louis I am not talking about our country taking you over. I know you would never agree with that and I would never propose it. I am talking about a merger with you and I sharing power with full rights of access of our citizens to travel back and forth across our former borders, with our military might equally spread across our great country providing protection to all of our citizens. We are in the process right now of drawing up our new Constitution which I would assume you would find basically acceptable as I see that you have modeled your Constitution very much after our former document. I bring this up at this time as I am fully aware of what is happening around the world and in some respects, I see your Hispanic America as a possible target for some of the more aggressive powers in the world today."

"Your land is rich in natural resources and some of these powers lack those resources. I believe you may know of whom I speak. The major culprit is now drilling just miles off the Coast of Florida operating out of Cuba. They are rapidly spreading their drilling rigs across the Gulf of Mexico in an arrogant power grab. Robert knew from Intelligence Briefings that the Chinese had been wooing Donley making very lucrative offers to drill wells in the fertile soil of New Mexico, Arizona and California as well as off-shore California. He acted as though he had no idea of the Chinese moves on Hispanic America. Robert continued, "I am not sure of what is going to happen in our coastal waters in the Pacific. They have taken over the independent islands of the Pacific and are knocking at the door of Hawaii. The Hawaiians have an independent streak a mile long and are not accepting our advice to arm up and we would provide the arms. I think they look at the Chinese as less of a threat than they do the United States of America. I am sure the Chinese are also looking at Alaska and I am receiving more interest from them in coming back into the Union than I am ever receiving from Hawaii. Now I don't expect an answer from you on this issue tonight or this week but I would like to know at some time in the near future if this is something that we could work on."

"Louis, I fully intend to make this very beneficial to you and to your people. A lot more beneficial than the deal the other powers would be offering you" Robert smiled and went on. "We have always admired the Hispanics in our country and have great respect for their strong family ties and their work ethic. I speak for the entire country when I say this. I would dearly love to see the country united again as Americans living in peace and harmony. Not White Americans, or Native Americans, or Black Americans or Hispanic Americans but as Americans. Do you have any comment at this point or would you rather delay that? If you would, I can certainly understand."

Louis Donley's expression had not changed as he listened to Robert present his case for unification of the two land masses. After a brief pause, he responded.

"Robert, I agree that there would be many benefits for both of us if we did reunite the country. I would not be against that move but my problem is that many in my Hispanic America would be very opposed to that. Now I don't know how long they would remain opposed, particularly if they saw benefits accruing to them by reunification. I have also been considering the Chinese threat as I am sure that you have as well. If they did take over Hispanic America, they would just keep on moving east and take over the entire country. I don't know if you could stop them from doing that but I agree with your proposition that it would be much more difficult for them to do so if our countries were united and fighting from combined strength. I will consider what you propose but I am not in a position now to agree or disagree with it. We would have to consider the manner in which our two countries were united and the political powers assigned to each. That would also affect whether my citizens would accept the agreement or not. I would be willing to enter into discussions regarding this matter but only on the condition that at this point in time, those discussions would be kept secret."

"Louis, I completely agree and we can and will keep such discussions totally secret. I will let you be the judge as to when the veil of secrecy can be lifted, if ever. If we do decide that joinder is a decent possibility, we could commence joining only certain tasks, foreign policy, military defense, and so forth. I suggest we each appoint a team of negotiators, say five men on each side and they could be titled an Economic Policy Board which should not raise too many flags. I will do so this coming week. If you can do the same, have their leader contact me here at Scott Field and they can meet in Denver or we can split locations or whatever they decide upon."

"Robert, I am agreeable with that. I will set that up and have them get in contact with you. By the way, what is your status with Texas? We have only limited involvement with them."

Robert laughed. "Our relationship is about like yours. They have agreed to be part of the United States of America and will have Senators and Congressmen but they also are very independent and have made that very clear. They were one of the first states before the collapse to let us all know that they were about to secede. They wear that as a badge of honor now and remind us of the fact that if they do not like what they see going on in the national government, they will secede again."

The two men talked over border matters that kept coming up over time and they were able to come to agreements that both concluded would not be raising major problems. At the appointed time, the limousine arrived to take Louis back to his quarters. Sarah had delivered his wife at the same time. The following morning, the Donleys boarded the VIP flight for the trip back to Denver. Everyone was pleased with the meeting between the two countries and all were hopeful that in time they could again be reunited.

Robert selected five men with experience in foreign relations and international negotiations to serve on the Economic Policy Board. When they were selected, Robert had them assemble in the administration building conference room. He explained that he had met with Louis Donley and after receiving assurances from those present that anything discussed at this meeting would be held in strict secrecy, he told them of the conversation regarding reunification.

"You are to hold yourselves out to the public as involved with economic issues providing benefits to both sides in the discussions. In truth, much of what you discuss will deal with just that. Overall, I want you to focus on the objective of the discussions which is to bring the two countries together under our Constitution. It must be fair, it must not favor one side or the other, always maintain an amicable relationship. If we are unable to unite our two countries, we at least want to maintain very good relations as we are joined at the hip and cannot afford to have unfriendly relations with them. In reality, they need us and we need them. They have resources that we need and we have material goods that they need. Likewise, they need our military support. One area that I would like to have you bring up early on in the discussions is the matter of their Southern Border with Mexico. We all know that the Southern Border remains porous and thousands or maybe millions continue to pour over that border every year. Many of those immigrants do not intend to reside in Hispanic America. They want the good life that is rapidly coming to the United States of America. We have beefed up security on the Colorado, New Mexico and Texas borders but every day, Hispanic America becomes less attractive as more unskilled workers flood into that country. If we reunite, we will be assuming all of those immigrants. Make them aware that the mass of unskilled labor coming in endangers the chance of unification."

Robert was also thinking about the situation with South Florida and the Cuban control of that area. He could discuss unification with Paco Morales but he was not hopeful they would be able to come to any form of agreement with them. Maybe in years to come, that would come about as a result of a peaceful discussion but Robert had his doubts. Robert did have Sarah confer with the Cubans regarding the Bayside residents that had elected to stay on the beach when the Exodus to Montana took place. Sarah reported that some were still living in the area and apparently the Cubans had completely stabilized the Melbourne area and businesses were again in operation and the people were living fairly well. Sarah had inquired as to the whereabouts of Jim McCleod but had come up with nothing. If he was still alive, Robert assumed he would have come to Scott Field by this time. It was possible that he had been killed in fighting against the FSP force that eventually took over the area that included North Farm. Carlos Moran ,who knew McCleod, said that he had never seen or heard of McCleod after the FSP took over that North Farm area around Jacksonville and that was years ago. Robert assumed that with the passage of time, McCleod was most likely dead. That was too bad as he would have been a welcome addition to the government Robert was attempting to build.

After Donley had left Scott Field, Robert's calendar was cleared for a few days so he decided to visit the Study Group to see how they were coming along with the new Constitution. When he walked into their meeting room, they were involved in an intense argument dealing with restrictions that would be placed on Freedom of Speech. Bill Phillips explained to Robert that two of the members were against any restrictions on the media with respect to what they could publish. They reasoned that whatever their position, there would be opposing views published elsewhere so why bother to limit ones views. Robert raised the issue of what if most or all of the media held a particular view and was opposed only by a small minority on the other side. This was the case in years past that propelled Turner's administration to the forefront ahead of all opposition. In fact, some of Turner's actions were virtually indefensible yet were basically unopposed as the entire popular media supported him. Should the media be denied the right to support comments that were clearly lies or at best, non-truths. What good does that do for the general public. Robert continued, "I know that to deny a person the right to publish his opinion is a dangerous restriction and should be used very sparingly, yet is it not justified in certain situations. I think we would all say yes in certain cases it is wise and justifiable to restrict publication of falsehoods that may cause disruption to the well being of the populace. It seems to me that what is needed is a reasonable, intelligent control mechanism that would prevent this restriction from becoming a tool to control thought. Possibly we could have a review group comprised of both sides involved in the issue with a couple of neutrals to decide by majority vote if the publication should be restricted. How you would ever find the people to make up such a group and have that group be accepted and respected by the citizens is beyond me. Maybe you members of the group may decide that there is no alternative proposal that is better than allowing all speech to be unrestrained or have better control mechanisms. I don't know. That is up to you to decide here. I may have other ideas but I want to know your thoughts."

Bill Phillips, the group leader, told Robert later that the way they had handled Study Group arguments in the past seemed to work most of the time and that was they would separate and the members would draft wording that they hoped would resolve the issue. Frequently it did and that was the end of the discussion. The members had also learned that you never wanted to get so involved in the discussion that you were losing control of your temper as that rendered one completely ineffective. When that did happen as it did on a few occasions, Bill Phillips would intervene and tell the offender to take five then come back with a cooler head. All members of the group were professionals and generally acted as such. When they did get a bit out of line, they always came back and apologized to the others for losing control.

Robert spoke with Phillips a few days later and asked if they had resolved the issue over Freedom of Speech. He said they had. They added wording to the effect that words that tended to incite violence or to increase hatred of a person or a group of people were restricted and would be denied publication. The other provisions of the First Amendment were acceptable as written. Robert was not convinced that this wording would solve the problem. As he saw the issue, Robert told Phillips, the problem was how to prevent critical speech, not necessarily hateful or prone to violence speech, but just critical comments directed at a person, a group, or an idea and the comments were not true. They were totally or substantially false. "Can wording be drafted in the Constitution to prevent such critical comment that is not true?" The two men continued talking for some time and finally both concluded that the wording offered by Phillips previously was the least ambiguous and least capable of causing further confusion. Robert decided he would give it further thought and bring it up again if he could come up with a proposal.

The group rewrote the second Amendment to comprise two separate provisions. The first being the State may have a well regulated militia and the citizens of the separate States shall have a right to bear arms and neither of these provisions shall be infringed. They concluded that the rewrite would remove all confusion regarding the right to bear arms as being related solely to the Militia. Robert was in total agreement with that position. The restrictions previously held with respect to where citizens could carry weapons were further reduced and clarified to allow less restrictive limitations on where one could carry a weapon.

The Fifth Amendment was rewritten to remove the requirement for a presentment or indictment in view of the fact that the Military was conducting all trials of Military and civilian personnel on the contention that the nation continued to be in a condition of "Public Danger". When that condition was removed and civilian courts were again handling criminal matters, the Fifth Amendment wording would be rewritten by the Study Group subject only to approval by the President. The change would not go through the much more difficult Amendment process. The other provisions of the Fifth Amendment were acceptable.

The Sixth Amendment was acceptable as written with the addition of the words "as allowed by the Rules of the Court Martial proceeding," following the wording relating to assistance of counsel.

The Tenth Amendment was clarified to give clearer understanding of the broad scope of the State powers and the very limited intrusion allowed the Federal Government into State matters.

The remaining Amendments were acceptable without any changes.

Following the drafting of the basic constitutional document, the Study Group began redrafting the criminal code that would be applicable to all citizens of the United States, civilian and military. They did not consider that the Constitution was a completed document as other provisions were expected to arise in the drafting of the Criminal Code. Also other provisions such as the Balanced Budget Amendment had to be drafted and incorporated into the document as a constitutional requirement.

"We the people are the rightful masters of both Congress and the courts, not to overthrow the Constitution but to overthrow the men who pervert the Constitution."

—Abraham Lincoln

CHAPTER TWENTY-FOUR

The proposed Constitution as drafted by the Study Group was finally ready for Robert's review and acceptance. He did add a few provisions that he had the Study Group consider and draft. One was that English was the only National Language and would be used in all Court Proceedings, Government notices to Citizens, Educational Presentations, and in all government media publications including print, television, and radio. Other languages or interpretations would not be added. Public school students were expected to know how to speak English. English lessons would be made available for non-English speaking students and for pre-school children. Another was that the National Government was given specific authority to punish any person or entity for spreading or publishing any inflammatory falsehood that was detrimental to the peace and well being of any person or entity including the United States Government. The Study Group considered this latter provision to be a potential source of conflict among the citizens due to its lack of specificity. Robert assured them that the prohibition was intentionally crafted to potentially have wide application covering many different publications of falsehoods. "It sounds like a 'catch all' criminal provision and that is what it is and it is needed in view of the present gaps existing in the new Criminal Code."

The new Constitution and Criminal Code were published in the Word of WestPac, now carrying the banner, Word of the nation. Both documents were the topic of the day in restaurants, coffee houses and in the homes across the nation. The main topics of discussion revolved around the reintroduction of religion into American life. There was really no reintroduction of religion, there was rather an end to the prohibition of religion in American life. In any event, this was quite a change after years of the media, television, radio and the movie industry doing their best to turn religion into a comedy act. Robert devoted his television address following publication of the new Constitution to some of the issues that were coming up. He explained his attitude regarding some of the more significant changes in the document from the wording of the original Constitution. "Remember my fellow Citizens, the problems that were created by gaps in the Constitution that created confusion in many aspects of our lives. Remember that confusion is the birthplace of bureaucrats. We have had enough of them. Look at the collection of buildings, among those still existing, in Washington, DC, standing as mute monuments to former bureaucracies crammed with people that were telling you how to live your lives. At least that is what they said they were doing there. Those buildings are used today for public housing and the people that would be there if we were still operating under the original document would be the same ones that are now out either complaining about the new Constitution or hopefully working in industry or retail or on farms. If they are out producing today that is something they never did before. Let me assure you, they are not coming back into our government to guide your lives. You don't need that and I don't want it either."

There were very few organizations that were out campaigning against the Constitution as there would have been in prior years. The main reason they were not there is that they would have been violating the law if they were assembling and protesting against the government without a permit. Permits of this type were sparingly issued at least during this time of relative instability. People were allowed to be against a particular government law or regulation but they were not allowed to publish their arguments of dissent nor were they allowed to combine into unified groups to carry forward their arguments of dissent without a permit. They could join together in support of a lawful measure that did not contravene a specific prohibition written into the law. This was becoming the new norm for the anti-government groups and it was totally acceptable to Robert. For example, the new laws denied those facing serious Court Martial trials the right to have their own Counsel defending them. They could have the assistance of an Officer of the Court to explain certain aspects of the case to them but that Officer, who was an attorney, was not allowed to argue on their behalf. This was quite a change from the former provisions of the Sixth Amendment case law where an accused was given notice that he had a right to Counsel and if he could not afford one, the Court would appoint one for him. There were few protests against this new provision of the Constitution due to the permit requirement but there were many meetings promulgating granting the former rights to the accused. These meetings were carefully orchestrated to avoid violations of the protest laws. This was one of Robert's temporary techniques for holding down dissent. He was fully aware that in time, this restriction would have to be dropped and there would be a full return to the right of free speech for all citizens.

This rather severe new treatment of the legal rights afforded to the defendant carried over into other aspects of the Criminal Trial and it was this treatment of the defendant that Human Rights organizations of prior years would have vigorously attacked with a vengeance. New protest groups who had been granted permits were growing in connection with the retraining centers. These were not all necessarily prisons in the old sense of the word. They were organized in varying degrees of increasing control of anti-social behavior. Varying from reeducation of older students who apparently had lacked an education on what was considered normal acceptable social graces to persons serving long or life time prison sentences for taking the life of their fellow citizen.

The conditions inside the retraining centers varied by the nature of the treatment being delivered to the inmate. Actually, in the lower levels of the centers, the inmates were referred to as guests and the conditions for the guests were almost, but not quite, acceptable. All inmates provided their own labor to cover the cost of their being rehabilitated or punished, whichever the case might be. It was also possible for some who had been sentenced to the more severe retraining centers to reform their lives and work their way down the ladder to those Centers more focused on rehabilitation.

The groups that were protesting the retraining centers were, again, not publicly condemning the Centers themselves, they were attacking them by alternate proposals for dealing with prisoners. For example they discussed rather publicly the fact that currently there were two million citizens confined to retraining centers and this was costing the National Government millions of National Dollars. A less costly solution would be to move all of the prisoners, including the lifers out of the Centers and onto farms where they would be raising crops and working with farm animals. A much more enjoyable past time than making license plates and furniture for government offices. Robert's attitude towards these groups was that if they didn't bitch about this, they would be bitching about something else and so far they had not created much of a ruckus. The figure of two million incarcerated prisoners did get his attention and he contacted Ross Perry to see if they couldn't cut those numbers down a bit. Many of the prisoners had been sent to retraining centers on indefinite terms and possibly many had just been forgotten. There was no doubt that was the case for some but hopefully not too many. Perry said he would have his staff check it out and see if they could not make a significant drop in the numbers.

The same day that Robert had spoken to Perry about the prisoners, he received a call from Sarah. "Robert, I spoke with an old friend of yours today."

Robert had been thinking of Jim McCleod and his name immediately came to mind. It was a pleasant thought and Robert eagerly said, "Who was it?"

"Irene Covington and she asked how you were doing."

Hearing her name put a sour note on the conversation for Robert. "Where the hell is that one? We haven't heard from her in a few years. I was hoping she was gone for good. She probably wanted to hear if I had been hit by a car or something, right?"

"Robert, now you know she wouldn't be thinking of that. She is in the Chicago area working with some social groups who are still trying to get parts of the city rebuilt. She did read the new Constitution and commented that it had your finger prints all over it."

"How perceptive of her. She must be in Chicago trying to organize a revolutionary communist youth league of some sort. She is not up there raising flowers. We all know that. What did she really want?"

"I think she just wanted to say hello and was probably waiting for an invite to Scott Field to apply for some position in management."

"Sarah, you have not lost your sense of humor, have you. No, even Irene knows that would not happen. In fact, we will have to keep tabs on her. There is no doubt that she is not up to any good especially in Chicago. I suspect we will hear more of her in relation to the new Constitution or the retraining centers. All of her old pals are involved in attacking those targets. Keep me posted if she shows up again."

Now that the Constitution had been published for over a month, Robert knew that the demand for elections would be the next public outcry. The new Constitution was not to take effect for another four years but its publication had a definite effect on how the citizens viewed their personal freedoms. Robert realized that over the course of the next few years, all of the former rights included in the earlier Constitution would become effective in the minds of the public whether their time had come or not. That certainly included elections which were not to take place for at least another year.

The Constitution did provide for the election of a President, Senators and Representatives. According to the Constitution, the President was allowed to appoint his Vice President and the members of his Cabinet. There was no review of his Cabinet appointments. He was also allowed to appoint the seven members of the Supreme Court and that did not require confirmation in the Senate until subsequent replacements were appointed. The intention of this provision was to give the first President the power to protect his actions from interference by the courts. Robert was thinking ahead when he had that provision written into the Constitution.

In view of the fact that Robert had seen nothing that prevented him from doing so, he had planned to assume the office of the President and would not be facing an election for four years. With his appointment of the members of the Supreme Court, he was assured of a full term of four years without interruption if he so desired. He had already decided on who the appointees would be for the Supreme Court and had little doubt as to their loyalty to the President. The Senate would select and pass on the District Court Judges and the Appellate Court Judges. That would keep them busy for quite a while and out of his hair for the foreseeable future. Remembering that the Senators were limited to two six year terms would somewhat dim their focus on harassing the President.

Robert was now getting up in years at sixty-five and he was beginning to look forward, hopefully, to a quiet four year term as President during which time period, he would devote his time improving the infrastructure of the country and increasing its overall stability. He knew this was going to be a difficult task but he had confidence in the staff that he had accumulated over the years to get the job done.

He still had to work out the issue of the West with Louis Donley and also wanted to bring Alaska back into the Union. Alaska would be a welcome addition with the tremendous natural resources they had buried under the tundra. He had Toni make arrangements for the Governor of Alaska to visit with them at Scott Field and see if arrangements could not be made to bring them into the fold or at a minimum to set up some worthwhile trade agreements with them to bring more petroleum and natural gas into the country. He had Toni arrange the same sort of welcome to the Governor as they had laid out for Louis Donley. Robert assumed that the Governor of Alaska would be more amenable to rejoining the Union than Donley had been as the Governor of Alaska seemed to be more aware of the ambitions of the Chinese, but then one never knew. Arrangements were made for the visit to take place in one month and Toni was busy working on the schedule with Clay Daley.

Robert did meet with the two leaders of the major political parties in the nation and announced that elections for all offices other than the President would take place in one year and advised them to prepare for that election. The two men had maintained their political party connections even during the FSP years on a less confrontational level and they were still looked upon by the party faithful as the key party figures. That was not an issue. They did inquire regarding the Office of the President and Robert kindly informed them that he would hold that office for the first four years of the country operating under the Constitution in order to provide stability to the government. After that it would be up for election and he would not be running. At least at this point in time it was not his intention to run.

In the meantime, Robert picked the members of his Cabinet and put them to work immediately. He assigned Sarah as his Secretary of State and appointed Anders as Vice President. Ross Perry became the new Secretary of Defense and for Treasury he assigned an economist from Stanford that he had consulted with on the gold issue. The other offices he would fill as time went on. In the meantime, he sent Sarah to Denver to meet with Louis Donley as he had indicated an interest in discussing some matters. He cautioned Sarah to work with Louis and get him to join forces and to do it absolutely fairly as Louis had always been fair with WestPac and the new nation. "Besides we need their oil." Robert, somewhat tongue in cheek, suggested to Anders that he might consider meeting with Boo Hicks in order to get some advice on handling the office of the Vice President. Anders replied that Hicks seemed to have handled the job quite successfully as he had ended his tenure as a very wealthy man. Robert commented that Boo Hicks was about to become a guest at Scott Field as his trial was fast approaching. His days of riding the gravy train were about over.

With the forthcoming elections coming up in months, the political season was rapidly gathering steam. The two main parties dominated national politics but they were not the only parties involved. There were splinter groups in the country with their own special interests and they all had their own political party. There was no way they would ever control the National Election but some of them did possess enough clout to win a seat or two in the legislative bodies both on the Federal level and also at the State level. The primary reason for the existence of splinter groups was that there was no doubt that the Constitution did not enjoy unanimous support among the voting citizens. Likewise the issue of Voter Qualification Requirements engendered a lot of dissent among the more liberal minded voters and the Liberal Party because it was their constituents that were primarily effected by reason of their lack of income and assets.

Many citizens were angered by the voter requirements and claimed that they were "just plain un-American". Robert made them a topic for one of his weekly broadcasts and explained his reasons for supporting what many were now calling the 'Jim Crow Laws'. Robert told his listeners that no longer would there be a large bloc of the population with "no skin in the game". His comment being directed at the majority of the population, pre-collapse, that paid no income tax yet were constantly demanding more benefits. It is very easy to criticize programs paid for by others when the complainer is not footing the bill. It is even easier for the complainers to demand that the programs be expanded to provide even greater benefits for them when they pay nothing. In fact, it is amazing to see how people can actually get angry with those who were paying the bills for not paying more. We saw a lot of that in the years before the collapse because the non-payers had the ear of the President and as long as he kept giving them benefits at no cost he owned their votes. When that bloc of votes represents over fifty percent of the voters, the demagogue owns the country and that was exactly what happened in the years before the collapse.

The result of the new voter qualification laws was to disenfranchise a large bloc of voters. They actually referred to themselves as the Jim Crow Party, a party without a vote. Robert didn't care what they called themselves; they were not going to vote unless they paid taxes at a certain level and showed a certain qualifying level of income or assets. He knew that if they were making money at the qualifying level, paying for a house, paying taxes, or running a business that they would no longer be demanding goodies for nothing. Furthermore, Robert made it clear that the citizens who associated themselves with the Jim Crow Party or other such group had no right to hold rallies or to disrupt any lawful public gatherings in furtherance of their demands for voting rights. Such activities would be in direct conflict with the express wording of the Constitution. He warned them that any organized activities along these lines would result in arrests and confinement. At the same time, Robert was fully aware that given time and with certain replacements on the Supreme Court, The Jim Crow Party would be holding the rallies they wanted to hold. While he thought they would eventually succeed in doing that, it would take a hell of a long time for that to happen. Having them succeed in changing the wording of the Constitution, however, was no easy task. The measure would have to pass the Senate and the House with sixty per-cent of the vote and then two-thirds of the States would be required to ratify the measure with a sixty per-cent vote. That was a high hill to climb.

Robert also made sure that there was no voter fraud as that was the most common voter recourse when they wanted to ensure their right to anything coming from the government. He ordered, and his legislature approved, a law requiring a fraud proof identification card given only to qualified voters. It verified citizenship based on reliable provable documents and showed that the possessor thereof was qualified to vote in Federal and State elections for a five year period. The cards were renewed every five years on the holder's birthday provided the holder of the card remained a qualified voter. During elections, polling stations were manned by staff trained to detect fraudulent identification cards or non-qualified voters with current identification cards and anyone attempting to vote based on a fraudulent card was immediately arrested and summarily sentenced to a Retraining Center.

This was just one more very punitive law that Robert had inserted into the Constitution to ensure the viability of the document and the preservation of the Union as it was conceived to be. Many people opposed Robert's hard line approach to Democracy but he always responded, "We don't have a Democracy, we have a Federal Democratic Republic and there is quite a difference. Read the Federalist Paper Number Ten which this country has claimed to follow since its inception. We have a representative democracy, not a pure democracy. Power to govern on the national level in the Congress is in the hands of elected representatives chosen by the States based upon population and in the case of the Senate, based upon an undemocratic calculation of two senators per State regardless of State populations. Congress is obviously the more democratic body compared to the Senate yet it is the Senate, and presumably the Courts, that primarily gives this nation its continuity. Furthermore the term of office of a senator is six years rather than the two year term of a representative rendering the senator a much more powerful figure representing his State than is the representative representing the population of his district. These aspects of a Federal Republic provide protections for its longevity that a pure Democracy does not possess. This is the primary reason the Federal Republic concept provided this country its initial longevity until its protections were overridden by the power hungry schemers that designed methods to circumvent the Constitution upon which it was based. Hopefully, our new Constitution with some of its safeguards will preclude this from happening again." Robert was always ready to speak at length as to why America collapsed. He would mention that Madison who wrote Federalist Paper Number 10 considered a Democracy as a form of government destined to collapse due to its inability to prevent a faction of special interests, the most common of which Madison referenced frequently as a faction of those 'without' assets desiring to share the assets of those 'with' such assets. People had that natural inclination to want what others had. That was inherent in human nature. Madison saw the unequal distribution of income and property existing in a free society as a faction in waiting. In a pure Democracy, it would burst forth and proceed to destroy the very Democracy that allowed its birth. People have different skills and consequently some are more adept at acquiring property than others. A Democracy provides the ones without property a ready-made path to acquire the property of the producers. Madison sought to protect against this occurrence and did so with the apparatus of the Republic. His protection consisted of primarily representative voting and the bicameral system with a less democratic senate holding down any signs of avarice from the house. Keep in mind, Robert would say, "Madison wrote Fed 10 when less than half of the citizens even had a right to vote. Compare that to pre-collapse times when virtually anyone could vote and a large bloc of those voters paid no taxes." Robert noted a contributing factor allowing factions to grow in this country before the collapse was the fact that when the protections were written into the Constitution by the Founders to limit the effects of factions, this country was united in language and culture, all descended from common ancestors and following the same basic religion, Christianity. Compare that to the population of this country at the time of the collapse. Why do you suppose so many people wanted the good life and were not even paying any taxes for it? He would exclaim, "Hell, why not?"

In the meantime, Robert's new policy of Study, Work and Succeed was producing an economic leap forward in the country. The American motto of work hard and succeed was again taking shape across the nation. Taxes were low. Regulations were no longer prohibiting economic growth. Businesses were booming. Profits were increasing and unemployment was getting to be a problem of the past. Temporary work permits were again in vogue for non-citizens as labor was getting in short supply. Problems were beginning to grow on the Western border with Hispanic America as illegals continued to flow into that country from South of the border. Louis Donley had not been able to stifle the flow of illegals into his country and they continued to try to pass on through to the land of opportunity, The United States of America. Sarah had discussed this issue with Louis Donley a number of times and was warning him that unification of their two countries was being threatened by the huge increase in unskilled labor flowing in from Central America. Sarah also warned Louis that they had to make a decision soon and they could not publicize the fact that negotiations were taking place as the illegals would immediately come flocking in hoping to be in place if and when Hispanic America became part of the United States of America. The economy of Hispanic America was better than it had been and certainly better than Central America but was well below that of the areas encompassed by the United States of America.

Sarah was finally able to work out an agreement with Louis to the effect that the two countries would be joined together as they were joined in years past with the change that Southern California would become a separate State and would have its own two Senators and the appropriate number of Representatives. Louis would also be named as a third Senator Pro Tempore from the State of Colorado to occupy that seat for one six year term with full voting rights. The other States of the west would have the regular allocation of Senators and Representatives. The result of these additions to the National government was twelve additional Hispanic votes in the Senate and a sizeable bloc of Hispanic Representatives in the House. This provided a strong voice for the citizens of Hispanic America in the senate and Congress of the United States of America.

An agreement was entered into with Louis Donley that Voter Identification Cards would be made available in Hispanic America to those that qualified under the financial or property requirements with a commensurate easing of the birth requirements. A Birth Certificate was not as commonly available for citizens of Hispanic America as it was in the United States and alternative forms of proof of birth were required. For those that could prove birth in the geographic area of Hispanic America and who otherwise qualified for the Voter card, they were given the Card. Qualifying birth in Hispanic America was proven using Church Records, hospital records, parental employment records, or credible affidavits of responsible parties who were themselves qualified to be citizens. All of these sources sufficed to document a legitimate birth. These documents proving birth were also utilized in the other States of the Union in those regions lacking the civic organization that was present in pre-collapse years.

Immigrants into Hispanic America that were unable to produce evidence that they had lived there for over three years would be considered illegal and would not qualify for the Voter Identification Card. If they possessed skills or property that would otherwise qualify them for the Card, they were allowed to stay in country and were permitted to take a qualifying study course for citizenship. The course extended over a six month period of time with classes held in the evenings. The remainder of the immigrants that did not qualify for the cards or for citizenship training were allowed to stay on work visas provided they had employment. In the event they did not have employment, they were required to leave the country unless their relatives would sign affidavits promising to support them and their families until they received visas and were gainfully employed. This was to be strictly enforced.

Another issue that was coming to the fore was that of pensions, government issued and private pension funds. Following the collapse, no pensions had been paid to anyone. Social Security was defunct as were all government pensions. Private pensions soon followed. As the economy in the new nation under Robert's leadership began its climb back to levels of prosperity, the outcry from those who had lost their pensions likewise began to climb. This demand for unpaid pensions involved a potential debt of trillions of dollars for the government and for many of the former companies that continued to exist in one form or another. There was no way the pensions could be paid and Robert, in one of his final orders as the leader of the country declared all pensions in effect at the time of the collapse of the country, some ten years previous, that were not being paid were no longer in existence and no claims would be honored for the payment of those amounts. There was a substantial outcry from the public as virtually everyone was affected but those who had some understanding of economics knew there was no alternative available other than voiding those obligations.

A further result of voiding the old pensions was that newer private pensions were no longer being issued. Social Security no longer existed but it had always been considered a successful program and the congress was considering reestablishing the program with some changes. One change would be that it would be the only retirement program covering government and private employees and would be financially supported by all citizens based on a flat tax on all income and all levels of income. Another change would be that funds paid in through taxes for Social Security would be invested in very conservative funds secured by the Treasury Department and there would be no borrowing from that fund by the government or private agencies. The fund would be subjected to annual audits to ensure that it was protected and preserved for its dedicated purpose, retirement benefits. A further needed change was that senior citizens over seventy years of age were given benefits at the minimum payment level under the new Social Security Program provided they had no other funds or assets available to reasonably provide for themselves.

The Senate and Congressional elections across the country had everyone's attention. The two parties remained basically the same as in years past. There was the Conservative Party and the Liberal Party. Their philosophies were diametrically opposed based on philosophical and economic beliefs. Due to the changes in the Constitution, the changes in voting qualifications and the conservative views of the Government, the Conservatives were the majority party in the elections. As Robert mentioned to Anders, "How the hell can the Liberals win when their base is comprised of people who either do not work or who have no or limited property. For the Liberals who do qualify to vote, they no longer are interested in whining their way to payoffs from the government that they will have to pay for themselves with their taxes. The population was working, there were no Unions; they were making good money, buying homes and new cars and sending their children to college. They were taking vacations and spending large sums of money in the West to the great satisfaction of Louis Donley and other Western leaders.

One major government project that had begun shortly after the retaking of the nation by the WestPac force was the rebuilding that was required as a result not only of the war but also as a result of years of neglect of infrastructure and lack of the funds necessary to make improvements. Cities like Detroit were wastelands of buildings in decay, everything in a state of collapse, debris lying in the streets. Residents wearing rags, half starved children without parents begging for food, rats roaming the streets and alleyways at night searching for scraps of food, no police, no security, crime out of control, gangs controlling everything, It was an absolute disaster area. Robert decided that they had to start somewhere and Detroit was a very good candidate. He had Perry move thousands of troops into the city to establish order. That alone took months as the gangs were firmly entrenched and the populace supported the gangs primarily out of fear. More damage to buildings was done in the process of restoring order and more citizens were lying dead and dying in the streets.

Captured gang members were sent to a secured location outside of the city. Some of Perry's toughest most battle hardened troops were placed as guards and monitors. That turned into another battle. Gang leaders had to be ferreted out and separated from their members who would do nothing without their leaders consent. Gang leaders that persisted in violent confrontations with their captors were treated harshly. The policy in the prison was if you wanted rough treatment, just let the guards know and they would comply. The Black gang leaders were difficult to deal with but nothing compared to the Muslims. The Muslims were motivated by their religious faith and that could sustain them during their most trying times. The Blacks were not into religion at least a religion that instigated violence. They were into acquiring material goods and drugs. Over time, the Black followers were segregated from their leaders and began adjusting to prison life. As a result, they became more amenable to rehabilitation and eventually began returning to society.

The Muslims on the other hand were not adjusting to anything and were only hardening their refusal to blend into society and adopt American values. Perry was of the belief that they should be shipped back to their countries of origin in the Mid-East, and the problem would be solved in that manner. He had his troops offer that as an option to the Muslim leaders in the prison and that immediately got their attention. They had absolutely no interest in leaving Detroit for a bare existence in Afghanistan, Iraq, Saudi or Yemen. They immediately began presenting a different attitude towards the guards and the prison program and it was clear that they feared returning to the Mid-East more than they feared abiding by the rules of law in the United States. Robert's suggestion was that they be monitored for a lengthy period of time and if they showed their old behavior again, just ship them back. If they were willing to abide by the rules, they could eventually be paroled but if they were returned to prison, they would be shipped back to their home country immediately. Some were eventually returned to their families in Detroit and they immediately spread the word that if they continued to disrupt, destroy and fight the government, they would be sent back to the Mid-East. This program appeared to work for a while but as time went on, the hard core Islamic Faith was again in full

swing and Sharia Law was again being forced on the Islamic neighborhoods and the old attacks on Christians and Jews again came alive. This
time, Robert ordered that Sharia Law was not allowed to be practiced in
the United States, at any level. The Koran was henceforth banned and religious services in Islamic Mosques were limited to the peaceful aspects of
the rewritten Koran. Services were henceforth monitored to ensure compliance. Any Muslim that violated these orders would be deported to the
Mid-East without a hearing. The general population of the nation accepted
these Orders without complaint as they had lost patience with their Mid-
East neighbors.

The rebuilding program in Detroit and in similar cities was a labor intensive operation. Prison labor utilizing convicts charged with lesser crimes
were housed in wooden barracks in the vicinity of the work areas and put
to work rebuilding the homes and businesses of the city. Prisoners were
being delivered from across the country to serve in the rebuilding program
and in the course of performing their labor function, they were paid a small
amount for their services and were also learning the trades involved. In
fact, education and rehabilitation were part and parcel of the rebuilding
function. Prisoners that began demonstrating a respect for the property
of others and for the law in general were considered eligible for work
release where they could continue working in the rebuilding program but
at apprentice level wages. In this manner they were able to build up a
reasonable nest egg and when they were given their final release they had
the funds available to assist them in establishing lives elsewhere or if they
chose, they could stay on the job as freedmen working up to journeyman
wages. There was a labor shortage in the northern tier of States which this
system also solved. Without the labor source of the retraining centers, the
cost of the rebuild would have doubled with the need for imported higher
cost labor.

Another benefit of the Rebuilding Program and the rehabilitation of prisoners was a sizeable increase in the number of inhabitants of the lower level criminally oriented retraining centers. Those were the primary sources
of the labor force that were involved in the rebuilding and these were the
members of the criminal world that were most likely candidates to eventually rejoin society. The other inhabitants of the retraining centers were
major offenders who were generally serving long prison terms. The major rebuilding effort was taking place in the northern tier of States where
the fighting had been the most damaging. Minneapolis was on the list as

were Des Moines, Madison, Chicago and some of the eastern cities. By far the worst cases were Minneapolis, Chicago New York city and Detroit. Those four cities required extensive rebuilding from the ground up and even though it was assumed the project would require years to accomplish, it was approved and work commenced.

"The whole basis of the Constitution was a restriction of power, and the whole basis of the federalist system was that there was not one sovereign centralized power from which all authority flows."

—Roy Moore

CHAPTER TWENTY-FIVE

B eth Sloan's educational curriculum had been in effect across the country for over two years and was already showing good results. Robert
was particularly interested in the morals training program and what effects
that was showing. He had Clay Daley compile statistical data on youth
crimes of violence and they showed the beginning of a definite decline.
Youth programs of a positive nature were also being developed that had
been cancelled in the years prior to the collapse. The 4H program for the
rural youngsters was operating in full swing and had reduced youth crime
in the farm belt to a negligible figure. The Cub Scout, Boy and Girl Scout
Programs were flourishing in the cities and were very popular activities for
the pre-teens and the teenagers. They had been shut down in years past by
the Liberal governments on the grounds they were elitist, sexist, and the
final closing allegation, "They were lacking comprehensive participation
in leadership by all non-religious elements in the society and all socially
and sexually deviant sociological groupings."

Since Robert had taken over the government and located it at Scott
Field, young boys that had achieved Eagle Scout ranking had a standing
invitation to visit Scott Field and meet the President. Many took advantage of this opportunity and Robert always took time to make their visit
memorable.

Honor Roll Students were popularized in the communities in which they
lived and were feted in annual recognition dinners and public events. The
Military Academies were again operating in the same locations as they had
in the pre-collapse era. The former "Ivy League Schools" were not quite
the same as they had been in earlier years. They were no longer the schools
focused on the sons and daughters of the rich and famous. They served the
same communities as the former community colleges had served in years
past and continued to serve. There were minimal tuition cost differences
between the so called Ivy League schools and the community colleges.

What allowed for this was the tremendous drop in pay for the professors in the former top ranked schools. In current times, all colleges produced educated students or their teachers were dismissed and room was made for someone that would educate the students. Likewise everyone had access to colleges but admission was based on test scores, class standing and grades. Ethnic background had zero impact on admission as did their social contacts. Any exceptions to these policies led to termination of those involved. Another change on college campuses from earlier days was that clubs, organizations, fraternities, sororities and other similar groups were not allowed to base membership on ethnic, religious, or financial grounds. To reduce the occurrence of the extremes that these policies could produce, any party filing a complaint for a violation was required to file a substantial bond in the event their complaint was determined to be unfounded or unproven. The measure of proof required in these matters was 'clear and convincing.'

In the early days of the new nation, attorneys again began to appear in the mix. Robert spoke to his Attorney General and they drafted a new set of laws which the Congress and Senate approved whereby the old rules of civil litigation were changed in a number of respects. Should the party that filed suit not prevail, the opposing party was allowed to recover their costs of suit including attorney fees. This had a marked effect on the number of cases filed. The filing attorney was also liable for the payment of that cost in the event his client was not able to do so. Should the attorney not be able to pay the cost, his license was suspended until the cost was paid. These changes further decreased an attorney's interest in filing suit on behalf of a client unless it was clearly a valid claim.

Malpractice suits were no longer allowed. In those cases persons injured by reason of the negligence of their doctor or other professional were able to recover a limited compensation on reasonable proof of injury from the professional board serving the professional and the responsible professional was subject to suspension or loss of license in cases involving gross negligence. Unions continued to be illegal pursuant to the provisions of the "Unlawful Gathering Act" which did not mention Unions but the clear wording of the Act obviously applied to them and was enforced against them. This was an ongoing topic of conversation among those working in the trades. In the meantime, employers were also subjected to the "Unlawful Gathering Act" and suffered the same consequences when found to be operating in concert with one another for their mutual benefit. This act benefitted Union members injured by unlawful acts of their employers and also injuries to the general public by concerted actions of corporations or companies. It was assumed that at some point in time, Unions would be permitted to function but when and if they were determined to be lawful there would be restrictions applied to the Unions to prevent the abuses of the past.

Robert had Sarah meet with Paco Morales in Miami to determine his interest in merging his area of control in South Florida back under the umbrella of the United States of America. Robert offered Paco the same arrangement they had offered Louis Donley, more Senators for their area of control and a new division of Florida into North and South Florida. Paco would be appointed the Senator Pro Tempore for one six year term and two other Senators would represent South Florida. That would give Paco the same arrangement as Louis Donley received and with great representation of his territory in the United States Senate. Paco would also be allowed to maintain his military units as National Guardsmen and the same arrangements for distribution of the Voters Identification Cards would be given to the residents of South Florida as were given in Hispanic America. Paco was definitely interested in the proposal and so informed Sarah. He was just not ready to commit at this time but according to Sarah, very likely would in the near future.

After the elections for the members of Congress and the Senate, there was a period of time where there was relative peace and quiet in the capital buildings at Scott Field. The capital structures were still in the process of being constructed on the outer environs of the Base. These consisted of a new Capital structure housing the House, Senate and Congressional Offices. A housing section very similar to the old military barracks concept was constructed to provide temporary housing for the Senators and Representatives when they were in Session. Staff quarters were also provided for staff serving the new government. The Capital and environs were all located on the secured Base and identification cards were required for admission to the Base which thereby excluded all lobbyists and others seeking favorable assistance of one form or another from Senators and Representatives. There was much grumbling about this restriction but Robert had no intention of making any changes.

The nation was to continue under the guidance and leadership of Robert Thomas through his term as President. He was not restrained by the new Constitution until the end of his term. Then the new Constitution would apply and the executive power would no longer be absolute. Nevertheless, the Senators and the Representatives began serving in their legislative roles immediately. They could perform duties commensurate with their positions but Robert retained the power to nullify anything they produced. He did not intend to do that unless he considered it to be absolutely necessary. A period of time passed without any executive orders from him attacking any of their product.

After a while, Robert realized that the Representatives and the Senators were starting to write new laws and regulations for the nation. He had no objection to that as long as they were working on matters that he considered in keeping with the objectives and purposes of the new nation. He had lately learned that they were in the process of reinstituting the Environmental Protection Agency which had wreaked havoc in the economy years before and apparently the people behind the new effort were intending to do so again. Robert called a meeting of the leaders of the House and the Senate in the large Conference Room adjacent to the President's Office. The new leaders of the legislative bodies were curious as to the purpose of the meeting and were all waiting quietly for the President to appear. A few minutes after the appointed time for the meeting, Robert walked into the Conference room and laid his notes down on the rostrum.

"Welcome to the New United States of America. Remember the old one? The one with all the laws and regulations that told us when, how, and why to do virtually everything. Well, those days are gone. We don't do that anymore. Sure we need some laws but let me tell you it will be damn few laws. You men and women are the new guardians of the liberty of the citizens of this country. You are not the parents of a nation full of kids. You are not needed to direct their every move. Our country was not founded on legislators telling everyone what to do. Now if you are going to pass a law I want you to know that unless it is damn necessary to have that law on the books in order to save lives because our citizens are too damn dumb to protect themselves; or people that are using their own good judgment to avoid problems are just too damn dumb to handle that responsibility and they are going to need that law to survive, I am going to veto it. We are not going to get back to a country filled with lawyers and bureaucrats watching their every move and telling our citizens what they can eat, how much and what they can see and what they can do, if that is what you want then you will go out in the same manner as the previous occupants of those great big empty buildings in Washington went out. We are not going to have the alphabet soup bureaucracy again and you people are here to make damn sure we don't. You are not here to be a co-conspirator in recreating that mess again. Make a note of this. There will be no regulatory agencies created period. If you study the new Constitution, you will find that is written in there. They are like cancers in our culture. They soon grew more powerful than our own Constitution. No more of that. If a business or an individual gets out of line, there are criminal laws that can be invoked. I consider it my ultimate duty to protect the freedom of our citizens. If you do not intend to honor the new Constitution, You will be removed from this legislature in a heart beat. This country is not going to put up with that crap again. Are there any questions? Good. Dismissed."

The word going around in the new government offices was that the President was not going to adopt the provisions of the new Constitution until the time came when he had to do so and that would be at the end of his term. Anders heard some of the gossip and commented on it to Robert. Robert laughed and said it was true. The country was presently in training to live under the new Constitution and he considered himself the guardian of the principles contained therein. There was no way in hell this country was going to revert to what it had gone through before and furthermore, he told Anders, I have also had a large number of calls from legislators to the effect that they agree with my view of what legislation is required and which is not. "So there are two sides to this issue and I am on the side that is right."

The media, with one exception, was not touching the issue even though they had been fully apprised of Robert's speech to the legislators. They knew that if they hopped on the story like they would have in the days before the collapse, they would have to find another job. Robert knew quite well that he was pushing the envelope a bit by telling the legislators what they could do and what they could not do but his primary concern was what was going to happen when he was no longer around. Hopefully, others would rise to the challenge and speak out when it was necessary to do so.

The one exception in the media that did print the story and then addressed it further in a very critical editorial was the New York Press. The editorial blasted Robert as assuming dictatorial powers over the legislative branch of the government and should be impeached. Robert called the Editor on the telephone.

"Mister Mathews this is the President and I read your editorial regarding my discussion with the legislative leaders. I take it you are aware that your editorial violates the law on dissent and furthermore I am not impeachable for the next four years. Sorry to tell you that."

"I didn't think I violated any law but if you think so, that is your business."

"No, I think it is your business Mister Mathews and do you see those three military men that just walked into your office?"

"Yes…Just what the hell, do you think you are doing?"

"OK. This is what I am doing. I am buying your newspaper and I am going to pay you one thousand dollars for every asset of your business including the cheap pens you have in your desk, all printing equipment, everything, the building as well. Now this is not negotiable so pick up your wallet, nothing else, and leave with the three uniformed troops. They are going to take you to a nice summer camp where you will be residing for a period of time until you gain more respect for the law and then you may find some other business to get involved with provided I let you out in a reasonable period of time. Goodbye Sir."

The three Rangers delivered the thousand dollar check to the Editor who refused to take it. They then cuffed the prisoner, stuffed the check into his shirt pocket and one of the men walked him out to their vehicle while the other two men announced to the staff that the newspaper had been sold but they could continue working. The Rangers advised the workers present that a new Editor-Manager would be arriving shortly. Some of the staff writers got up and prepared to leave apparently in protest at what they were witnessing. The Sergeant in charge of the Rangers told them, "If you walk out, take your personal items with you as you will not be coming back here." That stopped the parade to the door and the walkers quickly resumed their desk chairs.

News of the involuntary termination of the owner-editor spread rapidly throughout the newspaper industry. While the story created a stir among the editors, none chose to write about it in their own publications. Their take on the new government was that, yes, there was a Constitution but it did not control or restrain the present powers of the President at least during his term of office. The President was in a position of power and he did not fear using it. Possibly at some time in the future the Constitution would be the supreme law of the land, but not right now. Robert was aware of the limitations on his power as President but for the present time he was going to ignore them. He wanted to make sure that there was not going to be another runaway government and he would hold off on delivering full-fledged Constitutional government until he was convinced it would last. He was fully aware of the fact that he was pushing the envelope quite a bit with his treatment of the Editor but he would see that he was released soon and would be allowed to buy back his former property for the one thousand dollar purchase price provided he appeared to have learned his lesson.

The country had achieved a status of relative stability since the Muslim forces had been defeated in the Lakes Region. There continued to be occasional outbursts of fighting by remnants of Muslim forces that had continued resisting as guerilla units using hit and run tactics against truck or rail transportation of supplies across the country. They were more of a destabilizing nuisance than a viable threat to the nation, yet Robert told Perry to bear down on them and bring their attacks to a halt. That was difficult to do as the Muslims would attack at night and then melt into their communities by day appearing as just normal law abiding Muslim civilians. Robert fully intended to rule by fiat at least until the country was stabilized and secure. With the problems relating to the Muslims, he fully realized that this was going to take some time and he prayed that it would reach that status before his term of office expired.

Perry was of the opinion that the solution was to ship entire communities of Muslims back to the Mid-East or the problems would just continue. Again he met with the Muslim leaders in the unstable communities and warned them as to what the alternatives would be if the situation continued. That got their attention and for the most part the raids stopped. Perry warned them that if the raids were stopped on a temporary basis only, the ships would be loaded without any further discussions and the passengers would not be going cabin class. That cemented the situation and no longer were shipments by truck or rail put under attack. Similar problems developed elsewhere across the northern tier of States where the Muslims were represented in larger groups than in the South where they were seldom seen. Having learned how to deal with Muslims, Perry warned the leaders of those communities that they could be deported and the result was the same. When they were aware of what the risks were for them if the attacks continued, they became much more cooperative. That was classic Muslim response. If challenged seriously with punishment that they really feared, such as eviction from the United States of America, they would fold like a paper fan.

A very large standing army remained after the war against the FSP and the Muslim conflicts. Robert met with Ross Perry to decide on the size and type of Defense Force that they were going to have in the future. Globally, the main threat to the United States remained China but there had been no actual confrontations. China had survived the global collapse in much better shape than the other countries of the world due to their extreme authoritarian control of their population. Corruption in China was operating at a minuscule level compared to what had been occurring in the United States and Europe due to their very active secret police operation. Their economy had suffered during the collapse due to the decline in exports to countries such as the United States that no longer had funds available with which to make purchases of Chinese products and they were able to retrench more quickly on inventory levels and cost controls in view of the fact that the government controlled every business, large and small.

Following the collapse, China realized that they were in a much more improved position in the world than they had been just a year before due to the fact their competitors had suffered far more severely than they had. Their global confidence climbed rapidly and they began flexing their muscles to exert their influence with their immediate neighbors and those on the Pacific rim. They were not directly threatening Pacific area powers, they were just being much more subtle in their demands for concessions than they had been previously.

The disagreements were occurring more on the periphery of their areas of influence rather than in face to face meetings. The Chinese had exercised dominion over Taiwan by exerting their power and inserting their own people in the government of the island. The United States at that time was in the throes of collapse and made no response. The Chinese were also letting the Japanese and the Southeast Asians know who was running the show in the east. China looked to Southeast Asia as their source of raw materials and oil reserves and they let the countries of that region know that their natural resources were needed exclusively by China's rapidly expanding economy and they would pay a fair price for them. At the same time, China was putting the pressure on the Japanese to invite the Americans to leave their military bases in Japan and Okinawa as they had successfully convinced the South Koreans to pressure the Americans to leave South Korea. Most of those moves occurred during the Presidency of Frank Turner who was too busy filling his own coffers to worry about the security of the nation. In the last few years, China had made overtures to the Hawaiians to allow Chinese bases on their islands allegedly for the purpose of protecting Chinese interests in the Pacific. This matter was still up for negotiation which infuriated Robert.

The real reason for the Chinese actions in Hawaii was to advance their sphere of influence farther to the west into turf formerly possessed by the United States of America, their number one competitor. The Hawaiians acted as though they were honored by the interest the Chinese were showing in their Island homeland but had thus far not granted them permission. In the meantime, the Chinese were favoring Hawaiian markets with goods at lower costs than the Hawaiians could pay for them elsewhere, including from the United States. Possibly, in time, the day would come when the Hawaiians would lack the backbone to deny the requests of their new Chinese friends. The Chinese had also approached the Alaskan government with lucrative contract offers to mine for scarce resources and drill for oil which China needed badly for its rapidly growing industrial economy. The Alaskan government at the time was harboring some thoughts of going it alone and possibly entering into negotiations with other countries while at the same time pondering rejoining the United States of America as a member State. They were Americans at heart and had serious questions as to the real intentions of the Chinese. WestPac and now Scott Field were offering Alaska lucrative contracts as well as benefits for opting into the new United States of America. Alaska liked what they saw Robert Thomas and his Administration doing in the rebuilding of America. At the present time Alaska appeared to be favoring a reentry into the Union and was not accepting the Chinese offers. The visit to Scott Field had been a success and the Governor of Alaska indicated that he was ready to sign the agreement on the basis that South Florida and Colorado had signed. He had to convince a few of his people but he was sure it was virtually a done deal.

In any event, Robert and Ross Perry treated China with a great deal of respect. They were fully aware of what China was up to and they did not want to challenge China to any form of military conflict. They had concerns about the strength of their military vis á vis that of China. The population of China was rapidly approaching two billion people so there was no question China could raise a far superior Army to anything the United States could raise. The Chinese also had a very impressive military. They had recently built two very modern aircraft carriers equipped with jump jet stealth fighters capable of carrying substantial bomb loads with operating ranges of up to four thousand nautical miles at super-sonic speeds. Their armored land force was very impressive as was the equipment their foot soldiers were carrying. They had five very modern cruisers with long range guns and missiles. China had a very impressive fleet of nuclear powered submarines with global range and missile firing capability some of which were known to be operating in the Atlantic Ocean. If America was to defend against a Chinese threat, it would have to be by way of very modern technology. Robert had Perry convene a meeting of the top men and women in the science fields to prepare a defense that would hopefully shield the United States from an attack from the threats coming from the east.

Nuclear weapons were available to both sides but both Robert and Perry's opinion was that they would only be used if such weapons were used against them. There was no other logical use of such weapons against a force holding the same weapons in greater quantity. The United States currently had a slight edge in technology. It was possible that the United States could create a defensive system comprised of electronic and technical barriers that would cause the Chinese to think twice about an armed attack on this country, nuclear or otherwise that would trigger a response the Chinese could not defend. The United States had been working on missile technology ever since they had arrived in Riverton. Most of the scientists and technicians involved in the space program had convened first in Riverton and later in Seattle to continue their space technology efforts. There was also the thought that measures could be taken to make the United States a less attractive target for Chinese acquisition. Robert did not know how that would be done but he would turn that problem over to the University Professors to discuss and ponder. It was obvious to Robert that some areas of the world were considered more attractive to take over and control than others. He had his own opinions as to what it was that made one area particularly more attractive than another. He assumed wealth, natural and acquired, and natural resources would be major factors but there must be others as well. If the United States was willing to supply their bountiful foodstuffs to the Chinese at a reasonable price, possibly that would allay their appetite to own Nebraska. He would let the professors and scientists work on that problem.

Robert spoke to Sarah about taking steps to improve relations with China if that was possible. He knew that the Chinese were very watchful of the tremendous advances that were occurring in the American economy while theirs, while progressing at a very good rate, lagged further behind every year. Since the United States returned to manufacturing and were now turning out the top quality products, the Chinese were obviously envious. American automobiles, electronics, aviation products, tool and die products in demand the world over, medical appliances, home appliances that had triple the life of products from previous years and many other hard goods were in great demand by all countries around the world. Robert suggested to Sarah that she invite some of the Chinese economists to Scott Field to meet their counterparts in this country. They could discuss with them methods of improving their own production methods. The Chinese experts in various fields did come to Scott and meet with their American counterparts. Robert was certain that the reason for the accelerating productivity in America was due to the Capitalist economic system while the Socialist Chinese economy was hamstrung by bureaucratic regulation. Before the Conferences were held, Robert spoke first to the American engineers and scientists as to the prohibition against divulging critical technological knowledge to non-citizens and the fact that the prohibition applied to the forthcoming meetings. General suggestions were allowed but no specific data was transferred to the Chinese. The meeting with the Chinese was not a spectacular success but it was a success and it was a good start to hopefully improve continued relations between the two countries.

Sarah had suggested to the Chinese Foreign Minister that the United States was not going to raise an issue over the Chinese assumption of control over Taiwan and that it would be expected that China would cease threats against Japan aimed at removing American forces from the main islands and from Okinawa. That seemed to be working. The Chinese did not accept or deny Sarah's proposals but the veiled threats to Japan ceased.

As for the size of the standing Army, Robert and Perry decided to reduce the force from the present two million men and women under arms to a force of one million, five hundred thousand. They would increase the Air Wing to seven fighter wings, three transport wings including aerial refuelers, four Drone or unmanned aerial vehicle wings, fifty nuclear powered submarines, an Atlantic Fleet of destroyers, cruisers, two aircraft carriers and the same for the Pacific. This would be built up over a period of years and hopefully nothing of any great consequence would occur in the mean time.

Robert's plans for the nation were going to cost a large amount of money and he spoke with his Secretary of the Treasury as to how that would be paid for. The tax that had been assessed on every living American had been a five per-cent flat tax on all income. There was no distinguishing types of income. Interest Income, Dividends, Capital gains and ordinary income were now merged as were all other forms of income. Every delivery of cash to any person was considered income including inherited funds delivered to a beneficiary by a deceased relative.

The tax rate was very low which was very popular but everything was taxed which produced a large tax revenue. Barter exchanges came under the microscope and all such exchanges now required a statement of value. That statement of value was subject to review by the Treasury Department who would ensure that services traded for return services were dealt with as though they were paid for in cash. Barter was a fairly common occurrence in the small towns of the west and they complained the most. The tax rate had been five per-cent but with the city rebuilding programs and the buildup of the military, it was raised to ten per-cent. There were complaints to increasing the tax rate and Robert reminded the citizens in his weekly address that it also included the National Retirement Program. There were many people that were also clamoring for a National Health Program. Robert was against nationalized health services as he questioned that they were successful programs. Too many people just loved going to the doctor and taking pills. The cost would be huge and in order to make it work, laws would be required to control the unhealthy behavior of many of the citizens. Weight was a factor in poor health and the nation would have to be put on a diet. Smoking would be criminally penalized. The same would be the case with excessive drinking. Drugs were already outlawed but the penalties would have to be increased. All citizens would have to participate in physical exercise. The more Robert thought of the changes that would be required for a national health care system, the more he realized it was not going to happen. Americans were independent people. They ran their own lives. They did not tolerate a government that wanted to run their life for them.

Another area of the world that continued to be a tinderbox was the Mid-East. The instability in that region had never ceased from the pre-collapse years, right through Turner's terms as President, The FSP years and to the present. It was Robert's intention to end all dealings with that area of the world due to their irrational lack of stability and to acquire needed petroleum products from more stable suppliers including American Oil companies, Alaskan sources, Venezuela now that it was governed by pro-American interests, Gulf wells and wells in the Southwest and Mexico.

While American sources of oil were being used to power American industry, Robert was fully aware of the fact that at some point in time, it would run out. It was only a temporary measure to service the nation while other energy sources were explored. Robert commissioned a Blue Ribbon Group to study alternative measures to reduce oil consumption and to study methods of replacing oil consumption in the United States. Nuclear power sources were being constructed across the country that could be harnessed to provide electric power grids for all electrical needs. Some suggestions for alternate sources had already produced gains. One was to utilize the oft tried electric power sources from wind and solar as much as possible and to use electricity to power small personal vehicles and city transit systems. Solar was not producing electricity in quantities sufficient to cover its cost other than to power low voltage devices. Studies were done on ocean wave action to determine if that could produce electrical power economically. Other methods as imaginative were also being explored.

Rail lines were being rebuilt and improved to provide alternate transportation systems for commuter travel. Less oil was used per passenger mile in rail transit than in all other systems. The problem was in getting the public to use rail commuter service. All cities of fifty thousand population or more were now connected and serviced by people moving trains running at convenient hours. In the limited number of cities serviced by commuter rail, private vehicles were no longer allowed on the roads unless they had a waiver license to drive on routes with connections through or to commuter rail systems. Robert had a ten cent a gallon gas tax applied to gasoline and diesel sales at commuter gas stations to put pressure on the public to stop driving their own vehicles. These programs did have some effect. A second solution was to increase the use of economical electric buses running on schedules within cities and from cities out on some rural routes. Automobile use of petroleum had always been the greatest offender. For that reason Robert also pressured the auto manufacturers to increase the efficiency of automobiles and had raised the automobile gas usage average up to fifty miles per gallon of fuel for city driving and seventy miles per gallon highway. Automobiles that did not operate at those efficiency levels were not permitted on public roads and highways.

"If the freedom of speech is taken away then dumb and silent we may be led, like sheep to the slaughter."

—Washington

CHAPTER TWENTY-SIX

A continuing problem in America that had always irritated Robert was the issue of drug use. It was attributed primarily to the youth but that was not an accurate association as to who was involved in its use. Robert believed that it was a social disease that had spread across all parts of American society. All ages were involved in drug use, the only difference was the drug of choice for the different segments of American society. For the elderly, prescription pain killers were the preferred drug. For the professionals and the wealthier citizens, cocaine and some of the more transcending exotic drugs de jure were the trips of choice. The youth continued their age old favorite, cannabis, with some mixing of it with heroin or taking the final plunge and graduating to mixed heroin and finally to meth for those intent upon taking the short trip to the brick wall.

Robert had watched the various elements of crime fighters coming out with ever new plans to really crack down on the use of drugs and after a flurry of activity with no results, they would revert to their offices and stations followed by a long period of silence and then they would roll out another ever newer, ever better plan to finally crack down on the use of drugs. It was a rotating cycle of public promotion of their importance as the guardians of society and best of all it was a wonderful way to increase promotions in the departments. More Sergeants, More Lieutenants, more Captains but no changes in the plague that was destroying the country. Half the young people had glazed eyeballs at least every weekend if not all the time. Many of the younger crowd eagerly confessed that they were high right after brushing their teeth in the morning, or maybe they had stopped doing that as well.

Robert attributed the drug ills of the American people to just one more result of a total absence of any foundation of morals in their lives. Never taught in the schools, not at home with two working parents who were on drugs themselves, not exposed to any religious morals training as very few, especially of the young, ever went to church. Whatever the cause of the widespread use of drugs in American Society, Robert intended to end it by the end of his presidential term.

Robert met with Ross Perry and Sarah to discuss the problem. They knew they would never completely end the occasional use of drugs or the experimental use of drugs but what they wanted to bring an end to was the corporate massive scale distribution and sale of drugs. Some of the drugs were homegrown such as marijuana, meth and some psychedelics but the major source of criminal drugs such as cocaine were imported from Central and South America. Detection techniques for locating drugs in vehicles, trucks, trains and planes had advanced considerably in the past few years. There was a question if law enforcement really wanted to find the drugs. If they did there would be less police Sergeants, less Lieutenants, less Captains and so forth. Use of the military in fighting the problem could have a major impact on what the results would be. Perry was of the belief that if the military was not used as the major weapon against widespread drug use, it would just continue and grow worse.

The first target for the battle was the Southern Border with Mexico. Fifty thousand Rangers were sent down to guard the Southern Border and to man crossing stations. There had been a strong suspicion that many of the civilian Border Guards that were waving the trucks thru the border gates were becoming wealthy themselves. Inspection stations now under the view of the Rangers were expanded to allow the inspection of all vehicles passing through the border. None were waved through any longer. Cars, trucks, Semi-trailers, trains, planes, buses, people, everything was inspected to ensure that no drugs were passing through the border. As for the uninhabited areas of the border, drones were employed day and night in sufficient number to be on watch along the entire border for trespassers. Infra-red scopes were used for the night time traffic. If a person illegally crossed the border out where no one lived and was alive, he or she was observed.

When trespassers were spotted, the drones equipped with loud speakers told them to return to the border and cross back into Mexico or to come under attack from the Drone. Some refused to do so to their peril. They were then targeted by a drone and left where they fell. If there was a means available, as there sometimes was, to take the trespassers prisoner, that was done and then they were sent to prison camps for border trespassing for a period of five years working on road and highway repair, repainting County and State buildings, and building new schools for citizens, all services performed for minimum wages after deductions to pay for prisoner's food and housing cost in the County Jail. After that they were shipped back to Mexico and advised that if they came back, they would receive a ten year sentence.

The Canadian border then became the entry of choice together with ship and boat traffic into the east and west coast ports. Rangers were assigned to these locations and over time the cost of drugs in the States soared from ten dollars to a hundred dollars to a thousand dollars a hit. Marijuana experienced the same inflation in cost as aerial surveillance of crop lands was increased and where found, it was destroyed. Also employed was the new technique for following up the ladder from the user to the local dealer to the regional dealer to get the real culprits involved. The lower rungs of the ladder were advised that there was a ten year term for use unless they provided all the information on their source. If they did cooperate, they received a six month sentence for use which alone was an eye opener for the casual user. Upper rungs of the ladder were dealt with in the same manner but with longer terms.

Doctors that were caught basically dealing in prescription drugs immediately lost their licenses and were sentenced to terms in prison. The issue then focused on alcohol. Excessive use of alcohol was in many cases worse than the use of marijuana and needed to be dealt with as well. That was a more difficult problem to attack as drinking alcoholic beverages was as American as apple pie. The answer was to put on a massive campaign to stamp out habitual excessive drinking. Liquor stores were advised to be alert to large purchases of liquor by individuals. Records were kept and when such cases were observed, they were reported and interviewed by personnel trained to detect signs of dependency. When they were observed, the person was sent to a retraining center for treatment and when they were ready for release they were sent to an Alcoholics Anonymous group for further supervision.

After two years of the Ranger crackdown on drugs and alcohol, the drug users were facing huge price increases and they were like a boiling kettle with no relief valve, they were flooding hospitals and clinics for treatment of their dependency. They had exhausted their assets, cash and property trying to continue buying the evaporating drugs at the ever increasing prices. They had lost their jobs, their families, their houses and themselves in the process. The hospitals were instructed by Robert to offer assistance to them provided they admitted their dependency and provided the information as to the source of their drug supply. The hospital costs were paid for by the patient providing public services of an equal amount. The Government then paid the hospital bill. Another by-product of the drug crackdown was that city, county, state and federal drug crime fighters were sitting around the station houses playing pinochle with little if anything to do. The local governments could no longer afford to maintain the large police force when crime of all kinds had deteriorated to what it had been a century or more previous. Police captains became lieutenants, lieutenants became sergeants and sergeants lost their jobs. Burglary crimes, theft, and associated crimes almost disappeared. Assault and violence increased for a while before the former users finally exploded and ended up in hospitals.

The problem that Robert now faced was what to do with the teams of Rangers that had brought drug use to a halt. He did not want to leave them on drug duty for the rest of their career in the military and he knew that if he turned the operation back to the civilian Border Guards who had participated in the problem previously, he would be back at square one. He suggested to Perry that they maintain a watch on the problem and that new, more qualified, Border Guards, specially trained, properly supervised and fully warned that if they cooperated in any drug shipments they would be looking at long jail times with hard labor. Border Guards were hired on qualifications, intelligence, dedication, prior military service, recommendations, and test scores. There was no longer any affirmative action hiring or equal opportunity selections. Nor was there any favoritism of any sort allowed. If that was discovered, all participants were immediately fired. The new controlling policy was common sense. If a person was hired as a Border Guard and "it just made no sense to hire that guy or gal as a Border Guard" then the alarms would go off. No more mister nice guy for anyone involved in the battle against drugs. It had been destroying the wealth of the country along with the youth and many adults who made drugs part of their lives. An immediate by-product for the average citizen as a result of Robert's war on drugs was that they could walk down the street of any city and not be robbed. Street theft before the crackdown was so common place that citizens just didn't walk down the street. There were still gangs in the cities and these were being eradicated slowly but surely but they were still there. Perry had some of his Rangers walking down streets as decoys in areas of the cities that had this problem and when the punks would make their move, they were soon surrounded by teams of Rangers that let them know it was not smart to go after a Ranger. They were then picked up, hurled into trucks and carted off to retraining centers. There they learned to sing the National Anthem, to say the Pledge of Allegiance and they had to learn to memorize the entire Constitution before they could even begin their six month sentence. Every Sunday morning they attended church and after that they had what became known as 'circle jerk' where they sat around in a circle with a counselor and discussed what made them turn into such losers. The discussion would start off with the counselor asking, "Jefferson, tell everyone why you are such a jerk-off." The group at first could not believe what they were observing but after a while, they began to see the humor in it and all would chime in and ask Jefferson such things as to explain why he tried to sell the cop the drugs. "You really are a jerk-off."

Robert was quite pleased with the way everything was working out. Nothing was perfect but he did not expect that to be the case anyway. He still had two years left as President of the United States and he was beginning to look forward to the day when he could return to Florida and get back to fishing on the ocean. He was realizing that he no longer had the energy that he needed to do the job. He had spent his entire life working under rather adverse circumstances and it was definitely beginning to take its toll. He had enjoyed his work and still did but he was realizing it was work that required a younger man. As he thought about that, he called Sarah and asked if she had received any further word from the Alaska Governor or from Paco Morales as to what their intentions were. She said the Governor had reported just yesterday that Alaska was requesting readmission into the Union on the same terms as Colorado. Robert only commented, "Good, set it up. What about Morales?"

"I did talk with Morales a little over a week ago and he is about to commit but requested a little more time as he wanted to make sure his followers in the Miami area were in total agreement. He did not want to give us an affirmative response and then listen to gripes from his staff members. I expect Morales to be in full agreement shortly. I will let you know when it happens."

In the last year or so, Robert had become aware that a number of local state and city leaders across the country had been arrested or charged with absconding with public funds. In some of the cases the thefts were of very substantial sums of money and in some instances public land holdings were converted to private ownership, usually to public officials, free of charge. One of the defendants on the list of those charged with corruption was Bert Connors. Robert had to think for a moment to place the name but then he remembered the windbag bureaucrat from Oregon that he had dealt with in years past. They had warned Connors back then but apparently he just never learned the lesson. The more Robert thought about Connors and his type, the angrier he became. Connors was scamming his wealth at the same time young Americans were fighting to regain the country and getting their arms and legs blown off and in some cases their heads chopped off. Robert contacted Perry and told him he was familiar with Connors from the past and he wanted his fat ass put away for a long time. Perry told him that they had the goods on Connors and had been watching him for some time so, "Not to worry, that guy is going no-where."

The trials were all being held by Military Court Martial in the Riverton facility. Those found guilty, which was virtually all of them, were being sentenced to prison in the military stockade in the Valley. That facility was basically the Government Prison other than the special prison maintained at Scott Field. Special prisoners, mostly related to the Turner Administration, were housed in the Scott Field Prison which had been expanded for that purpose as there was a fair number of persons involved. State convicted prisoners were housed in State facilities across the country. One prison was not particularly better than another.

Stuart followed the media news on the defendants involved in these corruption cases as he was curious what type of individual would act in such a despicable manner at a time when the nation was coming out of very difficult times and opportunities were again appearing on the horizon. Most of the defendants were in mid to upper level management positions and were leading fairly comfortable lives. It was just one more glaring example of the lack of morals in the country. As he thought about that, he was reminded that he wanted to do something about what he called "the crap" that Hollywood was again turning out. The movie industry had been silent for years after the collapse and he knew that many of the principals had migrated to the South of France. He had been hopeful that they would restrict their activities to that area of the globe but they apparently were fascinated by Southern California. A person could not see a movie today that did not contain every four letter word in the lexicon of filth and every form of sexual perversion or coupling with man or beast that was physically possible. At a time when Robert was trying to instill moral principles into the psyche of the nation, Hollywood was doing their best to sell their depraved platter of delights to the youth of the country.

There was no doubt the movies were mostly attended and supported by the younger set and they were the ones Robert was most concerned about. He spoke with Anders and Perry about the problem and, of course, the first item to come up was that of Freedom of Speech. The three men all fully realized that the counter argument to doing something about the filth being conveyed by the Hollywood crowd would be their feigned concern for the freedoms endowed on this great nation. Robert suggested that they work with some of the more well grounded figures in the motion picture industry, and there were some, and develop a credentials committee that would review and rate movies that were being produced for the viewing public whether in theaters, rental or sales sources, or television. The ratings would be: Filth, Not Subject to Revision, Not Allowed Without Major Revision, and Acceptable Only to Adults Ages 21 and Older. Movies with ratings of Not Allowed without major revision, or Filth could not be published in movie theaters. Any movie without one of these ratings but bearing the credentials committee stamp could be seen by anyone, including children provided it showed the R symbol for having been reviewed. Announcement of the new movie rating system created a buzz among the citizens but soon died out as the public was obviously aware of the low quality of the movies being sent to local theaters.

As Robert was working in his office at Scott Field, Toni informed him that Sarah wanted to speak with him and she was in the outer office. Robert told her to send Sarah in. When she entered, he motioned to the chair in front of his desk and asked her how everything was going in the world. That was a standard question to Sarah from Stuart as Sarah always knew more of what was happening elsewhere than anyone else in the government.

"Actually Stuart, things are pretty quiet. The Mid-East is of course exploding in its normal manner and blaming us in the process but that is so commonplace I hardly mention it anymore. It does amaze me that they are able to blame us when we have so little to do with them anymore now that we are again producing our own oil from our own wells."

"Sarah, maybe they are thinking that we are drilling right over into their wells. Now that is something we should try to do. Anything else on fire, about to explode, a scandal coming up, anything?"

"I do have some information that I am sure you will find interesting, which is really why I came to bother you."

"And what, pray tell, is that. Sounds like some juicy gossip to me."

"Better than that, Robert. Your old friend is back in the news again."

"You have to be talking about Irene Covington. I thought she was dead. I have not heard anything on her for quite a while. What is that lovely lady up to now?"

"Well, this time she may have tripped and fallen on her political face in the mud. I think this time she has done it. Are you familiar with the group that carries the title, Americans for Democracy and Truth?"

"Yes but I am not an expert on them. I only know them as Radical Socialist trouble makers who are incensed that the country under my Nazi dictatorship is doing so well."

"Yes, that is the group. Or I should say that is the public persona of the group. What you may not know is the more secret side of ADT. Let me give you the full picture. Do you have time now or would you prefer I cover this later?"

"Hell no. You have me hooked. Let's hear it."

"Ok. As you know, Military Intelligence began following foreign email, digital and telephone comms some time ago between American political groups and foreign agencies or governments, depending upon what country was involved. We were mostly interested in the Mid-East but also began following China when their actions towards us turned a bit aggressive. ADT had been connected with some terrorist groups in the Mid-East with respect to their activities involving Israel. ADT was supporting some of these terrorist groups but always under the cover of educational or humanitarian assistance. The funds that were transferred to these groups always seemed to the military to be well in excess of what those purposes would convey."

"In the course of carrying out these efforts, the ADT came into contact with Chinese groups involved in the same sort of funding efforts. However, the Chinese efforts were more directly connected with bringing about the end of Israel, either through economic collapse by reason of interruption of commerce or blockades in the Mediterranean or shipments of arms to their enemies. The ADT representative guiding this operation was Irene Covington and over time, she managed to establish a very cozy relationship with the Chinese Security Chief, Chen Shi Yong. Actually from reviewing the messages back and forth, I have the definite impression that it was Chen who managed to set up the cozy relationship with Irene. I suspect he saw in her a very likely candidate for someone that he could work with in the States."

As the messages proceeded back and forth, Chen Shi was bringing out the fact that Irene had been treated quite unfairly in her efforts to protect democracy in the United States due to the lack of cooperation from Robert Thomas and others in the government. At first Irene was brushing off the comments but as time passed, she began voicing her own complaints of what she had been trying to do and had been frustrated in doing so by the autocratic methods of Robert Thomas in particular. Chen agreed, saying he had observed the entire sequence of events and sympathized with Irene for what she had gone through. Chen Shi then began dropping hints that if Robert Thomas had not been there putting up this wall, the United States today would be a much more democratic country than it was. Irene totally agreed with these comments and added some of her own.

Chen Shi then suggested that what the country needed was opposition to Robert Thomas and his gang of autocrats that he was not getting from the media. The new media were cowards in America and lacked the courage to speak the truth as their predecessors had. Sarah pulled out a file of message transmittals and began reading from them. She identified the source of each as Chen or Irene. She read from the first one. "What if we provided the funds for a clandestine newspaper published and distributed in the United States."

Sarah read from Irene's reply: "Chen, that would be against the law and they would land in your office the day of the first publication."

Chen: "What if there was no office and distribution was handled by our own people. The newspaper would be free and would be found where people were found. It would get the truth out to the public."

Irene: "Interesting but what would I have to do with that?"

Chen: "You could be the writer and publisher. We would pay you for this and your presence and participation would be unknown period. No problem. We would cover all costs and ensure distribution of the paper."

There were other messages detailing the involvement of each party and how the distribution would be conducted. The purpose of the newspaper, clearly laid out by Chen was to create a division in the American public leading to a peaceful overthrow of Robert Thomas and his staff.

Robert appeared a bit confused, "Sarah I have heard nothing of this newspaper or any clandestine newspaper, did they ever do it?"

"Yes, they did produce one issue of the newspaper and then we arrested all parties involved in the production of the paper and its distribution, including Irene Covington. She is being held right now in Riverton and was just arrested yesterday. Perry may not know this as the arrest was made by one of the investigating officers when he learned that Irene was making plans to depart the United States, presumably for China."

"What the hell is wrong with her? I thought she had a brain. She had a screwy outlook on what made the world go around but I find it difficult to believe she would sell this country down the river to the Chinese."

"Robert you will soon find out the whole story as it is going to a Court Martial here at Scott Field and she will be looking at a long prison term when she is found guilty. Notice, I did not say if she is found guilty. She is in serious trouble."

"Well keep me posted on what is going on there. She may have just been dragged into a bad deal she would never have gotten into on her own. I hate to say it, I almost feel sorry for her. I must be getting old."

"I'll let you know what happens. I don't think we will have to wait very long."

Robert was down to his last year in office as the President of the United States. All of the laws that he had put on the books were still there and would stay there until the House and the Senate set them aside and the new President did not veto those changes. Those laws could also be challenged by appeals on lower court decisions that could wind their way up to the Supreme Court but that could also take a long time. Maybe up to three or four years or in some cases even longer.

Robert was a bit skeptical that the nation would remain a free nation devoid of the cancerous effects of overgrown bureaucracy that had finally destroyed the sacred freedoms created by the Founders centuries ago. He had tried his best to instill a love of freedom in the citizens and into the sacred document, the Constitution of the United States, that had lasted three hundred years before it was overtaken by greed, corruption, and Administrative Laws that set up a collateral bureaucracy that eventually strangled it. He had counseled his friends in Government, whether in the House or the Senate to be alert that others would try to destroy the Constitution as others had tried before. What he was most concerned about at this time was who would become President to be the chief defender of the sacred document for the next four or eight years. He wanted a young man, one with the energy and the fight to take on all the legal challenges to the basic intent of the Constitution which was to protect the inherent God given freedoms every man, woman and child possessed.

Right now the nation's economy was booming and that was the first time since many years prior to the collapse when freedom still reigned in the country. The nation's economy was now booming because there were very few regulations existing as road blocks to prevent it from booming. Taxes were relatively low so that people could work, create profits, retain them or use them for further investment in their businesses. Already many in the nation were demanding higher taxes on others who worked harder or were more successful in their businesses so that they could pay for additional benefits for the complainers. The complainers were never complaining that they were not paying enough in taxes. It was just more of the same old mantra that Robert had heard for years.

So who to get as a viable candidate to serve as the next President of the United States. There were a few young men that Robert held in very high regard. One was Clay Daley who served in the Executive Department of the Government and was widely respected but he was not as well known as some of the others. He also needed more experience in the government. Jack Nix was very well known and was highly respected by all. Further-more he was one of the original Pioneers having made the difficult trek from Florida to found the new nation. He had served in the difficult battles that led to the retaking of the country and he was a no nonsense leader of men, respected by the Military and by all in the civilian realm. Monty Wyatt was another well known, respected Military Leader that was also one of the original Pioneers and his wife was a survivor in the collapse of the nation that took the lives of the other members of her family. They were two true patriots and were respected as such. Most of the others were like Robert, now getting up in years and as Robert had learned, this was a young man's job. The job tested you daily; you were under pressure 24/7; there was no let up in the challenges you had to face. Robert knew that the job was taking a toll on his health. He had experienced a few fainting or dizzy spells that were not noticed by others as they had occurred while he was alone in his quarters. This was the primary reason that he had firmly decided against being a candidate for President. Robert knew he had done a good job controlling the nation during very difficult times. But as good as he was, he questioned that he had been good enough. Yes, he had al-ways accomplished his goal but was he too quick to revert to autocratic methods to achieve it. He was heavily criticized for this but what were the alternatives. He sure as hell did not believe in the committee approach to solving problems which would have spread the blame. He had seen that fail too many times. He always considered Stuart as the truly great man in the re-creation of the United States of America. It was for that reason that he had the statue dedicated to Stuart and placed in the District of Columbia Memorial Park alongside the other great and well attended National Monuments. But then, hadn't Stuart played a bit fast and easy with truth in order to accomplish some of his goals? Robert knew he had but he also knew that Stuart only did that when there was no other alternative. Well, Robert thought, isn't that what I did as well. "I should stop being so hard on myself. I probably was a far better leader than others around the world. Sure as hell better than Turner." Robert smiled and stopped thinking about whether he had done a good job or not. That was a waste of time. He had often said that a person could beat himself to death with self criticism.

Robert inquired of the two possible candidates as to their interest in taking on the candidacy for President of the United States. Neither Nix or Wyatt was overly eager to take on the task as they were content with their present military duties and saw in them ample challenges sufficient to maintain their interest. Yet, both agreed to pursue the Office if they were asked to do so. Robert met with Anders, Ross Perry and Sarah to discuss the matter further.

Robert first inquired of Sarah if she would be willing to pursue the job. Sarah indicated that she would do so if the others refused or if Robert thought that she would be the best candidate for the job. Robert had always harbored a question about Sarah's dedication to principle when she had served as the Executive in Charge of WestPac after Stuart died. He thought that she had let others lead her astray on some important matters such as Roberts taking control of WestPac. Anders disagreed with Robert on that issue and believed that she was just outvoted by virtually everyone in Riverton at the time the decisions were being made. Robert had great respect for Sarah and dismissed his misgivings based on the opinions of Anders, Ross Perry, John Barnes and Matt Parker. All gentlemen that he viewed as men of personal strength, patriotism and personal courage and that he trusted completely. He decided that he would hold an interview session with each potential candidate and he and the four gentlemen that he consulted with respect to Sarah would pose questions to them and they could each weigh their answers and then vote. Robert had his own preference even before the interviews but then the others very likely did as well. That was only human nature but he as well as the others would have to stifle that preference and decide on the basis of their responses in the interviews.

They held the interviews in the Conference Room adjacent to the President's Office at Scott Field. The first person interviewed was Sarah and she did an excellent job of fielding the questions. She was the one most familiar with the structure of the government, the history and importance of the Constitution and the present situation of the country and the World at large. With respect to her opinions regarding how to deal with current and hypothetical threats, she had ready answers but Robert felt that she was almost too nice with respect to how she would deal with those who were attacking her. He did not let that color his opinion of her as he knew that he, himself, was considered as overly aggressive and even too mean to quote Irene Livingston, to be serving as President. The other interviews were likewise very impressive. All three possible candidates had a ready knowledge of government, of the duties of the president and of the problems the nation would be facing in coming years. When the interviews were over, and the candidates had left the room, Robert asked them what they thought.

The four men all looked at one another and Ross finally spoke up. "All of them looked damn good to me. I personally prefer Jack Nix. He is well known, very well respected, he is smart, knows what he is doing, is not a loud mouth and is a man of deep personal character and conviction. You can trust Jack Nix...now you can certainly trust Sarah and Monty as well. They are all good but I'd go with Jack Nix." Anders pushed Sarah as she had done the best with respect to her global view and knowledge of what needed to be done in government. Barnes was in favor of Monty Wyatt as Monty had worked with Barnes a great deal and Barnes thought the world of Wyatt and how he dealt with problems. Robert finally spoke up and he said that he favored Jack Nix. "He truly loves this country. The others do as well but I think Jack just has that boundless energy and love of this country that no one person or other country would succeed in destroying it while he was at the helm." The men continued talking for two more hours to make sure they were covering all bases with the three candidates. In the end, they all agreed that Jack Nix would make an excellent candidate to run for the Office of President. Now all he had to do was to win the National Election.

"All institutions are prone to corruption and
to the vices of their members."
—**Morris West**

CHAPTER TWENTY-SEVEN

R obert called Jack Nix to come to Scott Field so that they could talk over the coming election. Nix had been up in Riverton reviewing the training of new recruits with Mark Campbell and Roy Yates but caught the next flight to Scott to meet with Robert. When he walked into Robert's office, Robert told him to have a chair and make himself comfortable as Robert had a number of items he wanted to discuss with him. Robert told Nix that the leadership in the executive wing of the government all favored him to be the Presidential candidate in the elections coming up in one year. Nix was pleased that he was held in such high regard by the men and women surrounding Robert and he would be happy to serve as the candidate of the Conservative wing if that is what they wanted him to do. He would also be pleased to continue serving in the Military as he had been doing all of his life. It was clear that being President was not one of his major goals in life but if he was called to serve as President, he would make that his primary mission in life. Robert told him that he understood Nix's position on being a candidate for the Office but that he, Robert, was very concerned for the future of the country if a person with the necessary qualifications did not take over the reins of government.

"Jack, as you know, I have been tangling with various elements of this government ever since I became President and one thing I have learned is that no matter what sacrifices many have made of their own blood and treasure in creating or defending this great nation, there are still many people trying to destroy what so many brave people have done. I, and the others, supported you because we believe you have the brains, the drive, the energy, the courage and the principles to be the guardian of what this great nation stands for." Nix began to speak but Robert held up his hand.

"Let me finish, Jack. Whoever takes over my job is going to have a real battle on his or her hands keeping the wolves away from the door. There are so many attacks against this country daily that the President must work overtime just to be aware of what is going on. Attacks not from foreign powers, although those are beginning to increase, but attacks from internal agents, public figures, bureaucrats, contractors, whoever, trying to better their position, increase their own power or steal some portion of the national treasure. We just put two or three hundred executives in positions of power across the land and already we are prosecuting approximately sixty of them on serious theft and corruption charges that will put most of them in jail for many years. At the same time, there are hundreds or more likely thousands of our citizens that are criticizing us for being too aggressive and too mean in going after these hoodlums. That is one of the major irritating factors involved in being President. Constantly trying to do the right thing and constantly being blamed for doing it. You spend half of your time being angered by public officials using their position for their own advantage right after they have taken the oath of office to serve for the good of the community. Half of the time angry and the other half disgusted that the culprits continue to be out there even when they are aware that they are involved in a very risky enterprise of theft that most likely will be discovered. Disgusted not only at the scum balls that steal from the nation but also disgusted at the citizens who seem to think it just goes with the territory. Well, it doesn't just go with the territory."

"You have heard the term, 'the fourth estate' and it has had many meanings over the years though they are all somewhat interrelated. Most of us know that it refers to the Media but how it refers to the Media varies from person to person. The most recent and the one the media likes to use is that it refers to them as the guardians of the sacred institution of government. The media in the fourth estate concept sees themselves as the overseer or as the 'fourth estate' overseeing what the government is up to and that they are carrying out their sacred oaths of office. Nothing could be further from the truth. The media, generally the handmaiden of the Liberal Elite, microscopically examines what the opposition political leaders are doing but totally ignores what their scum balls are up to. In all of my years in government, in Westpac and here, I have never been alerted by the media to a single display of corruption by their liberal friends. Nothing, nada, zip, zero."

"I have been alerted when some Conservative strayed a bit off the line and they didn't have to stray far before they hit the front pages of all newspapers, radio, TV, what have you. Now I tell you this not to dissuade you from assuming the mantel as the Conservative Candidate but to be perfectly honest that this is one bitch of a job and most of the time you will not like it. But, on the other hand there will be supremely glorious moments when you will clearly know and realize that you were the only thing standing in front of the Constitution protecting it and you won. Those moments are worth the price of the ticket even though you may be standing alone and are the object of media sarcasm, insult and allegations that you are playing favorites. It is a tough job but there definitely are rewards. The reason that I supported you to be the candidate was that I knew you had the balls to do the job. That you had great self respect, principles and courage combined with a great love of our Constitution and the history of this country to stand up before the many people that will be willing to sell it all short for some relatively meaningless purpose or a piece of gold and to tell them no, that is not going to happen. Jack, one last thing and I have talked way too much, it is a lonely job. It is not like the military where you are clearly involved in a brotherhood. There is no brotherhood in being President. You are alone. You are on your own. When you stop by the club to relax and have a beer, there are no other Presidents standing at the bar. You are the only one and they will all be watching you, pandering to you, suggesting to you or maybe even laughing at you. Watch yourself because everyone will be watching you. Now, do you still want to be the Candidate?"

"You put it in a way that I could not refuse the offer if I wanted to do so. I love a challenge and you know that. You just laid out the ultimate challenge of our lifetime and I want to show you that I am up to that challenge. I had thought of some of the hills to climb that you just laid out but not all of them. Furthermore, I'm sure that if elected, I will discover other challenges that neither one of us had thought of before. Times change and new challenges come to the fore. Let's do it."

In the following months, the Conservative Party endorsed the candidacy of Jack Nix to be the nominee of the Party on the first ballot. The support was genuine and enthusiastic. Nix had always been a well liked and highly respected figure in the Military and in the government of Robert Thomas. As Robert sometimes put it, "Hell, he'd whip my ass if he ran against me."

The Liberal Party endorsed Senator Vince Clayborne of New York. He was now a United States Senator but in former years he had been a lower level administrator in the Turner Administration but he was considered an honest bureaucrat as he either was honest or he was very adept at dodging subsequent investigations sponsored by Stuart or by Robert in their house cleaning moves. Clayborne was a very articulate and knowledge-able politician adept at holding his own in a debate and very well liked in the Senate by those from both parties. He had most recently served as the Senate Minority Leader and while in a minority position, he was able to get many bills passed favorable to his party and his constituents. He was also considered a clean politician and not one to delve into the world of dirty tricks to win elections. From the point of view of the candidates, the campaigns started off quite well however the tone soon changed as the media became involved. Their immediate focus was to explain to the public that their public hero, Jack Nix was just another copy of Robert Thomas. There were cartoons with Robert holding the strings over the puppet, Jack Nix, and having him dancing to the music. It was really quite humorous but incensed Robert more than it did Nix. Nix could not conceive that it could be an effective advertisement for Clayborne but he had much to learn about political campaigns.

Jack Nix campaigned on Robert's record as President. The economy was booming, cities were rebuilding, unemployment was at four per-cent, profits and incomes were up, college costs were reasonably low and crime was down. It was a dream record for a candidate to claim as his own. Robert campaigned heavily for Nix as did Sarah, Anders, Parker and all of the well known leaders of the rebirth of the nation. Clayborne had a hill to climb but he had the backing of the Liberal media and the trades who wanted a return of the Unions and the teachers who it seemed were always liberal. The Military backed Nix but the rest of the country, other than those elements mentioned, appeared to be divided between the two men.

In the debates which were televised, Clayborne did very well. He was a debater by nature and had a ready grasp on many of the political issues of the day. He also immediately latched onto the Chinese issue as a problem that only he could solve which provided the media with yet another good opening to get at Nix. They immediately began claiming that Jack Nix would have the country starting a nuclear war against China if he were elected. This was vehemently denied by Nix but it did cost him some votes.

During the campaign the trial of Irene Covington began at Scott Field. She was incarcerated in the Scott Field Prison so she did not have ready access to the media, yet they did have opportunities to interview her prior to her incarceration at Scott. It was clear from listening to her comments in these interviews that she saw her chance for freedom as the election of Clayborne. Many of her supporters were involved with the Clayborne campaign and the candidate had devoted a number of his speeches to the unfair imprisonment of Irene Covington who had been a hero of the nation until Robert Thomas threw her in prison for an alleged violation of her constitutional rights to speak her mind on political issues. The media harped on the line that she had done nothing wrong other than to write words on paper which was an American civil right dating back to the late 1700's when Thomas Paine wrote "Common Sense".

As Clayborne's campaign progressed, the public was beginning to side with Irene Covington in her defense of the charges against her. In the debates the media moderators made it a point to always bring up the 'Covington Affair' as though Jack Nix somehow had something to say about the charges against her or the right to set her free. Nix would only reply that the case was before the Military Tribunal and they would examine the evidence and rule accordingly.

The Court Martial proceedings against Irene Covington came to a conclusion four weeks before the election. The decision when it came out was a guilty finding of consorting with another government to the detriment of the United States of America. It carried a maximum sentence of twenty years in prison

There was an immediate outcry in the media with a demand that Robert remit the sentence to time served. Irene had already been in prison charged with the crime for over two years. Robert had full authority as President to remit the sentence or to pardon Irene and release her from Prison. As the day of sentencing came, the media was in a frenzy claiming Irene Covington was a victim of Conservative Bias. Whatever that was. Following the sentencing hearing, Irene received a sentence of ten years in prison to be served at the Scott Field Prison. Robert and Nix discussed the case and the options available to reduce any damage flowing from it with respect to the election. Jack Nix was not interested in taking any steps to modify the Military Court decision or to pardon her. His attitude was that "she knew what she was doing and she chose to do it. Let it be."

On the evening before the election, Robert had her brought to his office under guard for a meeting. She had been making numerous statements to the media by way of her associates that were blatant lies concerning Robert's service as President and his service prior to that with Stuart. To her, both Robert and Stuart were Nazis intent on controlling the entire country. Robert found that almost humorous in view of the fact that here he was about to leave the office of President with nothing but his clothes and a savings account that had grown to a size sufficient to provide him a reasonably comfortable retirement but certainly would not allow him a lavish lifestyle. When they brought her in, he told her to take a chair. She had kept her mouth shut when she arrived at his office and Robert had the distinct impression that she may have thought he was going to pardon her the night before the election as a favor to Nix.

"Irene I hope they are treating you well in the prison. Are they?"

"Yes, I have no complaints. I would like to be free. No doubt about that."

"Yes. I am sure. You have a ten year sentence and I am sure you have been told that the Military Courts never remit or reduce their sentences, right?"

"Yes. That is what they say."

"Now I am not going to remit your sentence nor pardon you either but I want you to understand that if you are a good prisoner and stop insulting the future President and me and Stuart that there is a good chance you will receive a shorter sentence from Jack Nix and I am assuming he will win the election. That is what my pollsters are telling me. I wanted to tell you this so that you did not start blabbing about what jackasses we are and in the process be cementing your stay at Scott. Now if you do want to blab about what Nazis we are and how unfair we are, go right ahead and do that but be aware of what you are doing to yourself. Do you understand this?"

Irene smiled and would have enjoyed making another comment but refrained. "Yes, Robert. No problem. I will be very silent."

"Good Irene, and also be careful. If and when you receive an early release from Nix, there will be conditions attached, such as I just requested of you. Do not play games then either. You do not want to go through this process twice, right?"

"How right you are, Robert."

"Good, Irene. If you need anything within reason, have your guards contact me and if it is something I can do and should do, it will be done."

"I'm almost starting to like you, Robert."

"Keep working at it, Irene. Good luck and I will see you on down the road."

The election was becoming a very hot topic of most conversations and the main point of interest was the Office of President. The media was pushing heavily for Clayborne and that carried a lot of weight. Also, the trade groups were also as they were hopeful of getting Trade Unions back in power. Teachers groups unanimously supported Clayborne for the same reasons. Jack Nix had the support of the Conservatives and the majority of the Independents primarily because he was recognized as an honest man who served honorably in the military during some very difficult times. Robert was doing his best to push Nix's campaign to a successful conclusion and for that purpose, he accelerated the trials of the Nation's bureaucrats that had been arrested on various corruption charges. Most of the government officials charged with taking public funds or property were associated with the Liberal Party and Robert saw to it that the defendants associated with the left were all coming to trial at or before Election Day. There were also some Conservative Party defendants involved in the corruption mess and Robert saw to it that their trials were delayed until well after the election. The media was virtually forced to report on the trials of the Liberal defendants as they were the only ones going to trial in the days and weeks before the election. Some editorials did question why it was that the only defendants going to trial at this time were the Liberals. Robert merely commented that it was just a coincidence.

When election day rolled around, the weather was unusually good and the turnout was massive. In view of the great economy, peace across the land, high employment and families again moving back into new homes, the Conservatives carried the day. Twenty Senate seats changed to Conservative winners and two hundred four House seats were lost by Liberals.

The Conservatives ended up with clear majorities in both houses. Needless to say, Jack Nix won in a landslide. His charismatic personality, his illustrious war record, and his perfectly clean record in government assured him of a victory. There was much celebrating in the Executive Wing at Scott Field. Nix had been present at the gathering in the President's Office as the election results came in. It was obvious by nine p.m. that Jack and most Conservatives running had won their elections. The Liberal commentators were almost in tears which made the Conservative Victory all the more enjoyable.

Vince Clayborne conceded at ten p.m. and Jack entered his Campaign Headquarters in Saint Louis at eleven p.m. The crowd there was ecstatic and it took fifteen minutes or longer for Jack to quiet the crowd before he could speak. He thanked everyone that had worked on his campaign and thanked Clayborne for his kind words in his concession speech. He then took a moment to praise President Robert Thomas and all the work that

Robert had done to bring the country back from perilous times to the status of the great nation that it had been in years past. He then told the American People that much work had yet to be done and that all Americans should unite to continue the good work regardless of what political party they belonged to.

After the election, Robert began to make his plans for retirement. He had a few items to take care of before he left the Presidency and he did not want to leave any problems for Jack Nix. There were a number of residents of retraining centers that Robert had sent in for various infractions over the years and some remained incarcerated. Robert had Toni get reports from the Centers on the rehabilitation or lack thereof on the list of names that he had delivered to her. The reports that he received on all except for five names on the list were favorable for release. Robert immediately pardoned all of the others and wished them well in their new status as free men. As for the five, he commuted their sentences down to three more years on the condition that they provide evidence of their rehabilitation at that time. As for Irene Covington, he spoke with Jack Nix about her situation and the fact that she had already served three years behind bars including time served before her trial. He suggested to Jack Nix that he might consider pardoning her after one more year of time served. Nix suggested that Robert knew Irene much better than he did and it would be more meaningful if Robert pardoned her in his final days as President of the United States. Robert agreed to take care of that.

With about two months left on his tour of duty as President of the United States, Sarah informed Robert that both Alaska and South Florida were coming on board accepting their Statehood status under the terms previously discussed. That was welcome news to Robert especially with respect to South Florida as he had been envisioning himself in his boat headed out of the cut for the deep water and the big ones. He had missed his early years as a teenager when he had been going through the cut in his fishing boat heading for the deep water going after Wahoo and Grouper and he looked forward to getting back out there. Robert thought to himself, "Where had all the years gone?" It seemed like a short time ago that he was in the convoy headed west to Montana wondering if he was not in the process of making the mistake of his life. In retrospect, it was not a mistake. He had played a large part in bringing back the greatest nation that ever existed. That was not on his mind at the time as he traveled to Montana but it slowly became a goal much through the inspiration of Stuart

Martin who Robert continued to think of daily. It had been a very interesting life that he had led and he regretted no part of it. Every part had either been a great accomplishment or a great learning experience. There were tough times, but they were worth the price he had to pay for them. As soon as he was out of office, he knew exactly where he was going to go, back to Melbourne, the beach, find a good boat and enjoy life again.

Time flew and soon Robert was in the final week of his Presidency. He called the prison on the Base and had them bring Prisoner Covington to his office. When she walked in, it was apparent that she had lost weight and had aged quite a bit since she had been arrested just a few years before. Apparently prison life was taking its toll. "Irene have a chair. Are you coming along OK? You seem to be fatigued."

"Robert, it is not exactly a walk in the park but I will survive."

"Irene when you get out of prison, what are your intentions?"

"I don't really know. The situation in our country has changed so much in the years since we all left Florida. I don't know if there is a place for me anymore or not."

"What kind of work would you like to get back into?"

"Robert, I always enjoyed teaching and I would like to get back at that if it is an option. I don't know if my background here would prevent that or not."

"Irene, I think that depends on you. If you concentrated on teaching and stayed away from your leftist tendencies, you might be able to get along alright."

"This has been a learning experience, Robert. I think I am out of politics for good."

"Glad to hear that Irene. I'll tell you what I am going to do. I have always had sort of a love hate relationship with you but I have always respected your drive to do what you saw as a good goal. I didn't always agree with your goals as you well know. I am going to release you from Prison on the condition that you will not renew your associations with your leftist revolutionary friends. If you do, you will be back in Prison. I am also going to talk to Beth Sloan to assist you in finding a teaching job somewhere in the country that will not be a temptation for you to slide backwards if you know what I mean. Are you in agreement with this?"

"Robert, God…yes. I would appreciate that opportunity very much. I have been sitting in my cell watching my life slide by slowly in a complete waste of time and I know, I put myself there. Not you or anyone else. I appreciate that. God bless you, Robert."

Beth Sloan found a teaching job for Irene Covington in her home town in Iowa and she abided by the terms of her release.

In January, Robert began moving his personal items out of his office and having them shipped to Melbourne to await his arrival there. The swearing in of Jack Nix to serve as President would take place in the Scott Field Conference Center followed by a reception in the executive wing. At the conclusion of that event, Hans Frick was flying Robert to Patrick Air Force Base in Melbourne. Patrick Air Force Base was again serving as an arm of the Nation's Military and was now a fighter base and a drone operator training base. The drones in the Military were now being used primarily as border control weapons and in some cases as crime apprehension and prevention tools. Training continued, as well, at Patrick for the Drone operators and maintainers with respect to tactical combat operations which the military had found so effective in battling the FSP. Illegal immigration continued to be a problem in South Florida with illegals from Cuba and from Haiti being the usual target. The drones in Patrick were frequently being called out to monitor the Florida Straits which was the normal route taken by both the Cubans and the Haitians to gain admission to the United States. As Robert's flight was on final approach to Runway 02 at Patrick, the pilot commented on the lineup of drones along the side of the parking ramp by the hangars. It was an impressive sight. Robert mentioned to the pilot that the appearance of the base had changed a great deal since he had last been here. He tried to catch a glimpse of the old marina that supported the Bayside Complex but he could not make it out. There were some structures down there but he was not sure if those were the buildings that he used to operate his boats from or not. He was very eager to see what changes had been made since they had all left in the heavily guarded convoy for Montana. He had also made it a point to try and track down Jim McCleod as no one in government had heard from him after he had left for North Farm so many years ago. Most likely he was no longer alive.

When his airplane taxied up to the operations center at the base, there was a vehicle driving up to the door of the airplane and a stairway was set up for the passenger to exit. As he stepped off of the airplane, the base commander saluted him and welcomed him to Florida. Robert thanked him for his courtesies and accepted his offer of quarters at the Base until he was situated somewhere on the Island. The Base Commander was very eager to parade Robert around Florida on a meet and greet tour but that was the very last thing that Robert wanted to partake of. He wanted peace and quiet mixed in with some fishing, searching for old friends and visiting former places where he had lived or worked, including Bayside Complex. Many memories were there and Robert was looking forward to renewing them. One of his main regrets was that Stuart was not there with him. He knew how much Stuart would have enjoyed coming back to Bayside. Robert knew exactly where the spot was that Stuart had fallen unconscious on the island when Ross Perry had rescued him. Stuart had taken him there a number of times as it was just down the beach from Robert's marina office. It was just a nondescript part of the beach but a very important landmark for Stuart. That was where he said his life had really begun. In many respects, it was also the spot where Robert's life had also begun. Before then he was a professional opportunist, usually honest, but not always. He chuckled as he thought of his usual comment regarding his honesty. "I was always honest about the fact that I was lying." Over time he had actually been able to stop lying but he attributed that primarily to the fact that he had to. Back then, before he adopted truthfulness as one of life's principles, People were just not believing half of what he was telling them. He soon learned that he could not lead people if they did not believe that what he was telling them was the truth. After he had seen the light, he became a truly effective leader.

Robert had every intention of finding a small apartment on the beach somewhere but he soon discovered that was not a possibility. The entire world, it seemed, was awaiting his arrival in Melbourne. When he left the Base to look for property, he was met by hundreds of people wanting to thank him for his service or to introduce their children to him or for autographs or whatever. He soon realized that it just went with the territory and he tried his best to be patient. He finally realized that if he wanted privacy he was going to have to be tricky about it. That was right up his alley. He thought about getting a disguise but that was a bit extreme so he dropped that idea. He did contact a realtor and made the realtor promise that all of their dealings would be completely secret. He wanted to purchase a home on the water that would afford him privacy and further that would bear no sign that he lived there. It would have to be on the Intracoastal side of the water as if it were ocean side, he would not be able to keep a boat protected there from the waves, storms, and variable tides. He finally located a home which he purchased that provided quarters for an attending person to cook and clean as Robert had no intention of taking up those duties. The house came with a dock and a boat house large enough to handle up to a thirty foot long boat with a small cabin. He then purchased the boat and had it equipped with two motors and the appropriate fishing gear.

Robert's house was situated on the narrow part of the island so that the morning sun was visible as it peered over the ocean and the setting sun went down just on the other side of the Intracoastal. It was an ideal Florida location. As he sat in his living room in the late afternoon, sipping his Brandy and enjoying the view of the fantastic Florida early evening sky-line he thought he had died and gone to heaven. The setting sun sent its rays passing through the towering cumulous clouds bringing out every color of the spectrum and bathed the waters and land below in various shades of the rainbow. Robert would just sit in his lounge chair facing west sipping his Brandy and never tiring of the fantastic Florida sunset.

This was as great as it gets. He was fishing most every morning. Running up to the cut, then out the pass and on out to deep water where the Wahoo, Grouper, Snapper, and Amberjack lived. Sometimes he had friends with him but usually Robert enjoyed going out alone. As he told close friends, "I prefer the one I love." He said that almost as a joke but there was no doubt he had spent his life thoroughly enjoying his own special sort of humor.

As time passed, people of South Florida came to realize that Robert did not care to have dinner with people he did not know nor did he care to attend festivities as a guest of honor. This annoyed some people but most of the South Floridians understood exactly where he was coming from as they thought pretty much the same. The people he did care about, the Pioneers, Jack Nix, Sarah, Anders, Wyatt, Clay and all those wonderful people that rebuilt the country, they were always welcome at Robert's home and they had no trouble relaxing there as that was the name of the game. A good dinner, some drinks, a movie that Robert would usually sleep through, early to bed and a morning fishing trip with a cooler full of frosty beers or occasionally by the time the guests arose, the house was empty and Robert had already gone fishing. That was just Robert's style and his close friends were certainly not offended. That was the main reason they enjoyed being at Robert's home in Florida. There was absolutely no schedule and they could do as they saw fit.

Robert did pursue some loose ends once he was situated in his Florida home and had the time to do so. He was unable to find any information regarding the whereabouts of Jim McCleod and had talked with many of the former residents of North Farm who spoke glowingly of McCleod but lost sight of him after the FSP gained control of the area. He contacted Carlos Moran who he had come to know during the turnover of Bayside to the Morales Cuban Force and Moran had spoken with McCleod shortly before the FSP overran North Farm but not a word from him or a sign of him after that. Robert presumed the FSP had killed McCleod for fear he could become a thorn in their side. He did speak with Ross Perry by telephone at his office at Scott Field to see if there was some way they could inquire of Frank Turner regarding the whereabouts of McCleod. Perry doubted Turner would tell them anything about him as Turner had consistently refused to provide any information on any and all topics. One topic Ross had attempted to pursue had been the present whereabouts of the gold bullion that was taken from Fort Knox by operatives of the Turner Administration. It was a very large amount of gold that had been pilfered and in the current global market it was valued in the trillions of dollars. Turner would only smile and tell the investigator to "just go find it. It must be out there someplace," followed by a chuckle.

Robert did visit Bayside and as he drove up to the Complex, he was surprised to find that the exterior appeared very much the same as when he had last seen it with some cosmetic changes. There were no longer the concrete barriers to block the entryway to automobiles carrying unfriendly visitors and the concertina wire was no longer on the top of the walls surrounding the complex. Furthermore, the walls and buildings were now painted in a tourist inspired pastel color with an occasional flamingo painted in various poses to break up the monotony of the walls extending around the perimeter of the complex. The entry gate was now monitored by a security guard who waved Robert through as soon as he recognized the car and driver. Robert searched for a place to park his car in the lot adjacent to the administration building but the only open spot had a sign on it for the assistant property manager. The space was empty so Robert took it thinking he would not be there for over a half an hour. As he stepped out of the car he looked over the large parking lot and park like setting surrounding it that was apparently now converted into a playground area for the children with slides, climbing bars and swing sets. There also used to be a swimming pool there that was no longer in sight. Robert pictured how the grounds had appeared the last time he saw it. It was then a large training field for Perry's security force with troops marching and practicing tactical maneuvers. What a complete transition to how it now appeared. Robert

locked his car and walked over to the administration building and introduced himself to the property manager who had already been notified that
the President was on the property. Robert told him that he was on a déjá vu
trip to see his former home from years past. He told the property manager
that he had parked in the assistant's spot and hoped he was not getting into
trouble for doing that. The manager assured him that was no problem and
furthermore, the assistant was not coming back until the following morning. Robert toured the administration building and the complex grounds.
He soon realized that nothing was as he recalled it and it was just another
disappointing attempt to revisit a place that had meant so much to him in
years past. Even the bullet holes in the walls from the gun battles that had
taken place at or near the complex had been repaired and were no longer
visible. He inquired as to the marina on the Intracoastal where he had
spent so much of his time years ago and the property manager had no idea
what he was referring to. Robert asked if it would be alright if he explored
along the shoreline of the Intracoastal and the manager assured him he was
welcome to visit whatever part of the complex or adjoining property he
wished to see. Robert walked down to the shoreline on a sidewalk that was
not present when he had been working in the marina. There was a large
building on the site of the former marina and a number of recreational
boats, canoes, jet skis, and some smaller fishing boats secured to a permanent wharf in front of the building. None of these permanent fixtures dated
back to Robert's time at Bayside. He soon realized that there was nothing
here that had anything to do with the trying times of years past. At other
points in his life, he had revisited scenes from former years and in every
case, he had been sorely disappointed to learn that nothing remained from
his memories of the past. It was always a depressing experience for him
and reminded him that life was passing him by way too rapidly.

As he was pondering these dismal thoughts, he glanced down the shoreline in the direction of the spot that Stuart had come ashore when he was
fleeing the mainland. The property manager was with him and Robert said,
"Let's take a short walk; I want to show you something." The two men
walked along the shoreline about fifty yards and Robert stopped and pointed at the spot where Stuart's canoe had landed on the Island. He explained
to the property manager that, "This was where it all started. Stuart came
here, seriously wounded from a gunshot wound in the arm and shoulder,
crawled out of his canoe right here and collapsed on the sandy beach.
Ross Perry, who also lived here then, was on guard duty, saw him coming

ashore and then carried him up to the clinic that was set up in the Bayside Complex. They saved his life. Did you know that?"

"I heard he had been shot but I knew nothing as to where or when or what was done for him. This is very interesting."

Robert looked at him and wondered if the rest of the country also had as little interest in the history of those who had brought the country back from disaster as this fellow. "Yes, it is interesting. Why don't you go on back to your office. I want to sit here for a few minutes alone, if you don't mind."

"Sure, Mister Thomas. If you need anything, let me know."

Robert found a patch of grass up out of the sand on the beach and sat down. It was a pleasant afternoon. Not too hot and not too cool. He studied the ground as the water lapped the shoreline and looked across the water at the houses in the area where Stuart had most likely lived. There were children playing in yards over there now and it bore no resemblance to what it looked like back when everyone was fighting for their lives. Back then the smell of smoke and burning rubber was everywhere. Billowing clouds of smoke hovered over Melbourne and the sound of gunfire constantly rent the air. There were no children playing in yards then or families enjoying a nice day. It was so peaceful here now and relaxing with the rhythmic sound of the water lapping the shoreline that Robert made himself comfortable, leaned back and thought about how his life had changed so completely since the days that he lived in the complex and made his living selling on the black market. He laughed to himself as he thought of those days. No wonder people thought he was a crook. In many respects he was but he had changed. He ended his political career as a respected man dedicated to the country that he loved. As he thought about everything that had occurred in the country from those days to the present, he concluded that the collapse under President Turner was the best thing that happened to the country. Had there been no collapse, the country would never have been able to make all of the necessary changes that he and Stuart as well as the others had brought about. He knew that Stuart would be proud of him now. He always suspected that Stuart had some misgivings before, but he would not have any now.

Robert thought about how he had lived his life. He was proud of parts of it and he was embarrassed by other parts. When he was a young man, he had done things he was not proud of. He had taken advantage of people that were not capable of protecting their best interests. He was ashamed of that now but there was no way he could right the wrongs he had committed against so many people so long ago. As he thought about it, he also thought most other people had similar experiences. They did embarrassing things when they were younger but were saved from the embarrassment until they aged and became able to see how foolish and unfair they had been in their youth. He also thought about many people that he had known that he had respected his entire life for the way in which they lived their lives. They were honorable, trustworthy, respectable people. Why in hell couldn't he have been the same. Anders had told him that the people that he had such great respect for also had secrets and misgivings as to the way they had lived their lives. "Trust me," Anders said, "They grind their teeth at night just like everyone else."

Robert laughed recalling Ander's comment and thought that he must not be that bad as he did not grind his teeth at night. That reminded him of a common thought that passed through his mind during good years and bad, "I hope God has a good sense of humor." Most of the more colorful dealings that brought him wealth were actually quite humorous. He had sold one boat dealer one of his own boats. He had learned in his early years of shady dealing to find the greedy person with the money and they were an easy mark. It never bothered him to take such a person to the cleaners. Back then he had told himself he was just doing "God's work." Robert thought about God fairly often in his declining years and finally reasoned over time that God had to be what men frequently referred to as "a regular guy". So many of what preachers referred to as "Sins" were in Robert's view nothing more or less than the actions reflecting the human side of people and usually involved some hilariously stupid decision some of them or all of them made. "How could God get pissed at that?"

As he laid in the grass, it reminded him of the many women in his life that he had known over the years. He never did get married but that was definitely a benefit to the ladies he had known. Robert knew he was not the marrying type. He was too damned independent and too focused on himself. He knew he was considered to be a very selfish person but to him that just meant he was busy fulfilling his own goals which benefited him and the nation he was working to improve in one way or another. He could not understand men who doted on their wives. He admitted freely to others that he lacked the patience and dedication to be like them. His friends found his behavior somewhat humorous as he was a true iconoclast, certainly with respect to marriage, and this was just evidence of his attitude towards long term relationships. He would have preferred to have a friendlier, longer lasting attitude towards women but that was just not to be. He was what he was and fortunately for all the women that he had known, he realized it.

Robert continued to think of the people in his life as he continued to lay in the grass. He was supremely comfortable and there was little wind and now that the sun was down a very light breeze brought in cooler air and took the mosquitoes away. He had slept for a while and when he awoke, the stars were out. It was a beautiful evening and it reminded Robert that this was one of the main reasons he had wanted to return to Florida. And now here he was at the very spot that Stuart had come ashore after fleeing for his life. They all, Stuart, Robert, Sarah, Ross and the others, had started something great right here at Bayside Complex. They had fought back and had retaken the country from the likes of Turner and the others that had almost completely destroyed the great nation. Almost, but not quite. Those that fought the hardest to bring the country back had won the battle. Robert was proud of the fact that he had been part of that great effort. He knew his life was about over and now that he was up in years and definitely slowing down, he took great comfort in knowing that he had contributed something good in his life time. It was not all shady dealings or tricky business arrangements, he had helped a lot of people and he took a great deal of personal comfort in that. As he drifted off to sleep, he heard Stuart's words and could see his face smiling at him, "Robert, if it were not for you, we would not be here."

The following morning, the assistant property manager drove his car into the Bayside Complex and was irritated to find that someone had parked their car in his assigned parking place. He finally found a spot on the far side of the lot and marched into the administration building to the property manager's office. The manager was seated at this desk and observed the angry look on his assistant's face as he barged into the office. "Well, aren't we the happy camper. What's the problem today, Fred?"

They found Robert lying up on the grass along the Intracoastal. He appeared to be sleeping but there was no sign of life. He had apparently passed away in his sleep.

Robert was buried in the National Cemetery in Riverton, Montana, alongside his good friend Stuart Martin and the many thousands of West-Pac Rangers and fighters who had perished in the battle to retake the country. A stone monument was eventually placed on the site where Stuart had come ashore after fleeing for his life and where Robert had passed away.

At the dedication of the monument, protesters with their signs were present voicing dissent at the expenditure of funds for the monument when many citizens did not have adequate housing.

"It is surmounting difficulties that makes heroes."
—**Louis Pasteur**

Acknowledgements

I wish to thank John McClure of Signalman Publishing for his able assistance in getting *Finding America* published and Duncan Long for his great artwork on the cover. Their assistance and words of encouragement are greatly appreciated.

About the Author

R. Thomas Roe, the author of *Finding America*, sequel to *Searching for America*, is a retired trial attorney residing along the ocean in Florida. He also has a home in the mountains of Colorado where he usually spends the summers. Mr. Roe is a graduate of St. Thomas University and William Mitchell College of Law, both in St. Paul, Minnesota. He has written other fiction novels, *The Gaelic Letters*, winner of a Royal Palm Literary Award in Fiction/Suspense and *Palm Beach Gold*, a crime fiction novel. Mr. Roe enjoys reading and writing as well as mountain biking when at his home in Colorado.